STREAKING

Borgo Press Books by BRIAN STABLEFORD

STREAKING

A NOVEL OF THE FUTURE

BRIAN STABLEFORD

THE BORGO PRESS

MMXI

STREAKING

FIRST BORGO PRESS EDITION

Published by Wildside Press LLC

www.wildsidebooks.com

STREAKING

CONTENTS

CHAPTER ONE

Canny Kilcannon was playing in the top-table poker game, protected from kibitzers by carefully-arranged screens. His game was off, and he knew it. He was still winning, of course, but that wasn't what mattered. He hated playing badly, even if he still won. He won more when he was playing well than he did when he was playing badly, but the money wasn't the reason he played the game—not any more.

He played the game because he was supposed to be good at it: because he felt, when he won, that he deserved to win, that there was a legitimacy in his sense of triumph. At least, he usually did. Not tonight. Tonight, he couldn't get his act together.

Tonight, he had to rely on luck.

Four of the eight players at the table were smokers, and they were the kind of smokers who took a macho attitude to the vice. The obese American was smoking Turkish cigarettes whose tobacco was dark and dense with extra tar. The Arab, on the other hand, was conspicuously failing to enjoy a Havana cigar. The Slav who was so slender that was practically anorectic and the American who was pretending to be an ex-marine were smoking aromatic crap that was posing a real challenge to the overworked air-conditioning.

The haze of their compounded smoke, gathered beneath the overhead light, was grey and wispy, not somber at all, but Canny knew that clouds were still treacherous when they inverted themselves to show their silver linings on the outside, and he was paying attention to his gut feelings, alert for any rumble of alarm. There was nothing definite.

There was a feeling that something was about to happen, but no suggestive indication of what it might be. He stacked a third bad hand in a row, almost glad that the cards gave him no choice. Had he played them, one of them might have improved dramatically when the flop was dealt, but if it had gone to a showdown he'd have looked like a crazy optimist when he showed his hand, and that wasn't what he was. He was a Kilcannon—a *Credesdale* Kilcannon—and he had an image to maintain as well as a secret to conceal. He wasn't some stupid Candide, adrift in a world whose violence and misery he was impotent to escape, but that didn't mean that he had to come across like a smug clown who expected things to work out right even when he did them wrong.

When he was playing badly, the sensible thing to do was to play safe—not because he wouldn't win, but because he wouldn't seem outrageously lucky when he did. The people he was playing against would think that he was lucky anyway—they were the kind of people who never had any other excuse to offer themselves for their own lack of success, no matter how badly they had played—but at least they wouldn't think he was stupidly lucky or insanely lucky.

So he waited until he had a hand that was far better than average—the king and jack of hearts—before he bet again, and then he bet entirely by the book, forcing the issue with mechanical precision. When he won, it was obvious, not merely to the obese American who'd had the misfortune to call him but to everyone else, that he had always had the upper hand—that chance had favored him at the very start, so that all he'd had to do was follow its kindly dictates.

As the croupier began to deal again, one of the waiters materialized at Canny's elbow and whispered in his ear, telling him that an urgent telephone call had been put through to the casino manager's office. Canny folded his hand without looking at it and got up, leaving his chips on the table. He had accumulated about three thousand Euros, but he'd started with a thousand

and he'd been playing for five hours, so it was by no means an exceptional take. More than half of it had been won from players who'd left the table, so the seven who watched him go were hardly aware of the fact that they'd been stung; two or three of them were even further ahead than he was.

The waiter led him to Henri Meurdon's office, which was decorated in the same slightly raucous style as the casino itself, although the effect was considerably ameliorated by the paintings hung on the walls. The Delvaux was genuine, Canny had been assured, but the Khnopff was a copy.

"One can't have everything," the manager had told him, when he'd first been allowed to access to the private space, "and appearance is more important than actuality, in a casino."

Meurdon was sitting at his desk tapping at the keyboard of his computer. When Canny came in he immediately got up, as if to leave, but Canny raised a hand to indicate that there was no need. Meurdon nodded politely, and focused his attention on his screen to indicate that he would not be listening to anything that Canny said.

The caller was the night-manager from the hotel, relaying a message from Canny's mother. His father had taken a sudden turn for the worse; the apparent remission of his cancer had come to an end; the disease had come back, more aggressively than before.

Canny wasn't surprised that he hadn't had any obvious premonition of the turn of events, unexpected as it was. He wasn't entirely sure whether it qualified as good luck or bad—although Daddy would naturally have taken a very different view—and it wasn't exactly unexpected, even though the moment had come sooner than he expected. His father's cancer was, after all, the reason he was here: the reason why home had become even less bearable than usual.

"I have taken the liberty of connecting to the Air France website, Monsieur Kilcannon," the manager told him. "There is a flight from Nice at eight-fifteen a.m. which has first class seats available, connecting at London Heathrow with a ten a.m. flight to Leeds. Would you like me to make a booking?"

"Yes please," Canny said. Monte to Nice was approximately fifty kilometers; to check in at seven-fifteen he would have to leave at six-thirty or thereabouts. It was now three-twenty-five.

"Would you like me to pack your bags for you, sir?" the night-manager asked.

"No," Canny said. "That's all right. I'll pack them myself when I come back. Please order me a car, though—two cars, I mean. One to take me to Nice from the hotel at six-fifteen, one to pick me up here at...."

He hesitated. Even if he went back to the hotel right away he wouldn't be getting any sleep, and this was the last opportunity he would have to visit the casino—*any* casino—for some considerable time. Running away had saved him a lot of awkwardness, but it had also stored up a lot of hassle when it came to taking over the reins of the family affairs. He would be shuttling back and forth between Credesdale and Leeds, and between Leeds and London, for months on end—and when everything was in order again, it might be the kind of order that wasn't conducive to *all* the vices he'd spent the last ten years cultivating with such insouciant assiduity. Perhaps he owed himself one last flutter, one last flourish.

"...at four-thirty," he finished, eventually.

"Yes, Monsieur Kilcannon."

As Canny lowered the receiver back into its cradle, Henri Meurdon said "Bad news, Monsieur?" in his smoothest voice, wearing his most diplomatic expression.

"Bad news, Henri," Canny confirmed. "My father. He seemed to have responded well to the chemotherapy—he was really quite cheerful last time I spoke to him, swore blind that he had years of wear in him yet—but appearances seem to have been deceptive. He was always a man to nurse his pains secretly and never let on to the true extent of his fears and expectations—but I dare say that he's dying a little more rapidly than he hoped. His luck's been good while it lasted, but it seems to have run out."

"I'm very sorry to hear that, Monsieur."

There was a soft knock at the door. In response to Meurdon's invitation, the waiter came in again, carrying Canny's neatly-sorted chips in a plastic tray. Although Canny hadn't asked for them to be removed from the table, he accepted them graciously and returned a ten Euro chip by way of a gratuity. The seat would still be his if he wanted it, but now that he had the chips he wasn't sure that he did. Poker demanded too much concentration and he had been playing badly even before the news came through. It was time to change to a mindless game of chance.

"Trois milles deux cents quatre-vingts, Monsieur," the waiter reported as he backed away. The information was presumably intended for Meurdon rather than Canny, although it was difficult to be sure.

As the door closed again, Canny said to the manager: "Don't worry, Henri. I was playing poker—it's not your money I've won."

"I know that, Monsieur," Meurdon said. "It is of no consequence—if you placed it all on your favorite number at the roulette wheel, and won, I would be happy to lose the money."

Canny laughed. "Is that a dare?" he said. "I won't be back for a while, you know. I have responsibilities now. This was always going to be my last fling—although I'd hoped to spin it out for a few more weeks, if not months."

Meurdon shook his head. "No, Monsieur Kilcannon," he said, smoothly. "It is not a dare. I spoke the simple truth; you do me a better turn when you win than you would if you were to lose—which is perhaps as well, considering the amount you have won over the years."

Canny frowned. He knew about the screen-filled room on the upper floor where Meurdon and his security staff could keep watch on every bet laid in every game, and he didn't suppose for a moment that the manager had been using his computer to surf the web when he came in to take the call, but it still worried him a little to think that the casino might have a record of all his visits, and all his victories. When he played poker the house took its cut in seating fees and the flow of cash was utterly irrelevant, but when he played *chemin de fer* or roulette he played against the house—and Meurdon's house percentage was, in the long term, less powerful than his own.

"I've never had a spectacular win," Canny said, half-apologetically. "I've been very lucky—but I always bet modestly, compared with your more flamboyant clients, and any profits I've made must have been similarly modest."

"I know about your modesty," Meurdon told him, with a slight smile. "Which makes the consistency of your good fortune even more remarkable. I had you under observation for a while, when you played *chemin de fer*, in case you were a card counter. When I discovered that you were not, I was pleased."

Canny raised an eyebrow, but only slightly, He'd never realized that he was under surveillance, but it didn't surprise him. That, after all, was what the cameras in the hall and the screens in the upper room were for. "How did you convince yourself that I wasn't?" he asked.

"Your betting pattern," Meurdon told him. "Counters patiently place minimum stakes for hours on end, until they are convinced that the cards in the shoe are biased in their favor—then they begin betting far more heavily. You play your cards as you see fit, whether the shoe has been recently replenished or not, varying your stake in an entirely casual manner. If that were not proof enough, I've observed that the ratio of your stakes to returns is exactly the same at *chemin de fer*, poker and—most remarkably of all—roulette. I don't suppose, given that you might not be favoring us with your custom again, that you'd care to explain how you do it?"

Canny's surprise was magnified, but he felt no alarm. The atmosphere in the room hadn't darkened, and there was no nausea gathering in his stomach. He was not under threat from Henri Meurdon.

On the other hand, he thought, it was one thing for Meurdon to interrogate the record of chips he'd bought and cashed in order to check that he wasn't counting cards; it was quite another to take the trouble to have *all* his betting patterns analyzed and compared. Meurdon's question was, however, the kind of challenge that he was always prepared to meet.

He laughed. "Well, you seem to know more about that than I do," he said. "*Entirely casual*, you said—and that about sums it up. I've always been lucky. Yorkshire folk have called us the lucky Kilcannons since time immemorial, so I guess it runs in the family—except that poor Daddy's contest with the crab doesn't seem to have worked out so well. These things always even out in the long run, isn't that what they say?"

"They do say that," Meurdon admitted, "but all experience of life suggests otherwise. Even the so-called laws of probability, if properly interpreted, suggest that there are always winners and losers in the long run, and that breaking even is no less a statistical freak than any other result. The trick is to make sure that one ends up with the winners rather than the losers. I have the house percentage to make sure that the casino achieves that objective—but you have something more precious, I think. That is why I say that you do better for me when you win than if you were to lose."

For a moment or two Canny was frightened by the reference to *something more precious*, but then he realized that it was only a turn of phrase, connected with the latter part of the sentence.

"*Pour encourager les autres*," he murmured, with a wry smile. "I'm sorry that I haven't been a better ad, then. I fear that I've been a little too unobtrusive to persuade your richer clients to plunge more heavily."

"You have been a far better advertisement than you know, Monsieur," Meurdon said—and Canny knew, now, that he was not merely being polite. "One might almost say that you are the ideal advertisement. You are not as good-looking as your friend the football player, let alone the movie stars who honor us with their occasional presence. You are not even as well-dressed, although I would not dream of criticizing your sense of style—but you have something more valuable to me than looks or clothes: your *savoir faire*. You do not bet ostentatiously, but you do bet casually. You bet *lightly*, as if betting were as natural as breathing, and you always expect to win...which is not unnatural, given that you usually do. Whenever you lose, you smile, as if you know perfectly well that the reverse is temporary. Whenever you win, you do so gracefully, as if it were your entitlement. Can you understand what a role model like that is worth to me, Monsieur Kilcannon?"

"I hadn't really thought about it," Canny admitted. "It never occurred to me that people might watch me when there are so many colorful people around."

"People watch one another in different ways, Monsieur. Yes, everyone watches the sheikhs, the businessmen, the musicians and the sportsmen—but they watch them from afar, regarding them as specimens in the world of celebrity. No one ever thinks: *I shall bet like that in order to be like that.* They compete among themselves, of course, but what you would probably call the casino's *bread and butter* comes from the tourists who each have much less money to spend but are multitudinous in their numbers. They *do* look at you, Monsieur Kilcannon, and they think: *That is the way it is done; that is the way a man should bet, the attitude a true gambler should strike.* Yours is an attainable model, a copiable performance—in every respect but one. Unlike you, *they* lose. Not all of them, but more than enough, and always if they come back often enough. In order to sustain the kind of hope I need them to bring to my tables, I need authentic, consistent winners—and they are much harder to come by than you might suppose. In the bad old days, of course, we pretended, but the regulations are much tighter now and the employment of shills is strictly forbidden. We have reason to be grateful that there are genuinely lucky men around, and I shall be truly sorry not to see you again."

"I'll be sorry too," Canny said, softly—although any intention he might have had to return, once the estate was sorted out and the businesses were running smoothly again, had evaporated while Meurdon was speaking. "But I might be able to help you out one last time, before the car picks me up, if you don't mind."

It was Meurdon's turn to smile "Don't let me detain you, Monsieur Kilcannon. "And—*bon chance!*"

CHAPTER TWO

As soon as Canny stepped back into the larger room he felt the change in its atmosphere. The atmosphere really was subtly different, of course, because the air in the gaming arena was more carefully maintained—against much greater challenges— than the air in Meurdon's office, but in Canny's estimation the potential with which it was charged went beyond any mere mechanical conditioning. It was pregnant with possibility.

According to the family records—legends, as Canny had always defiantly thought of them—the Kilcannon luck always sank to a low ebb whenever the patriarch died, and remained at a low ebb until it was dutifully renewed, but Lord Credesdale wasn't dead yet, and while he was still ailing Canny's share of the family fortune might actually increase, as if it were flowing out of the old man's decaying husk into his still-vibrant flesh. The time was ripe for a *coup*—if he wanted to bring off a *coup*.

In a way, he did. But in another way, he didn't.

He did because he knew that this would be his farewell to the playboy lifestyle. He might recover some of the threads, but it would never be the same even if he did, because he wouldn't be the same. Once Daddy was dead, he'd be the Earl of Credesdale—no longer a son fighting for scraps of his a fortune that really belonged to his father, but his own man, in control of his own destiny. He would never again be the person he was now, and he couldn't deny a certain urge to celebrate that conclusion.

On the other hand, he had just been informed that other eyes were following his luck, not merely watching it but weighing it, not merely marveling at it but wondering what could possibly sustain it. In circumstances like that, scoring a spectacular win might qualify as an extremely undiplomatic thing to do, perhaps a stupid thing to do.

His father would have been horrified by the fact that he was even thinking about it—but Canny wasn't sure whether that qualified as an argument against or an argument for.

What the hell, he thought, eventually. *He was daring me, wasn't he?*

The potential seemed to hang most heavily of all above the roulette table, and it drew him with smooth efficiency while he put up no resistance. Stevie Larkin, the English football player Meurdon had referred to as Canny's "friend" was one of three team-mates playing the roulette wheel. They were sitting to the croupier's right, directly across from a trio of models, one of whom was said—if only by the tabloids—to be one of the ten most beautiful women in the world. Although the club the footballers played for was Italian, the other two were Croatian and Algerian; at the top level, the sport was a perfect model of twentieth-century globalization.

Canny had been casually acquainted with Stevie Larkin for a couple of years, because the footballer had sought his help as a translator at various Mediterranean social occasions. Stevie certainly seemed to think of him as a friend, even though the footballer was a Lancastrian and Canny was a Yorkshireman— which would have made them implicit rivals in their own land almost as surely as the fact that Canny was about to succeed to an earldom while Stevie hailed from an insalubrious area of a small industrial town. They had hardly exchanged five words tonight, but as soon as Stevie saw Canny gravitating towards the roulette table he nudged the Croatian and begged him to surrender his seat so that Canny could sit next to him.

The Croatian obliged, although he seemed a rifle resentful. So did the Algerian, who was currently serving as his companions' French translator—having presumably been brought along in the faint hope that he might be able to act as a go-between assisting one or both of his team-mates to pick up something tasty. Any of the models they were currently ogling would doubtless have done very nicely—although the footballers had probably no chance there, especially with Lissa Lo. Canny couldn't believe that Stevie could possibly think that one of the ten most beautiful women in the world would give him a second glance; unlike some of his ilk, the Lancastrian had his delusions of grandeur under control.

Canny sat down beside Stevie and said hello.

Stevie eyed the tray of chips as Canny set it down in front of him, but didn't comment on their value. For once, he had something else in mind. "Called into the headmaster's study, were you?" he said. "Caught cheating again?"

"Phone call from Mummy," Canny reported, laconically. "Daddy's taken a sudden turn for the worst. Got to go home and inherit the estate. No more carefree playboy lifestyle for me."

"Oh, I'm sorry, mate," Stevie said, repentantly. "Didn't realize it was serious. If you have to get away, go."

"Can't get a flight out till morning," Canny told him, tersely. "Won't be able to sleep. No mad rush. Might as well finish up here."

"Right," Stevie said, uncertainly.

"Next time you see me I'll be the Earl of Credesdale," Canny said, reflectively. "But friends like you can call me *my lord*." As he spoke, he counted off a thousand Euros in chips, then reached out and put the entire stack on zero.

It was the sort of gesture that could precipitate a moment's silence almost anywhere else in the world, but this was Monte Carlo. Everyone on the table saw what he did, but there wasn't a single sharp intake of breath. The croupier didn't even blink.

"I know you've had a shock, Can," Stevie murmured, "but don't you think you're overdoing the symbolism just a trifle?"

"Symbolism?" Canny queried. "I thought you left school at fifteen without a single GCSE."

"We all have our own personal sports psychologists these

days," the footballer told him, as the wheel spun. "Used to be we only got counseling when we got transferred—nowadays it's every time we lose. I know what symbolism is, mate—and you just lost a grand. Only Euros, but even so...."

The croupier called the number, and raked in Canny's chips with practiced ease.

Entirely casual, Canny thought. *As if it were as natural as breathing.*

He counted out another thousand, and placed it in exactly the same spot.

"I get it," Stevie said. "You called a cab, didn't you? You only have time for three shots, so you cut your stash in three. It's a penalty shoot-out—all or nothing."

Canny was slightly surprised by Stevie's ready interpretation, but he met the younger man's blue eyes with his own darker ones with carefully-feigned frankness. "That's absolutely right," he said. "The sports psychology is really paying off."

He looked away from Stevie as he caught something in the corner of his eyes and directed his gaze at the far side of the table. The three models were all looking at him, trying not to be obvious but not quite contriving to hide their fascination—even Lissa Lo.

Canny had never attempted to be the womanizing kind of playboy that Stevie Larkin thought he ought to aspire to be, but he knew that he was going to miss the presence of beautiful women—not as much as the click of chips and the rustle of cards, but enough to leave a gap.

If he decided to follow the dictates of family tradition, he was going to have to get married now. According to the advice of the records, he'd already put it off too long for his own good. If the records were mere legends—a tissue of hopeful fancies and silly mistakes—it didn't really matter what advice they offered, but whatever else Daddy found the strength to say to him, he was bound to get an earful on *that* subject, and then some.

Canny knew that Daddy wouldn't approve of the way he was betting now. Daddy had always advised him to go slow, to be modest in his aims and modest in his gains. *It's a gift*, Daddy had told him, time and time again, *and it has to be treated with due respect. Don't try to test the limits. You had your ration of playing the fool when you were a boy. You have to be a man now. Don't risk bringing the lightning down. Collect the house percentage, little by little. Don't ask for too much too quickly. When freaky things start happening, you never know when they'll stop.*

"Don't bring the lightning down," Canny murmured, while everybody placed their bets on rouge and noir, pair and impair, or bet on batches of four or eight numbers. There were a dozen other bets on individual numbers, but all of them were ten-Euro bets—there wasn't a single hundred, let alone another thousand. Lissa Lo hadn't bet at all; she was still watching him.

"What's that, mate?" Stevie asked. "Storm coming?"

"Just symbolism," Canny assured him. He wondered whether Henri Meurdon was watching him on the screen in his inner sanctum—and whether, if so, he was mildly disappointed that Canny had broken his pattern and his image by accepting his playful dare.

The wheel spun. The ball dropped. Canny lost.

He watched Lissa Lo collect forty Euros, and add it carefully to a stack that must have been worth more than a thousand. Had she started with half as much or twice as much? Her expression gave nothing away.

Canny immediately pushed his remaining chips on to zero. There were twelve hundred and seventy, which was two hundred and seventy over the official table limit, but the croupier didn't bother to seek permission from above to let the bet stand; he had the discretion to accept it, and he had his own notion of style.

"What the hell," said Stevie, putting down five hundred Euros. "I'll keep you company, mate—even though I don't have a country estate."

"You must get paid at least thirty thousand a week, plus perks," Canny pointed out. "And the estate's in a valley so shallow and narrow that it hardly qualifies as a dale."

"It's in bloody Yorkshire as well," Stevie said, feigning contempt, "but you'll have it till you die, and I might break a leg on Sunday. We have personal financial advisors too, you know. I lost my last club shirt in the dotcom crash. I'm a sensible investor now."

"If you were sensible," Canny muttered, "you'd bet the whole thousand. When it's all or nothing, the Kilcannons always come through."

"Is that the family motto?" Stevie asked, not moving a muscle to add to his stake—but Canny watched Lissa Lo reach out a delicately manicured hand, and place five hundred Euros of her own on zero. On another night, with a slightly different crowd, she might have started a rush, but it was four o'clock in the morning and tired sanity held sway. Nobody else joined in. Canny didn't know whether to be glad or not.

Well, Daddy, he said to himself, silently, *this is the end. From now on, I'll be just like you, at least for a while. No more grandstanding.* But he was very keenly aware that there was one more spin of the wheel to go. He really wasn't certain that he would win, when the croupier spun the wheel and dropped the ball—but as soon as he saw the streak he knew that he'd been a fool to doubt himself.

Visually speaking, it was a beauty. It wasn't the brightest he had ever seen, but it was certainly the most complex. Given that he was about to win more than forty thousand Euros at long odds he might have expected it to be brilliantly white, but it had all the colors of the rainbow in it, not ordered into a spectrum but fragmented and mingled in a kaleidoscopic effect that was literally dizzying. The physical sensations accompanying the visual were equally complex; as expected, there was an element of euphoria and a rush of supreme self-confidence, but they were part of a compound whole whose other elements were unnamable. Some of them, at least, he had never felt before. He felt as if he had been moved sideways and wrenched out of shape, but he hadn't really moved at all. He was sitting perfectly still.

The experience was all the more thrilling because he knew

that no one else would have the slightest memory of the experience; if they felt it at all, or saw anything at all, it would leave no trace.

Afterwards, the heady cocktail of immediate sensation gave way to the customary wrench of nausea and the surge of objectless fear—the "aftertaste of triumph" his father had always called it—but he was well used to steeling himself against the possibility of collapse.

While the inner wheel of the machine spun, its glossy black casing surrounded it with a halo of reflected light, making the whole ensemble seem a mirror of wayward fate.

Then the silver ball dropped meekly into the zero slot.

This time, there was an audible effect—not a communal intake of breath, but an abrupt collective exhalation.

"Bugger me," Stevie murmured. "You did it. Thanks, boss."

Even Lissa Lo permitted herself a slight smile—but she wasn't looking at Canny any more, and she studiously ignored the stacks of chips that the croupier was counting out, one by one, before raking them out. She was whispering to her companions, whose expressions suggested that she was bidding them an apologetic farewell.

Canny calculated that thirty-six times one thousand two hundred and seventy was forty-five thousand seven hundred and twenty—ten Euros shy of forty-seven thousand, including the stake. The croupier had already signaled to one of his peers, who came to collect the chips on Canny's behalf. A brief nod sufficed to confirm that it was his intention to cash up. Canny took back a hundred Euro tip and tossed it to the man at the wheel; it seemed the least he could do.

As natural as breathing, he reminded himself, as he stood there watching the boy, savoring the prospect of the walk to the cashier's office. *Set a good example, now—leave them wanting more*. He half-expected Henri Meurdon to emerge from the office to shower him with felicitations, but Meurdon had an image to maintain too. *Forty seven thousand?* he imagined the manager saying, in his slightly perfumed English. *People walk out of here with that sort of money every day of the week. You could too, if you were lucky—and we'd be glad of the ad.*

Before he moved off, Canny permitted himself one last glance at the three models. Two of them were staring; one wasn't. It was the one who wasn't to whom he addressed himself, although he didn't look directly at her and spoke distinctly enough to be heard by everyone at the table. "I need an early night," he said, carefully making his apologetic tone ring false. "I have to go home—Daddy's so ill that he might not last the week, alas. Henri will have to do without me for quite a while, I fear—I hope he won't miss me too much."

The frowns that greeted this speech were all male. Canny heard a whispered Arabic phrase, and had seen enough of the Makhtoums at Ascot and Epsom to know that it meant "the luck of the devil". He smiled. There was no need to take it personally. Long experience had rammed home the lesson that no one ever credited his own good fortune to the devil, or anyone else's to the angels.

Having observed her whispered conversation, Canny wasn't entirely surprised when Lissa Lo got up too. He didn't read anything into the coincidence; it wasn't unusual for women to get up and follow him when he left a table—many of the women he encountered on a day-to-day basis loved winners, and not a few were masochistically intrigued by evident disinterest that wasn't overtly queer—but Lissa Lo was in an altogether different class. It was said that she never got out of bed for less than Stevie Larkin got for playing a game of football, but that you couldn't get her into one for what he got paid for a whole league season, whoever or whatever you might be.

As Canny walked away from the table, though, the model moved on to a convergent path. He didn't look around to see what kind of expression Stevie Larkin was wearing, but he could imagine it easily enough.

"I'd better call it a night too," the model said, as they made their way over to the cashier, walking in step but not quite together. "The boat's waiting to take me to Nice—the jet has to be in the air by six. I have to put down at some ridiculous RAF base west of York, so that a fast car can whisk me off to Harewood House for a shoot."

Canny frowned, partly because of a momentary confusion as to the significance of the word "shoot" and partly because her reference to the RAF base west of York rang such an eerie bell. "Do you mean Church Fenton?" he said, as he stood politely aside to let her cash up first.

"Yes—do you know it?"

He only hesitated for a moment before answering. "The family pile's only twenty miles away," he admitted. "Approximately north by north-east—a little place called Cockayne. Church Fenton's practically local—two hundred miles more local than Heathrow, at any rate"

"Cockayne! How charming." The model's delicately-etched eyebrows increased their curvature slightly, delicately but firmly implying that she was fully capable of savoring the resonance of the name. "In that case, I suppose I ought to offer you a lift."

The rainbow quality of the streak took on new meaning as Canny calculated the possibilities implicit in the invitation. The rules forbade him to waste his erotic energies on frivolity, of course, but the majority of his ancestors had taken a very dim view of the supposed pleasures of the bedchamber, so that wasn't surprising. They were Yorkshiremen, after all. The fact that his father had always sided with the rules probably had as much to do with the Earl of Credesdale's disapproval of his son's attitude to life as with any real fear of diminishing the brightness of the family's lucky streak.

Well, why not? Canny thought. *If Daddy's share of the pot is all but exhausted, why shouldn't I be able to turn a thirty-six-to-one hit into a thousand-to-one shot? And why shouldn't I treat myself, if the opportunity does arise?*

He was careful, though, not to take too much for granted. It was entirely possible that all he was being offered, by Lissa Lo and Lady Luck alike, was a lift to Church Fenton.

"I have to go back to my hotel," he said, in a deeply apologetic manner that—for once—wasn't feigned. "There mightn't be time to get up the hill, pack my cases and get back down again before your boat casts off."

"Why don't you try?" she said. "The boat's practically on the doorstep. I'll hold it for you for...oh, an hour should still leave plenty of time. Not a moment longer, though."

"If you really wouldn't mind," Canny said, in frank astonishment, as the cashier rammed wads of bills into a leather-clad bag.

"I really wouldn't," she assured him. "I'll probably try to take a nap on the boat, but I can never sleep on planes—I'd be glad of the company. It's a pity that the news about your father has spoiled your lucky day." She glanced at the cash that was stacking up in the bag, but she obviously meant the outrageous good fortune that had thrown him at the feet of a woman whose private jet was landing two hundred miles closer to his home than the scheduled flight he'd intended to catch.

"Yes it is," he agreed, prepared for the moment to regard the coincidence in exactly that light. "They say that these things always balance out in the long run, but there's no compensation for losing a father."

"Mine died some time ago," she said, "but I know what you mean. People who think that things always balance out don't understand the real nature of chance, do they?"

She turned away as she said it, denying him not only the opportunity to answer the rhetorical question but also the opportunity to look into her lovely eyes in the hope of figuring out exactly what she meant to imply.

CHAPTER THREE

Stepping out of the air-conditioned casino into the warm night air was like stepping into a bath. Sweat immediately began to form on his brow. The Mediterranean coast benefited from sea breezes, of course, but the sea never cooled enough to impart any real freshness to them. In Paris, it was said, thousands of people were dying from the heat every week. That was partly because so many doctors and other medical workers took their holidays in August, just like everyone else, but it was mostly the fact that the temperature never got much below blood heat, even at night. In Bordeaux, so rumor had it, even the age-old habit of throwing all the doors and windows open in the darkness before the dawn and then sealing the shutters tight against the sun wasn't saving the populace from cooking slowly in their skins. Even in England—in Yorkshire, no less—the temperature was ten degrees above normal. No wonder his father had run out of energy with which to fight his cancer.

Mercifully, the cab was air-conditioned. It got Canny to the hotel in less than fifteen minutes, despite the tight bends it had to negotiate as it climbed the sheer face of the lavishly-overbuilt cliff. The driver was perfectly happy to wait for him, in order to make a return journey to the quay.

A breeze was stirring the foliage of the syringas in the garden as Canny made his way up the old stone steps, but it made little difference to the cloying warmth of the night. It seemed, in fact, to have a more tangible effect on the shadows gathered around him, which rippled and swayed in a curiously serpentine fashion. The soughing of the wind in the branches was easily imaginable as the hissing of snakes.

Canny always tried to listen to what the shadows were trying to tell him, but he couldn't help wondering whether Stevie's sports-psychology symbolism was playing games with him. He still felt a little nauseous, and a little fearful, but that was only to be expected, given the violence and complexity of the streak. Sometimes, darkness was perfectly natural, even when it shifted restlessly as he passed by.

The night-manager was waiting at the desk to see if Canny needed anything further, and Canny explained the change of plan.

"I'll just pack the essentials in a single bag, if that's okay," Canny said. "Could you have the rest packed up properly in the morning and send them on? I'll send Bentley to pick them up at Leeds airport."

"Of course, Monsieur."

"Thanks. Can you get the stuff from the safe and have my bill ready in twenty minutes?"

"Yes, Monsieur."

Canny went up the stairs two at a time rather than waiting for the elevator. He only had to go up to the first floor.

Because it looked out on to the elevated rear garden—the monks' garden, it was called, although Canny doubted that the hotel had ever been a convent—the room didn't have the feel of a first-floor room. One could easily jump from the balcony to the lawn without serious risk of injury. The balcony doors were closed, of course, and the curtains were drawn, but the first thing Canny did was to draw them open and open the door to let the breeze in so that the stuffiness did not become too oppressive as he packed. He switched on a bedside lamp and then switched off the strip light, so that he wouldn't be displaying such an obvious beacon to every moth in Monaco.

He pulled out the smallest of his suitcases and placed the leather-bound bag from the casino in it before going to his drawers. He'd been on the move for more than two weeks, so he had a fairly extensive survival kit, but he had a reserve ward-robe at home so he didn't need to worry too much about the possibility that his luggage might not follow him as quickly as it ought. He stripped off the clothes he was wearing, though, and put those in the case. Before getting dressed again he went to the bathroom to use the facilities and collect his shaver and toothbrush.

When he came back again there was a black-clad figure in a ski-mask standing by the bed, pointing a gun at him.

Canny's first thought was that he had been an utter fool to let the intruder in, given the serpentine quality of the shadows that had pestered him on his approach—whose real symbolism now seemed far more obvious than he had carelessly assumed. Even by the muted light of the bedside lamp, though, the shadows that were actually congregated in the room didn't seem panic-stricken. His unfocused fear hadn't amplified itself into alarm, let alone panic. The gun-toter didn't seem to have any imme-diate intention of shooting him—and probably wouldn't form any such intention, unless he did something stupid.

Canny tried hard to judge the expression in the bandit's eyes, but it wasn't possible. There was uncertainty, of course—but in a situation like theirs, there would always be uncertainty. In a situation like theirs, there would always be scope for chance to take a hand, for action to be inhibited or encouraged by a wayward whim.

"Don't move," was all that the intruder said, in a voice so neutral in its quality that Canny couldn't be certain whether it was male or female. Canny knew that the thief had already spotted the leather-bound bag in the suitcase, imperfectly obscured by a crumpled shirt. *Now's the moment*, he thought, as the other moved to take the bag containing the forty-seven thousand Euros—but he didn't move a muscle. He felt safe, as long as he didn't precipitate another streak, and safety seemed enough, for the moment. He had already won one gamble at long odds—even if the highly-colored streak had contained some bad omens as well as bright ones—and it would undoubtedly be pushing his luck to conjure up another. He was five or six inches taller than the thief, and just as athletically built, and he had the Kilcannon luck on his side, but a gun was a gun and money was only money.

He did as he was told, and didn't move.

The intruder picked up the bag containing his winnings and weighed it carefully, but didn't bother to open it. He—assuming that it *was* a he—put out his right hand to flip aside the breast of the jacket Canny had discarded, exposing the wallet in the inside pocket, but he couldn't take it out without putting down either the gun or the bag containing the forty-even thousand Euros. After a moment's hesitation, he left the wallet where it was and turned back to Canny.

By that time, Canny had thought of several good reasons to justify his decision not to move. It simply wasn't worth it; the money might be slightly more than a drop in the ocean, but it wasn't anything he needed desperately—it certainly wasn't a sum worth risking his life for the mere possibility of its salvation. Then again, the streak he'd invoked in order to win it might well have generated aftershocks in the fabric of reality, of which this might be one—and even if the people were wrong who believed that there was some kind of ultimate account-book to be balanced, he couldn't take it for granted that the corollary disruptions of probability would all go his way. Nor could he be sure, now that his father was fading fast, whether the records were right to declare that his luck was heading towards its minimal level, or exactly when that minimal level would be reached. If he were now a mere victim of chance, just like anyone else, it certainly wouldn't be a good time to play the hero or the fool.

The reasonable thing to do—the *only* reasonable thing to do—was to let the thief take the money, slip through the curtains and vanish into the dark garden, saying "easy come, easy go" in the casually cavalier fashion that was, it seemed, the very essence of his public image.

But at a deeper level, Canny understood that none of those

reasons was the *real* reason why he was standing still. While all of that was going through his mind, he knew that he was letting events take their course because he was paralyzed by fear. In some respects, he was only human. He could be startled, shocked, frightened...even petrified. Gambling *was* as natural as breathing to him, but the manner in which he played with cards and chips was still an act, a role, a performance. When he was precipitated out of that public persona by an event as outrageous as this one, his habitual self-confidence sometimes deserted him, leaving him with only the same instincts and reflexes to guide him as anyone else.

He didn't move because he couldn't. He was stuck.

He didn't even say anything. He waited in vain for chance to intervene in his favor regardless—for the thief to stumble and drop the gun, or for the police to burst in and spring a trap— but nothing happened. The flow of causality seemed inexorable, immune to the superimposition of a more generous alternative.

After a slight hesitation, perhaps born of trepidation and anxiety rather than any uncertainty as to what he ought to do, the intruder grasped the black bag tightly, moved smoothly across the room, and exited via the balcony. The curtain prevented Canny from seeing him jump, and the monks' garden absorbed the sound of his footfalls. It was as if he had vanished into the shadows like one more virtual serpent in a swarm.

Canny's thoughts immediately became unstuck. He snatched up the phone and pressed the button that would connect him to the front desk. The night-manager's response was immediate.

"You have intruders in the grounds," Canny said. "In the monks' garden. One is dressed entirely in black, with a ski-mask and an automatic pistol. He's carrying a rectangular leather bag about fifty centimeters by thirty-five."

"I have pressed the alarm, Monsieur," the manager told him. "The police will be here within fifteen minutes."

"I don't have time to talk to the police," Canny told him. "Can you put me through to Henri Meurdon at the casino."

"Yes, Monsieur."

Meurdon was just as quick to reply. "Henri?" Canny said. "It's Canavan Kilcannon. I think you might have a spotter in the casino—or might have had when I left. When I got back to my hotel there was someone waiting to relieve me of my winnings. Nobody knew I had them till five or ten minutes before I cashed up, so they must have worked very fast indeed. Check your tapes to see if anyone left within the last half hour—and take a close look at the crowd around the roulette table. You might be able to identify him, or at least narrow the field. I can't hang around—I'll have to leave it with you."

"I shall take care of it, Monsieur," was all the Meurdon said. "You will get your money back, if it is humanly possible." There was no surprise in his voice, just grim concern—but that was part of his standard performance, and what Canny had just told him hadn't been nearly sufficient to shock him out of it.

Canny didn't waste time wondering whether it might have been Meurdon who had tipped off the thief. Even if everything the manager had earlier said to Canny about being delighted to see him win had been so much bullshit, Meurdon couldn't afford to get involved in anything so stupidly brutal. He couldn't have people lurking in his casino to tip off muggers, either. Forty-seven thousand was a very tiny sum compared to the losses he might sustain if a rumor like that got around; it wasn't as if he was short of competition in Monte Carlo.

"Don't worry about the money, Henri," Canny told him. "I just thought you'd appreciate the warning, in case you do have a snake in the grass. I hope it's a false alarm."

"Merci, Monsieur."

Canny rang off and resumed getting dressed. The most important thing of all, he thought, was not to let the unfortunate incident disrupt his plans too badly. It would be adding insult to injury if he were to miss Lissa Lo's boat, and not just because it would save him ten or twelve hours by comparison with Air France's flight to Heathrow and its British Midland connection.

He carried the suitcase down the stairs; it wasn't heavy enough now to require the elevator, although it felt a little better once he'd added the items he'd stored in the hotel safe. He signed the account and the credit card slip.

"The intruder was about five-four—sorry I can't do that in metric—and slimly built," he said. "That's all I can tell you, except for what I said before. The lock on my balcony door hasn't been forced, although I can't be certain that he wasn't in the room before I opened it. You might want to check the wall and the balustrade, in case he left anything behind when he was climbing up."

"What did he take, Monsieur?" the night-manager asked, insouciantly.

"Nothing of any importance," Canny said. "I might have disturbed him, panicked him into running before he'd had a chance to go through my stuff and move on to other rooms. The bag wasn't mine—it belonged to the casino."

"Ah oui," said the night-manager, nodding his head. "Monsieur Meurdon will doubtless take his own steps to recover it."

"Apologize to the police on my behalf," Canny said. "Explain about my father. I have to get down to the quay before the boat leaves, or I'll lose half a day. That could be the difference between seeing him once more and...."

"I understand, Monsieur," the manager assured him. "I will take care of everything. Good luck, Monsieur."

Canny thanked him, and hurried out. The cab pulled away from the curb just as the police car was arriving, but the police made no attempt to interrupt its departure.

CHAPTER FOUR

The journey downhill was even more rapid than the journey up, but it still gave Canny time to think.

Had he noticed anyone in the casino who might be the spotter for the thief? No.

Could it possibly be anyone he knew? Certainly not.

In another life, Stevie Larkin might easily have become a petty criminal, but in this one he was a star; he probably didn't know what Canny knew about the casino's security, but that wasn't an issue.

Could the cab driver have been involved? No. He would have recognized the bag for what it was, and would have known that it must contain a tidy sum, but he certainly did know what Stevie didn't about the kind of resources Meurdon could mobilize.

It had to be someone far less obtrusive than the driver or any of the players at the table, and far more reckless—almost certainly outsiders; almost certainly nomads. What kind of accent had the thief had? Impossible to tell, from just two words, just as it was impossible to be sure whether it had been a man or a woman.

It wasn't until all these thoughts had run helter-skelter through his head that Canny began to curse himself, silently, for being such a fool. Even if he had done the right thing in letting the thief take the money instead of chancing the Kilcannon luck in some kind of lunatic defensive exercise, he had been a fool. He had said nothing; he had observed no more than was superficially obvious. If he had only persuaded the mugger to issue a further warning or instruction, he might have had a far better chance of identifying his country of origin. If he had only looked harder, more searchingly, at the cut of the black clothing, or the dimensions of the automatic pistol, he might have identified some telling detail that would assist in the hunt.

Henri Meurdon wouldn't come back to him for more information, of course—Meurdon had his pride, and his own brand of serene confidence—but it wouldn't have done the least harm to his own image had he been able to take out his mobile phone now, call the casino, and say: "Oh, by the way, there's one crucial detail I didn't mention before...."

Mobile phones were banned from the casino, of course, but the spotter must have had one. Whether he had used it inside or waited until he was clear, he must have moved with suspicious rapidity to a place where he couldn't be observed. Meurdon would surely pick him up on the CC-TV tape—and the casino's system was state-of-the-art, far more capable of facilitating an identification than anything to be found in an all-night petrol station, or even a bank. If the spotter didn't get out of Monte very quickly, the Union Corse would be on to him in a matter of hours—and he and his companions would have to travel fast and far to exceed their eager reach.

Was it conceivable, Canny wondered briefly, that the spotter might be making his escape by the same route as he was? Lissa Lo couldn't possibly be involved in the robbery, but she must have had her own minders at the casino, who would be with her still. She was too valuable a property, with or without her winnings, to be allowed to wander around the Monte Carlo waterfront at four o'clock in the morning without protection. It didn't seem likely that her bodyguards would cross that kind of line, though—or that they'd have had some kind of set-up in place, waiting for an opportunity to strike.

It took a while, but he finally arrived at the logical end-point of the postmortem, which was that he should never have placed the three fatal bets.

Don't bring down the lightning. Not, at least, for an item of cheap showmanship like the one he'd pulled. Even a midfielder like Stevie Larkin had been able to see that it was a stupid symbolic gesture—a silly farewell to a childish lifestyle, inspired by the fact that Mummy's bad news had hit him harder than he cared to admit.

He'd known that his father's death was coming soon enough, of course, but he hadn't been ready for it at all. The timing was unexpected, but that was a matter of detail. The simple fact was that he hadn't been ready for it at all. It meant too much to him. He'd been in denial. This whole trip had been a symptom of his denial. In his own eccentric fashion, he had been asking for some sort of rude awakening; he ought to be grateful that it was just a common-or-garden-robbery by some idiot who should have known better, which might not even cost him forty-seven thousand Euros. Once the Union got on to the case they'd probably pay him back the full amount, less a ten-per-cent commission, even if the stolen money had been half-spent by the time they caught up with the perpetrators—and in spite of the fact that he wouldn't dream of insisting that they make any kind of redemption, or make any kind of a fuss if they didn't. The Union had an image and a reputation to maintain, and its members were doubtless even more fanatical in its defense than they had been in the days before Communism had collapsed.

Lissa Lo's boat was still moored at the end of its jetty when the cab came to a halt on the quay; there were still ten minutes to spare before the deadline the supermodel had set.

Canny gave the driver a hundred-Euro tip, and thanked him sincerely for his effort.

"You're welcome, Monsieur," the driver assured him. *"Bon voyage."*

Canny was slightly disappointed—but also slightly relieved—when the purser showed him to a cabin, and apologized for the fact that Miss Lo had already retired to her own, in order to rest for a while before boarding the jet. Canny tried to take a nap himself, but even if the heat hadn't been so oppressive there was far too much buzzing in his head to let him rest, even though none of it was streaky in a meaningful sense.

He made every effort to put the mugging out of his mind, but that still left thoughts of his dying father to clash inconveniently with images of Lissa Lo, all caught in the net of an acute awareness that his former way of life was coming to an irrevocable end, within a maelstrom of possibilities and impossibilities that was dragging him inexorably along into an unanticipatable future.

Okay, he thought, as he tried to focus his mind. *So she isn't in any hurry to make beautiful music. Maybe she is just offering me a lift because Daddy's at death's door. I'd still be ahead of the game. On the other hand, if this were the beginning of a friendship that might turn into a relationship...well, there are cases to which the rules simply can't apply. Some women are just too gorgeous to pass up, if the opportunity arises.*

He had never been in love. He didn't know whether that was an aspect of his consistent good luck or not. If it was, the reduction of his luck to its lowest ebb following is father's death—if the testimony of the records could be trusted on that point— might give him the opportunity to fall head over heels. If not... the opportunity might still be there. It wouldn't be sensible to fall in love with someone as beautiful as Lissa Lo, of course, but if he were to receive the slightest encouragement, being sensible would be the last thing on his mind. How Stevie Larkin would envy him, in spite of all the groupies he entranced with every spot-kick!

The boat was fast; it skimmed over the placid waters of the Mediterranean with consummate grace, bumping over the waves in a near-regular rhythm that set up a surreal contrapuntal relationship with the throb of its motor. The darkness of the cabin enhanced the insistence of Canny's remaining senses, which gave the journey a dreamlike quality even though he never did manage to drift off into sleep. Eventually, he got up from the bunk so he could stare out of the porthole. He was on the starboard side of the boat, so he could see the lights on the shore, and could even make out the dark contour of the horizon against the sky, whose blue was already beginning to brighten slightly as the dawn approached.

"Goodbye, Riviera," he murmured. "I had a good time, while it lasted, but responsibility calls. From now on, when there's trouble at t'mill, it's down to me to sort it out. Maurice Rawtenstall probably doesn't think I'm up to it, but his predecessor probably thought the same about Dad. It's traditional, after all. Maybe I'm not—but with luck, I will be, and luck's something I've never been without."

He shut up then, feeling slightly foolish even though the drone of the boat's engine would have drowned out his words before they reached the ear of a listener stood directly beside him.

Nice was lit up brilliantly, as a modern twenty-four-seven city ought to be; the Promenade des Anglais seemed endless. The heat in the cabin was stifling, but he remembered only too clearly what had happened last time he'd tried to let in a breeze and he knew that it wouldn't last much longer. He let the porthole remain shut, and used the towel that had been carefully placed at the foot of his bed to mop the sweat from his face.

He felt a sudden pang of nostalgia, not merely for Cockayne but for Cockayne in Autumn, when the shadow of the Pennines wasn't quite enough to keep the chill out of the low-lying dale and the sky was as grey as slate and the smoke-blackened stone of the terraces was like a sponge soaking up the moisture from the foggy air.

Soon, it would all be his: his own little Utopia, insulated from the hurricane of change that was sweeping the world by the mass and pressure of all the Credesdale traditions.

For a moment, he could almost believe that he belonged there, cultivating his own narrow garden with infinite patience and stoicism. But then he thought of Lissa Lo, and everything that she symbolized, not merely by her beauty but by her glamour and fame, and told himself that there would be time enough for gardening in Utopia when he had wrung the last few drops of delight from the blazing glory of Cosmopolis.

And then the sun came up, rippling silver across the placid waves of the Mediterranean.

CHAPTER FIVE

Although Lissa Lo couldn't have had more than two hours sleep, even if she'd tumbled into slumberland before Canny had stumbled across his friendly neighborhood mugger, she was as bright as a button by the time the two of them clambered up the steps into the back of the jet and fastened their safety-belts.

They were running more than half an hour behind Lissa's original schedule, but once they were in the air the captain turned in his seat and leaned out of the cockpit to give them a thumbs-up sign—a promise that he could get them to Church Fenton on time, given the kindness of the weather and the co-operation of French and English air traffic control.

Canny assumed that Lissa Lo had that effect on everybody—everybody who was male, at any rate. Her face was immaculately made-up, presenting a truly fabulous appearance, and even her casual clothing was cut to the millimeter...but Canny wasn't sure that it was wise to expose himself to so much titillation.

Even though he knew that the information was irrelevant, Canny took time out to study the model's discreet companions. They weren't as ostentatiously big as the minders most successful models trotted around as status symbols, but they compensated for their lack of vulgar mass with an easy arrogance suggestive of immense skill in esoteric martial arts. Canny couldn't pinpoint their origins, although he was normally able to tell Chinese, Japanese and Filipinos apart—but then, he couldn't pinpoint Lissa Lo's origin either; she had a curiously cosmopolitan quality even though she didn't seem to have a single drop of Western blood in her veins.

The bodyguards took up positions at the back of the cabin, far enough away to sustain the illusion that whatever Lissa might say to Canny, and he to her, would remain entirely private.

The model didn't bother to apologize for the fact that there was only freshly-squeezed orange juice to drink, so Canny didn't have to explain—truthfully, although it always sound like a lie—that he didn't like drinking alcohol in airplanes because it had such a dehydrating effect. It was one of the few occasions when the conscientious abstemiousness demanded by the rules didn't seem in the least onerous, thus allowing him to assume a tokenistic attitude of compromise with their requirements. Given that he wasn't drinking, he felt that he was entitled to a certain latitude in matters of lust.

Lissa, seeming perfectly at ease, told him all about the photo-shoot she'd be doing at Harewood in some considerable detail. He would have prompted her if she'd needed it, but she didn't. Although high fashion wasn't really his sort of thing, Canny listened attentively, feeling privileged to be the recipient of so many words fallen from such exquisite lips. By the time she asked him whether he minded talking about his father, he was sufficiently relaxed not to feel too awkward about doing so.

"Not at all," Canny said. "To tell the truth, we've never been close in the usual sense of the word, even by dour Yorkshire standards. We respect one another, of course, but the old man always saw most aspects of parental responsibility as a matter of stern duty, and he brought me up to see my filial obligations the same way. If we ever did love one another, we've learned not to show it. He wasn't always the mean disciplinarian I grew up with, mind. It always sends a shudder down my spine when anyone calls me a chip off the old block, but rumor has it that Daddy was a little on the wild side himself, before I was born to sober him up. The word in the county is that he didn't calm down until his own father died, and then underwent a complete personality change. That prospect frightens me a little, but I figure that I'm my own man. I don't have to go down the same route."

"So your father was a gambler too?"

"He certainly was," Canny said, wondering whether she had something more wide-ranging in mind than the closed book-makers accounts and the bans imposed by White's and the Victoria Club. "So long as I've known him, though, it's just been Lloyd's, the Stock Exchange and life in general."

"Was he badly hit by the crash?" Her voice was light, for all the world as if she were making polite conversation without actually caring at all what she was saying.

"Everyone's been badly hit by the crash," Canny said, warily. "Luckily, Daddy never got into dotcoms—not his sort of thing at all."

"Will you have a lot of business responsibility to take over?"

Canny could have read all kinds of hidden meanings into that awkwardly-phrased enquiry, but he didn't want to, and he told himself that it would be ludicrously oversensitive to do so. "Oh yes," he admitted. He decided that it would be a good idea to choose his own ground rather than let the string of questions extend into hazardous terrain. "I'll have to give up on Monte, and Paris, and the season, at least for a couple of years. We're not expected to make a meal of mourning where I come from, but taking care of business is another thing entirely. Time was when the Mill was just a mill, churning out textiles like all the rest, but it would have gone bust fifty years ago if it hadn't moved on and diversified. There are only a handful of farms on the estate, but they've had to move with the times too—putting a few sheep out to graze the moor isn't nearly enough to qualify as a living these days, and even that's a more complicated busi-ness than it used to be. Then there's the village. Collecting the rents is child's play, but managing the pace and direction of its development...the elders are supposed to do all that, of course, but that only means that they create a deluge of demands that I have to act upon. I should have been getting involved in all of it for years—since I left university, I guess—but it was so much easier to play the prodigal son, and to let it slide and slide. Well, it's fatted calf time now, and when the feasting's over the grind begins. Grief is optional where I come from, but seriousness isn't, once there's no one else to shoulder the burden. It's simply *not done* to go on playing the black sheep of the family once one becomes the thirty-second Earl."

"The thirty-second?" Lissa echoed, flirtatiously. "Is that a lot?"

"Not really. A fair few of England's hereditary titles go back to the Norman conquest, although many are more recent. Henry IV created quite a few when he displaced Richard II. Ours is one of the odd ones intermediate between the two. We'd probably have been stripped of our entitlements when the Lancastrians hammered Richard III in the Wars of the Roses, and might have lost the estate to the anti-Catholic purges of the Puritan era, but somehow we came through—the benefits of obscurity, I suppose. The Crede's more beck than river, one of the least of the Wharfe's tributaries—and Cockayne itself wasn't built until the early nineteenth century, to house the twenty-fifth earl's newly-imported mill-workers. The name's second-hand—there's a hamlet of the same name in the North York Moors—and stealing it was false advertising of the most outrageous stripe. Credesdale was even less like the mythical land of Cockayne than the other Cockayne's idyllic setting even before the Mill was built; now it's a parody. The industrialist earl probably didn't know what the name signified, though."

"He wasn't being ironic?"

"Unlikely. Until I came along, the Kilcannons didn't do irony. We're not effete and corrupt like the aristocracy down south. We're Yorkshire folk—genuine Yorkshire folk, not Johnny-come-latelies like the Viking settlers of the Dark Ages. The twenty-fifth earl might have jumped belatedly on the Industrial Revolution bandwagon by building the mill, but we were never the kind of people who made up proverbs about muck and brass. We've got roots all the way down to the county's core. Daddy's fond of saying that we'd probably be seriously rich if our remoter forefathers hadn't taken such a caning during the Roman Invasion and the Viking Settlements, but even our relatively well-kept family records don't go back to Anglo-Saxon days, so we only have legends to draw on with respect to its early days. Personally, I don't care whether we're ultimately descended from Celts, Picts or Neanderthals—it's a cosmopolitan world nowadays, I tell him—but genealogy has always been an obsession of ours."

"It's very fashionable nowadays," the model observed.

"Sure—but we're not about to give it up for that reason, no matter how hard we and the village elders might try to resist the pressure of modernity."

"Family tradition is a valuable asset," Lissa Lo assured him.

He gave her another sharp look, but the comment seemed harmless enough. "So it is," he agreed. "But it can be overdone. I keep telling Daddy that the world has changed forever, and mostly for the better, but he just shakes his head, in a way that none but a true Yorkshireman can. I'm sorry to see him go, of course, but he's had a good innings. He's only seventy-five, which doesn't seem that much now so many people live to be a hundred, but he was in exceptionally good health until the crab got to work in his guts—didn't look a day over fifty until the middle of last year."

"You must have been a very late first child," Lissa Lo observed.

"My arrival was more than a trifle belated," Canny admitted, "although I look a little younger than I am. Daddy's first marriage was a complete disaster—his description, not mine; I never met the lady. There were no more kids after me, even though the second was better. I suspect that he was glad to stop, once the continuity of the family name was assured. Other titled families take out insurance by having younger sons, then have to send them into the army or the church to get them out of the way, but not the lucky Kilcannons. One's almost always been enough for us, and we've never been excessively afflicted by daughters."

Canny realized that his determination to fill up conversational space without exposing himself to too many questions was making him babble like an idiot, and wondered yet again whether the old man's impending death had disturbed him more than he cared to admit, but he put it down to the fact that he wasn't used to sitting this close to women as beautiful as Lissa Lo. He'd always tried to avoid fantasizing about such encounters, but he'd never been entirely successful. He'd always been prepared to tell himself that the rules had been soured by traditional misogyny, and that his father's recent conservatism in that regard must have been caused, or at least excessively influenced by the failure of his first marriage.

He wondered, briefly, whether his father had seen a dark streak before the tumors started to reclaim his flesh, and whether, if so, he'd guiltily attributed it to his own failure to keep the rules in his youth—but he set the thought aside and hauled himself back into the moment. It was impossible to think of a lift in Lissa Lo's hired jet as anything but a generous stroke of fortune, and one worth following up as far as he might be allowed.

He studied Lissa's face as she paused, having no new question ready. He had always thought her exceedingly beautiful, whenever he had caught a glimpse of her at Henley or the palace, but now that he was so close to her—without a roulette wheel to distract him—he realized that there was something about her beauty that was just as magical, in its own way, as his own gift. Canny was used to the close proximity of lovely women, and had thought that long practice had accustomed him to the necessity of withstanding most of their beguilements, innocent and ingenious alike, but he could see very clearly that Lissa Lo was in a class of her own.

"I suppose you'll have to start thinking about the next heir now?" the model observed, when their search for conversational inspiration had dragged on a few moments too long. If it had been any other woman in the world—even another of her own seriously spoilt kind—Canny would have taken that for a blatant tease or a baited hook, but from Lissa Lo it easily passed for polite and disinterested conversation.

"The old man is certainly going to say so, in no uncertain terms," Canny admitted. "He might well get very intense about it, no matter how much morphine he's on." He hesitated, but eventually decided that he'd never forgive himself if he didn't try, and bit the bullet. "Would you like to take a look at the estate while you're in the neighborhood? The house isn't in Harewood's league, but it's got some interesting features."

"I'd love to," she said. "I might not be around long, though. My agent's fixed up something in Venezuela."

"Tonight, if you like, when you finish the shoot," Canny said, indicating with the slightest possible shrug of his shoulders that he wouldn't be offended by a polite refusal.

"I'd like that," she said, with all apparent sincerity. "I don't know what time we'll finish, though—photographers are an exceedingly unreliable breed."

"That's okay," he assured her. "Come if and when you can. No need to call ahead—cook's always able to stretch dinner if unexpected guests turn up, or lay on a little late supper. Shall I draw you a map?"

"It's not necessary," she told him, flatly. She didn't even bother to ask for an address; she was obviously the kind of person who took it for granted that she'd always be able to find her way to wherever it was that she wanted to go. Canny couldn't help wondering exactly where she did want to go, and why. A man in his position had to be even more careful about reading too little into coincidence than he did about reading too much.

"Don't expect too much of a welcome," he warned her. "Daddy will be delighted to see you, if he's conscious, but Mummy's bound to be a bit distracted."

"No problem," she said serenely. "Is there anything I shouldn't mention?"

Even that could have passed, just about, for a polite and disinterest enquiry—but this time, Canny got the distinct impression that there was something not quite right about this entire situation, and that he was being pumped for information that he'd be better off keeping to himself.

"You mean the bet I placed?" he said. "Well, yes—it might be as well if you didn't mention that. Mummy would think better of me if she were allowed to assume that I came straight home rather than sitting down for one last dip on the roulette wheel. Stevie Larkin will probably be spreading the story all along the coast for the next six months, but Mummy leads a sheltered existence, so it won't get back to her any time soon if you and I keep quiet about it."

"My lips are sealed," she said.

He might have made a joke about lipstick, but he didn't. She was, after all, one of the ten most beautiful women in the world—and her best assets were perfectly natural.

CHAPTER SIX

Having been forewarned of his arrival, Bentley was waiting with his namesake at Church Fenton. The butler was chatting amiably to the drivers of the two hire-cars that were waiting to collect Lissa Lo's party and whisk her away to Harewood House; he watched the company disembark with an affected air of quiet amazement.

Customs and Immigration were less officious than usual, even though their people had been called out. Canny's bag was the one they elected to rummage through in search of illegal stimulants; he knew better than to joke about it, and simply stood patiently by until they had gone through the motions.

After the dry and artificial atmosphere of the plane the Yorkshire air seemed cool and fresh enough, but it wasn't moist and the sky was clear. The heat wave hadn't relented yet. Lissa and her entourage were already busy loading up their vehicles, and Lissa couldn't tear herself away to bid him a fond farewell. She did wave, though, and flashed him a smile as bright as any benign streak. Canny did his best to reciprocate.

"You were fortunate to obtain a lift, sir," the butler observed, when Canny finally settled into the passenger seat beside him.

"Careful planning," Canny said. "It's always best to have a supermodel and a private jet standing by, just in case one's cancerous father happens to take a sudden turn for the worse."

"Of course it is, sir," the butler agreed, effortlessly matching his sarcasm. "Is the lady an intimate friend?"

"That's not the kind of question loyal servants are supposed to ask," Canny pointed out, "Even if they have known the young master since he was in nappies. I'll be the Earl of Credesdale soon enough—I might have to make some changes around here if I can't get the respect my position demands."

"Yes sir," Bentley said. "Would you like me to make out a list of suggestions, or should I leave all that to the village elders?"

"No—I'm relying on you to keep the village elders at bay. And no, she's not an intimate friend—but I *have* invited her to pop round tonight when she's finished her shoot. I don't know what time she'll arrive, and I'm not absolutely certain that she'll arrive at all, but I'm sure the staff can cope if and when she does."

"The staff can cope, sir," Bentley assured him. "It's your mother you have to worry about. And I hope you'll remember to tell your father that you don't know the lady intimately. He's not well enough to be allowed to jump to distressing conclusions."

"I suppose he's instructed you and Mummy to draw up a list of eligible brides for me?"

"If only she and I had been able to do so, sir, it would doubtless have set his mind a little more at rest. Your mother and I have put our heads together but the county isn't what it was."

Bentley had steered north towards Ulleskelf rather than west towards Barkston, but he had to swing left now towards Towton. The country was flat hereabouts, but now they were pointed in the right direction Canny could see the hills that shielded Cockayne in the distance, and the moors forming the horizon behind them.

"It's a bigger county than Daddy seems to think," he assured the butler. "If it were necessary to go as far into the untracked wilderness of Bradford or York, it could be done without the aid of native trackers. Richmond might be difficult, though. I'm sorry he's been on at you. I suppose people of his antiquity are entitled to get bees in their bonnets, but they shouldn't used them to sting the people around them. It's my business, and I really don't know why he cares so much about something so ridiculously old-fashioned as *the succession*, but we'll just have to keep stalling."

"It might make him feel better if you were prepared to pretend," the butler suggested. "Or at least to make it clear to him, if Miss Lo does accept your invitation, that you were merely making polite reparation for her kind offer of assistance in returning home more speedily."

"I'll do the second bit," Canny promised, "but I'm not going to start spinning him a line abut some hypothetical Yorkshire lass I've got me eye on. Mind you, there's bound to be someone eligible in the village. There's a girl I was at primary school with—Ellen, the oldest of the Proffitt sisters, it was—who showed me her knickers once. She married Jack Ormondroyd, who runs the fish and chip shop and captains the cricket eleven. Her eldest daughter Marie must be sixteen going on seventeen now, just about ripe. Another four or five months and she'll be exactly half my age. She'd do, I dare say. Handsome family, the Proffitts. Maybe we ought to invite her up for tea."

"The fact that a young lady's mother indulged in a little harmless exhibitionism when you were five years old is hardly a basis for lifelong commitment, sir," Bentley observed, lowering his baritone voice a little further, "although I dare say that Mr. and Mrs. Ormondroyd would be very proud indeed to know that the gesture had enhanced their daughter's desirability."

"Oh, stop pretending to be John Gielgud in that third-rate American movie," Canny said. "It's bad enough when you come over all Jeeves-y, without taking it to silly extremes. Anyway, how is the old fart, apart from his neurotic anxieties about the succession?"

Bentley dropped his act immediately. "He's not good, sir," he said. "The relapse took us all by surprise. He knew that the chemotherapy hadn't worked, apparently, but he gave firm instructions to Dr. Hale and the consultant at St. James's to say nothing, even to me. He decided that the power of positive thinking was his only hope. He was probably pushing himself a little too hard, pretending even to himself that if he only put on a good enough act he night actually get well again. When the illusion was punctured he went from one extreme to the other, although he has rallied a little in anticipation of your return. I'm sorry we had to call you back from your holiday."

"It used to be a lifestyle," Canny complained. "Now a trip to the Riviera only qualifies as a *holiday?*"

"Things have changed, sir," Bentley said, meaning that Canny's lifestyle would have to change, whether Canny liked it or not. "Your mother really is going to need your support—the staff can only do so much."

"I know," Canny said. "I'm her son. It's my job, not yours. And even if it weren't my job, *I'm her son.* He fooled me, too. I thought he really was getting better, at least sufficiently for me to risk one last fling. We Kilcannons get into the habit of taking our legendary luck a little too much for granted." He could talk relatively freely to Bentley about the Kilcannon luck, even though Bentley didn't know the whole truth, or even the half of it. Bentley was the kind of family retainer who never worried about how much of the truth he knew and didn't know, and would never say a word out of place, even—perhaps espe- cially—if he knew more than he ought to.

The Bentley swept majestically through Towton, but the natives didn't bat an eyelid. If asked what they thought, they'd probably have opined that Bentleys weren't really Bentleys any more, now that they had to be manufactured by Rolls Royce. They'd probably have felt the same even if Rolls Royce hadn't been taken over in its turn by Germans. Canny couldn't help wondering whether the Bentley driving the Bentley was any more authentic than the car, in a world where servants were an anachronistic affectation rather than a necessity of civilized existence, but it would have been churlish to voice the thought.

"Did you have good luck in Monte Carlo, sir?" the butler enquired, innocently, as the car went over the Cock Beck Bridge and began to climb towards the ridge of the dale that hid the Crede.

"Swings and roundabouts," Canny said tersely. "Look—I might be getting a phone call or two from a guy named Henri

Meurdon about a matter of considerable delicacy. I'd rather Mummy and Daddy didn't get to hear about it. There was an incident—a robbery. It was nothing serious, and I don't want anyone worrying about it. The Union Corse will take care of it, if there's anything that can be done."

"The Union Corse, sir?" Bentley echoed, the question mark at the end of the sentence was hardly perceptible.

"It's a kind of insurance company," Canny told him, although he had no doubt that Bentley could easily come by a more accurate account, if he cared to take the trouble. The butler's computer had a broadband connection, just like the one in the library. "It's also possible," Canny added, "that a story might get reported in the gossip columns involving Stevie Larkin, Lissa Lo and a little flutter on a roulette wheel. It might be better if Daddy didn't get to hear about that either. I'll warn Mummy not to say anything if she comes across it in one of her magazines."

"That would be Mr Larkin the football player?" Bentley said. "The one who's reported to be coming back to England?"

"Yes, it would—although he didn't say anything to me about leaving Milan. And no, I don't know him well enough to get his autograph for any of your multitudinous nephews, or to put in a good word for Leeds United if he is thinking about a transfer. We just happened to be sitting next to one another in Monte, right across the table from Lissa Lo, and we all happened to bet on the same number. Pure coincidence—but you know what the papers are like when an opportunity comes up to get two celebrities' names in the same sentence, especially if one's male, the other's female and they're both sexy."

"If only you were five years younger, sir," Bentley observed, flippantly, "you would doubtless have sparked rumors of a fascinating *ménage à trois*. Were there no film stars present to add spice to the mix? Members of the royal family, perhaps?"

"I'm afraid not—unless you count royal families from the United Arab Emirates. I know you don't usually, but as they're moving Royal Ascot to York next year, I thought you might be prepared to be flexible."

"Very amusing, sir." Bentley had slipped back deep into mock-Wodehousian mode, if not all the way back to American sitcom parody, but Canny didn't mind. He had said what he needed to say, and he knew that the butler would have taken note of the salient points.

The car was already turning into the driveway of Credesdale House. The early morning sun was lighting the Great Skull from the side, making its shadowed eyes seem even more sinister than usual; Stevie Larkin would doubtless have thought its symbolism horribly excessive.

Canny got out in front of the house before Bentley took the car around to the old stables. He let himself in, and paused in the hallway to hug and kiss his mother. He was in no hurry to rush upstairs, but his mother was so enthusiastic not to delay him that he felt obliged to set aside all other possibilities.

"He's been asking for you for hours, Canny," Lady Credesdale said. "Hasn't slept a wink. You mustn't mind if he curses you a little—he wouldn't take his morphine until he'd seen you, and now he's in dreadful pain. Ring as soon as he decides to take it—Bentley will give him the shot."

"It's okay, Mummy," Canny said. "I don't suppose he's got anything new to say—he just wants to make sure that I'm on board. It won't take long." He knew that it was an optimistic judgment, but it was what his mother needed to hear. He went upstairs resolutely, nodding derisively to the lugubrious ancestors whose eyes seemed to be following his course.

You might have hooked and landed me, he said, silently, *but you haven't gutted and filleted me yet—not by a long way. Just you wait and see who'll be coming up these stairs with me tonight."*

CHAPTER SEVEN

Lord Credesdale seemed more angry than pleased to see him, but that was just the pain. The old man was propped up on three voluminous pillows, but he was having difficulty holding himself steady.

"What's all this about you flying over in a private jet?" he demanded, as Canny pulled up a chair so that he could sit as close to the bedhead as the beside table would permit.

"I got a lift, Dad," Canny replied, brightly. "A real stroke of luck—I wouldn't have got here till late afternoon if I'd flown Air France and British Midland via Heathrow. The streak's still holding, you see."

"Well it won't hold much longer, if the diaries are reliable," the sick man snapped. "I might not last through the night. This is the acid test, Can. This is when all your fine talk and snippy attitude will have to confront the reality of a situation."

"Just like you did, Daddy," Canny said, trying to make his voice sound soothing, "forty years ago. Hard landing, rude awakening, sobering experience. I know. I'm ready. If the luck really does run low, I'll be able to tell all right—and I'll take whatever action seems warranted. Trust me."

"Trust you! How...?" The old man's voice gave out under the strain. His ravaged face was tormented, as much by anger as distress. Canny rose to his feet and poured a glass of water from the decanter on the bedside table. His father tried to refuse it, but that was sheer stubbornness, and Canny eventually persuaded him to sip it.

"How can you trust me?" he said, softly. "I can see the difficulty, Daddy—and I know you're right. All my life, I've had the family gift to draw on. It's always been there, and I've taken it for granted while I've felt free to doubt it, scoff at it, resent it, kick against its discipline, throw tantrums about its sillier rules. But now the crunch will come. If the records are right, the luck will fade away to dormancy—unless and until I renew it, by following the rules. I know all that, Daddy—everything I need to know. I really will try to learn from your experience as well as my own. If things do go sour, I'll be as desperate to get things back on track as you were."

His father had settled back on the pillows, and had closed his eyes momentarily—but not because he was relaxing. Lord Credesdale was fighting his pain, fighting his anxiety—rebelling, like any true Yorkshireman, against whatever presented itself for resistance. As soon as Canny finished and sat down again, he rallied.

"*If*," he echoed, contemptuously. "Always *if*. After all this time, all you've seen and been, it's still *if*. Trust me, you say—but you won't trust *me*, will you? You won't take my word, or my advice."

The old man tried to raise his hand in order to point an accusing finger, but he couldn't do it. Canny took the hand in his own, startled by its frailty. The skin seemed slack and dry, lying upon the bone like ill-secured wrapping-paper. He couldn't remember having held his father's hand since he was a child, and he had no clear memory of how it had felt, but he knew that it must have been solid and strong, with a grip as firm as a carpenter's vice. His father had been a tyrant then, a thunderous man of whom even Bentley walked slightly in fear, and more than slightly in awe. Now, he was a shell about to be shed by a monstrous molting crab. It was terrible—more horrible in confrontation than any mere diminution of the family lucky streak could possibly be.

"I believe you, Daddy," Canny told him, squeezing the fragile hand as hard as he dared. "I always did. It's just that...sometimes

I have trouble admitting it to myself. It doesn't mean that I won't take care of things. You did. You tested it to the limit—but in the end, you took care of things. I know you haven't always thought as much of me as you wanted to, but am I really such a disappointment to you that think I won't take care of things? I have Mummy to look after, and the estate, and everything else. I know how much it all adds up to. There's no *if* about that. I'll do my best, Daddy. I'll take care of things."

That speech seemed to have the desired effect. It couldn't do much to calm the physical pain, but it did seem to set the old man's mind at rest, just a little. Canny knew that it was what his father had wanted to hear, had needed to hear. While Lord Credesdale composed himself, Canny glanced around the bedroom, taking note of the extent to which his father had reclaimed it since his last return from hospital. His mother's attempts to modernize the decor and modify the ostentation of the Georgian furniture with a few light touches of the twentieth century had been carefully undone, although the modifications had stopped mercifully short of replacing the Alma-Tadema over the fireplace with one of the ancestral portraits from the upper landing. Even Daddy, apparently, could do without the cold stare of some censorious forbear zeroing in on his helplessness.

"You shouldn't have run off like that," Lord Credesdale muttered, eventually. "Gave the wrong impression. And no matter how skeptical you are about the family history—and I've been through it myself, so I know what I'm talking about—you'd be a fool to tempt fate too far. You should be engaged by now, if not actually married. Waiting nine months to reignite the streak would be bad enough. How long's it going to take you now? Two years? Three?"

Canny couldn't help sighing, but he stifled the sound. "This is the twenty-first century, Daddy," he said. You can get mail order brides practically by return of post, even in Yorkshire. Half the female population of Bridlington would marry a lord, sight unseen, faster than a Kosovan party girl would hitch herself to a British passport-holder."

"Very funny," the old man growled.

"Actually, it's rather tragic," Canny told him. "And if there's one thing in the records that's almost certainly based on blind prejudice, it's the insistence on marrying so close to home." He knew as the words escaped from his mouth that they would probably undo all the good work he'd just put in, but the old habit wasn't about to die yet. Fortunately, his father's reaction tended more to the plaintively maudlin than the righteously wrathful.

"That's what I thought," the dying man said, "and look what happened to me."

Canny couldn't actually "look" even in memory, because he hadn't been born until his father had been safely hooked up with his mother, who was a Garforth girl, but he had heard the story of his father's first wife a thousand times.

"It wasn't because she was from outside the county that she couldn't have children, Daddy," Canny said. "There are as many barren women in Yorkshire as anywhere else, and at least as many fertile ones in every corner of the globe. The prejudices of the first dozen earls are based in the fact that not one of them ever went abroad any further than York, for lack of public transport or any desire to test the supposition that the people living south of Sheffield were all secret cannibals. We live in a cosmopolitan world now. The county has no official existence any more. Our postal address is in *West* Yorkshire now."

"It's not a matter of postal addresses or local authorities," Lord Credesdale declared. "Calling the bottom end of the east riding Humberside doesn't make it part of Lincolnshire. Yorkshire's Yorkshire and always will be, even if Bradford looks more like West Pakistan."

"You're being ridiculous, Daddy. Anyway, breaking the rules didn't do you any harm in the long run. I arrived in my own good time, and I for one am glad that it worked out that way. The matter's not as urgent now they've invented antibiotics, and I'm not even going to mention IVF and nuclear transfer technology—but if it'll set your mind at rest, I'll promise to start courting just as soon as I can, starting in Tadcaster and Wetherby. When Mummy puts it about that I'm well and truly on the market, the local gentry will be hurling their daughters at me with catapults. The only difficulty will be persuading them to form an orderly queue."

The tone of this speech might have been provocative on another occasion, but Lord Credesdale had grown used to Canny's little ways over the years, and was not devoid of a certain dry wit himself. The old man condescended to make an effort to smile, although the expression he actually contrived was something of a travesty.

"And the gambling?" the old man said. "You haven't got a habit, have you? You can let it go, when your luck dries up?"

Canny didn't challenge his father's use of "when" rather than "if", although he still remained unconvinced that the allegedly inevitable diminution of the family gift following the death of an earl was anything but a patriarchal myth intended to prey on the minds of guilt-ridden scions. "An addiction, you mean?" he said, scornfully. "No—I'm as clean as a whistle. I can leave off for a year, or ten years if it's necessary, and not feel a pang. I'll run the portfolio defensively and keep the mill ticking over, until everything's well and truly sorted. Or would you rather I put all the shares in a blind trust and gave the village elders *carte blanche* to oversee the mill's businesses the same way they oversee the village shops?"

"Good god, no! At least you've got brains, even if your luck deserts you. Stockbrokers are all crooks, and the village elders are all fools. You can rely on Maurice Rawtenstall, though. He's probably crooked, but he's discreetly crooked, and it's better to have a clever crook in charge of your cash cows than an honest idiot. If he creams a little off the top, that's fine—just make sure we get all the milk. Keep everything under control. Use a tight rein, until you've done what you have to do. *All* of it."

"I'll follow the family motto," Canny assured him, sourly but not entirely insincerely. "No matter how absurd it seems, it's best to do it *just in case*."

There was a sneer in his voice, but that too was what his father needed to hear. If he'd said it piously, Daddy wouldn't have been able to believe it, but saying it as if it were something nasty that he had to swallow regardless, he could be convincing—or as close thereto as was humanly possible.

Canny could remember a time when his father wouldn't have cared a tuppenny toss whether Canny intended to follow the rules or not, just so long as he got the lion's share of the luck he'd renewed by siring a son as the rules required—but he didn't doubt the sincerity of the old man's conversion. Daddy really did care about the succession, about the continuation of the Kilcannon streak, not because he thought the Devil would have him if the bargain weren't properly extended, but because it was the done thing. As men like Lord Credesdale approached death, they cared more rather than less about the state of affairs they were leaving behind: its order; its propriety; its continuity. Canny wasn't at all sure that he wouldn't go the same way himself, especially if the course of events did knock him off his high horse, and persuade him of the wisdom of following the rules *just in case.*

If parental tyranny had achieved nothing else as he'd grown older under its spur, it had certainly inculcated the habit of doing his petty penances and performing his petty rituals because compliance was far less troublesome than non-compliance. He hadn't had the benefit of Stevie Larkin's personal tuition, but he'd read enough psychology to know how easy it would be to take aboard the age-old obsession with lineage and continuity along with all the rest of the petty rituals once the responsibility of managing the family luck was his alone. He wasn't under any delusion that Daddy's death would free him, or that burning all the portraits of his ancestors would render their commanding stares impotent.

Canny had never met the thirtieth Earl, but he had a strong suspicion that Daddy had turned into a replica of his own Daddy—and now that he was looking down at the hollow wreck of the man his father had once been, it was all too easy to imagine that he might be forced into the shoes of the departed tyrant, possessed as he had been by exactly the same obsessive ghost.

"I'll ring for Bentley, Daddy," Canny said, softly. "It's time for your shot. You need to rest."

"Bugger that," said the old man, hoarsely. "I'll sleep when I'm dead. Right now, it's not pleasant dreams I need. Look, Can, it's hurting me to talk to you almost as much as it hurt me to stay awake fidgeting, fretting that you wouldn't get here, but if I take the morphine I'll be away with the fairies till supper-time. The least you can do is hear me out and save your smart remarks and sarcasm for someone who appreciates them."

"Yes, Dad," Canny said, meekly. He always shortened "Daddy" to "Dad" when he was making a show of being serious. He released his father's hand and sat up straighter in his chair.

"You think I'm going to give you the usual load of crap about your responsibilities, don't you? To your mother, the estate, the villagers. Well, I'm not. You're not the only one who's noticed that it's the twenty-first century. Your mother's as tough as an old boot and the villagers are perfectly capable of looking after themselves in spite of the fact that we've kept them wrapped up in cotton wool for the best part of two hundred years. The mill was never a part of the family heritage, and the patchwork pig's ear it's turned into is an irrelevance. It wouldn't matter a damn if the entire folly went up in flame tomorrow, as long as the insurance was paid up. What concerns me is you, Can, and what you make of yourself."

The dying man had to pause for breath then, but Canny knew that he wasn't supposed to interrupt. He waited, patiently, for his father to find breath enough to continue.

"You've probably always thought of yourself as a means to an end," Lord Credesdale went on, eventually. "That the only reason I ever had a son was to renew the Kilcannon streak. And you've probably always thought that I resented having to share my luck with you as much as you've lately come to resent having to share yours with me. Well, there's no denying it—

you're absolutely right. You were a means to an end, and I *have* always resented the sharing. But that's never been the whole story."

Again, Canny waited out the pause.

"You're my son, Can. I don't know how other men feel about their sons, or other sons about their fathers, but it seems to me that nobody actually needs a streak like ours to mix up their motives and complicate their feelings. As far as I can see, it's normal. Other people have their rules just as we do, and benefit in their own ways from sticking to them even while they seethe with frustration. I want you to get it right, Can. I very nearly didn't, and maybe you'd say that I never did, as a husband or a parent, but either way, I want you to do better. I want you to succeed. That's why I'm telling you, as firmly as I can. not to test the system to destruction. You've had the luck all your life, and maybe it won't seem too different at first to be without it, for a couple of months or a couple of years—but in time, the cumulative effect of being without that house percentage will take its toll. Believe me, I know.

"To begin with, I dare say, a little common-or-garden bad luck might seem like a novelty. You'll be able to bear it easily enough—but over time, it'll wear you down. Oh, you'll always be able to look around at your friends and neighbors, and see most of them getting by perfectly well under the dominion of honest probability—but it's the ones who aren't that you need to study carefully. Look at the ones who lose more often than they win, not just at their predicaments but at their attitudes. You and I know that their misfortunes are just a matter of chance, and so do they—but that's not the way they feel. They feel victimized, Can. They feel tormented. They feel that fate has it in for them. Only a few of them get around to thinking, consciously, that they must have *deserved* the bad things that happen to them, but it doesn't matter whether they get that far or not, because it's just as bad thinking that they didn't deserve it as it is thinking that they did."

Canny felt the expression on his own face setting hard as the words got through to him. Even his father it seemed, had drunk his fill of popular psychology. Even his father had worked out the elements of psychological probability. The old man's eyes were as dark and taut as they had ever been—no slackness or hollowness there!—and they were boring into him with all the fervor of a mind that desperately needed morphine to ease its distress but wasn't prepared to compromise, for the moment, between raw wakefulness and sugared dreaming.

"If it's like that for them, Can," the old man went on, relentlessly, "imagine what it's going to be like for you. You'll be the thirty-second Earl, Can, at the tail end of a winning streak that's lasted *eight hundred years*. Imagine what it's going to feel like if things go wrong for *you*! Whatever you believe now about the necessity or otherwise of following the rules, you won't be able to forgive yourself if things go awry after you've decided to break them. Oh, you'll tell yourself that it's just a coincidence, not your fault at all...but you'll never be able to believe it. You've been favored by fate all your life, and for you the dominion of probability really would be victimization by neglect. For you, it really would be torment. Believe me, Can, *I know*. I came back; I saved myself—but I've been to the kind of Hell that's specially reserved for people of our kind, and I'm telling you that it's a place to stay out of if you can possibly avoid it, and that it's certainly not a place to spend your entire life."

The sick man finally trailed off, and slumped back against the heaped-up pillows, exhausted and agonized. Canny knew what an effort it had cost him to say all that, and exactly what his father now needed to hear—but he also realized, belatedly, that there were certain things he could only say to his father, and that the opportunity to say them would soon be lost. On the Riviera it had seemed easy enough to be alone with his burden, his doubts and his questions—but now that he was home again, it suddenly seemed very much harder.

"Thanks, Daddy," he said, sincerely. "I know you needed to say that, and I did need to hear it. You probably think I've never loved you as much as I could and should, because I always resented sharing my luck, blah de blah de blah, but we can cut that crap now. We're in the same boat. Your luck's running out, and so is mine. Maybe if I wasn't benefiting from my half of the partnership, that crab would never have got its claws into your guts. Who knows? We've both looked long and hard at the family tree, and we know that our kind of luck isn't the kind that guarantees long life. How could it be? Renewability implies death. If any father had ever outlived his son, the streak would have ended there and then, according to the rules. The death of the father, before or soon after the marriage of the son, is part of the pattern."

It was his turn to pause, without fear of interruption.

"Cancer of the liver and pancreas isn't a pretty way to go," he continued, "and it certainly isn't a painless way to go, but we have morphine now. Maybe that's an aspect of the Kilcannon luck—a gift of fate to ease our passage, which just happens to be useful to millions of others as well. Maybe all the progress of the last eight hundred years has been the spin-off of fate's partiality to the Earls of Credesdale, and a few others like us with whom we're careful never to meet up, let alone compete. So, we're in the same boat—my loss of luck may be temporary and repairable, while yours is permanent, but I can still look at you and see my own future. At seventy, or seventy-five, or maybe eighty, I'm going to be lying pretty much where you are, suffering the same ultimate indignity, feeling *victimized* as well as tormented, wondering whether I somehow deserved it. A pity, isn't it, that we can't find the first Earl's magic formula, to summon up the devil for a second time and renegotiate a few key clauses in the contract?"

He was speaking metaphorically, of course. None of the last ten earls had believed in the literal truth of the family legend that credited the Kilcannon streak to a thirteenth-century pact with the devil. However the first earl had contrived to start the streak, it had been no formal agreement signed in blood—but that didn't mean that the metaphor wasn't sound.

"What's your point, Canny?" Lord Credesdale whispered, his

voice as ragged as a well-worn dishcloth. He always switched from "Can" to "Canny" when he relaxed the sternness of his posture. He never called his son by his full name, any more than Canny ever addressed him as "Lord Credesdale".

"My point," Canny said, this time letting his sigh be heard, "is that I understand you better than you seem to think, Dad, and sympathize with you more than you seem to think. For what it's worth, I also need you more than you seem to think, and I'd really like to talk to you about the family secrets while I still can, and while you're still up to it. We're not only in the same boat, Daddy, we're the only ones in it. If we can't help one another, nobody can—and this isn't the kind of situation where we can draw lots to decide which of us gets to eat the other one—all that's been taken out of our hands. We are what we are, where and when we are. I want to try to make the best of that, and I need your help—more help than just one lousy lecture. I'm sorry that I ran away, Daddy, but I'm back now. I'm not going to run away again. Can I call please Bentley to give you a shot? I think you're suffering a little more than you need to, now—and I need you to sleep so that you can wake up a little stronger a few more times before you give up the ghost. Besides, I may have a little treat for you later, and you'll be better able to appreciate it if you take a nap first."

Lord Credesdale looked up at him, breathing awkwardly. The old man tried to say yes, but in the end could only manage to nod his head. Then he tried to say something else, but only contrived to form the ghost of the word "keys".

"It's okay, Daddy," Canny said, as he got up to ring for Bentley. "I understand about the keys. We'll do it tonight, if that's what you want, after your surprise—or tomorrow, if you prefer. Either way, we'll talk again. We'll get things straightened out, for both our sakes. That's a promise."

CHAPTER EIGHT

Whether the photographer's generosity or Lissa Lo's manipulative talents deserved the credit, the model made it to Credesdale in plenty of time for dinner. She drove herself, unaccompanied, in a hire car she must have commandeered from someone at the shoot.

"Are you allowed to dump the minders?" Canny asked, when he went out to greet her, having had advance warning of her approach from the eagle-eyed Bentley.

"They don't pay me—I pay them," she told him. "When I say *get lost* they vanish."

Even though Canny had been careful to mention the possibility to all concerned, Lissa's arrival at Credesdale House made quite an impact.

"Your father will have a fit, Can," said Lady Credesdale, as soon as Lissa had gone into the guest bathroom to freshen up. "She's *Oriental.*"

"According to *Hello!*, the *Sun* and Ellen Ormondroyd in the fish-and-chip shop she's one of the ten most beautiful women in the world, Mummy," Canny pointed out. "She's rumored to be distantly related to the royal families of Persia, Bhutan *and* Siam—and don't tell me that two of those places don't exist any more, because we Kilcannons disapprove of almost everything that's happened in world history during the last thousand years, let alone the last hundred. Anyway, we all came from Africa in the beginning. The lady and I are just friends—not even *good* friends. We must have been in the same room half a dozen times, but until we happened to find ourselves at the same table last might I'd barely exchanged ten words with her. Technically speaking, we've never even been properly introduced. We're not an item; everybody knows that supermodels only date movie stars. And Daddy will love her—trust me on this."

"Well, Can, you certainly ought to be thinking of becoming an item with somebody," his mother retorted, changing tack as effortlessly as ever in the face of manifest criticism. "You know how paranoid Daddy is about *that*."

"This is the twenty-first century, Mummy," Canny told her, his voice falsely sweet. "These days, a chap can go through three or four barren marriages and still impregnate the nurse hired to wipe his arse. And I do wish you wouldn't call Daddy 'Daddy'. When I do it, it's cute and accurate; when you do it, it's faintly obscene."

"I don't know what happened to you, Canny," Lady Credesdale complained. "You used to be so loving as a child."

"Sorry, Mummy," Canny said, repentantly. "I'm just a bit edgy. You know how it is."

Actually, Canny knew that his mother hadn't the slightest idea how it was. She had to know, of course, that there was a family secret, but she had long ago given up hoping to be let in on it. She was of the old school of Yorkshire womanhood, and she could accept that kind of thing. Sometimes, Canny wished that she hadn't been so accommodating, or that his father had taken a more relaxed attitude to that particular rule. He hadn't yet made up his mind what to hope for or expect from his own future wife, but he hoped that she might at least be curious about the skeletons lined up in the Credesdale cupboard. He had no idea what the results of blabbing might be, but he'd certainly seen what *not* sharing the big secret could do to a family's internal dynamics, and he wasn't sure that he could subsume that kind of strain under the heading of things to be done *just in case*.

Mercifully, Lissa didn't come back into the drawing-room until his mother had had time to turn her frown upside-down, but Canny still had to weather the storm of Lady Credesdale's unspoken disappointment as the three of them continued the conversation along conventional lines.

Lissa congratulated Lady Credesdale on the internal decor, politely overlooking its manifest hideousness, and his mother graciously took credit for it, although it had mostly been in place before she arrived—save for such oddments as the occasional table and the magazine rack—and was maintained entirely by the servants.

Lady Credesdale, in her turn, made banal and blatantly insincere comments on the exhausting nature of a model's life, and Lissa assured her that the excitement alone was more than adequate compensation for the trouble, and that privacy was an overrated privilege.

Canny watched the two of them bring their mutual dislike to full maturity with interest, marveling at the amazing rapidity with which their hostility matured. Occasionally, he stirred the pot with a casual remark about Lissa's bodyguards or Mummy's book group—but in the end he saved the situation by offering to take Lissa for a turn around the grounds. He was unsurprised, but delighted nevertheless, when the model accepted with enthusiasm.

"You mustn't mind Mummy," Canny said, as Lissa contemplated the absurd neatness of the lawn and the mildly surreal quality of the topiary, turning her lovely face reflexively to catch the faint breath of the evening breeze. "She has exactly the kind of life she always wanted, and she feels guilty about not being able to enjoy it. She isn't nearly as idle as she thinks she is, but she's never been able to think of her commitments in the village as work. I'm going to devise a suitably-labeled executive position for her once I'm in charge of the empire, to see what she can do with some real authority. I think she might surprise herself."

"I'll probably become envious of younger women myself as I get older," Lissa said, lazily. "And I'll probably dislike myself for my shallowness. Faces and breasts fall much faster than minds decline; it's something we all have to live with, but nobody likes it—not in my line of work. Is your gardener really a Barbara Hepworth fan, or doesn't he have the patience to carve the crenellations of the hedge into peacocks and rabbits?"

"This is Yorkshire," Canny told her. "Jebb doesn't do *twee*. He doesn't really do abstract expressionism either, but we're all too frightened of his probable reaction to mention the phrase in connection with his endeavors. How do you like the gargoyles? They're not authentic Gothic features, alas—just fashionable Victorian frippery—but they do have spectacularly ugly faces. The hellhound and the worm are supposed to be the best, but I rather like the one that looks exactly like the twenty-eighth earl." He pointed out the relevant monstrosities as he spoke; they were still close to the north-western corner of the house, so they could see the side as well as the façade, although the walls still loomed over them in a satisfyingly intimidating fashion.

Lissa didn't make any comment about Canny's use of the term "worm" where she would surely have used "dragon", but she'd already demonstrated that her mastery of English extended as far as the appropriate use of the word "crenellations", so he wasn't in the least surprised.

"Isn't that one supposed to be the devil?" she queried, instead—speaking of the one that Canny had identified as an ancestor.

"Yes it is," he agreed, "but the twenty-eighth earl was definitely the model—you didn't have to go past his portrait to get to the guest bathroom, but I'll point it out later, Believe it or not, the ones on the stairs are the better-looking Kilcannons. I'm the exception, of course—I got my luck from Daddy and my looks from Mummy. I shudder to think how I might have turned out if it had been the other way around."

Thus far, Canny had navigated their stroll in such a way that the Great Skull was obscured—although she must have seen it as she drove towards the house—but once they had passed through the wooden gate in Jebb's ornamental hedge the oddly-shaped rock formation on Cockayne Ridge was clearly in view, looming ominously over the grey slate roof and neatly framed by Credesdale House's twin chimney stacks. It immediately became the obvious topic of conversation.

"Who would have expected to find a death's-head dominating the Land of Cockayne," Lissa said. "Your ancestors must have been exceedingly unsuperstitious men, to build a mansion house in the shadow of something like that—or men whose superstition worked in peculiar ways. I suppose family curses must be routine in this part of the world."

"No family in Yorkshire is complete without one," Canny assured her. "Isn't it much the same in your part of the world?"

"Superstition works in peculiar ways there, too," she agreed, "and no family is complete without its...unfortunately, Mandarin and English don't run parallel in that respect. There isn't a word in English that encapsulates our notion of such things. *Curse* gives the wrong impression."

"You're Chinese, then?" he asked, delicately.

"Not according to my passport," she said. "In my part of the world, though, nations come and go in much the same way that conquerors used to come and go. Mandarin always endures and thrives regardless. It's the language of wisdom and bureaucracy, the precious relic of the oldest empire of all."

"The language of wisdom and bureaucracy?" he echoed. "You wouldn't find many people in the West who'd yoke those two concepts together."

They were strolling up the hill now, and Lissa paused to look back at the house. From this angle, it had always seemed to Canny to be direly reminiscent of a set from a particularly corny Hammer horror film, but the model made no comment as he dutifully pointed out its worst features.

"Tacky Victorian mock-Gothic has its virtues, of course," Canny observed, angling his languid hand so cleverly that it took in the ornamental portico and the flying buttresses at the same time. "It passes for quaint nowadays, and the house must have been even uglier before, to judge by the surviving walls. Great-great-grandfather's diaries always refer to the replacement of the patched-up Tudor pile that preceded it as 'the

Restoration', although he must have known perfectly well that the Goths who conquered Rome never got as far as Britain. At least no one ever thought of replacing that beautifully coarse Yorkshire stone with red brick. The family's even older than the title, if legend can be believed—the records claim that the land was ours long before the first Earl was ushered into the Upper House—but any house that was here in the fifth century can't have been much grander than a wooden shell. Given that the Romans must have been perceived as the enemy, its occupants presumably took pride in the absence of a bathroom."

"It *is* beautiful, in its own way." Lissa's own ancestors, he supposed, must have lived in a great many exotic palaces if the assurances of *Hello!* could be trusted. Considering that she'd spent all day posing in what Daddy would have called "posh frocks", in front of the grand facade at Harewood, the model's generous approval of his own humble abode seemed to Canny to be a substantial compliment. He didn't have the feeling that he was being teased. Whatever Lissa Lo's agenda was, it wasn't anything obvious—but if she had been attracted by the fact that he was an unusually lucky man, she wasn't going to be able to cut herself a permanent slice, if the rules could be believed. If the rules could be believed, his own luck was about to take a turn for the worse, and no matter how seductive she decided to be she wasn't the right person to help him renew it.

If the rules could be believed.

Now that he was with Lissa Lo instead of his father, the force of that *if* had returned to its full and proper magnitude. In any case, what greater luck could there be in the world of the twentieth century, for a virile young man like himself, than to get together with Lissa Lo for as long as she was prepared to indulge him...*if*, that is, she were prepared to indulge him at all.

Even if she were, he reminded himself, the questions would remain, unanswered and perhaps unanswerable. How much of the supposed precedent set out in the diaries was mere legend, lies and special pleading? And even if it were true, how much time was available to him for pleasurable dalliance before he settled down?

"The place does have a certain grotesque charm," Canny agreed, negligently, "but I wouldn't want to live here full time. I've always regarded the London flat as *home*. I suppose I won't actually need it, now that Tony's abolished my right to sit in the Lords, but I'm certainly not about to give it up. Daddy was one of the most dedicated of the absentee hereditaries, although he could always be relied on to turn out for any vote to relax restrictions on gambling, but even he made abundant use of the flat while I was too young to stake my claim to it."

Lissa smiled, rather mechanically. Canny wondered whether he could think of a joke that would produce a stronger reaction, but thought it unlikely. In his experience, supermodels had even bigger stocks of hilariously filthy jokes than Hollywood producers. Traveling the world still had certain advantages over waiting in lordly fashion for the world to come to you.

From the top of the ridge they had a perfect view of the Crede meandering down the dale to the village—whose Yorkshire stone seemed rather funereal, caked as it still was in the ancient grime of the Industrial Revolution. The village elders had been discussing the possibility of a general clean-up for a generation and more, but whenever the words "Hebden Bridge" were mentioned, enough lips curled contemptuously to have the motion shelved. Personally, Canny thought that it was the proximity of the motorway that had spoiled Hebden Bridge, not the sandblasters, but he'd always stayed out of the debate. He was privately glad, though, that the ridge and the Great Skull had shielded Credesdale House from the worst effects of the soot and the acid rain that had given the walls of the contoured terraces their distinctive color—3-B black instead of 3-H grey—and their unevenly pitted texture.

"I'll show you the village, if you like," Canny said, as they set off down the slope again, having found the air on the ridge only slightly less enervating than the somnolent atmosphere of the dale.

"Is there time?" Lissa countered, strongly implying that there couldn't be.

"We wouldn't be able to walk down there and back before dinner," Canny admitted. "Another time, then. It may look a bit grim, but there are home-owners in Leeds who would kill for the opportunity to be mere tenants in Cockayne. The county council occasionally tries to reduce the elders' privileges, but the family has a lot more influence there than one democratically-elected representative, so we're clinging like limpets to our eccentricities. Some outsiders call Credesdale the last bastion of degenerate feudalism, others the last flourish of Victorian philanthropy, but the villagers like to think of themselves as ultra-patriots of the one true fatherland—Yorkshire, that is— and last-ditch defenders of an endangered way of life. We're all insane, of course—but we're Yorkshire mad, not common-or-garden mad. Daddy should have woken up again by the time we've had dinner, by the way. He'll be thoroughly morphinated, but more-or-less *compos mentis*. Would you like to meet him? Don't feel obliged—he's not at his best, by any means."

"I'd like that," she said. The shoes she was wearing weren't designed for walking up and down grassy slopes whose paths were rough-hewn and strewn with rabbit-droppings, but she moved with an unearthly grace, almost as though she were flowing. The turbidly creeping waters of the Crede came off a very poor second best. It was enough to make Canny catch his breath, and fix his eyes upon her back until he grew dizzy.

Canny felt unprecedentedly awkward. He knew that it would be a dire conversational error to bring up the awkwardness that had developed before they stepped out into the evening air, but the compulsion to babble had come upon him again and he was temporarily bereft of appropriate subject-matter. "Better to be formally introduced to a dying man than try to do girl talk with Mummy," he said, in a stupidly mock-jocular fashion. He regretted it as soon as the words had spilled out of his mouth.

"That's not it," Lissa assured him. "I really would be interested to meet your father—if *he* doesn't mind."

"I'm sure he'll be delighted," Canny murmured, wondering

exactly how far her interest and curiosity might extend, if he gave it scope to operate freely. "If my guess is right, a visit from one of the most beautiful women in the world is exactly the kind of thing that might give his morphine dreams the perfect lift— and I'm a very good guesser." They had reached the gate again now, and he overtook her swiftly so that he could unlatch it and hold it open while she passed through.

"So am I," Lissa said, as Bentley emerged from the house to summon them to the table with all the imperious obsequiousness one could expect of an authentic English butler with a passionate interest in bad Hollywood representations of authentic English butlers.

CHAPTER NINE

Canny was uncomfortably aware that the food was no better than moderate, but he took refuge in the thought that Lissa probably wasn't going to eat much anyway. The mediocrity was only to be expected, given the short notice and the fact that the village shops managed their stocks much more economically than any town-based supermarket. On the other hand, the '73 Pomerol was one of the best the cellar had to offer, and Canny took due note of the appreciative way that Lissa sipped it. After consuming two glasses she refused the sweet Bordeaux—and, of course, the dessert it was supposed to accompany. She also declined to partake of the brandy. Although she'd made her way through a perfectly adequate portion of the main course, Canny was glad to observe that she didn't visit the bathroom in order to throw it up again.

Fortunately, Canny's mother was perfectly well-behaved during dinner, and never once mentioned her gnawing fear that Canny might be gay—which she usually confided to all his female acquaintances, in the faint hope that one of them might have contradictory evidence and a willingness to share it. She called him "Canavan" once or twice, apparently spoiled for choice between her own preferred diminutive and his, but he didn't mind that.

"You know that Daddy wants to give you the library keys tonight, don't you, Can?" Lady Credesdale said to Canny, when he and Lissa Lo stood up together to go up to his father's room. "He thinks it might be his last chance to do a formal handover, although Doctor Hale keeps telling him that he might live for another month."

"He might, no matter how big a liar the old quack is," Canny said. "He's always been tough—too tough for his own good, perhaps. I'll take the keys with all due solemnity, but I'll let him take a look at Lissa first. He'll enjoy that, and we might as well share what we can, while we can."

Lissa Lo smiled at that too, but her motives were still profoundly unclear to Canny. Her body moved in interesting ways as she preceded Canny up the staircase, pausing more than once to study the portraits hung on the left-hand wall. He'd told the truth when he'd said that they were the best of the bunch, although that had more to do with the talents of the painters than the features of the sitters. The spectacular awfulness of the ones that had been retired to shadowed corridors on the third floor couldn't possibly have been *entirely* due to the ugliness of the subjects.

"Did they ever smile, or did they simply feel an obligation to glower at their painters by way of intimidation?" Lissa asked.

"They certainly didn't think of sitting for a portrait as any kind of fashion shoot," Canny replied. "It was a matter of duty, to be faced in the same purposeful way as checking the accounts and sleeping with their wives. I'm different, of course—too much television, Mummy says."

The model made no comment, but Canny could imagine what she was thinking as she scanned the faces of his ancestors. The Kilcannon luck had never extended far in the direction of good looks. Canny was, indeed, the cream of the crop in that regard. Not for the first time, Canny cursed the reflexive flicker of mad optimism which said that there might be something in this encounter for his long-suppressed hormones, as the hostile stares of his forefathers told himself to pull himself together. Wile he was in the presence so many ugly Kilcannons, he didn't dare believe that someone as beautiful as Lissa Lo might be seriously interested in his body. It seemed far more likely that she was here on some kind of quasi-anthropological field-trip, like a Brave New Worlder visiting the Savage Reservation.

Lord Credesdale looked terrible, and he wasn't entirely coherent at first, but Canny had been right about the sight of Lissa Lo giving him a lift. He rallied, in spite of the depressive effect of the morphine—and once his tongue was loose, he began to string sentences together with reasonable fluency. After half an hour of aesthetic appreciation and idle chitchat, though, the thirty-first Earl asked the model, very politely, whether he could have a few moments alone with his son and heir.

"I won't keep him long," the old man promised. "Family matter—might not have another chance."

"I can't believe that," Lissa said. "A mind as strong and capable as yours isn't about to lose its grip just yet. But of course you must have a moment with Canny. I'll wait downstairs for a while. I promised to be in my hotel in York by eleven, because I need to catch up with my sleep before taking the long haul out to Venezuela, but I won't go without saying goodbye unless I have to."

It was the first time that she had spoken Canny's nickname; Canny was profoundly glad that she hadn't called him "Can" or "Canavan" in spite of hearing both from his mother's lips.

"Thanks, Lissa," Canny said. In the circumstances, her promise to wait seemed to him an extraordinarily generous offer.

Lissa closed the door behind her, very neatly.

"You know what these are, don't you?" said the dying man, drawing the keys out from beneath his pillow, where Bentley must have placed them.

Canny knew that it wasn't a good time to say "Of course I do", let alone "Get on with it". It wasn't as if he'd never been in the library before, although he'd never been in any hurry to take up the burden of scholarship on which his father had always urged him to make an early start. He could have picked up the keys from their resting-place any time he liked, rules or no rules. The formal passing was purely symbolic—just another little ceremony, insufficiently burdensome ever to have been put to the proof—but Canny made no objection. He said his lines dutifully, trying not to sound weary—although his lack of sleep the previous night would certainly have given him an excuse.

"That's almost certainly part of the ninety-nine per cent of it that's bullshit," Lord Credesdale told him, forthrightly, when they finally returned to normality. "I wish I'd been able to figure out which is the odd one per cent, but I couldn't. You might do better. I hope I didn't use more than my fair share, if it turns out to be a wasting asset, but you know how it is—they don't all win, and when the tide's going out it's sometimes hard enough to stay even. You haven't been fucking that tinted Sindy doll, I hope?"

Canny shook his head and pursed his lips. "She's not a doll, Dad," he said, curtly. "She's heard of the Land of Cockayne, she uses words like 'crenellations' in everyday conversation, and she's prepared to compromise her diet for a '73 Pomerol. She thinks the Restoration's beautiful, in its own way, and rumor has it that she doesn't go in for fucking at all—not even photographers or footballers. She's got where she is on looks alone, without pimps or producers' casting-couches. And of all the great Yorkshire traditions, the casual racism is the one least worth preserving—I'd really rather you didn't die with a sin as stupid as that one staining your soul. Now you've seen her at close range you know how believable her reputation is."

"So what does she want with you?" was the brutal counter to that.

"She's certainly not after my money, Daddy—or the family secrets. She's no more a Mata Hari than a Sindy doll. I doubt that she wants anything at all—but that's not mutual. On the other hand, I'm not desperate. Even if I never get to kiss her, I like her a lot. Okay?"

"I'm sure she's a lucky girl in every respect," said the dying earl, with the faintest of sardonic smiles. "I'm sorry. Can't help worrying. I suppose you're free to make your own arrangements, while you've nothing to lose, but there are warnings in the journals against sirens."

"She's not a siren, Dad. She's not a Mata Hari, or a Jezebel, or a Delilah, or any other kind of *femme fatale*—and the only reason the earls of old were so bitter about female beauty was that they couldn't get any half-way good looking woman to give them a second glance in spite of their money and status. Lissa's a woman like any other—except that she can have any man she wants, and has no reason at all to pick me. She's just curious, bored with her usual entourage and her usual routine. Let it alone, will you? Can I go back to her now?"

Yet again, his father could only contrive a nod now that the reserves of bile had spilled out of him. He'd been able to talk to Lissa Lo with an approximation of charm and fluency, but he still hadn't mastered the art of talking to Canny with the aid of any other motive force than resentful disapproval.

"Tomorrow," Canny murmured, determined not to let it go just yet. Then he went to say goodbye to Lissa Lo, and to tell her that she was welcome to drop in any time she liked.

She had obviously been crossing words with his mother again; to judge by their respective expressions, Lissa had scored all the palpable hits.

"Thanks," she said, when he had offered the invitation. "It's a fascinating house, and I was interested to meet your family. Sometimes, I miss having a home—but my mother's been a nomad for years now and I hardly remember what it was like to have a real home. She's in England at present, but we might relocate to the USA next year. It's so difficult to choose where to settle, given the rate at which the climate's changing."

"I really am very grateful for the lift from Monte Carlo," he said, as he walked her to the stables, where her car was waiting. "The hours it saved me might turn out to be precious. No matter what Old Hale says, Daddy will be lucky to last the week, and there are things we need to settle."

"I understand," she assured him. "I don't suppose we'll be bumping into one another on the Riviera again, but while mother's in England I'll be popping back as often as I can. I'll ring you, if there seems to be a chance we could get together."

The last few words reverberated in his mind, and in his body too. *If there seems to be a chance we could get together.* It was explicit, then: there *did* seem to be a chance. Except that, given her reputation, he couldn't be sure what "get together" was supposed to imply.

He opened the door of the hire-car for her, but he dared not make any further move. He waited for her to turn her face towards him, and to lean forward to kiss him lightly on the cheek.

There was no passion in it at all, but it thrilled him more than any other kiss he had ever received.

"I'd really like that," he said. "Any time. Any time at all. Have a good time in York—and Venezuela. Drive carefully— the roads around here can be awkward after dark, at least until you get on to the A64."

"I always do," she assured him—although there was something in her tone that made him uncertain as to whether the assurance was believable.

CHAPTER TEN

Having had no sleep at all the night before, Canny felt quite exhausted, but his mind was still racing. His father's impending death and the new sense of urgency it had engendered would probably have been enough to keep him awake, but Lissa Lo's visit and the promise seemingly implicit in her farewell amplified the problem. The engine of his life seemed to have moved up a gear, and he knew that he would need to wind down before he could contrive to sleep. He felt that he had to take a solemn look at his new heritage, to complete the unspoken part of the ritual, but he lingered in the drawing-room until his mother had gone upstairs—fortunately, without offering any further comment on Lissa Lo.

Bentley had never before approached him to ask permission to retire, but he did so now. Apparently, the ceremonial handing over of the keys had been duly noted, even though the butler could only have the vaguest idea of its true significance.

"Of course you can go to bed," Canny said. "I think I'll go to the library for a while, but I won't be needing you again."

"Thank you. sir," the butler said, without any hint of caricature.

There were three keys on the iron ring that Canny's father had handed over so ceremoniously; one of them fitted a conventional Yale lock, one a modern mortise lock, and the third a much more ancient device.

That third key was by far the simplest at the business end and by far the most ornate at the other. The part that turned in the fingers was very intricately-worked, inlaid with all kind of arcane symbols. Anyone, seeing it for the very first time, would immediately have identified it as the key to a wizard's den.

The library's basic design had been carried forward with the antique lock; like any respectable wizard's den it had an outer chamber with a supposedly secret door hidden behind a section of book shelving—only "supposedly", because anyone with half an eye could easily work out where it was—and within the room behind the "secret" door there was a further chamber, better hidden now than ever before by the fact that its door no longer looked like a real door, but more like an item of bizarre decoration. Obedient to the well-known occult rule of three, the library's inner sanctum had an inner sanctum of its own, where its most intimate treasures were kept.

There were few shelves inside that second inner sanctum, and they were not filled with dusty incunabula; what they bore instead was a strange assortment of mortars and pestles, stone jars and glassware, moulds and candles, long brass pins and ornamental daggers. There was also a cupboard made of seasoned wood, so old that it was as hard as iron, and a desk that was just as sturdy, with a rack for pens and two sockets where porcelain inkwells had once been set. The cupboard was where the Kilcannon diaries were kept, along with more precious items of ritual apparatus: the vestments parodying those worn by priests; the speculum and the astrolabe; the idol, with gemstones for eyes.

In times gone by, Canny knew, the library—or its equivalent, in the house before the house before last, and any earlier edifices—would have been reckoned a wizard's den in a perfectly literal sense. In the days before printing, only two kinds of people were reputed to possess books: monks and sorcerers. That was because there were reputed to be two types of books: holy ones and unholy ones. The holy ones were indisputably real, the unholy ones merely their virtual shadow; insofar as there ever had been any actual volumes that passed themselves off as grimoires or textbooks of Satanic magic, they had probably been forged to prove their own existence for the benefit of those who would condemn them.

There was little of that sort in the Kilcannon library—nothing at all that seemed remotely plausible to Canny—although the earl who had commissioned the fake Restoration had dutifully accumulated a substantial stock of Rosicrucian follies and fake Hermetic tracts. There was no more evidence of any authentically diabolical text, in fact, than there was of the legendary contract than the first earl had reputedly signed, after exhaustive negotiations with the devil—whose own negotiating skills, later Kilcannons had proudly claimed, if only in secret, had increased markedly as a result of the experience.

Although several of them featured elaborate explanations as to what might have become of the "lost" diaries that had probably never existed at all, the actual diaries went back no further than the eighteenth century. They had all been written in volumes already bound, designed for the keeping of financial and public records, their pages made out of humble paper rather than parchment or vellum, vertically lined in various patterns as well as horizontally ruled to guide a pen.

Only one of the surviving texts, as far as Canny could tell, had been written before the invention of the steel nib. The Kilcannons seemed to have lacked the kind of resolution that drove monkish scribes to write when parchment was ridiculously expensive and the quill-based technology of literary reproduction required hard labor as well as considerable technical skill. No wonder they had fallen in so enthusiastically with the ideological thrust of the Industrial Revolution!

Before 1745, it seemed, the Kilcannon legacy and all its multifarious rules had been a purely oral tradition. Canny could only wonder how much educational labor had been saved when the nineteenth Earl had devised the ceremony of the handing-on of the keys, after writing down everything he "knew" about the history and mechanics of the Kilcannon luck, with as many exemplary anecdotes as firm instructions and as many philosophical conjectures as stern warnings. It had been the Age of

Enlightenment, after all—philosophical conjectures were very much *de rigeur*, even for the beneficiaries of age-old diabolical pacts.

Canny didn't bother to lock any of the three doors as he passed through them on his way to the desk. His mother presumably knew where he was as well as Bentley did, but she would no more dream of disturbing him there than any of the servants. If the house were to catch fire and Bentley had to ensure his safety, the butler would probably stand in the doorway of the outermost library and call out very discreetly: "I'm sorry to disturb you, sir, but would you mind running for your life, closing the doors behind you as you go?" Or words to that effect.

He didn't want to work, of course—indeed, he hadn't ever wanted to do any of the kinds of "work" that most of his forebears had thought essential to the maintenance of their defiance of the laws of chance—but he did feel a need to get the feel of the heart and soul of his legacy. The library might be a shrine to all kinds of folly but, in symbolic terms of which Stevie Larkin or any similarly-half-educated amateur would surely approve, it was the place in which the luck of the Kilcannons resided.

Tonight, Canny felt that he ought to be in that residence—not so much because the passing of the keys demanded it, but because he needed to feel the presence of that luck and breathe in its atmosphere.

It was his, now, to cherish for a few more days and then perhaps to revive, after an interval of a year or two—or ten, if he could wait that long or unkind fate insisted that he must—for the sake of continuity and preservation, and for the sake of avoiding a greater sin than any specified in the catechism or the Decalogue: the sin of *waste*.

After all, if the first earl really had sold his soul so that his descendants might confound the leveling effects of chance unto the fiftieth or the hundredth generation—no one had ever pretended to know exactly what duration he had demanded, or exactly how far the devil had beaten him down—it was up to those descendants to ensure that he had got full value for the price he had paid. A Yorkshireman, as Yorkshiremen had always been fond of saying—or at least hearing—was like a Scotsman with the generosity squeezed out.

Canny leafed patiently through the nineteenth earl's diary, congratulating himself on his ability to decipher the appalling handwriting, as black and coarse as Cockayne stone.

The rituals he was supposed to perform in connection with his father's funeral didn't seem too taxing. The fasting wouldn't be fun, but the rest of it wouldn't hurt him in any other way than making him feel silly. The ancient "wisdom" didn't call for any serious self-mutilation until the marriage ceremony—the private one, not the one that would take place in church—and the birth of his first-born son.

"I wish I could believe that you'd simply made the whole thing up, you old fraud," Canny whispered to the old man's non-existent ghost. "What a hoax that would have been! A story to knock any Gothic novel into a cocked hat and make Defoe's history of the pirates look like sober journalism. But you believed every word, didn't you? Every word that your father had handed down from his father before him, and so *ad*-not-quite-*infinitum*. Even as you questioned it, and brought your Enlightenment sensibility bravely to bear on all its heaped-up absurdities, you didn't dare to do anything but believe it, maintain it, and hand it on. You wrote it down and locked it up in your wizard's den-within-a-den, along with your crazy apparatus, but that's as far as your daring went.

Having had the benefit of a modern education, Canny understood only too well how the age-old logic of superstition worked, and how it persisted in a supposedly enlightened era. He had seen it at work in many a sporting dressing-room and all the places he had ever been where gamblers hung out—which were very numerous indeed.

We did *that* when we won, the argument ran, so let's make sure we do the same again, but we did *that* when we lost, so let's declare it taboo until the end of time, *just in case*.

He knew from long experience as well as patient observation

how easy such rituals were to start, and how hard they could be to put aside. He knew how they tended to accumulate, even within the space of a sportsman's brief career or an untalented gambler's hectic ride to ruin.

Given centuries to run riot, as in the case of the Kilcannon inheritance, their bulk and complexity could hardly help becoming horribly oppressive.

Sportsmen and gamblers rarely had any fate more terrible in mind than losing a game or losing their money—and even sportsmen with as much at stake as Stevie Larkin, and gamblers playing with the entire wealth of Arab emirates, had to figure that life would go on in the wake of those sorts of disaster. Children's rhymes came closer to the texture of the Kilcannon legacy when they endeavored to lend credulity to the ghoulish idea that you could break your mother's back by stepping on a crack. Given the perceptibility of vivid "streaks" whenever fate lent a particularly conspicuous hand to a Kilcannon, it wasn't at all surprising that the family luck came elaborately hedged about with sinister rumors of "black lightning"—not to mention the gnawing paranoia of the suspicion that the "cosmic balance" might one day be righted at a single appalling stroke, whose divine judgment would immediately deliver all the presumptuous Kilcannons into Hell.

"But it's all just *fear*," Canny said to the Kilcannon ghosts. "It's all guilt, anxiety and psychological probability."

Canny owned several books on psychological probability, by everyone who'd ever considered the phenomenon in detail, from John Cohen in the 1960s to Martin Ellison in the present. He understood that the human brain was preprogrammed by natural selection to look for patterns and induce generalities— that being the mental foundation of rational expectation—to the extent that it could not admit to itself that sometimes, there really were no significant patterns to be found. Even people who knew perfectly well that every spin of a roulette wheel was independent, so that red coming up four times in a row had no influence at all on the probability of its coming up again, were still more inclined to bet on black. Mere knowledge was insufficient to overturn the built-in hunger for order, for pattern, for balance, for even-handedness.

He understood, too, that the human brain was also preprogrammed to reward successes to a greater degree than it penalized failures, especially if the successes were few but large and the failures frequent but small, so that even people who knew perfectly well how heavily the odds were stacked against them could not resist the temptation to feed money into slot machines, or buy tickets in the National Lottery, in the hope of hitting jackpots.

He knew all that as well as anyone—but he knew better too. He knew that the Kilcannons had a gift that enabled them to beat the odds: a "house percentage" granted to them by some cosmic whim; a plenary indulgence protecting them from the mercurial wrath of mathematical probability. If common men were vulnerable to superstition, how much more vulnerable was a Kilcannon? If common men made the sign of the cross before feeding money to one-armed bandits, or fondled their lucky rabbit's-feet as the roulette-wheels began to spin, even though the house percentage always worked against them, how much more inclined was a Kilcannon to indulge in ritual, given that he was *guaranteed* to come out ahead if he did?

Canny sighed, and closed the book.

What he wanted, more than anything else in the world, at that moment in time—more even than a chance to savor Lissa Lo's naked body—was a chance to avoid being sucked into the vortex of anxiety and obsession that had consumed his father. So far as he could tell, that same vortex had consumed his grandfather too, and twenty-nine other Earls of Credesdale before him, exacting a price for their uncanny luck that was as heavy as it was ironic. If he couldn't avoid that fate, he reminded himself, then what he had—or had had, and might yet recover—couldn't be regarded as a gift at all. It would indeed become the family curse: a diabolical pact contracting him to a perverse kind of torment.

It was a challenge he had to meet. If he couldn't do it, with all the intellectual resources of the newly-born twenty-first century at his disposal, who could? His own son? The son, that is, that he would be forced by superstition to sire, in order to renew the lucky streak that would be damped down by his father's death and not return to full strength until it could once again be shared by a father and son—who would hardly be able to help loving and resenting one another at one and the same time.

Canny glanced at his watch, and saw that had been reading for longer than he thought by the light of the bull's-eye lantern mounted on the leather-topped desk. He had been seated at the desk for an hour, when he should have been in bed catching up with a night's lost sleep.

And yet, he still didn't feel that he could go to sleep. His mind was still seething.

He sighed again—and then he suddenly looked up.

Lissa Lo was standing in front of him, on the far side of the desk, watching him curiously.

CHAPTER ELEVEN

"That's very clever," Canny said, trying to sit still even though his heartbeat had accelerated with distressing suddenness. "I never heard a sound." *Or saw a warning cloud of symbolic darkness*, he didn't add.

"It's just a matter of knowing how to walk," Lissa Lo assured him. "If you'd bothered to lock the front door, though, I'd have had to ring the bell. I never believed what they say about country folk not feeling the need to lock their doors, but I guess it must be true after all."

"No it's not," Canny said. "It must have been a misunderstanding. Bentley must have thought the *handing on of the keys* meant that I'd be assuming responsibility for the whole house—that's why he came to ask permission before he went to bed. I didn't realize." He paused then, not knowing which of two possible interpretations he ought to put on the remarkable fact of Lissa's unexpected return.

Either she was far hungrier for his body than she had seemed, and far hungrier than could ever have seemed likely—or she was avid for something else entirely.

She wasn't offering him any obvious clue. She just stood there, waiting.

"It's only a matter of hours since I gave Mummy and Daddy my solemn word—or at least my solemn opinion—that you weren't a Mata Hari," he said, "but here you are, Matahari-ing away like an expert."

"And if you'd locked the door to this strange little cupboard," the model added, "I'd have had to knock—or pick it. It's a terrible lock, by the way—I could open it with a nail-file. I should have rung the bell anyway, I suppose, but it's late. I didn't want to wake the whole house. No, that's not true. I didn't want to wake the creepy butler. I wanted to see *you*, in private."

"That's very flattering," Canny said. "the stuff of wet dreams, in fact—except that I've a sneaking suspicion that it wasn't the prospect of hot sex that brought you back. Twice or three times I *almost* had suspicions, but I kept telling myself not to be silly."

"What kind of suspicions, Canny?" she asked, mildly.

"I never show my hand until I'm called," Canny said. "If you want to beat around the bush, I can beat with the best. You did seem unusually curious, and I'm not quite stupid enough to flatter myself with the notion that it might be my sex-appeal that excited you. I hoped that you were serious about seeing me again, of course, but I certainly didn't expect you to change your mind half way to York and come back tonight. For that, you'd need a more powerful reason than anything ordinary."

"I couldn't help myself," she told him, with all apparent frankness. "I drove away because that was the rational thing to do—the *safe* and *sensible* thing to do—and then I turned around and came back. Perhaps I'm just a typical fickle female." The last comment was saturated with sarcasm.

"You still haven't told me why," he pointed out.

"It was your ability to beat the odds that interested me," she admitted, finally laying her cards on the table face upwards.

"That's what I figured," Canny conceded.

"Can I sit down?" she asked.

"I'll get you a chair," he offered.

"No need," she assured him. She stepped back through the door to collect one from the intermediate room, and placed it opposite his, with the desk between them. It looked like a businesslike arrangement, and her attitude seemed businesslike too. He couldn't help regretting that.

"What tipped you off?" he said. "It wasn't hitting the zero— you half-expected that, didn't you? Was it Henri Meurdon?"

The last question seemed to surprise her, and Canny realized belatedly that he'd given away more than he should have done.

"No," she said. "You told him?"

"Of course not. He'd been studying me for a while, with the aid of his trusty computer and a well that I'd returned to at least once too often. I don't understand why *you* decided that my luck might be something out of the ordinary, though. You haven't had the same opportunities."

"I wasn't sure until I saw the world smear," Lissa said, calmly, as she recomposed her sitting position, as if she were posing for a photographer. "Before that, it was just a gathering sensation. It takes one to know one, isn't that what they say in England? I hadn't expected the disruption associated with your hitting the zero to have the same after-effects as it would have done if I'd deconstructed the moment myself—but I hid it well, don't you think? Better than you, perhaps?"

The fact that she had to turn away momentarily to reposition the chair exactly as she wanted it allowed Canny to make some attempt to hide the effect that this bombshell had on him. The casual way she'd referred to the world's "smear" implied that she didn't realize quite how appalling the claim would seem. Deconstructing the moment! He'd never thought of calling it that, but it had a certain charm. Calling it a "streak" was Yorkshire bluntness, of which Canny had never entirely approved. "Smear" wasn't much better, though.

He thought about denying everything, but that seemed to be the least sensible way to play the scene, given that he was surrounded by the trappings of his strange calling. He'd learned long ago that when anyone raised the possibility that his luck was unnatural in an earnest manner, the best strategy was to play along, but never to seem to be taking it seriously. This was an unprecedented situation, though, and perhaps an impossible one. If Lissa Lo were lying about what she was, she must know far more about his own gift than anyone he had ever met before. If she were telling the truth, she might be more dangerous still.

"What after-effects do you mean, exactly?" he asked, warily.

"Do you want a demonstration?" she countered. "Isn't my lifestyle proof enough of what I am?"

Canny did want a demonstration, but he knew that it might be dangerous to demand one. As for lifestyle...well, he'd run around with a great many rich and beautiful people who'd never had to give their luck a helping hand. Stevie Larkin was rich and famous, but he certainly wasn't a streaker, just a big kid who could kick a ball with more than usual precision. Streakers—especially if they heeded the kind of advice he'd just been reading—tended to be more moderate in their habits and demands than footballers or movie stars...or models.

On the other hand, he thought, the rumors about Lissa Lo's sexual abstinence suggested that she did practice some kinds of self-restraint, and he'd often given in to temptation himself. He didn't want to jump to any conclusions just yet.

"You got a first at Cambridge," Lissa Lo said, when Canny didn't answer her question. "My guess is that you didn't do much work, but the right questions came up in the exams. Your father wanted you to do economics, but you thought pure science was the way to go. You studied genetics, because you thought the answer might be there—but if it was, it didn't stop you following in the family tradition by becoming a habitual gambler, in which role you've enjoyed considerable success. That's all gossip, by the way—I haven't done anything as stupid as hiring a private detective, and I strongly advise you not to do that either. As I say, last night wasn't the first time I wondered about you, but it was the first time you planted yourself right under my nose, and the first time you placed a bet so ambitious that I could be certain you were the cause of the deconstruction. I had other reasons for my suspicion, of course. You're very abstemious by the standards of your kind, they say. No drugs, very little sex. I can relate to that. Are you sure you don't want to set up a demonstration? I know your father's not dead yet, but as long as we don't enter into any kind of contest I don't see what harm it can do. We don't need to risk anything in competition, Canny—not while we have the option of wanting the same things."

Canny wasn't at all sure that he and Lissa Lo did—or even could—want the same things. He had to say something, but he was completely at a loss. In the end, he became desperate.

"You didn't by any chance, have anything to do with the fact that I lost that forty-seven thousand Euros as easily as I'd made it?" he asked.

Her face registered her astonishment with what seemed like revealing clarity. "I didn't know you had lost it," she said. "When?"

"Last night," he said. "I was mugged when I went back to the hotel."

"Oh! And you think that I...oh, I see! You're not accusing me of complicity in the mugging, just of complicity in the disruption of probability. You think my presence might have put a twist on the smear! I never thought of that, but it *was* a peculiar one, wasn't it? Maybe we've already done the demonstration, then. Did things get tangled because I bet on zero with you, do you think, or do you suppose that my simply *being there...?*"

Canny was glad to see that she was capable of confusion too. "I don't know," he said. "There's a lot I don't know. Apparently, there's a lot that you don't know either."

She recovered her composure with remarkable swiftness. Within five seconds she was as calm as if she had simply changed poses. "*Did* you get any answers from genetics?" she asked, eventually.

He was delighted to discover that he had recovered his own composure too. "The only clear answer I got from genetics," he told her, "is that any gift or curse that might run in my family has to be determined by a gene on the Y-chromosome. It's always been father-to-son, not just with us but with all the others my forebears have knowingly run into. Which makes you doubly anomalous—and maybe doubly dangerous, if you really are what you say you are." It wasn't just a Mata Hari she wasn't supposed to be, he remembered; it was a Delilah, a Jezebel, or any other kind of *femme fatale*. Salome and the Biblical Judith, he recalled, really had been woman enough to cause men to lose their heads.

"Are you sure it's genetic?" Lissa asked him. Her eyes travelled suggestively around the shelves. She used her gaze as a pointer, picking out the jars and the mortars as well as the books stacked in the open cupboard."

"They're nothing very exotic," he assured her. "You might have noticed a few commentaries on the Kabbalah on your way in, but the treatises allegedly inscribed in blood are actually written in red ink, the alchemical journals are records of unalloyed failure, and the grimoires are all fake. I suppose, if you add all three rooms together, it's one of the largest collections of books on ceremonial magic and the occult sciences in the country—but I've turned enough pages in the next room to know what rubbish it all is. Even the more credulous of my ancestors left copious marginal annotations—they probably reduced the commercial value of the collection by forty per cent, but they show up its true worth with terrible clarity. Different earls preferred different euphemisms, but the gist is always the same. *Trichardy. Japeworthy. Poppycock. Workless. Meaningless. Worn out. Probably trivial. Utter crap. Whatever does the job, it isn't this.* Take your pick."

"And genetics is no better?" she persisted.

"I used to be sure that it had to be genetic," he said, carefully, "but all my ancestors took it for granted that it was magic—even Daddy, once he'd got his fingers burned in a metaphorical rather than a literal way—so I suppose I might be wrong. How about you?"

"It was first explained to me in terms of yin and yang," Lissa Lo told him, "but it's a cosmopolitan world now. Our horizons get wider all the time, as they must. I have to say that I admire all this scholarship. Would you believe that with us it's always been strictly oral? Never a word written down. Those are manuscripts in the cupboard, aren't they? How far back do they go?"

"Not far," Canny said. "It was oral with us too, until 1745. The Enlightenment."

"Ah! It didn't reach my part of the world, I fear. We thought we were enlightened enough already."

"We had steel nibs and a phonetic alphabet," Canny told her. "It might have been more difficult for your ancestors, stuck with paint-brushes and all those Mandarin pictographs. No wonder Confucius expressed his philosophy in aphorisms. So how does the story work out in terms of yin and yang?"

Lissa sighed, but she seemed to recognize the inevitability of making the running. She was the guest, after all. She must suspect—as he and his immediate forefathers had—that any magical account she'd been given was almost certainly codswallop.

"The cosmic balance," she said, touching her delicate chin with a well-manicured fingernail. "Opposition and continuity. Fortune and misfortune are unequally distributed among the living, but there has to be a overall evenness; our good luck has to be obtained at the expense of others. The gift has to be passed on, but it can only be doubled while the inheritor is a child; as the child grows to adulthood, she takes an increasingly bigger share of a fixed pool, while her mother ages and eventually dies. The cycle has to begin again, after a suitable interval, or the chain breaks. But the luck always has to be guarded, lest it dissipate. Each new recipient has to cast the spells, maintain the rituals and deny herself certain self-indulgences, especially sexual, except in very particular circumstances. Is that how it works with you Kilcannons?"

"Pretty much," Canny admitted. He didn't elaborate—not so much because he was being discreet, but because it didn't seem that there was much to add. He could no longer doubt that she was exactly what she said she was, and that she knew him for exactly what he was.

The question was: where did they go from here?

CHAPTER TWELVE

In the short term, at least, where they went was deeper into matters philosophical and theoretical. Of numerous unsafe alternatives, that seemed the safest to Canny—and, apparently, to Lissa too.

"It all seems to make a certain sense, to my mother at least, in the context of what your bigoted father might disdainfully call Eastern Mysticism," the model told him. "In her equally-bigoted view, it doesn't seem to make any sense at all in terms of what she derides as Western Materialism—but you and I have both grown up in a world whose scientific establishment is entranced by quantum mechanics and the uncertainty principle, so we know better than either of our respective parents or any of our ancestors, where the opportunity for a proper explanation might lie. The hereditary aspect is puzzling, though. If there were a gene for good luck—passing over the question of how on Earth the biochemistry could work—surely it would give its possessors such a massive advantage that people like you and I would be far more common than we are."

Lissa's beauty seemed even more mesmeric to Canny now, in the shaded lamplight, than it had aboard the neon-lit jet or the twilit ridge. He knew, though, that the ever-problematic possibility of sex had now become extremely problematic indeed.

She might still be lying, Canny told himself, although he couldn't believe it and it was more deliberate distraction than serious proposition. *She might have been very thoroughly briefed by someone else—someone of my kind in a narrower sense. But if there is a male streaker involved, he's playing a dangerous game....*

"It's not be as simple as that," he told her, trying hard to keep his tone relaxed and matter-of-fact. "There are some genes that are only advantageous if they're rare. Don't bother trying to come to terms with the paradoxes involved in groups of lucky people playing zero-sum games—just think about those harmless hoverflies which mimic dangerous wasps. The mimicry only protects the hoverflies if there are so many more wasps around that the predators are able to learn that black-and-yellow-stripes are associated with stings, so the mimetic coloration of the hoverflies can only be favored by natural selection along with genes that maintain their relative rarity by restricting their reproduction.

"Cuckoo-strategies might be a more relevant example. Cuckoos can only get away with laying their eggs in other birds' nests if they don't become too common. As their numbers increase, so does the pressure on their victims to develop the ability to detect and destroy their eggs, so the price they pay for getting other birds to raise their offspring is that they don't lay very many eggs. In their case, natural selection works in favor of a strict avoidance of reproductive excess. Sometimes, selfish genes have to be exceedingly prudent in order to maximize their own selfishness."

"And you think it works the same way with us?" she said, apparently following the argument easily enough. "You think that the genes producing our luck, however they might accomplish it, have to be packaged with other genes that make it difficult for us to reproduce?"

"Without any supportive biochemistry it's just so much sociobiological flimflam," Canny admitted, "but the logic seems sound enough. You're still young, but you've been around long enough to know how much hatred there is in the envy that people try so hard to hide whenever they smile at people they credit with the luck of the devil. Sometimes, I think people as lucky as us use up ninety per cent of their luck just keeping themselves alive, so that they can reap the full benefit of the other ten per cent. Their rarity is a precious asset."

"Have you ever met another?" she asked. "Before me, I mean."

"Maybe," he admitted. "I've certainly thought so, more than once—but if there's one thing the journals are very clear about, it's the necessity of caution. The last thing a lucky Kilcannon wants to do is to come into conflict with someone who also has luck on his side—and you seem to have been given the same warning. The diaries record numerous anecdotal instances of things getting very freaky, usually with ruinous results—although the darkest warnings of all must be products of paranoia, because there's no way anyone could have survived to compile the records. If I'd thought that your interest in me might be generated by a similar talent, I might not have dared to set foot on your jet—and I'm astonished that you let me do it, given what you knew."

"Mother would be horrified," the model admitted. "But the world changes so quickly, doesn't it? My generation has so little respect for the wisdom of its ancestors."

"I've been tempted too," he admitted. "Throw discretion to the winds and challenge the gods to do their worst! After all, it can't really be magic, can it? Almost all of the so-called evidence of disasters befalling the foolishly bold is anecdotal hearsay—but on the other hand, there's hardly a portrait on the staircase that doesn't have one seriously weird tale hanging invisibly from its frame. Irresistible forces don't mix—and so far as I know, they've always been rare enough, and exercised so discreetly, that they've only had to demonstrate their immiscibility to my ancestors once or twice in every century."

"That's what our tradition says," she agreed. "If it were genetic, though, you'd have to look at the matter differently."

"The Kilcannon women only have to be fertile, so far as I can judge," Canny said. "They don't have to be carriers. The lucky ones only have one son apiece, of course—although there are some interesting accounts in the diaries of sons that weren't lucky...admitting cuckoos into the nest, one might say, if one were to extend the earlier metaphor. If you'd been a man, I probably wouldn't be talking to you like this—but I suppose the fact that you aren't raises possibilities I never had to consider before. Some temptations are hard to resist, as you must know very well."

"I think I've met other females," she said. "I was warned about not keeping close company with them—but I wasn't warned about men like you. Other kinds, of course, but never ones like you. That's very strange, don't you think? If the gift really has been handed down through hundreds of generations, there must have been other meetings like this one, not just same-sex encounters."

We all came from Africa in the beginning, Canny thought, *but we went our separate ways. If there are two different genes, they could have emerged independently, in the latter stages of the story, one in the East and one in the West. The female variant could be sex-limited in its expression. It's a cosmopolitan world now, but it hasn't been that way for long, and cuckoos have to be prudent to survive and thrive.*

"I suppose there must," he said, aloud. "Maybe they didn't dare talk as freely as we have. Maybe they were blinded by their preconceptions, and couldn't even get this far without running for cover. Or maybe the multiplication of freakish possibilities really did cause some kind of a storm that wiped them out. Maybe we won't survive the night—the clouds could be mustering the black lightning even as we speak. You have been warned about world-shattering catastrophes, I suppose?"

"Deconstructed moments can't always be reconstructed," she said, with a lightness that was probably feigned. "The illusion of Maya sometimes dissolves and expels that which has troubled its harmony. Things fall apart. That sort of thing?"

"That sort of thing," he agreed. "It must have sounded far more ominous in the days before high explosives and modern seismology. Do you always get by on two hours sleep a night, or is it one of your...ritual privations?"

She smiled at that. "Tired or not, I ought not to stay any longer," she said, with a mischievous smile, although her relaxed posture suggested that she was not yet in a hurry to leave. "My people will be missing me in York, and they know where I was bound even though they didn't come with me. I wouldn't put it past them to come looking for me—or even to phone mother, which would really whip up a storm of sorts. Do you think I dare come back another time, if the black lightning leaves me the choice?"

The way she said it implied that she'd already got what she had come back for: confirmation of his nature. She hadn't been sure, and she hadn't been able to bear the uncertainty, but she was absolutely sure now, in spite of his calculated flippancy. It was a different ball-game now, and they both had to take aboard the possibility, however slim, that there was a zero on the wheel that really might wipe them both out. Canny knew why he might be willing to take the risk, but he couldn't see what was in it for her. She was one of the most beautiful women in the world, but he was a very long way from being one of the ten sexiest men.

"Do you want to come back?" he riposted, wondering what answer he ought to hope for.

"Will you let me in if I do?" she parried.

Canny didn't want to answer that in case he over-committed himself. "All my ancestors thought it was magic," he said, carefully. "They didn't have our oh-so-modern flexibility of mind, or the lesson of the uncertainty principle. But they did contrive to renew their lucky streak over and over again for at least thirty generations. How many other families had something like it, but lost it through carelessness? We don't know. You and I might be wiser to take what precautions we can, and stay in different hemispheres from now on."

"I wasn't betting against you at the table in Monte Carlo, even before the last bet of all," Lissa said. "That's the beauty of roulette—you can bet on possibilities that aren't mutually exclusive. If you hadn't decided to pull off that coup on the zero, I could have bet with you without being so obvious—by betting on the color of your chosen number, or whether it was odd or even. You could have been more discreet than you were."

"True," he admitted. "But I didn't know that there was a risk of tangling my streak up with someone's else's. You did, apparently."

"I still couldn't be entirely sure," she said, without specifying how long she'd been suspicious of him, "but I was sure enough not to bet against your zero. Twice running I let my chips stay where they were; the third time, I went with you. Would you have done any differently, in my situation?"

It was a genuine question, but it was one that Canny couldn't answer. "I'm not sure I'd have thought it was a good idea to offer you a lift in my private jet," he said. "Even though we wouldn't be in any kind of competition...."

"Yes you would," she said, confidently. "You wouldn't have been able to resist the temptation—and for once, I'm not talking about my face and figure. In view of everything you've told me tonight, I'd say we're now running even in the silly risk stakes."

"In that case, it might be sensible to stop now," Canny said, dryly.

He knew that he was the one who was in greater danger. His father was upstairs dying, and if history was any guide at all, his own streak would dwindle away with Daddy's frail flesh. Unless Lissa was much older than she looked, her mother was probably in perfectly good health, having only begun to lose her looks a couple of years ago. But he also knew that he didn't want Lissa Lo to walk out of his life forever, no matter what the risk might be.

Maybe, Canny thought, he should have gladdened his mother's ignorant heart by making sure that he had a potential bride waiting in the wings—a bride he could impregnate as soon as the ink was dry on Daddy's death certificate. Some of his more recent ancestors had been careful to do that, although others had loudly sung the praises of the education gained during the "doldrums phase." Some of the ones who'd rushed into marriage—including, he supposed, his father—hadn't been as fortunate in their choice of brides as they ought to have been, if their lucky streaks had applied to all matters equally. But what difference could it have made to his present situation if he'd been engaged, or even in love? It was probable, Canny supposed, that Lissa Lo still thought of her discovery of his gift as one more stroke of her own good luck—but he had to bear in mind the potentially-ominous fact that neither of them had had any previous inkling of the possibility of any such meeting.

The model must have been doing her own share of thinking, because she said; "Maybe we'd simply neutralize one another if we entered into competition. Restored balance. Yin and yang. That's likely, I think. But if we were to work together...to lay the same bets...."

"We still don't know whether your presence added a twist to my streak," Canny pointed out. "If it did, and if the mugging was part of the twist...betting together might not have the effects we'd expect. Synergy might work in mysterious ways."

She smiled at him. "I really do have to go to Venezuela," she told him. "The jet's ferrying me down to Heathrow tomorrow morning to pick up a 747. I have to go now—but I'm glad I came back. We will talk again, won't we?"

"I'll be tied up here for quite a while," Canny countered. "I've got a father to bury—and a hell of a lot of reading to do, if I take his advice."

"That's not an answer," she pointed out. "But that's okay. I'll come back anyway, and take the risk of being turned away. I won't try to alter the odds in my favor—but I still can't believe that you can turn your back on me now."

"If that's what you want," he conceded, knowing that she held all the cards, and that she knew it—and also that she might be the better judge, if only because she were subject to the lesser temptation.

"It is," she told him—and he couldn't help his heart quickening at the sound of the words, as if they were a promise of unsurpassable joy.

CHAPTER THIRTEEN

Canny went straight to bed, but couldn't sleep. Given that turning the pages of the old diary hadn't relaxed him, it was hardly surprising that his unexpected conversation with Lissa Lo had woken him up to the full extent of which he was still capable—and even though her departure had let him down again dramatically, he couldn't let go. The food for thought she had fed him had given him terrible mental indigestion, and he couldn't even begin to attempt its coherent organization, but he couldn't fall asleep. Eventually, he began to dream while he was still awake, and his dreams were hectic.

He didn't drag himself out of bed until eleven-thirty the next day. Bentley didn't call him for breakfast, and probably wouldn't have called him for lunch either if he hadn't made it on his own.

"How's Daddy?" was the first thing he asked of his mother, when he went into the living-room to read the morning paper.

"Asleep," she said. "Everyone appears to be keeping strange hours now. Actually, he seems much better—or, at any rate, much calmer. I don't know what you said to him yesterday, but you obviously set his mind at rest. If only you could have...."

"Well, I couldn't," Canny said, cutting her off. "It wasn't what I said so much as the timing. I'll have another chat with him later—and I'll try not to make things worse again."

"You, on the other hand, look dreadful," Lady Credesdale observed, by way of retaliation.

"Thanks," he replied. "I'll try to pull myself together before I go up to see Daddy again. Are you at home for lunch?"

"Yes, but I have to go down to the village this afternoon. The servants pass on all the available gossip at light-speed, of course, but I'm the source of official news. Everyone waits on my reports—even Maurice Rawtenstall at the Mill and Father Quimper."

Mercifully, it wasn't until his mother had left on her mission to inform that the telephone rang. Canny was still in the dining-room, lingering over a second cup of black coffee.

"Henri Meurdon," Bentley reported to Canny, who was feeling slightly better now that lunch had revived him.

"Thanks," Canny said, as he went into the drawing room and picked up the receiver. He waited for the butler to close the door behind him before saying: "Henri? You have some news?"

"Yes and no, Monsieur. The matter is more complicated than we thought."

"What do you mean?"

"You have doubtless been distracted by the matter of your father's illness, Monsieur, or you would have realized yourself that there was no time for the robbery to be arranged *after* you won the forty-seven thousand Euros. The thieves must already have made careful arrangements for getting in and out of your hotel, and your room. This was not an opportunistic crime. You, not the money you won that night, were their intended target; we suspect that they had been stalking you for some time, before you even arrived in Monte Carlo."

Canny understood immediately that Meurdon had to be right, As soon as the casino manager pointed it out, Canny realized that he had been distracted by other matters from giving any significant thought to the mugging; in effect, he had handed over all responsibility with a single phone-call, and had promptly banished it from his mind. Now that it had been stated forthrightly, it was obvious that the gunman in his hotel could not have got there from some distant point, identified his room and found a means of discreet intrusion within the interval that had elapsed between his winning the money and his arrival in the hotel.

"You mean they intended to rob me anyway, no matter how much or how little I came away with that night?" Canny said. "But if I'd left immediately after receiving the call from home, they'd only have got three thousand. It wouldn't have been worth the risk."

"No, Monsieur Kilcannon—when I say that *you* must have been the target, that is what I mean. I suspect that they intended to kidnap you—but they changed their minds, and took the money instead. You were right about their having a man in the casino, who did indeed tell them that you were carrying the money—but he must also have told them what you said to the people at the roulette table as you left."

For a moment, Canny couldn't remember having said anything at all—but then he did. *Daddy might not last the week*, he'd announced, trying to sound uncaring. That—and the prospect of a forty-seven thousand Euro consolation prize—might have been just enough to subvert a kidnap gang's scheme. Demanding a ransom from a man who was ill was one thing; attempting to demand a ransom from a man who might have died before the demand arrived was something else.

"Are you sure about this, Henri?" he asked, hesitantly.

"No, Monsieur—how can anyone be sure of such a thing? But we are not dealing with common fools, Monsieur. We are endeavoring to recover your money, and I think we might still succeed—but my associates do not normally operate as far afield as England, and you might like to make some enquiries of your own."

"What? You mean the kidnap gang was *English*?"

"No, Monsieur. Eastern European, I believe. Since the collapse of communism, the Riviera has become the Wild West. But if you were a target, you must have been identified by something more than your reputation here. Someone in your own country—your own locality—might have given information as to your suitability. So it seems to me, at least. I cannot be sure... of anything. Kidnapping was a crime in danger of extinction in Europe only fifteen years ago, even in Sardinia, but things have changed. People in the old Soviet Republics watched too many bootleg American movies; they seem to model themselves on the worst sorts of imaginary gangsters. We shall do what we can, of course—but these are dangerous men, Monsieur Kilcannon. Perhaps you ought to take precautions of your own. I will call again if I have any further news—especially of your money."

"Yes, of course," Canny said. "Thank you, Henri. I appreciate your help—and your advice."

When he had put the phone down he rang for Bentley. "This may seem like a stupid question, Bentley," he said, "but does anyone in the village have any contacts in Eastern Europe? The former Soviet republics, in particular?"

"Yes sir," the butler replied, promptly. "I believe some of the units in the Mill have extensive dealings with that part of the world. We have received trade delegations in the village, and our own representatives have visited such places as Kiev, Riga and Tbilisi. If you had paid more attention to...."

"You can forget the delicate criticism, Bentley. I take the point. Fast-changing world, fast-changing businesses. Daddy's been banging on at me for years to get involved at the Mill, so I'd be ready to take over when the time came, but the pressure only served to increase my native stubbornness...and now the chickens are coming home to roost. So what kind of business is it? Not money-laundering for the Russian mafia, I hope."

"I doubt it, sir—although I dare say that if there were anything clandestine going on, I'd be the last to hear of it. I believe that the former Warsaw Pact countries and ex-Soviet republics have become a significant market for the plastics and polymers units."

"Really? Well, I suppose that Cockayne has to move with the times, just like everywhere else. And I suppose that if you live in Uzbekistan or Albania, the whole EU is the new Wild West."

"Has something happened, sir?"

"Nothing important, probably. During my recent farewell trip to the Mediterranean coast I appear to have been targeted by a gang of East European kidnappers. When they heard that

Daddy was dying they became anxious about the viability of a ransom demand, and decided to settle for a forty-thousand Euro heist instead, just to cover expenses. It was lucky for me that I happened to come by the alternative—but it was a bad move on their part, because I got it from a casino that pays protection to the Union Corse, who are already royally pissed off by the way that vagrant aspirant mafias are casually muscling in on their traditional territory, and tend to get very resentful indeed of rivals operating on their actual premises. The trouble with being lucky is that it's a rare warm wind that blows no one any ill... and I guess that includes Daddy as well as the outlaws. Shit! Of all the times to discover that I'm living in interesting times...."

He trailed off, realizing that the most interesting aspect of his suddenly-interesting times was Lissa Lo, whose advent still did not seem at all unfortunate. Swings and roundabouts, as he had said to Bentley only yesterday...or yin and yang, as she might have put it. That multicolored streak he had seen in the casino had obviously sent ripples in every direction, stirring up all kinds of craziness.

"I thought the Union Corse was an insurance company, sir," Bentley said, mildly.

"And I thought you knew what I meant," Canny retorted. "They're the Riviera's most efficient racketeers—have been for a century and more, having settled in long before crime first got organized in America. They've never had total control, of course, but they've always considered themselves a cut above the gangs who followed *southern ways*. They're not really Corsican any more, in spite of their name, but they have a sense of tradition and they still define themselves partly in terms of rivalry with Sardinia, where the local bandits used to be much more heavily biased towards such practices as kidnapping. It's almost as complicated, in its way, as Yorkshire and Lancashire, and far more bizarre in its implications. The Union Corse will try to hunt down the people who stole my money because it's a matter of honor—they take their protection racketeering very seriously—and *pour encourager les autres*. By which I mean that they'll want to send a message to any other Eastern Europeans ambitious to muscle in."

"I understand the Voltairean reference sir. A matter of hanging admirals, I believe. What you're trying to imply is that someone *here* must have given away information about your family—not just its wealth, but about its situation, Only son, father ailing, old-fashioned concern about the succession. If anyone did, sir, I'm sure they had no idea what they were doing. It's the sort of information that an unscrupulous inquirer could easily glean from casual gossip. The villagers are always proud to talk about Cockayne's unique circumstances, enthusiastic to explain them to new business-partners. I don't think you need assume that anyone you or I know was actually part of a plot to kidnap you. That seems very unlikely to me."

"Unlikely," Canny echoed. "Yes, you're right. People do talk, quite innocently. And people listen—sometimes anything but innocently. We live in a cosmopolitan world, where there's scope for all kinds of new commerce, and new misunderstanding. The spectrum of probability isn't something constant. Being lucky is a much more complicated business than it used to be."

"Pardon me for saying so, sir, but are you sure that Monsieur Meurdon is a wholly reliable source of information?"

Canny laughed, briefly. "Of course I'm not sure," he said. "He may run an honest casino, but he pays protection money to the Union Corse. His situation is complicated. He practically dared me to place the bet that won me the stolen money, and he's already investigated my betting patterns. Maybe he did set up the robbery, and made up all this stuff about Eastern European kidnappers as a cover story to distract me. I can't be *sure* of anything—and to tell you the truth, I don't give a damn about the forty-seven thousand Euros. I could do without any further complications and twists of fate, just for the time being."

He knew as he said it that he was lying. What he really wanted was to pick and choose his complications, his twists of fate. He only wanted to hide from *some* essentially unlikely contingencies. Kidnap gangs and muggers he could do without;

Lissa Lo was another matter. He wasn't sure, any longer, that he could do without her...and if there was a price to be paid in strange ripples of uncertainty and whatever they might stir up, it was a price that he might have to pay, for the sake of simple curiosity as well as not-so-simple lust.

Bentley probably knew that he wasn't telling the *whole* truth, but Bentley was used to that, and to being content with it.

"Your father is awake now," the butler said, in a softer tone. "if you'd like to see him, I think you'd find him in a receptive frame of mind."

"Yes, I would like to see him," Canny said. "Thanks, Bentley. I appreciate what you're doing—all of it. You're a real tower of strength, and I don't know what Mummy and I would do without you. Sorry about the clichés—but they really do mean what I want to say."

Bentley nodded his head, to signify that he understood.

CHAPTER FOURTEEN

"Hello, Can," Lord Credesdale said, when Canny went into his room. "I feel a little better today—in myself, that is. This bloody body's still collapsing on me, but I slept well for the first time in weeks. To judge by the look of you, you didn't."

"Jet lag," Canny said, trying to sound laconic. "Or too much excitement. I'll be okay in a day or two." He studied his father's face with mild amazement. His mother had not been exaggerating; the thirty-first earl looked much better. Canny was modest enough to take it for granted that it was the morphine rather than his own words that had brought a new tranquility to the old man's brain, but he was aware of the fact that the drug hadn't been able to achieve that effect before. Maybe it was mostly a matter of timing, of arrival at the threshold of death—but it wasn't improbable that he had played a part in facilitating the process.

"Did you go to the library last night?" his father asked, when he had settled into the chair, conscious of the contrast between his own awkward pose and the ones that Lissa Lo had adopted during their confrontation in he library.

"Yes, Daddy," he said. "It was a far more enlightening experience than I expected."

"You don't have to lie to me because I'm dying."

"No, Dad—I know that. In fact, I think perhaps I ought to tell you a little more of the truth than I'm normally inclined to do. I think I might have done something rather stupid. I wasn't going to tell you, because I didn't want to trouble you with it—

but you're the only person who might be able to see the implications, in the context of the family gift, so you're the only person who might be able to give me advice. Can I tell you the story, even though it might hurt you a little to hear it?"

"I'd far rather listen to you than tell stories of my own," his father said, trying to sit up a little straighter. Canny helped him to rearrange his pillows, then stood over him for a moment before sitting back down, trying to figure out what kind of reaction he might get to his tale—and whether it might, in fact, undo whatever good work he had done the previous day.

"Go on," the old man said.

Canny nodded his head. He told his father about receiving the telephone call at Meurdon's casino, what Meurdon had said to him, what he'd done when he went back to the roulette wheel, the exotic streak he'd seen when zero came up at the third attempt, what had happened when he went back to the hotel, and what Meurdon had just told him on the phone.

"Stevie Larkin's amateur psychoanalysis was right on the button," he said, by way of conclusion. "The call hit me harder than I thought. The triple bet was way too symbolic. I think I might have called down the lightning, Daddy. Waves of improbability are radiating in every direction." He didn't mention Lissa Lo's return to the house, or what she'd claimed to be. That was something he still hoped to figure out on his own, if he could.

Lord Credesdale remained perfectly calm—unnaturally so, by his own volatile standards. It couldn't just be the morphine, Canny thought. There had been a change in him that cut far deeper than any mere anesthetic.

It must, Canny concluded, have been the handing over of the keys. Even though both of them had known how meaningless and arbitrary the ceremony was, its symbolism had taken effect. The old man had been relieved of his formal responsibility, and his anxiety had evaporated; he really did feel that he had been unburdened—that he could look at the problem that Canny had set before him with a dispassionate eye and weigh it objectively, without any attendant dread.

"It wasn't so stupid," Lord Credesdale said, after a few moments' thought. "It's always safer to use the house percentage discreetly, of course—although this Meurdon character seems to have noticed it anyway, thanks to his computer—but it was only a bet, at the end of the day. Nothing really significant. If the streak that went with it caused a massive disruption, it can't have been a piddling thousand Euro bet that provoked it, even at odds of thirty-six to one. Even if all this stuff about kidnap plots is bullshit and Meurdon's playing his own game, things had started to go awry before you placed the bet—and we always have to remember that shimmers in the fabric of reality aren't something we *cause*, any more than the lightning that blasts a tree is *caused* by the tree. Fate twists itself, for reasons we can't comprehend—we just attract a tiny part of the spin-off, and we're victims as well as beneficiaries. So don't waste time regretting what you did. You need to ask yourself whether there's anything you can do *now*, before the deadline expires on the better part of our collective bounty."

Yesterday, Canny thought, *he could hardly string words together. Now he can talk about the deadline expiring on our collective bounty. He really is in a different place.* He knew, though, that the more significant part of that sentence was the earlier part, and its use of the word "you". For the first time in his life, Lord Credesdale was looking at his son's situation as something that did, indeed, belong to his son and not to him.

"There's not a lot I *can* do," Canny pointed out, "except for trying a little harder to understand. Consulting the diaries really isn't much help."

"Don't underrate them, Can. The old earls weren't fools."

"I'm sure they weren't. But that doesn't mean that their ruminations are relevant to me—to *us.*"

"If the diaries are mostly rubbish," his father told him, "so is most of that pop psychology crap you read."

"Some of it, yes. But we do have to be aware of the seductions of psychological probability. There's a danger of falling into the same trap that claims people who think that they can derive a system for winning at roulette by searching the record of results for patterns that aren't really there—and I think that far too many of our ancestors got well and truly stuck in that one, without ever realizing it."

"Even so...."

"There's another reason the diaries aren't much help, Dad, even if we set aside matters of psychological probability. The thought occurred to me as I was talking to Bentley just now that the spectrum of probabilities changes over time, qualitatively as well as quantitatively. The implications of *being lucky* are very different now from what they were in the nineteenth earl's time, let alone the first's. Do you see what I mean?"

The old man furrowed his brow. His eyebrows were still dark although the hair on his head was almost all white, and the line they formed now was like the careless stroke of a marker pen across his pale face. "I'm not sure that I do," he said.

"What I mean is that there are a great many more opportunities open to people nowadays—and a great many more things that can go wrong for them. If the first earl really had made a deal with the devil, the devil would have to be working overtime to keep up with the technicalities of delivery. Once upon a time, a title, a narrow strip of land and a pot of gold would have been the height of any man's aspirations—but people have very different expectations nowadays. The land and the title aren't worthless, but they aren't worth nearly as much as they once were, relatively speaking, and the gold's had to proliferate in all kinds of strange ways, into shares and property, businesses and bonds. On top of that, there are all kinds of other rewards and prizes that didn't exist a couple of centuries ago—or that nobody cared about in those days. The first earl might have wished for a wife and son, but it would never have occurred to him to ask for a wife he could love, and who would love him—and the idea of asking to be *lovable*, if only in being handsome, would hardly have figured in his calculations. He might have asked for some kind of cleverness, but how could he have imagined the kinds of intellectual skills that people aspire to nowadays? He might have asked for fame, but how could he have imagined modern celebrity? Not that he actually did make a formal contract with fate or the devil, of course—but you see what I'm getting at, don't you? Sometimes, I wonder whether the Kilcannon luck is really keeping pace with the times—and what the implications would be of its catching up."

"Don't complicate things too much, Can," his father said, after a pause for thought. "At the end of the day, luck's luck, and we've got more of it than most—always provided that we can protect and prolong the streak."

"That's the Yorkshire way to look at it, all right," Canny conceded. "But things can't always be simplified to that extent. What I'm trying to get at is that luck isn't *just* luck. It's not a quantifiable thing you simply have less or more of—it's much more complicated than that."

"It *is* just a quantifiable thing," Lord Credesdale insisted. "Everything, at the end of the day, is just probabilities. It's all just electrons orbiting atoms, statistics and uncertainty. What we think of as the world—everything we perceive through our senses—is just an image. The reality underneath is mathematics, equations, probabilities. That's where our house percentage is based."

"It's not where we experience it," Canny objected—but he spoke uncertainly, realizing that his father had a point, and not one that he had expected the old man to make. The Kilcannon luck showed up in all sorts of ways, but the way it showed up most clearly, so that even other people could discern it on occasion, was in gambling. That was where it was most at home, where it operated most comfortably. Where there were numbers, and money, the dividends of the family gift were easily perceptible, and easily delivered. When it came to avoiding kidnap attempts, or avoiding cancers, the calculations and outcomes weren't nearly as straightforward—but that didn't mean that they weren't a matter of juggling probabilities and resolving uncertainties. Maybe the things he thought of as qualitative really were reducible, in some final analysis, to quantitative matters-to the mathematical intricacies of subatomic physics. If so....

"The one thing you *can* do, if you really have been caught up by some weird chain of circumstances that might yet carry you into deeper trouble," Lord Credesdale said, "is to make plans to renew the streak as soon as possible. This kidnap threat might have gone away, but it might not—and either way, it serves to illustrate the kind of dangers that are always around us, lying in ambush. All this stuff about celebrity and lovability is to do with your reluctance to treat the succession as a purely practical matter, isn't it? Having your head turned by supermodels is just a symptom. What you're saying is that you might not be able to *feel* lucky if you don't get the kind of rewards that modern romantic fiction promises to lovers, no matter how much money you have."

"Am I saying that?" Canny recognized, again, that his father might have a point.

"I've been there," Lord Credesdale reminded him. "And before you say it, I know what your next move will be. Just because it didn't work out for me, you reckon, it doesn't mean that *your* love-match won't work out. Well, maybe not—but even if Lissa Lo were willing, you must be able to see how long the odds are that it could ever work out. We're talking about a myth, Canny. Forget my experience—look around at the rest of the world. How many people *really* get lucky in love? And for how long? How many people can sustain that kind of so-called luck for a lifetime, let alone thirty-two generations? You're right; the first earl wouldn't have thought to ask for it if he really had made a deal with the devil, because he didn't live in the modern world—but that doesn't mean that he was wrong. Maybe you shouldn't ask for it either. Maybe you should be content with the luck you have at cards, and in business, Maybe you should just take the money, Can, and forget the rest. Let the luck deliver what it *can* deliver, and don't push for the impossible."

"That's easier said than done," Canny told him, although he realized that his father must have given the matter far more thought than he had ever imagined. The mood might be new, but the philosophy wasn't.

"Nobody's ever said that it's easy," the old man reminded him. "I never told you that, and none of the diaries make any such claim. Quite the reverse. You might think the rituals and the petty self-mutilations are silly, but they have their symbolic value if nothing else. It *isn't* easy. Luck isn't free; it has to be bought. If you really did come to me for advice, that's what I can offer. Life's a bitch, and if you don't have the luck it can turn rabid. Find a wife, Canny. Conceive a son. Renew the streak. Not Lissa Lo, or anyone like her. Stick to the rules."

"You don't know anything about Lissa Lo, Dad," Canny told him.

"I know enough."

"I don't think you do."

Canny hesitated for a long time then, fearing that he might undo all his good work—but he had the library keys now, and his father was off the hook. The morphine could take care of the old man's pain, now. And when it came down to it, it wasn't the business at the casino about which he really needed advice— the subject on which he really needed advice was much more important than that.

If his father hadn't be dying, Canny knew, he would never have dared to make the confession that he was about to make— but the time when he needed to keep his secrets seemed to be past, and the one he'd just parted with by way of testing the waters hadn't caused any sort of storm.

By the time he'd made up his mind, his father was grimly expectant, and it would have been too late to back down in any case.

"Spit it out," Lord Credesdale said. "I can take it."

"She's like us, Dad," Canny said, slowly. "She's a streaker— or so she says."

He had expected a reflexive cry of "That's impossible!" but none materialized. Lord Credesdale had certainly been taken aback by the utterly unexpected news, but the old man took it aboard more thoughtfully than Canny could have imagined.

"How did she know what *you* are?" his father asked, eventually.

"She says that she suspected before, but that she didn't know for sure until she saw the world come apart when I hit that zero—*deconstructing the moment*, she called it. Nobody's ever been able to see it before, Dad—some feel a twinge or a shudder, but she saw it. In her part of the world, she says, it's passed from mother to daughter—but the rules seem pretty similar, to judge by her sketchy description."

"And you think that because she's female you don't have to stay away from her? You think that because she's female, you don't need to *compete*? You think that she's your ready-made soul mate? You think that if you can only find true love together, as lonely people should, you might be twice as lucky together as you are apart?"

The scorn increased with every rhetorical question in the sequence; it hurt, but Canny knew that it was something he had needed to hear. It was what he had come to his father's room to find.

"I think it's a possibility," Canny said, quietly, although he realized how feeble the statement must sound to a cynical audience.

All Lord Credesdale said was: "What kind of bet is that, Canny? What kind of risk do you think it amounts to?"

"A kind people take every day," Canny told him.

"And lose, over and over again. You'd have to deconstruct more than a moment, Can. You'd have to pull the fabric of reality to pieces and remake the whole bloody garment."

"You don't know that, Dad." Canny warmed to the developing contest. He had come to make his own case, as well as to listen to his father's.

The old man thought long and hard about that before he finally gave way and said: "No, I don't. What I do know is that the odds are way too long. It's a bad bet."

"Sometimes," Canny said, "the only bet worth making is the

one where the odds are long." But that was where the tenuous rapport between them became overstretched. He knew full well that everything his father had tried to tell him, throughout his life and in the last few minutes, was that the only bets worth making were the ones most likely to win—the ones the universe could concede without tearing apart the unfolding pattern of causes and effects.

Even so, his newly-transfigured father didn't get angry. The morphine had numbed that along with the pain, now that he had parted with the keys to the family fortune. "It's not so, Can," the old man said. "Only fools think like that, and you've gambled enough not to be that kind of fool. If she's what you say she is, you have to stay away from her. You know that, without me having to tell you. It doesn't matter how beautiful she is—and in the dark, she'll be no different from all the rest. Make the sensible bet, Can. Leave the big lotteries to the idiots who can't calculate the odds like rational men."

"It's not that simple, Daddy," Canny said.

"Yes it is," the old man insisted.

"Maybe it was, in the days of the earls who never left the dale, even to go to Leeds, let alone London," Canny said, as much to himself as to the dying man. "In those days, it made sense to stay within narrow horizons, and to cling to the illusion that what lay beyond them was irrelevant. It's a different world now, Daddy. A global village. There's so much more to be done, so much more to be *tried*...."

"And so much more to go wrong," his father told him. "When the risks increase, the canny man plays even more carefully than before. Are you a canny man, Canny? That was always the intention, always the hope. That's the way I tried to bring you up. Did I really turn you against me to that extent? Is that why you wanted my advice—so that you can go and do the exact opposite?"

"No, Daddy," Canny said. "That's too simple as well. I really do need to work this out—but I'm not an old man, who auto-matically thinks of anything new as dangerous. You can see that, can't you?"

"I can see it," Lord Credesdale agreed, "but I don't have to like it. I'm giving you the best advice I can, son. Play safe. Follow the rules. Don't tangle your luck with anyone else's. It works—not very extravagantly, I'll admit, but it does work. Everything we know about other strategies tells us that they usually don't." His eyelids were descending even as he spoke, but he wasn't dying yet. The morphine was extending its grip upon him as his energy-reserves ran out. He might not have said his last words, but he wasn't going to say anything different if and when he woke again to say a few more.

Canny stood up. "Thanks, Daddy," he said, more sincerely than he would have imagined possible. "I think I need to lie down myself, now—and I think I might actually be able to sleep."

"You're welcome," the old man murmured, as he drifted away into his final, inescapable dream.

CHAPTER FIFTEEN

Canny went back to bed—and this time, he was able to sleep. It wasn't that his mind had ceased to buzz with anxieties and dilemmas, and it certainly wasn't that he could see any kind of a solution to his difficulties, but at least he had a clearer idea of the dimensions of his problems, and the kind of choice he had to make.

He woke up in time for dinner, but he went back to bed again long before midnight, and had no difficulty returning to sleep.

The next day, in spite of what he'd said to his father, Canny did take his problems back to the library. He did study the diaries, just in case there was something in them that would give him an insight. He delved into the early twentieth century, and then into the nineteenth, searching for evidence that some of his ancestors had grappled with similar problems before, on an intellectual level if not a practical one.

Some had, but their grappling did not seem to have been very productive. Not all the lucky Kilcannons of the past had taken it for granted that the family's negative curse was a kind of magic. Even before the Industrialist earl several of them had been more inclined towards primitive versions of the scientific method—hence the endless experiments with spells and rituals, and variations of spells and rituals, and all the marginal notes in all the so-called text-books, condemning the spells that were followed by failure as bullshit, or whatever similar vulgarity had then been in vogue.

In the Age of Reason, inspired by Blaise Pascal, one Earl of

Credesdale had apparently seized on probability theory like a gamekeeper's bulldog closing its jaws on a poacher's leg—he it was who had realized that the streak was a matter of coming out slightly ahead of the expectations of chance, and that there was no profit in considering each winning bet or stroke of good fortune individually—but the conceptual breakthrough had merely been added to the register of hearsay, never methodically investigated.

Even after the great conceptual leap forward, the methodology followed by subsequent experimentally-inclined earls had been routinely flawed by the assumption that each spell or ritual had to be correlated with the specific event most closely following in its train, and no matter what the results of their experiments had been, they had all fallen prey to the "safe" strategy based on the proposition it was better to do too much than too little.

Unfortunately, it seemed that the Kilcannons had never been as ruthless in their philosophical methods as they sometimes had in business. The conclusions at which they had arrived—whether by way of argument or experience—did not seem at all convincing to Canny, even insofar as they concerned mere matters of mathematical probability.

With regard to other kinds of rewards—matters of quality of life—the diaries were even more confused. His father had not been the first earl to be attracted to a woman who did not fit the specifications of tradition, nor even the first to marry one. Among the earls who had followed the specifications faithfully in matters of marriage, several had tested the limits of the supplementary rules regarding sexual abstinence and fidelity by falling in love and taking mistresses...and every one had come out of it badly in the end, and had castigated himself for his foolishness.

But what if they had been ordinary men? Canny wondered. What if they had been everyday victims of the laws of chance, with no special luck to aid them? Would they not have loved and lost in exactly the same fashion, and given vent to resentful misogyny in exactly the same way, and issued warnings to their sons and descendants to put such foolishness aside and stick to making money?

One thing that did seem certain, however, was that the Kilcannon luck was limited to quantitative matters. It had never been a qualitative matter. The Kilcannons had become rich, and they had stayed rich, but they had never obtained much evident happiness from their wealth. If anything, their raised expectations had made them more prone to misery than common men when those aspects of their lives that remained unprotected had gone badly.

Read in that way, the testimony of his ancestors gave every support to his father's advice. Play safe. Stick to what you know. Collect the house percentage. Don't howl for the moon.

"But times *have* changed," Canny murmured. The idea wouldn't let go. Whatever the diaries or his father said, times surely must have changed. Thus far, the Kilcannon luck had not changed with them to any further extent than diversifying the business interests of the estate—but did that necessarily imply that the Kilcannon luck was immutable, unexploitable in any other way? Could it be used to other ends, if only one were prepared to make the effort in an enlightened way?

There were also accounts in the diaries of encounters between Kilcannons and other lucky men: of card games, feuds and duels in which probability went crazy; of business deals that unwound in bizarre fashion. Again, the stated conclusions were unanimous, piled one atop another as an accumulation of bitter reflection. Stay out of such contests, if at all possible. Avoid such men, if at all possible. *Play safe.*

There was not a word about lucky women. If any had ever been encountered by any previous earl whose testimony had survived, she had passed unnoticed, or at least unidentified. There was no precedent for Lissa Lo—but his father's reaction to the notion had been no mere personal whim. All the diarists, and all their predecessors who had contributed to the oral tradition summarized in the earliest writings, would have agreed with the thirty-first earl. A new risk was even more dangerous than those encountered before and judged too dangerous to take. It ought not to be taken, and ought in fact to be fled, removed from the realm of temptation, and hence from the realm of possibility. A Kilcannon had to play safe. A Kilcannon *always* had to play safe.

But if every new risk were to be refused, Canny thought, then every new opportunity would perforce be lost. If every danger were to be avoided, what new achievement was possible?

Was the house percentage enough to compensate for the closing down of every other possibility? Did he really want to live his life in the same manner as his forebears, knowing what the testimony of the diaries was in regard to the price they had paid for their success?

The problem had become even clearer in his mind—but he was no nearer to a solution, as yet.

If there was progress to be made in understanding the scope and limitations of the family gift, Canny decided, it could not be made by following his father's advice. It had to be won by trial and experiment. But what if there really was no progress to be made? What if all the experiments failed? What if all the trials turned into errors?

There had been other experimentalist Kilcannons, calculated and uncalculated, and all *their* trials had failed—or so, in the end, they had concluded. They had all arrived, eventually, at the same attitude of mind. They had settled for what they had, for what fate seemed to guarantee. As long as what they did succeeded in renewing the streak, it had ceased to matter to them whether ninety-nine per cent of what they did was objectively irrelevant. All that really mattered, they had decided, was that in amongst all the rubbish they somehow did whatever was objectively needed to keep the Kilcannon luck running—and whatever the Kilcannon luck failed to deliver, that which it did deliver was far too precious to jeopardize. The inevitable result of that invariable settlement, however, had been that no one had ever tested the limits of the rules *scrupulously*; after thirty-one Earls of Credesdale and who knew how many earlier Kilcannons, no one was really any the wiser as to whether *any* of the customs and rituals had ever been objectively necessary... or whether there might have been so much more luck to be enjoyed, if only the rules had been properly refined and wisely elaborated.

The diaries and the portraits on the walls of Credesdale House were supposed to be testaments to family success, family triumph and family fortune—but they also told another story.

Didn't they ever smile? Lissa Lo had asked.

Maybe it *had* been just a matter of propriety that compelled his ancestors to glower at their portrait-painters—but Canny couldn't believe that. The simple truth was that they'd never been *happy*, or even content with their lot—even though wild horses would never have dragged the admission from them.

The diaries told Canny that they'd never understood why, in spite of their wealth and status, they hadn't been happy—but of the fact itself there was no doubt. They'd been miserly with the kind of luck they had and had refused, in the end, to count the costs they were paying in currencies that didn't show up on a balance-sheet.

By the time he'd turned twenty-one, Canny reflected, he had already managed to convince himself, more or less, that none of the magical mumbo-jumbo could be necessary and that the secret of the family fortune had to be a gene carried on the Y-chromosome. He'd firmly resolved, then, to do what one of his ancestors had never had the nerve to do for more than a year or two: to stand firm against the pressure of superstition and abandon all the spells and rituals, including the insistence that he mustn't marry outside the county.

He still wanted to stand by that decision, now that he had official custody of the library keys. He ought to wait politely for his father to die, of course, but when that *coup-de-grâce* was accomplished, he would be free. He would be free to experiment, to apply the scientific method...to pursue Lissa Lo, or at least to consent to be pursued, since that was the way things seemed to be working out.

If he entertained doubts, he told himself, they ought to be rational doubts, not irrational ones. They ought to be based in the analyses of probability theory, and the theory of psychological probability, not in the miserly insistences of his ancestors.

There were, of course, doubts of that kind that had to be taken on board. For one thing, his genetic hypothesis didn't seem so compelling now that evidence had been presented to him that there were streakers in the world who couldn't possibly have got their luck from a Y-chromosome gene. Was that a stroke of luck, or something else? He certainly hadn't seen a colored streak or felt reality shudder when Lissa Lo had dropped her bombshell; the world had not been re-ordered in the least by the revelation alone.

But those kinds of doubts only made the experiment more intriguing, and its corollaries more various.

Didn't they?

That afternoon, Canny went back to his father's room again, and found him in the same serene frame of mind. He tried not to talk about the issues he had raised the previous day, but that proved impossible. His father wanted to reiterate the advice he had given, as often as possible.

Play it safe.

DON'T TAKE ANY CHANCES.

When Canny asked his father, curiously, whether he'd had a happy life, the old man said: "Of course I have—what kind of a question is that?" But he didn't smile. He seemed to Canny to be protesting a little too much.

It wasn't a question that Canny could put to his mother with any greater expectation of an honest or considered answer, any more than he could ask her questions about any other aspect of the Kilcannon luck. She had always known that there was a mystery surrounding that luck, but she had always been content to leave it uninvestigated. Canny couldn't admire her for that, but he wasn't tempted to break the rule that specified that she must never be told—and he didn't ask her, either, whether she and his father had been happy. Like Bentley, he figured—who had a butler's gift for not seeing what he was not supposed to see even when he was staring right at it—Mummy was entitled to her hard-won ignorance.

The more pertinent question he put to his father was: "Do you wish you'd done anything differently?"

The old man did him the favor of thinking seriously about that one before answering.

"I'd be a fool if I didn't," Lord Credesdale said, eventually. "Hindsight always tells you which bets you should have laid but didn't, and you can't help but wish you'd laid them. But that doesn't mean that the losing bets you did lay were *all* mistakes, even if a few of them were. You have to make your choices as best you can, and you have to accept that some of your bets are going to lose. You have to be content with the house percentage. I did what I did, including a few things I shouldn't have done, but I came out ahead in the long run. If I'd followed the rules, maybe I'd have come out a lot further ahead—but hindsight can't tell me that. You *will* make mistakes, Canny—there's no avoiding them. Just try not to make too many stupid ones."

"That's not what you'd have said to me last week," Canny observed.

"No," his father admitted, "it's not. And maybe that was one of my mistakes. This dying is turning out a more complicated and time-consuming business than I'd expected. I don't feel quite myself, you know—but I do feel a little better, even though I know I'm worse. That old saw about *putting your affairs in order* is total crap, you know. I thought I was doing it—had done it—but it isn't even something I can do, discreetly or otherwise. It's something over which I have no control at all. Am I making any sense?"

"Yes, Daddy," Canny assured him. "You're making sense."

"You needn't say it as if it were the first time ever."

"That's not what I meant," Canny assured him, although it had been exactly what he meant.

"At least you gave me something to chew on," the old man

said, "even if I can't swallow it. Is the room getting darker, or is it just me?"

"I can't see anything, Daddy. It's clouding over outside, though."

"I wasn't talking about a streak. I'm hardly in need of omens, am I? And there's nothing for a bright streak to promise, short of a miracle. It is getting darker, though. If I go to sleep, will you sit with me for a while?"

"Yes—do you want me to fetch Mummy?"

Lord Credesdale tried to shake his head, but he couldn't do it. "No," he said. "You're the one with the luck, after all. If a miracle's on the cards, I'll need you here. If not...we've always been in this together, Can. Always."

Canny waited until his father's eyes had closed before he murmured: "Not any more, Daddy"—and even then, he said it too quietly to be heard.

CHAPTER SIXTEEN

Bentley woke Canny at six-thirty on the following morning to tell him that his father had died during the night—peacefully, in his sleep.

"I'll need a few minutes alone with him," Canny told the butler, when he got to his father's room and saw the dead man lying on the bed.

"Yes, sir," Bentley replied. "I've called Dr Hale—he's on his way, but he won't arrive for at least a quarter of an hour. I'll wait a few minutes before I wake your mother."

"Thanks," Canny said. He completed the first phase of the rituals he'd promised to observe without any difficulty, and still had time to stand back and look down at the old man for a few minutes more. There was nothing to see; it was just a lifeless body. When his mother came to join him, she was steadfastly stoical. No tears were shed; life had to go on. The doctor, who had anticipated the moment, was equally businesslike.

The funeral plans were already in place; all that remained was to set the ball rolling—and once it did start rolling, it moved with irresistible momentum.

The time was set; the invitations were mailed; the coffin was installed in the chapel of rest in the village.

The thirty-second Earl of Credesdale eased into his inheritance as comfortably as he could have been expected, and the flow of condolences consumed his attention so completely that he hardly had time to ask himself whether there was any evidence as yet that the supernatural component of his luck had all-but-vanished from his existence, as prophesied by legend and secret scripture alike.

The routine of public grieving was so rapidly established, and so insistent in its claims, that Henri Meurdon's second phone call—which came through as he was about to set out for the church—seemed a bizarre bolt from the blue.

"There have been developments, Monsieur," Meurdon informed him, while he stood in the drawing-room in mourning-dress. "Rumor has reached me that two of the four individuals who appear to planned your kidnap are now deceased. What became of the other two, I cannot tell; if they are wise, they have returned to their own country. My associates recovered some, but by no means all, of the money—some fifteen thousand Euros. It is not much, I know...."

"It doesn't matter, Henri," Canny said. "Please ask them to keep it, with my compliments, as some small compensation for their trouble. I thank them for their efforts, but I was the one who was careless. I'd rather the matter were closed now, if honor is satisfied on all sides. My father is dead, and I'm about to go to his funeral service; I regret now that I was moved by the news of his illness to place the bet."

"If that is your wish, Monsieur," Meurdon said. "I'm sorry to have disturbed you at an inconvenient moment. Please accept my condolences."

"That's my wish," Canny confirmed. "And thanks. I don't know when I'll be able to get to the Riviera again, but you can be sure that I'll call in if and when I do. Thanks for letting me know what the situation is."

"You are welcome, Monsieur."

Well, Canny thought, as he hung up, *if it was all a pack of lies and you're now forty-seven thousand Euros richer, I wish you well of it.*

"Canny?" his mother called, from the hallway. "The car's here."

"I'm coming, Mummy," he said.

There was, of course, no real need for a car. St Peter's Church was within easy walking distance, in the nearer outskirts of the village—but the Kilcannons had abandoned the old-style procession in the nineteenth century, at the behest of the Industrialist Earl, and it was the recent custom that they now followed. Canny travelled with his mother; there were two spare seats in the car but they would be occupied on the return journey.

St Peter's had been remodeled in the 1820s, with enough wooden benches fitted to accommodate the entire population of Cockayne and a few to spare for special occasions. That population had actually declined somewhat in the interim, owing to the fact that the villagers had fewer children nowadays. Even so, the church was full to overflowing because of the vast influx of outsiders—to the extent that many of the villagers had to wait meekly outside during the service.

Canny knew that four hundred formal invitations had been sent out, which must have drawn in a thousand people once spouses and children were added to the total, but he estimated that there were at least fourteen hundred people gathered in and around the church, almost all of them keeping a respectful distance from the family pews and the graveside stations. He nodded to a great many people as he moved through the crowd to take his place, but spoke to no one. The service was brief, according to his father's instructions.

Everything remained stiff and formal until the burial ceremony was completed, but everything then became utterly hectic as the meeting and greeting began in earnest.

Canny didn't realize that Lissa Lo was present until the crowd had gathered round him, and he knew when he spotted her in the distance that he wouldn't be able to speak to her for quite some time. She wasn't alone; she had apparently thought it politic to travel with a companion as well as her usual minders, and Canny was only momentarily surprised to observe that she was side-by-side with Stevie Larkin. There was a certain symmetry to the arrangement that made him smile wryly.

At the time, he was being introduced to a man and a woman he couldn't remember ever having seen before, although the woman was quick enough to say: "It's good to see you again, Canny. It's been a long time." When he hesitated, she was quick to add: "I'm Alice—the youngest of the Proffitt sisters—you were in the same class as our Ellen at the primary, but by the time I started school you were about to move on to Ampleforth."

Recognition was then immediate, as he connected the slender, dark-haired woman who stood before him with an even skinnier, bespectacled child. He knew immediately that he shouldn't have forgotten her, even though they he hadn't seen her for at least fifteen years, at which time she must have been thirteen or thereabouts—fourteen at the most. She had always been the most clamorous, though not the most glamorous, of the three sisters.

"I remember," he said. "You were the brat—the one who was always insulting me."

The woman blushed. "I was the youngest," she said, apologetically. "I had to try twice as hard to be noticed. I was the clever one too—you might have remembered that—and they weren't insults, as such, just witty remarks of an unusually frank nature." She blushed again. "Oh hell," she murmured, before raising her voice to begin again: "This is my husband, Martin Ellison."

Canny had shaken the man's hand and murmured "pleased to meet you" before the implications of the name struck home. Even then, he took a second look, to make absolutely sure that this was a Martin Ellison who might plausibly hold a post in a university psychology department. The man was younger than he would have expected—surely no more than thirty—and he was built like a rugby-player, but there was a certain gravitas in his manner. "The Martin Ellison who wrote *The Personal and Historical Implications of the Oedipus Effect?*" he asked, uncertainly.

"Why, yes," Ellison said, his astonishment palpable. "Do you really keep track of the people in your village to that extent? Even the ones who leave to go to university and never come back?"

"Oh no," Canny said. "I had no idea where Alice went, or who she married—but I'm interested in psychological probability. I've read your work."

"I'm flattered. I'm sorry for your loss."

"Very kind," Canny aid, reflexively. "Look, if it's not too much trouble, I'd like to talk to you about your work some time, when all this has blown over. Will you be coming up to the house? It'll be just as crowded, I fear, so we'll be mostly in the garden, and just as busy—but we might be able to have a brief word later, to fix up something."

Martin Ellison seemed to have been taken completely by surprise, and was obviously flustered—but Alice was quick to accept the invitation. "That's very nice of you," she said. "Actually, we were hoping to have a word with you ourselves." There was a momentary pause, and then she hurried on: "You must be quite overwhelmed by all this—when I was a kid we always thought Lord Credesdale was a bit of a recluse, but look at all these people! That's Stevie Larkin over there, with some model in tow! How on Earth did your father know a footballer?"

"Actually," Canny told her, "It's me that Stevie knows—not well, but he happened to be there when the news of Daddy's relapse reached me. He and Lissa Lo aren't an item—they're just flocking together, the way celebrities do when they're confronted by a crowd."

"Try telling that to *them*," Alice said, pointing at a gaggle of avid paparazzi positioned on the slope outside the cemetery. They were armed with telescopic lenses, but there were no barriers holding them at bay; they were keeping their distance for diplomatic reasons. "We mustn't take up your time now, though," Alice added. "See you later, I hope."

Ellen Ormondroyd and her husband were a dozen places further back in the queue of people waiting to offer their condolences. It was difficult to believe that she was Alice's sister; she was two inches taller and a great deal more voluptuous, although she didn't yet qualify as fat in spite of the temptations inherent in her vocation.

"I'm truly sorry, Canny," Ellen said, after her husband had mumbled something incoherent. "We all thought—hoped—he was getting better."

"He let us all think that," Canny said. "Even Mummy. It's the kind of man he was. You never mentioned that your little sister had married Martin Ellison."

"Alice?" Ellen look surprised. "I didn't think you even knew Alice—she was just a kid when you went to university. She went herself not long after, and moved down south. She was always the clever one. Martin's some kind of professor now, but he was hardly more than a lad when she met him at university in Bristol. They were in Canterbury for years, but he's just got a job at Leeds. Lydia's here somewhere, with her Ken—you must remember her. They're in Manchester now."

Canny remembered Lydia well enough to picture her at the age of seventeen—but that memory must also have been at least fifteen years old; her present whereabouts were of little interest. He wondered, instead, whether the word that Alice and Martin Ellison wanted to have was about the possibility of moving back to the village. The elders didn't usually approve of commuters, but if Alice were to say that she'd like to work at the Mill they'd probably overlook the fact that Martin was working in Leeds, especially if Canny put in a good word for them.

"Jack reckons you ought to turn out for the team before the season ends," Ellen said. "All the Earls have played, he reckons—and he's got scorebooks going back to World War One to prove it."

Jack seemed deeply embarrassed by this revelation, or at least by the unsuitability of the occasion—but Ellen Proffitt had never been intimidated by Canny Kilcannon, and Ellen Ormondroyd was only making it clear, in her own fashion, that she wasn't about to be intimidated by the thirty-second Earl of Credesdale either.

"Thanks for letting me know," Canny said. "I'll call in at the fish shop if I fancy a game."

The queue moved on and Canny did his best to remember

as many faces as he could: mill workers and tradesmen from the village, bank managers and brokers from Leeds, aunts and cousins from Tadcaster and York, gentry from Harrogate and Selby. There didn't appear to be any Eastern Europeans present, though.

The churchyard slowly emptied, but Canny's head was buzzing with the confusion of it all. He saw no streak, but he certainly felt the kind of disorientation that usually accompanied one.

Lissa Lo waited until everyone else was done before she came to greet him, bowing politely to the dowager Lady Credesdale before introducing her to Stevie Larkin.

"I think you're attracting some attention," Canny observed, nodding in the direction of the not-so-distant photographers, who all had their equipment aimed and ready.

"Sorry about that, mate," Stevie said. "Bloody vultures. My fault, I suppose. I told a few people where I was going."

"It's nobody's fault," Canny assured him. "An England midfielder, a supermodel and a newly-elevated Earl all in the one shot is too tempting a prospect. If the pros weren't here, some lucky amateur from Leeds would be seizing his chance to strike it rich."

"I could ask the sergeant to get rid of them," his mother put in. "Technically, they're trespassing."

"Mention it to the butcher's lads and you won't need to trouble the police," Canny said. "No—only joking. Best let them be, unless they try to get into the grounds of the house. At that point, we can point out to them, very reasonably, that they've already got something saleable and really ought to give us some privacy. I'll warn Bentley."

"I can ask my people to help with security at the house, if you like," Lissa said. "I didn't realize that our coming here would cause you any difficulty."

"It hasn't," Canny assured her. "You and Stevie will be the ones denying the rumors tomorrow—but I expect you're used to that."

"Oh aye," said Stevie. "No probs. Won't do Lissa's image any good, though, to be seen with a clown like me." He blushed as he said it, obviously feeling that his own image could obtain nothing but benefit from the imagined association.

"You'll both come to the house, of course," Canny said. "There'll be a bit of a jamboree out on the lawns, but once we're inside it won't matter where they stand with their telescopic lenses."

"With any luck," Stevie said, "they'll park themselves on top of that skull-shaped rock and lean over a bit too far."

"You came past the house on the way in, then?" Canny deduced. "I thought of you when I got back from Monte. How do you like the symbolism?"

"Bit too obvious, in the circs," Stevie muttered.

"I think we ought to be getting back, Can," his mother said. "Maurice Rawtenstall and his wife are waiting by the car."

"Yes, Mummy," Canny replied, dutifully. To Lissa, he said: "You can bring your car round to the old stables, if you like. I've got to go back with Mummy and the manager from the Mill, but we'll meet up in the grounds. Thanks for coming—and you, Stevie. I really appreciate it."

"I was in the country," Stevie mumbled. "Not far."

Canny's mother actually took his arm then, and steered him away. Maurice Rawtenstall and his wife were, indeed, waiting by the car.

"Went well," Rawtenstall commented, as the two women got in.

"It's a funeral, not a wedding," Canny said. "There was never much danger of drunken punch-ups."

"Aye," said the manager, "but we don't allus get what we expect." Canny took that as a veiled reference to Rawtenstall's anxiety about having the devil he didn't know replacing the devil he did in the capacity of boss.

"This is Cockayne," Canny said, as he took his own seat. "The land of peace and plenty. Nothing ever changes in Cockayne, and everything always works. Don't worry, Maurice—I know

I haven't done my homework yet, but I'm keen to catch up as quickly as I can. In the meantime, I'm sure you're doing a great job. Everything will be okay—you and I will make a good team."

"Mebbe," said Rawtenstall, philosophically. "Any chance of yon lad joining Leeds United, do you reckon?" Obviously, he thought that there would be time enough to discuss the business—and Canny's lamentable ignorance of its intricacies—on Monday morning.

"I didn't even know that Milan were looking to sell him until Bentley tipped me off," Canny replied. "We just bump into one another in casinos now and again—or used to."

"Canny!" his mother said—rather unfairly, as he'd only been answering a question. "It's your father's funeral."

"I know, Mummy," he said. "I know."

CHAPTER SEVENTEEN

As Canny had anticipated, Alice Ellison wanted to ask him about the possibility of moving back to Cockayne. She didn't barge in immediately when he began to make the rounds of the garden, the way she would probably have done at thirteen, but she was quick enough to take an opportunity of talking to him when it arrived. Presumably, she no longer thought of him as a stuck-up public schoolboy who needed to be taken down a peg or two, but she hadn't yet begun to think of him as a lord of the manor who ought to be regarded with awe and spoken to in hushed tones.

After some of the conversations Canny had forced himself through, it was rather a relief to be faced with someone with whom he had once exchanged childish banter in a comfortably mischievous fashion.

"I know you've probably got a waiting-list a mile long," Alice said, apologetically, "and I haven't exactly been a regular visitor since I moved down south, but I have missed the old place— more and more, actually, as time's gone by. Martin and I are thinking about starting a family, and I've always told him that Cockayne is the perfect environment in which to bring up kids."

"As it happens," Canny told her, "you might be in luck. I think I can probably manage to persuade the elders that Martin would be an asset, even though he's not in an honest trade. There's nothing vacant at the moment, and I doubt that I'd be able to move you to the very top of the queue, but I think I might be able to steer them in the right direction without seeming to be trying to throw my newly-acquired weight about. You're a Proffitt, after all—your Mum and Dad are pillars of the community, and Jack and Ellen's shop is the second most important gossip-well in town, after the Eagle."

"That's very kind of you, Lord Credesdale," Martin Ellison said.

"Not at all," Canny assured him. "I really am interested in your field of study, and I'd certainly like to talk to you about it some time. Are you working on a new book?"

"Of course. It's about popular superstition. Alice has...."

"Do you really think you can swing it, Canny?" Alice put in. "can I still call you Canny, now you're the earl?"

"You might have to work locally to keep the elders sweet, at least for a while," Canny said. "Would you mind that?"

"Actually," Alice said, "I was hoping to curry favor in a slightly different way. My degree's in history, and I've been doing some post-grad work. How would the elders take it if I approached them with a proposal to write a book about the early history of Cockayne? How would *you* feel about it, given that I'd need access to your records?"

"I think they'd like it," Canny said, after a moment's thought. "I think I could see my way clear to giving you access to some of the documents in the library—not the secret ones, of course, but the ones that relate to the village. Perhaps you could both come over for dinner in a fortnight or so, so that we could talk about it. Do you have a card with your telephone number, Dr Ellison?"

"Martin, please," Ellison said. He fished out his wallet and extracted a business-card from it. "Printed them out on my PC just the other day. We only moved up a few weeks ago—we're hoping that our present accommodation will only be temporary. The university's excellent, of course, but after Canterbury...."

"The neighborhood's a bit of a shock," Canny finished for him. "A stroll along Woodhouse Lane isn't quite the same as a morning constitutional in the Garden of England. I'll do my best to make sure that it *is* temporary. I'm looking forward to talking to you about the Oedipus Effect."

"You really have read Martin's book, haven't you?" Alice said, in a slightly puzzled tone.

"Of course," Canny told her. "I suppose you're surprised because Ellen's told you that I'm a playboy—a wastrel with the brains of a flea and morals to match."

Alice blushed crimson. "Oh no," she said swiftly. "Ellen's always said that you were really nice—she wouldn't ever say a word against you. She's always spoken up for you when...." She stopped abruptly.

"I'm glad to hear it," Canny said. "She and I have always had a certain rapport, ever since she showed me her knickers when we at primary together. Must have been the other gossips, then—I suppose the funeral set them all off. *Pooer owld Lord Cre'esdale—real gemmun, not like that son of his, allus off down t'Riviera.*"

Alice burst out laughing at his preposterous parodic accent. "Even I can do a better one than that," she said, *"an' ah bin 'obnobbin' wi' t'gentry in Canterburry these last se'n year'n'mooer."*

"Obviously, you can't," Canny said. "But I appreciate the gesture. Actually, nobody in the village seems to be able to do it properly any more. Too much TV, I suppose. The BBC gets to us all in the end."

"Well," said Martin Ellison, evidently deciding that it was time to move on before the tone of the conversation began to plumb unacceptable depths of irreverence, "I'm delighted to hear that you know my work, and I'll be delighted to talk to you about it some time soon. I'm sorry for your loss."

As Martin watched them move away, his mother homed in on him again. "Who *is* that girl, Can?" she asked.

"The youngest of the Proffitt sisters, Mummy," Canny said. "Married, I'm afraid. Sorry to disappoint you. They all are—all the Proffitt sisters, that is. I dare say you've taken care to invite a few Tadcastrians who aren't."

"Don't be silly, Can."

"I'm sorry, Mummy. I thought you'd come over to interrogate me as to whether I'd interviewed any of Bentley's suggested bridal candidates yet, and whether I thought any of them were up to the job."

"We can stop pretending now, Can," she said, "Daddy's gone. I don't care what you do—it's entirely your own business. Have you invited that Chinese girl to stay the night?"

"I don't think she's Chinese, mother, although she can speak fluent Mandarin. No, I haven't had a chance to invite her, yet. Will you mind terribly if I do?"

"It's *your* house now, Can. You can invite whomever you please."

"Oh, stop it Mummy. I'm sorry I made the joke about the Tadcastrian debs. Anyway, I'll have to go to London in a few days, and I'll probably be spending a lot more time there than Daddy did. You'll be Lady of the Manor till the day you die, which won't be for a long time yet, and you can run the place however you like. Unless, of course, you were thinking of remarrying?"

"That's cruel, Can," she said—but there were no tears in the corners of her eyes.

"Sorry, Mummy. A reaction against the strain of having to be so polite to everyone else, I guess. At least Ellen Proffitt was prepared to act naturally, although I don't think her husband approved. Even Alice is a bit subdued, although that might be because she's mellowed since she was thirteen. She wasn't over-awed, though, the way some of the others are pretending to be."

"You'll never overawe the Proffitt girls," Lady Credesdale observed. "They knew you when you were in short pants."

"So did practically everyone in the village over the age of thirty," Canny pointed out. "And not one of them has forgotten. That's why so many of them are pretending so hard to be humble forelock-tuggers, although they seem to have done their fair share of complaining about my wayward lifestyle while I was away. Too much imagination by half, I fear. The crowd's thinning out quite nicely now, wouldn't you say."

"Nicely enough," she agreed, looking around the gardens with a sternly calculating eye. The result of her calculations obviously included a note of anxiety, but Canny guessed that she was merely wondering what Jebb would have to say in the morning about the tragic state of his lawns.

"I'll tell Bentley to make sure that the booze-supply dries up fairly soon, although there's bound to be a handful who won't take the hint. You'll have to take care of your side of the family, though."

He was being slightly cruel again, but Lady Credesdale didn't have an opportunity to complain because Stevie Larkin was coming over. He was unaccompanied now; Lissa was still in hiding inside the house.

"I've got to get back to the folks on the other side of the moors, Lord C," he said, apologetically. "It was nice to see you again—hope it's in happier circumstances next time. I'm not expecting to be in Milan much longer—my agent reckons I've done my time in the sun and ought to head home again, and it's easier to get picked for England if you're actually *in* England. Liverpool or Blackburn would be nice, or even Man City."

Canny deduced from the slightly wistful tone of this list that Stevie's real ambition was to play for Manchester United, but that he didn't think it likely that they would be making him an offer. "Thanks for coming, Stevie," he said. "It's good to see you, too."

"Well," said Stevie, "it's like Lissa says—fate threw us together that night. Did the cops ever find out who mugged you?"

Canny raised an eyebrow at that, slightly surprised that Lissa had told him. "I didn't have time to call the police," he said. "It was no big deal. I think the casino's security people managed to identify the inside man who tipped off the mugger. He won't be operating out of their premises again."

"Well, that's something," Stevie said. "G'night, milord. Hope it all goes well for you. Never liked funerals myself, I'm afraid—way too much symbolism in the ashes-to-ashes stuff."

"What was he talking about?" Lady Credesdale demanded, as soon as the footballer had turned away.

"Symbolism, Mother," Canny retorted, deliberately misunderstanding. "Sportsman that is born of woman hath but a short career, and time's winged chariot is always hovering on the touchline. The poor guy's seven or eight years younger than me, and already he's worrying about his legs letting him down. He's no fool, though—he's probably put away a very healthy nest-egg by now. He'll be okay, even if he doesn't collect many more England caps and ends up at Man City."

"You know what I mean," she said.

Canny sighed. "I was mugged, the night I flew back home. As I said to Stevie, it's no big deal. I just handed over the money, and that was that. End of story."

"Does—did—your father know?"

"Yes he did—but he didn't think it was a big deal either. I'm sorry Stevie let it slip."

His mother shook her head, but she made no further complaint about not having been told. "You have to be careful, Canny," she said.

"It won't happen again, Mummy. I won't be tempting fate like that in future. No more casinos at four in the morning for me. As I told Maurice Rawtenstall, I may have neglected my homework in the past but I'm determined t catch up as soon as I can—and from now on, I'll keep my money in the bank, where it belongs."

"You don't have to lie to me, Can," she said. "I'm just your mother. You're the earl now—you can be as reckless and secretive as your father was, and never confide in me at all. Just treat me like part of the furniture. I'm used to that." This time, there *were* tears in the corners of her eyes. Canny would have hugged her, if he had thought that it would do any good.

"Come on, Mummy," he said, instead. "We've got a fair few goodbyes still to say. No rest for the wicked, eh?"

CHAPTER EIGHTEEN

It took Canny a further half-hour to escape from the garden, and even longer to escape the drawing-room, but in the end he was able to seize an opportunity to go to the library.

Lissa was waiting for him in the outer room, sitting in an armchair reading *The Personal and Historical Implications of the Oedipus Effect* by Martin Ellison.

"Quite a coincidence," she observed, as she rose to her feet, "his turning up at the funeral like that."

"A coincidence is what it was," he said. "I'd no idea he was married to a local girl."

"A pretty thing," said Lissa, in a dismissively disdainful fashion. "She seems to like you."

"She wants something—access to the library, it seems. I'll have to be careful about that one. Anyway, they all like me, even if they do make disapproving remarks about my imagined lifestyle. I've always been popular in the village, ever since I gave up playing for the cricket team. How was Venezuela?"

"Replete with tar sands and illicit loggers, reportedly. A speculator's dream and an environmentalist's nightmare. From where I was standing, though, it was just one more unit in the global village. How does one address the Earl of Credesdale, by the way? Sire? My lord?"

"As you're obviously still convinced that it's safe for us to be in the same room," he said, as he unlocked the door to the inner sanctum, "you might as well stick to Canny—although I'm not at all sure that there's anything canny about my letting you in.

Are you staying over? I ought to tell Bentley to have a room made up if you are."

"I can't. I have to be in London by six a.m. I shouldn't really be here, but when I bumped into Stevie and he told me the news, it seemed only right."

"You brought Stevie along because you knew that it would give the paparazzi something to get their teeth into, didn't you?" Canny said. "He's a smokescreen."

"He was all in favor of putting in an appearance," she said. "It has a certain symmetry, don't you think? The three of us all bet on that zero, when you said goodbye to your old life. Fate bound us together that night, didn't it?"

"You seem to have persuaded Stevie of that, too," Canny observed.

"I was surprised to see everybody standing around a grave," she said, blithely changing the subject. "I thought English lords were buried in crypts—in fact, after seeing your house the other day I was rather expecting a Gothic mausoleum."

"We Credesdales have always been buried in the churchyard, in graves marked with discreet stones, without so much as a cross or a stone angel. Tradition, you see."

"The church isn't small, though. The bell-tower's quite impressive."

"So's the organ—but the choir isn't what it used to be. There's always a very good turn-out at mass, but the church isn't the heart of the community any more. Changing times."

"But you don't go to mass yourself," she said, presumably implying that he didn't take communion, or go to confession.

"No," he said. "Neither did Daddy—although Father Quimper came out on Daddy's last day to administer extreme unction, apparently. *Just in case*, I guess—his motto, if not the family motto. Mummy let him in and out while I was in the library. I don't know why they were so secretive about it; it's not as if I'd have had any objection. You haven't mentioned meeting a male streaker to your mother, I suppose?"

"Do you think I'm mad?" she said. "She doesn't suspect a

thing. So far as she knows, I'm just attending a funeral, out of politeness. It's my business, not hers."

"I told Daddy," he confessed.

"That doesn't matter," she said. "Not any more. What did he tell you to do—never let me darken your doorstep again?"

"Pretty much."

He closed both of the inner doors carefully behind them, making certain that they would be undisturbed. The chair she'd brought into the inner sanctum on her previous visit was still there; she sat down in it as if it were her own, and made herself comfortable. She still had Martin Ellison's book in her hand, but she closed it now and set it down on his desk.

"You're not taking his advice," she observed.

"I haven't quite decided," he said. "You're sure that it's safe for you to be here, are you?"

"Of course I'm not sure," she told him. "I've decided that I'll take the risk—just as you have. The fact that we haven't a clue what the risk is, or how freakishly it might express itself if it ever does, makes it all the more piquant, don't you think?"

"Since Daddy died, my lucky streak is supposedly dormant," Canny told her, knowing that he wasn't giving anything away. "I'm normal now, almost. I thought when I saw you last that the loss of my luck might put me at a disadvantage, if it really does happen, and make me more vulnerable than I'd otherwise be, but it might have the opposite effect, mightn't it? It might make it safe for us to meet."

"Perhaps it will," she agreed. "Is that what you want to be— safe?"

"I'm talking to you," he pointed out. "I'm alone with you in the inner sanctum of Credesdale House. That's not what Daddy would have considered safe. Your mother would presumably take the same view."

She didn't smile at that. Her mood seemed to have became more serious, and he regretted making the reference to her mother. Outside, in the sunlit churchyard, she had seemed to be taking everything lightly, but now they were in the gloomiest part of the library she was becoming taut and stiff—which was the opposite of what he wanted, especially if they were going to talk about safety and risk.

"I think we're probably safe enough," he reassured her, "unless and until I decide to renew the Kilcannon lucky streak."

"Unless?" she queried.

"It has occurred to me," he admitted, "that I don't actually need any more *unusual* luck. I could live quite comfortably on my accumulated capital."

"Are you saying that you'd give it all up for me?" she said. Outside, she'd probably have said it with a broad smile, but there was a hesitation in her teasing now. "After thirty generations and more, you'd stop? Because of me?" She knew that the world was full of men who would make or break a deal with the devil at her request—but that wasn't what she was getting at.

"Maybe not," Canny said, trying to sound casual. "After all, if I weren't a streaker you'd never have glanced at me twice, would you? If I were the kind of person who could contemplate letting it go, I might not be interesting any longer."

The bantering tone didn't evoke a response. Lissa had decided that it was time to approach the problem in earnest. Canny decided that he had better be earnest too.

"It really might be safer if I didn't try to renew the streak, at least for a while," he said. "If you and I are going to put our heads together, and try to figure out how it really works, it might be best if one of us were...de-activated. And if you look at it from an objective point of view, I really do have enough."

"Don't be ridiculous," she said, dismissively. "How could you ever have *enough*? Are you really saying that if your ability to deconstruct the moment were still active—as it might be, for all you know—you'd avoid me? Knowing what I am, could you simply turn your back on me and forget that I exist?"

She was obviously asking him questions she'd already asked herself.

"I don't know," he confessed. "Probably not. How about you?"

"I'm not sure that I could ever have enough, if I didn't try to follow this through," she said, flatly.

"And what would *following it through* involve, exactly?" he asked

"Well," she said, "we both know what view our parents would take—but that's not our style, is it? My mother's right when she says that one shouldn't tempt fate, of course, but there are some temptations that are simply irresistible, aren't there?"

The way she was adding rhetorical questions to her statements told him that she was still uncertain, still fearful, still searching for an endorsement of her boldness.

"I suppose there are," he agreed.

"Do you mind telling me how, exactly, you're supposed to renew the family luck, according to tradition?" she asked. "You confirmed that it worked according to much the same pattern as the one I'm supposed to follow, but you were understandably vague about the details."

"Fortunately," Canny said, thinking that it might be wise to lighten the mood again, "it doesn't involve human sacrifice beneath the stony gaze of the Great Skull. It's as simple as you suggested, apart from a few recitations and trivial ceremonies that probably don't have anything to do with the actual effect. It's basically just a matter of siring a male child on a good Yorkshirewoman. When the child begins to be lucky, there are other ceremonies, which...." He trailed off, unwilling to say too much.

Lissa completed the sentence for him, but she didn't pick up his attempt to lighten the tone. "Which permit the parent to claw back a portion of the child's burgeoning magic," she said, evenly, "provided that the parent is neither too greedy nor too self-restrained."

"That's about it," Canny confirmed, although he would never have used the phrase *claw back*, no matter how conducive to festering resentment the situation he'd described might be.

"I won't ask for any more details," she said. "We have our rules of secrecy too. But I'll compensate you for your hazardous honesty, if you like, by telling you how I think it works."

"Please," Canny said.

"I agree with you that there must be a genetic component to the hereditary process," Lissa said, smoothly, "and that we have to look at it more scientifically than our ancestors could. Our tradition has always placed far more importance on the existential and psychological significance of mother-daughter bonds than on mere biology, so we see the hereditary aspect more as a matter of personal contact or learning—passing on a very particular kind of accumulated wealth—but that's just a cultural bias. The biology has to be the bottom line. As to what the genes actually *do*—I think it has to involve the physics of uncertainty. I'm not good with the mathematics, so I'm strictly an amateur, but it seems to me that if observers really do have a crucial role to play in bringing actuality from a probabilistic blur of potentiality, then it stands to reason that some observers must be more privileged than others. The margin might—indeed, must—be very tiny, but it's enough, in certain kinds of situations...or *un*certain kinds of situations...to tip the balance of probabilities in favor of a preferred outcome. However we inherited the privilege, and however we contrive to maintain it, you and I are better *observers* than our fellow men—not in the sense that we notice more, but in the sense that our needs outweigh theirs by a slight but vital margin."

"Our needs?" Canny echoed. "Isn't it more a matter of our desires?"

"That's a rather masculine distinction," Lissa told him. "Our needs shape our desires, and remain implicit within them—although, if your family is like mine, there's a strong tradition of careful restraint."

"Don't howl for the moon," Canny quoted.

"I was thinking more along the lines of *be careful what you wish for, you might get it.*"

"You can't always get what you want," Canny quoted, whimsically, "but if you try sometimes, you might just get what you need. Actually, that's the Rolling Stones—but I always did wonder about Mick Jagger. I often do wonder about anyone touched by glory, even though keeping a low profile has always been the Kilcannon way. If it is a gene, though, or more than one, there might be lots of people carrying them unawares, who break the rules without ever suspecting that there are any. They presumably have meteoric careers...and then the phenomenon presumably becomes dormant again, for a few generations. What really sets us apart is knowing what we've got, and being able to manage it—to preserve our status as privileged observers, if you're right about the uncertainty business."

"Exactly," she agreed. "What sets us apart is knowing what we've got—and being determined to make the most of it."

Except, Canny thought, *that being determined to make the most of it isn't at all the same thing as being able to manage it... and might turn out to be its opposite.*

"I've thought a lot about what you said the other night," Lissa went on, "and it does make sense. Especially the bit about your family having one gene, and mine having another. But even if it weren't genetic—even if it *were* magic...our meeting still raises interesting possibilities, don't you think?"

"I've done little else but think, these last few days," Canny admitted. "What are you proposing, Lissa? How do you think we ought to approach the investigation?"

The model hesitated for a moment, but only for a moment. "You're still thinking in masculine terms. I don't think we should *approach the investigation* at all; I think we should cut to the chase. What if your gene and my gene—or your magic and my magic—came together? Perhaps, as you say, it's safer for us to be in one another's company while your luck is reduced, awaiting renewal—but if it's a gene, you're still carrying it, and if it's magic, you still have the potential. The only way we can really find out what's possible is to have a child. That would fit in with your desires, wouldn't it? The trial, if not the child."

His own hesitation was far more deliberate, and far more extended. "Is that a proposal of marriage?" he asked, eventually, as casually as he could.

"I don't think we need to go to that extreme," she said, with a calculated coolness that must have been as false as his own laconism. "It's an experiment, not a love-match."

For you, maybe, he thought. "Were you thinking of a male or female child?" was what he said aloud, trying hard not to feel offended or hurt by her immediate rejection of the possibility of marriage. He was trying to maintain a flippant tone, but he knew that the artificiality of the flippancy must be obvious to her.

"It would be interesting to discover what chance would decide, wouldn't it?" Lissa said, her voice carefully neutral. "That's partly what the experiment would be about, after all."

Just because we aren't both male, Canny thought, *it doesn't mean we're not in competition.*

"One doesn't have to leave such matters to chance, nowadays," he observed, aloud. "If it's just an experiment, pipettes and Petri dishes might be the way to go. Perhaps we ought to aim for one of each: non-identical twins."

"It's not a joke, Canny," she told him, unnecessarily. "I'm serious about this. I've thought about it a great deal."

"Were you thinking of hopping into bed with me right now?" Canny said, with an edge in his voice that certainly wasn't humor. "If we hurry, you'll still have time to get to London by six?"

"Not right now," Lissa said, defensively. She paused before adding: "I'll have to clear a space in my schedule to accommodate a pregnancy. I have obligations."

The conversation didn't seem to be going quite as well as Canny had hoped when he first came into the library, in spite of the fact that she was offering him exactly what he'd thought he wanted, if not quite on the terms he'd wanted it. *Be careful what you wish for*, she had said, *you might get it*. She hadn't been trying to warn him against her—not consciously, at least—but it had been a warning nevertheless.

Lissa Lo's coolness and stylishness had seemed exciting before, but now the coolness seemed to be escalating into coldness and the stylishness was becoming rather mechanical. Canny knew that she wasn't really as unemotional as she was trying to seem—she was hiding her own uncertainty and trepidation—but that didn't make the awkwardness any easier to bear.

"So what kind of schedule did you have in mind?" he asked, quietly. "And what do you want from me in the meantime?"

Lissa stood up, not because she'd said what she'd come to say—although she had—but because she was as acutely conscious of the tension inherent in the moment as he was.

"Don't be in too much of a hurry to get engaged to be married, Canny, no matter what your family tradition dictates," she said. "I'm not asking you to wait forever, but I'd like you to give the idea serious consideration. If you decide that it's an experiment worth trying, I'll need a few weeks, perhaps months, to...put my affairs in order. I can't give you a date right now. We both know that it would be a risk—but it seems to me that the potential rewards outweigh the danger. You don't have to give me an answer now. You can think it over, and do whatever you want in the meantime—but I'll come back when I can, to ask the question again. Think about it."

Her stance left no further doubt as to the fact that she had said what she had come to say—and was sufficiently fearful of his reply to leave the matter undecided while she beat a hasty retreat.

Canny could understand well enough why Lissa might be afraid—but he wasn't certain which of the various possible reasons was the most powerful. Was she afraid that she'd simply gone too far—that the black lightning might have been hunting her down even she spoke? Or was she afraid of his response? Was she worried that he might turn her down, given that he had far more at stake than any other man she'd ever teased and tempted, and that the rejection might hurt?

She knew that the world was full of men who'd make or break a deal with the devil at her request—but she might not be sure, as yet, that he was one of them. And she had to know, given that she'd thought about it so intently, that he would be taking a greater risk than she in several different ways...and that he would be able to see those additional risks quite clearly, no matter how his desires might blind him.

Given that he wasn't sure himself whether he might be capable of rejecting her, if he persuaded himself that the risks were too great, her uncertainty was understandable.

"There might be a case for taking things more slowly," he said, mildly. "there are other co-operative ventures that we might try, to begin with."

"There might," she answered, her tone making it perfectly clear that she didn't believe it, "but I'm not a dabbler by nature. When I make a decision, I don't like to procrastinate."

"I can understand that," Canny said, wondering—a trifle optimistically—whether he might be reading too much into the situation. She had known since their first conversation in the library—and must have assumed, even before then, that the rules pertaining to his gift were likely to be similar to those pertaining to hers—that his luck was supposed to run low when his father died, while hers would remain strong for as long as her mother lived. For the moment, her luck allegedly outweighed his, and in any competition he was likely to come off worse. If they were to have a child *now*, rather than waiting until he had renewed his own luck, and were content to leave such matters as its sex to the dictates of "chance", it was far more likely to work out to her advantage than his...or so she must be calculating.

On the other hand, given that the only way to renew his own streak was to marry, and father a child, what was there for him to gain by procrastination but a tangled mess of complications? And given the nature of his desire, the pressure of his need....

Canny rose to his feet without saying another word. He went to open the door, and politely stood aside to let Lissa Lo precede him. Then he opened the two outer doors that let them out of the library.

It wasn't until Bentley had brought Lissa's coat and summoned her minders from the gate, while Canny escorted her to the door of her hire-car, that he gave her anything resembling an answer to the question she'd posed. "I'll think about it very seriously indeed," he promised. "How shall I contact you when I have an answer?"

"Don't try," she said. "I'll come to you, when I can."

"Fine," he said. "If I'm not here, I'll be at the flat in London. This is the address." He handed her a business card as he pronounced the last sentence

She put it away without glancing at it. "I'll find you," she said, with the total confidence of someone well used to finding her way wherever she wanted to go. "I know that I can count on you, Canny. I'm sorry for your loss, but I know that things will get better. There's a whole world of opportunity out there, waiting to be seen by the right observers."

"Thanks," he said. "I'm sure you're right."

CHAPTER NINETEEN

When Lissa had driven away into the gathering night, Canny decided to walk down to the village—to clear his head rather than to survey his domain. As he walked, he wondered what the consequences might be of accepting Lissa's offer. In the worst-case scenario, it seemed to him, she would walk away with the reward: a doubly-blessed child, available for her exploitation and hers alone. Was that possible, given that it contravened the rules by means of which her family streak had been cultivated? Was it what she intended, even if it were possible? Would it matter, even if it were to happen, even if the transgression were to cost him any chance of renewing his own streak? Hadn't he spoken the truth when he said that he had enough to get by, even if he never enjoyed another stroke of exceptional good luck as long as he lived? And what if her intentions were not entirely cynical—or, even if they were, that they might be modified by time and experience? What if they were to form a new collective, unlike any that their ancestors had ever known: an authentic triad, all equally able to share in the superabundant luck of their miracle child, whether it turned out to be a boy or a girl?

There might, as Lissa had said, be a world full of opportunities out there, waiting to be opened up. Perhaps she was sincere. Perhaps, after all, she might learn to love him.

Next time, he thought, *I really must show her the rest of my little fiefdom, so that she can measure me for what I am, rather than what I seemed to be in Monte Carlo.*

It was easy enough to imagine that she was beside him as he

walked beside the Crede, and what he might he have said to her as they approached and entered the village.

"The Industrialist earl wasn't the first, of course," he might have said. "The situation of the mill having been dictated by the flow of the Crede, he needed to house his workers, so terraces of houses had to be built one way or another. Utopian fantasies were in vogue, and Titus Salt was already hard at work in Shipley, building Saltaire. The old Industrialist introduced a few wrinkles of his own, though. From the very beginning, he planned to keep much tighter control over his property and his people. He instituted—and all his successors retained—a policy of letting the accommodation at rates below the market price, and instituting a system of variable rebates that made the accommodation even cheaper to everyone who was seen to be making a positive contribution to the local economy or the provision of local amenities—which is why there's still a butcher's shop in Cockayne, and a baker's, and a carpenter's shop—not to mention a good primary school and an excellent library."

How could she fail to be impressed?

"It hasn't been easy, of course," he might have told her, proudly, if only she'd given him the time. "Salt's Mill is a museum now, and so is Saltaire. Shipley's other mill was demolished long since. Daddy used to tell me that when he was a boy he could sit on top of the Great Skull and see the tops of a hundred factory chimneys surrounding him, in the distance, all belching smoke into the air to create a haze that never really cleared, all the way from Bingley in the far east to Rotherham in the far south. They're all gone now, including ours—but when our chimney was toppled, the Mill kept going. It's always been busy, no matter how many economic metamorphoses it's had to undergo. It was a munitions factory during World War II, a plastics factory in the fifties and sixties, and then got broken up into smaller units specializing in various kinds of technological enterprise—plastic components for aircraft, cars and domestic machinery; switches for telephone systems; optical fibers...I haven't kept up, I'm afraid, although I'll have to start. I think we've even diversified into software and ceramics—individual projects have folded by the score, but we've always been lucky in cutting them off at the right moment and replacing them with something new, always maintaining our elasticity. We've never been conspicuously innovative, but we've never been far behind the times either. We've always valued long-term stability over the short-term escalation of profit, never sought outside finance... and it's paid off—not spectacularly, but inexorably.

"In the meantime, we've fostered the old Industrialist's quasi-Utopian ideals in the institution of a highly idiosyncratic form of local democracy. It conflicts to some extent with the demands made of us by local and national government, but we've always managed to compromise, thanks to good representation on the county council and family influence. The village elders have gladly collaborated with the family in conserving the valley, and they take great pride in what they've done now that their age-old habits have become fashionable. We don't have a super-market, a cinema or a railway-station, but we do have a village green with a cricket square, a thriving marketplace, a local slaughterhouse and the Spread Eagle. The old ranks of outside toilets were converted into garages during the great renovation of the fifties, but private cars are still a relative rarity—the vehicles they house are mostly commercial."

"And it's all yours, now," she would surely have said.

He would have feigned pride, even though none of it had had attracted any significant fraction of his attention—but he was a changed man, now. He intended to make up for lost time as quickly as he could. so that he could take his father's place as the chief architect of Cockayne's future. It was all his now—not just the property and the income, but the responsibility to decide which aspects of its commerce and environment should hasten into the twenty-first century with all possible progressive determination, and which vestiges of the nineteenth century should be jealousy preserved and hoarded.

As if to endorse his flight of fancy, twenty-three people had offered respectful greetings to him by the time he reached the market square, and a further fifteen greeted him deferentially while he paused there, looking around at the darkened shops and imagining that Lissa Lo was by his side, hanging on his every word.

One shop, of course, was still blazing with light in spite of the fact that it was nearly eleven: the fish-and-chip shop. Customers were still trickling in, mostly one by one, and trickling out again—more than usual, thanks to the hangover from the funeral—but Canny could see through the window that there were four people who remained in the shop, not eating but chatting: Ellen Ormondroyd's sisters and their respective husbands. Ellen and her husband were behind the counter, as usual.

Eventually, Canny left the ghost of Lissa Lo behind and walked into the shop.

"Haddock and chips, please," he said, as he approached the counter.

A slightly uncomfortable silence had fallen when he walked in, and he judged that it would not be easily broken, so he took the burden upon himself. "Nice to see you again," he said to Alice and Martin Ellison. "Hello Lydia—you must be Ken. I hear you're in Manchester, now. Thanks for coming over. It's been a very long day. I had to get out of the house, away from the atmosphere. I didn't have time to eat at the reception, even if I'd been able to stomach it—my appetite's only just getting back into gear."

That speech invoked several sympathetic nods, but even Alice was casting about for something to say that wouldn't seem rude or stupid.

"I used to come in here once a week when I was a kid, you know," he went on, addressing himself to Alice's Martin and Lydia's Ken. It was before Jack's time, let alone Ellen's. Daddy used to give me money to pay for my supper, but what was more important was being allowed to walk down here on my own, even after dark. It wasn't like going to school—it was real life. Sometimes, it was the only part of life that did seem real—but that's not a complaint. I always knew how lucky I was. Always."

"Are you all right, Canny?" Ellen finally plucked up the courage to ask, while Jack Ormondroyd sprinkled salt and vinegar on his fish and chips.

"I'm fine," Canny said. "Sorry if I'm rambling. Long day.

"Open or closed?" Jack asked.

"Open," Canny said.

"You can send Bentley down to collect now," Jack observed, as he arranged the paper artfully into a basket. "That's what your Dad allus did, when the fancy took him, on cook's night off."

"He would," Canny said.

"Do you want to turn out for the team on Saturday, Lord Credesdale?" Jack asked. "I think we're one short."

Canny remembered his casual offer to drop into the shop if he wanted a game; Jack had obviously mistaken his motive.

"You would be one short if I said yes," Canny said, handing him a five pound note. "Thanks for asking, Jack, but I don't think so. Maybe I'll come down to watch the game, though— hang around the score box making a nuisance of myself, the way I used to."

"You'd be very welcome," Jack said, dutifully counting out his change.

Canny nodded, and nodded again to Martin Ellison as he turned away. "I'll ring you," he promised. "Bye, Ellen, Lydia, Alice, Ken."

By the time he'd reached the end of the catalogue of names Canny was already in the doorway. Their murmured answers combined into a ragged chorus as the door swung shut behind him.

Canny made his way slowly back through the village streets, eating as he went. His appetite had indeed got back into gear, and he realized that it really had been a long time since he'd last taken the opportunity to eat. A further dozen people greeted him politely; he didn't try to count the pairs of eyes that watched his progress from afar, or to estimate the thoughts that might be going through their minds as they contemplated their new landlord.

"This is what it's like, you see," he said to the ghost of Lissa Lo. "This is the greater part of the Kilcannon luck. It hasn't just been a quantitative thing, reflected in shrewd gambles and good business. This is what we've made of ourselves. We're not glamorous, by any means, and we don't do a lot of smiling, but we're worth something. We're solid."

By the time he finished that imaginary speech, however, he'd passed beyond the reach of the street lights into the gloom of the path that ran beside the stream to the bridge that carried the approach-road to the house over the beck. The night was fairly clear, but the moon wasn't full and stars seemed weak. He could find his way easily enough, but he still, seemed to be walking through a vast and ominous shadow. For the first time, it seemed to him that he could feel the absence of his luck, the failure of his early-warning systems.

He had no idea what Lissa Lo intended, in the longer run. He had no idea whether she would have any further interest in him, once he had given her the child she wanted.

He had no idea, either, how the outcome of that experiment might affect them, if they were indeed to be punished for their temerity in challenging the rules of fate.

But the haddock tasted wonderful, and the chips had exactly the right texture.

"We all live dangerously," he said—aloud, since there was no one who could possibly overhear him—"who live at all. And we all die but once, no matter how good or bad our luck might be. How many men are lucky enough to get the chance of intimacy with one of the ten most beautiful women in the world, under any conditions?"

There was, of course, no answer—but none was needed.

CHAPTER TWENTY

The next day was the busiest of Canny's life, and the one after was little better but he coped well enough. He spent all day Monday at the Mill, and returned again the following morning, but Tuesday afternoon was spent in Leeds, at the three banks where his various companies held accounts, and the offices of the two solicitors who handled various aspects of the family business. As five o'clock approached, however, he found time to call in at the headquarters of Robert Stanley and Associates, a firm of inquiry agents that his father had employed to carry out various kinds of research. He was immediately ushered in to see the top man, and asked him to put together a dossier on Lissa Lo and her family.

"Use publicly-accessible sources, as far as you can" he said. "Don't do any kind of digging that would advertise the fact that you're on the job—but I need facts, not gossip. Pay particular attention to her matrilineal ancestry—I'm not interested in her father's family."

"It might be expensive, sir," Bob Stanley warned him. "If you want me to go deeper than journalistic crap and the kind of fluff that comes up when you type a name like hers into a search engine, I'll have to use contacts outside the country. I've got links with good agencies in Hong Kong, the U.S.A. and Bangkok, but the cost...."

"Check with me if it looks like running over five thousand," Canny said, "but for that kind of money, I expect a thorough job. I need it done quickly. As soon as humanly possible."

Stanley, once he was reassured that Canny knew what he was committing himself to, agreed readily enough. He didn't ask what Canny's interest in Lissa Lo was, and gave the impression that the former Earl of Credesdale had given him tasks to carry out that were odder by far. The bank managers, too, had given him the impression that their dealings with the Kilcannon family had never been excessively mired in orthodoxy and expectability—although Canny had been glad to find, when he went through his father's private papers, that his newly-acquired business interests were all perfectly legal. A family as lucky as the Kilcannons obviously had no need, any longer, to be involved in anything more than slightly shady.

He spent Wednesday in London, traveling back and forth by train, and Thursday at the Mill. Friday was again divided between the Mill and Leeds. Every evening was spent reading, although none of his reading material came from the library shelves.

By Saturday afternoon, Canny felt in such desperate need of a break that he decided to take up Jack Ormondroyd's second invitation and walk down to the green to see how the cricket team was doing.

He arrived no more than an hour and a half after the match had begun, but it seemed that he had already missed the greater part of the crucial action. Cockayne's players were in the field and the visitors were seven down for sixty-five, which the local spectators thought a highly satisfactory score. Frank Langsgill, the butcher's eldest son, had bowled an entertainingly aggressive spell but had now retired, red in the face, to long leg, where he was patiently awaiting a mistimed hook.

Canny sat down in front of the pavilion to watch for a while, Only one more run had gone up on the board when Ellen Ormondroyd came bustling out of the back room where she'd been helping with preparations for the tea interval and said: "Have you heard?" There was a catch in her voice which told him immediately that the news was bad.

"No," he said. "What is it?"

"It's Alice's Martin. He's dead." The word "dead" fragmented into a strangled sob.

"What?" Canny felt his heart lurch, but that was only natural. "When? How did it happen?"

"Last night. He caught two lads breaking into his car—just kids, they think, although they haven't caught them. He tried to stop them—you saw what a big bloke he was, for a professor, so it must have seemed the right thing to do. One of them hit him with a crowbar—five or six times, although he must have been knocked silly after one or two. Fractured his skull. The hospital's only a mile away, but the ambulance couldn't get him there in time. Dead on arrival, they said."

Ellen had been standing up while she spoke, but now she flopped down on the bench beside him. Tears were rolling down her face.

"Jesus," was all that Canny could find to say. He put his arm out tentatively, making as if to put it around Ellen's shoulder, but withdrew it when her teenage daughter, who had come out of the pavilion behind her, sat down on the other side and took the responsibility upon herself.

"You shouldn't be doing the teas, Mum," Marie said.

"Alice said not to go over to hers," Ellen said—to Canny, not to her daughter. "Mum's gone, but Alice said she didn't want a crowd. Carry on as normal, she said—and Jack wasn't about to miss his cricket unless he absolutely had to, and Alice gave him the excuse he needed, so I thought I'd best take it too, in spite of...well, Dad's minding the shop, so I...only I thought you'd want to know, with you having read his books, and invited him to dinner and all. Sorry about the waterworks."

"That's okay," Canny told her. "Marie's right. You shouldn't be here, even if Jack can't let the team down and you're not needed in the shop. Shall I walk you home?"

"I've go to get the teas," Ellen said.

"It's all done but what Ginny I can take care on, Mum," Marie told her. "Look—you're distracting Dad."

Jack Ormondroyd was indeed peering at them from mid-wicket, even though the bowler had begun to run in.

"It's silly," Ellen complained, mopping at her face with a screwed-up handkerchief. "It's not as if I knew him right well. Only met him half a dozen times."

The batsman took a mighty swipe at the ball, hitting it high and wide. Canny winced in expectation of its arrival before realizing that it would fall within the field. Frank Langsgill was already running round to position himself beneath it, while Jack Ormondroyd bellowed: "Catch it!"

The shout was counterproductive. The butcher's boy fumbled the ball and it went to ground. The spectators groaned.

"That's not the point," Canny assured Ellen, when he was able to return his attention to the more urgent matter. "It's Alice you're feeling for. She's your little sister."

"Go on, Mum," Marie said, again. "Go home. I'll see to the teas."

Ellen consented to be raised to her feet. Canny took her arm, although he knew that every pair of eyes that had previously been fixed on Frank Langsgill was now on them, and would remain on them until the bowler contrived his next delivery.

"Come on, Ellen," he said. "It's not far. Jack will understand." He led her around the side of the pavilion and away from the green.

"It's such a stupid way to go," she said. "Young bloke like that—only thirty, younger'n you and me. At the university and all. Beaten to death by a Chapeltown yob over a car stereo. It's not as if you can get anything for them any more—worse than TVs. So stupid."

"He was unlucky," Canny said, feeling an oddly foul taste in his mouth. "It could happen to anyone."

"You see it every day on the news," Ellen went on, aimlessly. "People run down by their own cars, stabbed to death for a few quid or a bag of shopping. Old ladies beaten up. They wanted to come back to Cockayne, Canny—Alice thinks it's the last safe place on Earth. It used to be, didn't it? Still is, I suppose, if only because everywhere else has got so much worse."

"Things don't seem to be improving," Canny agreed. "I was mugged myself a little while ago."

"Not *here*?"

"No—in Monte Carlo. I was lucky. The mugger just took some money I'd won at the casino, and didn't shoot me. If I hadn't had the money...who knows what might have happened? Poor Alice. Will your Mum bring her back here?"

"If she'll come. Knowing Alice, she won't. Doesn't run away, our Alice, Not that it would be running away, but...well, you know how things can seem."

They reached the door of the fish-and-chip shop. When Canny opened the door Ellen's father lifted up the counter and came out to meet her. She collapsed into his arms.

"Make her a cup of tea, Jem," Canny said. "She'll be okay— it was my fault. She saw me and thought she had to tell me what had happened, but when she told me...it all broke loose."

"Thanks, Lord Credesdale," Jem Proffitt said, a trifle warily.

"His name's Canny, Dad," Ellen said. "We're his friends— aren't we, Canny? We've known one another forever."

"Yes, we're friends," Canny said. "If there's anything I can do...."

"That's okay," Jem Proffitt said, swiftly. "Everything's taken care of. Madge is with Alice. I'll see to Ellen."

Canny nodded, and backed away.

"Thanks, Canny." Ellen said. "Best get back to the game— that lot won't last much longer, and us'll knock off the runs in no time. You could have played, you know—wouldn't have made any difference.

"It would if I'd been at long leg instead of Frank," Canny said. "I'd have caught it." *With my eyes shut*, he didn't add.

"Aye," said Ellen, not at all skeptically. "I bet you would, at that."

Canny didn't go back to the green though; he headed up the slope instead of down. As soon as he got back to the house he went to the library, where he'd left the business card that Martin Ellison had given him. He looked at the phone number for a few seconds, then reached for an A-Z of Leeds and looked up the address.

He decided that it might be a trifle ostentatious take the Bentley to a murder scene, so he looked into the living-room to ask his mother if he could borrow her Citroen.

"Why?" she asked.

"A man I know was murdered last night," he said, shortly. "I ought to see the widow."

She frowned, but didn't ask for more details; she went to her purse and handed over the keys.

"Will you be in for dinner?" she asked.

"Probably," he said. "Don't wait if I'm not back, though."

The Citroen seemed very cramped by comparison with the Bentley but it handled the narrow roads much better and accelerated smoothly enough once he hit the A64, which took him all the way in to the junction with Woodhouse Lane. He found the street easily enough, although it was closed to traffic, so he had to park in the next street along. The taped-off area containing the car that Martin Ellison had presumably died defending was thirty yards further on than the address on the card, although there was no competition for parking spaces now.

The policeman on duty at the end of the street stopped him, but he only had to mention his name and explain his relationship to the population of Cockayne to be allowed through.

No one answered the door when he rang the bell, but he waited and then rang again. At the third attempt the letter-box opened and a female voice he didn't recognize told him that Mrs Ellison didn't want to talk to anyone.

"I'm a family friend," he said. "Canavan Kilcannon—the Earl of Credesdale."

The door opened, but only by a crack. "ID?" the voice asked.

Canny slipped his driving license through the crack. He heard the voice call out, announcing his name to someone at the back of the house, but the reply was muffled.

The door swung open to reveal a young woman, no older than Alice and perhaps a little younger. "Sorry about that," she said, as she looked up and down the street to make sure that Canny was alone. "I'm P.C. Willis, the family liaison officer. Come in. Mrs. Ellison and her mother are in the kitchen."

Alice and Mrs. Proffitt looked at him in open astonishment, even though they had been told of his arrival by the police-woman. "Ellen told me about Martin," he said, briefly. "I'm very sorry. She said that you wouldn't come home, because you thought it would seem like running away. She thinks you'd be better off in the village—so do I."

"I've been telling her that for hours," Mrs. Proffitt put in. "Maybe she'll listen to you."

"Why?" Alive snapped at her. "Because he's a bloody lord?"

"No," Canny said. "Because my father died last week, and I think I understand how you might be feeling."

"You've no idea," she retorted. "No idea at all."

"Why?" Canny countered. "Because Daddy was old and Martin wasn't? Because Daddy was ill and Martin wasn't? Because Daddy died peacefully in his sleep, and Martin didn't? Or because I'm just a son and you're a wife? Believe me, Alice, it doesn't make a lot of difference. Dead is dead. Left alone is left alone. Feeling guilty is feeling guilty."

All three of his listeners seemed startled by that.

"Why should I feel guilty?" Alice asked.

"You shouldn't," Canny said, fearing that he would sound crass but plugging on anyway. "But you probably do. I don't know exactly what about, but I dare say you've found some-thing. Maybe it was you who parked the car in that particular spot, or didn't stop him when he went out after the men who were breaking into it. Maybe you assured him that it would be okay to live here for a while until you found out whether it would be possible to move to Cockayne, when he expressed doubts. It doesn't matter what—you'll probably have found something you did or didn't do that would have made things work out differ-ently if you hadn't or had done it. You shouldn't stay here. You should come back to Cockayne with your mother. Ellen's there, and Marie, and Jem. The police don't need you to be here any more, do they?"

He looked at P.C. Willis as he asked the last question.

The policewoman shook her head.

"It's only twenty minutes away, in any case," Canny said.

"I can't use the car," Alice said. "It's evidence in a murder inquiry. Mum came on the bus."

"I'll drive you both," Canny said. "Pack what you need, and I'll drop you both at your Mum's door. Then I'll leave you alone. Your Mum will look after you. Ellen too."

Alice stared at him, uncomprehendingly. "I didn't go to your father's funeral to pay my respects," she said, distantly. "All I wanted was to get you on our side so we could move back."

"Well, *that* certainly wasn't what got Martin killed," Canny said. "I don't mind. What do you think she should do, P.C. Willis?"

"I think she should stay with her mother for a few days," the policewoman said, promptly. "It's better than having her mother stay here. You won't be able to keep the reporters and TV cameras from pestering you here. You might not even in Cockayne, but at least your mother's house isn't thirty meters away from a murder scene."

"We can make sure that the reporters keep a respectful distance in Cockayne," Canny said, without specifying how. "It's not running away, Alice. It's just the sensible thing to do."

Alice threw up her hands. "Well, if the lord of the bloody manor says so," she muttered, in a martyred tone. "I'll go pack."

CHAPTER TWENTY-ONE

"She doesn't mean it," Mrs. Proffitt said, when Alice had left the room. "She's upset."

"Understandably," Canny said. "Any progress?" he asked P.C. Willis.

"I can't...," the policewoman began, before Mrs. Proffitt cut her off.

"If you mean have they caught the little bastards, no," she said. "They will, though. They've got descriptions. They were off their own patch, you see. This isn't Chapeltown—everybody round here hates Chapeltowners. There'll be witnesses who'll stand up in court. They'll get caught—though what the courts will do I shudder to think. Slap on the wrist, I dare say. Probably sue Alice because they got blood on their crowbar."

Another thing that P.C. Willis couldn't do was rise to that sort of bait, so Canny said: "It doesn't really matter how long they go to jail for, Mrs. Proffitt. It won't bring Martin back."

"Drug addicts," Mrs. Proffitt said, as if she were spitting acid. "Murdering little bastards. Ought to be hanged."

"I understand how you feel," Canny said, and left it at that. He didn't, though. His own feelings were far less straightforward. He had had not the slightest inkling that the tragedy was about to occur, but that wouldn't have been surprising even if his gift had been at its fullest strength. Even so, he couldn't help wondering whether Martin Ellison's death had had something to do with him—if it had been spun off somehow from the climactic flash of disruption that had accompanied his roulette win. There wasn't the slightest reason for thinking that there could be any connection, however tortuous its logic might be, but that didn't prevent him from wondering. As he had pointed out to Alice, even ordinary people tended to feel guilty when bad things happened around them; people who were supposed to be masters of their own destiny were bound to have an even more exaggerated sense of their own agency. Even if the event had not been connected in any way with the unfolding consequences of that moment in Monte Carlo, there remained the question of whether Canny could have prevented the murder, if only he had cared enough to receive a presentiment of its possibility.

When Alice reappeared clutching an overnight bag P.C. Willis asked Canny where he was parked, and volunteered to walk them to the car.

"It's good of you to do this, sir," the policewoman murmured, as they moved out into the street and stood to one side while Alice locked up behind them.

"It's no trouble," Canny said. "I've known the family for a long time—I grew up with the three sisters. Do you want to come with us?"

"No," the policewoman said. "I'll come out as soon as we have some news—I know where Cockayne is. I've been through it." She repeated this to Alice as Alice was getting into the Citroen's front passenger seat. Canny held the door while Mrs. Proffitt clambered into the back.

As they set off, Alice said: "Ellen put you up to this, didn't she? She asked you to come and get me—just to show off that she could."

"Ellen just told me what had happened," Canny assured her. "She doesn't even know I'm here. She didn't think to ask, and she didn't have to. I told you the truth back there. I do know something of what you must be feeling."

"Why should you feel guilty about your Dad dying?" she retorted. "He had cancer."

"I shouldn't," Canny agreed. "I shouldn't feel guilty about

Martin's death, either—but I even feel guilty about that."

"Why?"

"Because I was mugged a few days ago myself. The mugger surprised me in my hotel room. He had a gun. I just stood there, helpless. There was nothing I could do. He took my money, and he left. He could have shot me, but he didn't. He probably would have, if I'd moved, and he might have anyway, because he was nervous. It was just my good luck that he didn't. I could have been killed, but I wasn't. Martin was. It wasn't his fault—on another day, he'd have blocked the first blow and taken the crowbar off the kid. He didn't do anything wrong. It was just bad luck. It could easily have been the other way around—I could have been shot, and he could have grabbed the crowbar and chased the kids away. I feel guilty because I was lucky and he wasn't, and I know just as well as you do how ridiculous that is—but it's no more ridiculous than you feeling guilty because he's dead and you're alive, and that's what I mean when I say that I understand."

"You patronizing bastard," Alice said, contemptuously—although Canny felt that he'd been more insensitive than patronizing.

"Alice!" Madge Proffitt complained.

Canny paid no heed to the interruption at all. "You see," he went on, "I can't help thinking—or feeling, at any rate—that there might be some kind of weird cosmic balance in which every bit of good luck I have is balanced out by somebody else's bad luck—in this case, Martin's. I'm a lucky Kilcannon, after all. I *expect* to have good luck—and if the universe can do me favors, it seems to stand to reason that it can do other people bad turns, and probably does, by way of compensation. It makes no sense at all, in terms of the calculus of probability, but psychological probability is a very different ball game—as Martin knew very well."

"Very clever," Alice said, bitterly. "You're telling me that Martin would understand how I feel better than I do, just like you do. Well, maybe he would—and maybe you do too, having lost your Dad so recently. Doesn't alter anything, does it? At least there's no possibility that the little savage who smashed his head in was his long-lost son, so you don't have to start lecturing me about the fucking Oedipus Effect, do you?"

"Alice!" Mrs. Proffitt complained again, her voice more agonized than before.

Canny drove north through Roundhay instead of picking up the A64, intending to go through Scholes and Barwick-in-Elmet rather than taking the main road. It seemed more fitting, somehow, to take the quieter route.

"I'm not lecturing you, Alice," he said, feeling that he ought to try to keep the conversation going in spite of the difficulties. "I'm telling you the simple truth. I've always felt guilty about the Kilcannon luck. You grew up in Cockayne, so you know all the stories, the whole rich stock of local legends. You can't tell me you that never heard anyone say that our good luck must be someone else's bad—with an exemplary tale to back up the claim. Don't tell me you never heard anyone say that the family have a pact with the devil."

"I never believed it," Alice said, contemptuously.

"Always told the kids that sort of stuff was rubbish," Madge Proffitt chipped in. "Never tolerated that sort of talk in our house, me or Jem. Ellen won't have it neither."

"I don't doubt it, Mrs Proffitt," Canny said. "The point I'm trying to make is that people say those things to express their feelings about the unfair way that good luck and bad luck are distributed within the world. The fact that they aren't true doesn't stop them affecting the way I feel—the way I've always felt, since I was a kid. Ellen understood that, I think—a little. You were telling the truth, weren't you, Alice, when you said she'd never say a word against me, and always defended me if someone else did?"

"Aye," said Alice. "Just like you were telling the truth when you said she showed you her knickers when you were at the primary."

It was Canny's turn to murmur "Alice!" as there was an

audible intake of breath in the back seat.

"Oh, sorry Mum," Alice said. After a moment's pause, she added: "You too, Canny. Got carried away. Stupid."

"It's okay," Canny said. "My fault."

"No, it's not," Alice said, after a slight pause. "It was good of you to come, Canny, even if Ellen did send you. She'd have come herself, if Jack hadn't been playing cricket and she was down to make the teas. If it had been Sunday and all she'd have had to miss was church there'd have been no stopping her—but *Jack's cricket* is a different matter. Lucky you didn't say yes when he offered you a game, or you'd have been stuck there too. Take a braver man than you to cry off after he'd picked you ahead of someone who can actually play."

"It's Jack we're talking about," Canny reminded her. "He'd have been only too pleased to call up the twelfth man in my place. He only invited me out of respect for tradition. Anyway, I was never that bad. My batting average was in the twenties. I was the best snicker in the village. Ask your Ellen."

The sheer bizarrerie of the last remark teased a wry smile out of Alice's repentant expression.

"We'll probably have won the match by now," Canny told her, glad to have found a topic that didn't annoy or hurt her. "The other lot weren't making much of a score. Frank Langsgill demolished their batting, although he blotted his scorebook later by dropping a sitter. They probably didn't get a hundred— and we certainly won't have needed to bat all the way down to number eleven to knock those off."

It was at that point, incongruously enough, that Alice finally broke down and began weeping. Maybe, Canny thought, Jack Ormondroyd had offered Martin a game too. Maybe Martin had been a good player, and had been looking forward to joining the team if and when the Ellisons were able to move to Cockayne— or maybe he was as useless as Canny was, and had had to make his apologies. It seemed more likely, though, that Alice had simply run out of annoyance and resentment, and had nothing left with which to shield her pent-up grief. The car crossed the

A64, heading into Scholes.

"I brought his book," Alice said, eventually, between sobs. "It's in the bag."

"What book?" Canny said.

"His new book. His book on superstition. I thought you might want to look at it, being interested and all. It's only a rough draft, mind, and not finished."

"Ah," Canny said. "That wasn't necessary, Alice. But thanks for the thought."

"Oh, I didn't *think*," she said. "I just did it. You wouldn't be here, though, if it weren't for the books, would you? You never gave Lydia's Ken a second glance—but as soon as you found out who Martin was, you were promising to get us a house—and I thought how lucky we were. How absolutely fucking *lucky*."

Madge Proffitt sighed audibly, but made no other protest regarding her daughter's bad language.

What Alice had said was true enough, Canny knew. If it had been Lydia's Ken who'd been murdered, he wouldn't have driven to Manchester. It *was* because Martin Ellison had been Martin Ellison that he had felt compelled to respond to the news of his death and his widow's distress—and Alice had packed Martin's latest, unfinished book in recognition of that fact, even without thinking.

"Martin was a wise man, Alice," he said. "I found a lot to admire in his work. I'm sure that we would have been friends. It's a terrible waste of a fine mind. Is there anything more I can do, when we get back?" The car was heading for Aberford now, and the Roman Ridge. They would be within sight of Credesdale very soon.

"No," said Alice. "I phoned his mother. She'll let his brother and sister know. They all live down south—Gloucester and Somerset. Didn't see much of them after we moved to Canterbury, but I suppose they'll want to bury him down there. If we can bury him at all, with him being murdered. Holds thing up, I dare say—especially if they don't catch them right away. That policewoman seemed confident, though. Impulsive crime, you see—not planned. They were seen. Just a matter of time. Nothing to do but wait."

"Well if you need anything," Canny said. "Mrs. Proffitt?"

"We'll let you know, Lord Credesdale," Madge Proffitt said, mechanically. "Thanks."

"Yes," said Alice. "Thanks. Sorry about what I said before. Not you I was angry at, really. Stupid."

"It's fine," Canny said. "You can insult me any time—it just bounces off. You must remember that, even though it's been a while."

"I haven't forgotten," she said. "Mistake, though—only used to make me try harder."

"Well, you'll have to try a lot harder now," he assured her. "The skin's got even thicker over the years. Takes a lot to get under it nowadays. You need someone to take it out on, you know where I am. Better me, maybe, than Ellen or your Mum."

"I'll remember that," Alice said, although her voice was devoid of gratitude. "Very kind of you, I'm sure. You must be busy, though, having just inherited the Mill. Not as if you'd spent a lot of time there recently, so I hear."

"There's a lot to catch up on," Canny admitted. "Here and in London. But the offer stands. Shall I drop you at home or the chippy?"

"Seven Berridge Street," Mrs. Proffitt was quick to say, although she must have known that Canny knew where she lived. "Thank you very much, Lord Credesdale."

"But next time," Alice said, as the car drew to a halt in Berridge Street and she opened the passenger door, "bring the Bentley, will you?"

"It's not a real Bentley," Canny told her. "They've been fake ever since Rolls Royce took them over, and now that the Germans have taken over Rolls Royce...."

She didn't want to play, even though she'd started it. Her face had became haggard and drawn again, "Thanks for the lift, Canny," she said, as mechanically as her mother, before she slammed the door.

"You're welcome," Canny said, inaudibly, before backing up and driving home.

CHAPTER TWENTY-TWO

On the following morning, not long after breakfast, Canny and his mother were reading the *Sunday Times* in the living-room when Bentley told him that Alice Ellison was asking to see him.

"Show her in," Canny said.

His mother offered Alice her condolences and conventional assurances of support, which Alice accepted gratefully—but when Alice said "I've brought you the book, Canny," Lady Credesdale took the hint and left the room.

It was on the tip of Canny's tongue to say "What book?" but then he remembered.

"You didn't...," he began—but Alice was already thrusting the typescript at him.

"The bit about you is just a set of notes," Alice said. "Martin hadn't really had a chance to get started on it."

Canny felt a sudden thrill of alarm, and looked at the typescript more attentively. The head sheet bore the title *The Legendry of Luck*. He scanned the contents page, then began riffling through it. There were only a hundred pages of actual text, but there were a further thirty pages of printed notes, all of them heavily annotated in blue ink. He found the page to which Alice had referred without much difficulty—it was headed "Kilcannon family"—and ran his eyes swiftly over it. He still had sufficient presence of mind to say "Sit down, please" and Alice eased herself down on to the sofa, perching on the edge as if she wanted to be ready for a quick getaway if Canny turned nasty.

Canny resumed his own chair, and replaced the page relating to the Kilcannons in the stack of A4 pages. He noted that the chapter of which they were to have been a part already had a title. All the chapter-titles on the contents page were taken from popular expressions; there was one on "Lady Luck", one called "Fortune Favours Fools", one on "Lucky Numbers", and even one on "Lucky Streaks". The chapter which was to have featured the Kilcannons was, however, "The Luck of the Devil".

"Where did he get this stuff about us?" Canny asked, slightly bewildered by the unexpected turn of events.

"From me, of course," Alice said. "He hadn't had the chance to talk to everyone else—not even Mum and Dad, let alone the anthropologist's traditional ideal informant, the oldest inhabitant. Look Canny—I wanted to say that I'm really sorry."

"About what?" Canny said, mystified by the change of tack.

"About all the things I said yesterday. That lord of the manor crack, the patronizing bastard remark—all of it. I treated you like some kind of adversary, when all you were trying to do was help. I was upset, angry...I shouldn't have taken it out on you. That was silly, as well as wrong. It really was good of you to help—and Ellen told me that it really was your idea, and that she never even thought of asking you to fetch me. I'm really sorry."

"No problem," Canny said, dismissively. "I was babbling like an insensitive idiot myself, because I was too embarrassed by the situation to keep my mouth shut. Can I assume from this that you and Martin wanted to move to Cockayne because you *both* wanted to do research into my family history?"

Alice seemed to be startled by the question, or perhaps by the earnest tone in which he'd phrased it. "It wasn't our main reason," she said. "As I told you, we wanted to start a family. I thought Cockayne was the right place to do it. My project was just an excuse, really—something I could put to the village elders. When I thought about it, I realized that it really would be an interesting bit of history to write up and that I really might be able to get access to some interesting sources here at the house, but it wasn't a priority. Martin only put you into his book because you seemed to fit—when I told him about all the local legends about the Kilcannon luck, he was delighted. He really was looking forward to talking to you, though—in fact, he nearly told you when we talked after the funeral, but I cut him off. I got embarrassed about having told him all those stories, and you not knowing that I'd done it. He did want to follow it up, but only as an example of his grand theory. It would make a nice case study, he said—as you've probably guessed, this was supposed to be a more popular book than the others, appealing to general readers as well as academics. He needed anecdotal material—anything you could give him by way of interesting documentation—but it wouldn't have been any big deal. It wouldn't have been *prying*, and he certainly wouldn't have published anything without your approval. He couldn't believe his luck when you told him you were interested in his subject—I think he wanted to bounce some ideas off you."

Canny felt slightly numb. The Kilcannons had always hidden their secret in plain view; they had always joked about their luck, always admitting to it in a jocular fashion. That was one custom he'd followed almost unthinkingly—but times changed. Henri Meurdon had used a computer to analyze his betting patterns. Lissa Lo had seen the streak that had accompanied the wrench of probability that had made his last bet on zero a winner. And Martin Ellison, respected scholar in the field of psychological probability, had married one of the Proffitt girls, who had a rich fund of listener-friendly folklore concerning the Lucky Kilcannons. Suddenly, hiding in plain view looked like a strategy past its sell-by date. People were getting close— perhaps too close—to an awareness of exactly how lucky the Kilcannons really had been.

Martin Ellison had been desperately unlucky to be killed in such a futile fashion—but now Canny had to tell himself, sternly, that it couldn't possibly have had anything to do with the Kilcannon streak. Since his father had died, the streak had become dormant, inoperative, impotent.

Or had it?

Wasn't his luck tangled up, now, with Lissa Lo's streak? Wasn't he seriously considering the possibility of taking that entanglement to a new level? Hadn't he already ventured into uncharted waters, unprecedented situations? If his interaction with Lissa Lo was *already* making things freaky, what would happen if and when...?

He became aware that Alice was staring at him. "Are you all right, Canny?" she said. "I honestly didn't think you'd mind. If I'd thought it would upset you, I wouldn't have mentioned it, let alone brought the damned book to show you...but I thought you'd be interested. You said...."

"I am interested," Canny said, trying to sound soothing. "Sorry, Alice, it just...took me a little aback, I suppose."

"You don't *really* have a deal with the devil, do you?" she said, heroically trying to make a joke of it.

"Of course we do," he told her, automatically. "We have to sacrifice a virgin every full moon to keep the family fortunes rolling in."

"I'm no good to you, then," Alice said. "I guess all three of us were lucky to survive the cull, for we're safe enough now. Marie too, if appearances can be trusted."

Canny shook his head, dazedly. "I shouldn't have said that. I don't know why I did. Daddy's dead, and Martin...and I'm making jokes about sacrificing virgins. It just slipped out. Sorry."

"I fed you the line," she pointed out, "and I ran with the joke. I'm the one to blame. I came here to say sorry for letting my mouth run way with me yesterday, and off it goes again. It was the same at your Dad's funeral. You must think I'm terrible—a typical third child, no self-control at all. The brat of the family, just as you said."

"No, it's okay," Canny said. "There's only one of me, so I don't have any excuse. I'm a self-made brat—always have been. I'm trying to give it up, but...well, I guess I'll just have to try a little harder."

"Me too," she said. "Doesn't go with the widow's weeds, does it? Do you know what I wish?"

"No."

"I wish Martin and I hadn't fucked around with all the family planning, all the waiting until we were in the right place to bring up a child. Because now...we won't ever have one, will we? We tried to control the future, to organize it...and it spat in our faces. Is that a sort of Oedipus Effect? I can't even ask him any more, can I? Who's going to answer all my questions now? My Mum? My big sister? Not the same, is it? Not the same at all."

"No, it's not," Canny said, ruefully. "I had a whole lifetime to ask Daddy questions—questions that needed to be asked—and I never got around to making a start till he was on his deathbed. Now, there's no one who can tell me the answers. He'd have been wrong about almost everything, of course—he always was—but that's not the point, is it? They'd have been *his* answers, and now they're lost forever. I thought I was alone before, but now I really *am* alone. I've got Mummy, of course, and Bentley...but as you say, it's really not the same."

Half a minute passed in awkward silence before Alice took on the responsibility of changing the subject. "Your friends are all over the papers," she said, flicking a negligent forefinger at the *Sunday Times*. "The tabloids, anyway. They reckon that Stevie Larkin's agent's trying to make a deal with an English club to bring him home, so the thing with Lissa Lo's even more newsy than it would be otherwise. Photos taken at your Dad's funeral are all over the place, even now, but they've sort of airbrushed the funeral out so as to conceal the fact that the pictures aren't fresh—no gravestones, no mourners...just the happy couple, at an anonymous *social function*."

"I can't say I'm sorry," Canny said.

"About what?"

Something in her tone made him look at her sharply. "About the fact that they've left out the funeral," he said. "What else?"

"Even when the pictures were fresh and you were in them

too," she observed, "not one of the pieces I read mentioned that they didn't leave together. You said they weren't an item, didn't you?"

"I don't think they are" Canny said, mildly. "If the papers can't get any new shots to update the story, that rather suggests that they're not, doesn't it? Does it matter?"

"Not in the least," she said. "But Ellen says that Lissa Lo didn't leave the house till *much* later than everyone else. You were on your own when you came into the chip shop, of course—but you did seem a little strange. I thought at the time that you looked the way you did because you'd just buried your Dad—but you'd just said goodbye to Lissa Lo, hadn't you?"

"Jesus, Alice," Canny complained.

"I thought we were confiding in one another," she said, disingenuously, "and not bothering overmuch about being insensitive. Actually, though, I am being sensitive. I figured that if you'd just been dumped by a supermodel as well as burying your Dad, I might be a more useful confidante than your mother or you butler—just as you might be more use to me than Mum or Ellen."

Canny wondered whether Alice had some sort of agenda in mind, or whether she was babbling to cover up her own feelings. He decided that the latter was more probable.

"I'm not sure this is the sort of conversation people are supposed to have at nine o'clock on a Sunday morning while they're stone cold sober," Canny said. "Would it be any business of yours if I did have some sort of relationship with Lissa Lo—unlikely as that might seem?"

"You're probably right," Alice admitted. "And no, it wouldn't. I just thought you'd like to know what kind of gossip's buzzing around the town. Not our Ellen, mind—she's telling everyone that you're a not a playboy at all, and that you and Lissa Lo are just good friends."

"Thank her for that," Canny said. "Tell her that Stevie Larkin and I are just good friends too, and that I've no idea who's likely to buy him. On second thoughts, tell them all that he's a cert to join Leeds United. It's not true, but it might help stop them speculating about the reasons why Lissa Lo left the funeral so late."

"There is a rumor, apparently, about the three of you—Lissa Lo, Stevie Larkin and you, that is—bringing off some kind of betting cup in Monte Carlo. Nearly half a million Euros, it's said."

"Shit," Canny muttered. "I told you yesterday—I was mugged the moment I got back to my hotel. It was forty-seven thousand, not four hundred and seventy thousand. Lissa and Stevie won less than half as much. It wasn't exactly a coincidence—they bet the number because I did—but it wasn't any kind of *coup*. This is how those stupid stories about the Kilcannon luck get started—and blown out of all proportion. It's just silly folklore, Alice—you know that."

"Yes," she said, humbly. "I know. Sorry—I should have kept quiet about it. I just thought you might like to know what's being said. I'm being selfish, I suppose. If I go back home—to Mum's, I mean—there's no way at all I can avoid my own problems, and church would be even worse. If I let them drag me to eleven o'clock mass, every eye in the place will be on me and Father Quimper's bound to ask them all to pray for me. I just thought it might help if I could talk about you for a bit. More *misery loves company* than *a problem shared*, I'm afraid. You said I could, remember? I thought you'd understand—far better than anyone else, at any rate, because of your Dad. I'll stop it now."

"I did say you could and I do understand," Canny said. "You don't have to stop. Straightforward insults are easier to take, though—the sort you used to hurl at me when you were thirteen."

"Witty remarks," she reminded him. "I just wanted to be the court jester. The position's still unfilled, I suppose."

"You obviously don't know Bentley," Canny said. "He does the best impression of an English butler I've ever seen. He'll make a fortune in Hollywood if they ever find out about him. Mummy and he are probably thinking of working up a double act, now that Daddy's dead, but they're keeping it a secret from me so I won't feel left out."

Alice smiled, dutifully. "Do you want to go for a walk on the ridge?" she asked. "I'm getting restless legs just sitting here. With a mouth like mine, I shouldn't be suffering pent-up anguish, but I guess the well's too powerful to cap."

Canny felt guilty, although he wasn't sure why.

"Yes, if you like," he said, coming to his feet. "It's Sunday, after all. There'll be time for you to get back for mass, if you want to."

"I already told you that I don't," she said, as she preceded him towards the door. "I haven't been for years, Martin was an atheist—not even a Catholic atheist."

"Even so..." Canny said.

"People will expect me. It'll give them a chance to let me know they're on my side, and it'll give me an opportunity to make my peace with God. I've heard it all, Canny—don't you join in as well. You're on the other side, remember?"

"No, I'm not," Canny said, quietly. He paused in the hallway to tell the expectant Bentley where he was going, and that he would be back in an hour.

The butler nodded, without the least hint of disapproval, and promised to inform Lady Credesdale.

CHAPTER TWENTY-THREE

As Canny and Alice made their way through the grounds at the back of the house, heading for the path up to the ridge, the Great Skull loomed over them with a recently-reinforced symbolism that Stevie Larkin would have been only too eager to point out.

"A couple of well-placed sticks of dynamite would do wonders for that thing, Canny," Alice told him.

"It's not so bad, if you look at it in the right ironic light," Canny said, insincerely. His ancestors had always tolerated the baleful visage because the family rules included stern warnings about the extreme unwisdom of any interference with its grim aspect, but he had always harbored a faint hope that one of the Langsgill boys, armed with a can of white aerosol paint, might pluck up the courage to modify it with a few deftly-placed graffiti.

"Well, September sunshine doesn't work. I suppose you could hire an ambitious local artist to turn it into Yorkshire's answer to Mount Rushmore."

"Whose face did you have in mind?" Canny asked. "Geoff Boycott? Richard the Third? Arthur Scargill?"

"You're right," she agreed. "It's probably friendlier the way it is. Are you going to tell me what went on between you and the supermodel now?"

"I thought we'd exhausted that topic of conversation," Canny said, frostily.

"Really? I thought you were just playing for time in case

the butler was eavesdropping. If it's too painful to talk about, that's okay. I've been dumped in my time, difficult though it is to believe—and rejected too."

"She didn't reject me, let alone dump me," Canny said, defensively. "We were just having a conversation. We have...interests in common."

"She's a probability freak too, then?"

For a moment, Canny almost panicked. His stomach lurched, much as it did after a particularly jagged streak, and he wondered momentarily whether there had actually been a rift in the pattern of causality. Then he realized that it was just another joke—a reflexive witticism as utterly innocent as all the rest, offered in the spirit of an amateur court jester. Even so, he paused on the slope, breathing deeply, and looked back down at the house. The Great Skull looked sideways at him, as if it were leering contemptuously. The dynamite, he thought, might not be such a bad idea after all—and now that he was the earl, there was no reason why he had to tolerate its rudeness if he didn't want to.

"More than you know," he said, eventually. He said it soberly, not simply out of habit. "Are you fishing for gossip, Alice, or is this strictly between the two of us?"

"I won't tell a soul," she said. "Not even Ellen. Especially not Ellen."

"Okay," Canny said, carefully assuming the lightest tone he could contrive, so that she wouldn't be able to believe a word of what he said even if she suspected that he might be serious. "She wants to have my love-child, in order to cut her slice of the Kilcannon luck, but she won't marry me. She doesn't want to get too involved; she reckons that the pregnancy will take enough time out of her busy schedule without any further complications. I'm feeling a trifle insulted by the prospect of being so casually and callously used—but she is one of the most beautiful women in the world, and I have the same hormones as the next man."

Alice looked at him in a mock-admiring fashion. He

assumed—but couldn't be absolutely sure—that what she was pretending so conspicuously to admire was his skill as a liar.

"Don't take this the wrong way, Canny," she said, "but if I looked like Lissa Lo and wanted a stud to father the perfect baby, I'd want a slightly better-looking peer of the realm. I don't think luck's hereditary, although superstition might be."

"There aren't that many of us peers around," Canny told her. "We're all lucky of course, but very few of us are even as good-looking as me. Once you'd set your heart on a genuine English earl, you wouldn't settle for a common-or-garden French Comte or American billionaire, would you? If you were Lissa Lo, that is."

Alice had to think about that for a minute or so. When she'd finally formulated her answer she tried to garnish it with a broad grin—but she couldn't quite do it justice. "I think I can figure out the full story now," she said. "The pride of *Vanity Fair* plans to use all the benefits of modern biotechnology to fabricate the perfect child. She's shopping around for the perfect sperm, and she thinks she might get it if she can only splice the genes for Stevie Larkin's looks and athletic ability into your blue-blooded base. And the reason you're so pissed off, being a Yorkshireman, is that she wants to splice you with a footballer instead of a cricketer."

"That's about the size of it," Canny agreed, readily.

"Bit of a sickener if the biotech wizards cocked it up, though," Alice went on. "Although I suppose a sperm with your lack of grace and athletic ability would never...oh shit, I said I wouldn't do that any more, didn't I? I'm sorry, Canny. I didn't...."

"It's okay," Canny assured her. "I said you didn't have to stop. Call me all the names under the sun. Insult me. Hate me. Pretend I'm the universe. I honestly don't mind—and you're quite right about nobody else understanding. I'll take it as a compliment that you came to me."

She shook her head slowly. "I'd just feel guilty about it later." she said. "That would give me a excuse to come back and apologize again, of course, so that I could have another go...but you're right. This isn't the sort of thing I should be doing on a Sunday morning, stone cold sober. I'm sorry I asked about Lissa Lo. We'd be better off discussing Stevie's transfer prospects. How much is he worth now, do you think? Five million? Ten?"

"He would be, if his contract with Milan had longer to run," Canny said. "He seems to be close to his peak, so he's probably got five or six more years at the top if he can stay injury-free, and a few years after that while he'll still be an asset in the premiership. Given that he'll be a free agent next season, though, I figure that he's affordable—his agent's probably trying to involve half a dozen clubs in the auction."

"Shit," she said. "I didn't *really* mean that we should talk about football—and cricket's out too. What about Cockayne? Any new broom-type plans for the village? The Mill? Strictly between us, honest."

"Afraid not," he said. "It doesn't seem to be broke so I ain't planning to fix it. Maurice Rawtenstall and the unit managers are doing a first rate job, so far as I can tell, and the village elders are doing their best." They had reached the top of the ridge by now and were heading northwards. The Roman Ridge was visible in the west, on the far side of the Crede, while the terrain to the east undulated gently in the direction of Cock Beck.

"Does that mean you can go right back to being a playboy as soon as the traditional decent interval has elapsed?" Alice asked.

"I'm afraid not. Just because everything's running smoothly doesn't mean that I can duck out of it. I have a part to play, even if I don't intend to rewrite it. I'm a cog in the big wheel now—no more early morning roulette for me."

"And no more girls laid end-to-end all the way from Nice to Monte Carlo?"

"No," Canny said, shortly.

"Laying them all the way from Tadcaster to Garforth doesn't have quite the same ring to it, I suppose. Less comfortable too, given all the bumps and hollows—and the ground's not very even either."

"Mummy wants me to settle down," Canny said. "It was Daddy's dying wish, too. I guess it goes with all the other estate duties. You do know that it's all nonsense, don't you? I'm a gambler, not a womanizer. If they really say that about me in the village, it's just fevered imagination."

"You don't have to make excuses to me. Has your mother got a likely gel lined up for you? She seemed to have a fair crop of cousins and nieces at the funeral—quite a contrast with the Kilcannon side of the family."

"She made an effort, but I don't think her heart's in it. She's probably delegated the job to Bentley, who'll probably put his plans into action as soon as Bob Stanley's completed background checks on all the likely candidates."

"Who's Bob Stanley?"

"An inquiry agent in Leeds. Daddy used him all the time."

The Kilcannons have their own *private detective*?"

"Of course. No one in business can do without one nowadays. I blame the Internet myself. He's not just ours, though—he's Robert Stanley and Associates nowadays. I could put in a word if you need a job. It's perfect for a historian—all trawling through archives, except for the occasional stake-out."

"Is he looking into your mugging?"

"No, that's over and done with. Storm in a teacup. Case closed."

"Come on, Canny—you're not trying. If things are really that boring, make something up. How much did the mugger get?"

"About thirty grand. It wasn't really my money, though—I'd just won it at the casino. I hadn't got used to thinking of it as mine, so it didn't seem like a terrible loss. Anyway, I think the inside man at the casino who tipped the gunman off is dead now. The local heavy mob are very careful of their house percentage—they don't like foreigners operating scams on their turf."

"Foreigners?"

"Eastern Europeans, or so it's rumored."

"So you hired a French hit man instead of getting your friendly neighborhood inquiry agent to investigate?"

"I didn't hire anybody. I really wasn't that bothered—but I thought I ought to tell the casino manager that he had a rotten apple in his barrel. He didn't hire anybody either. He didn't have to. Nobody likes the Russian mafia—and if it was the Uzbekistani mafia, that would be adding insult to injury."

"No," Alice retorted, abruptly losing the mood she was trying so hard to sustain. "Two teenagers from Chapeltown with a fucking crowbar is adding insult to injury. Compared with that, the humblest tea-boy in the Uzbekistani mafia is Professor fucking Moriarty, the Napoleon of crime."

"Sorry," Canny said. "I talked my way round in a circle."

"No you didn't—I did. If you're lying. by the way, and you've got the hit man's number, let me know...and don't tell me I can't afford him. Martin was insured, and we never got around to producing the dependants it was supposed to be protecting. Sorry."

"It's okay," Canny said. "But a hit man isn't the answer. I don't know what is, but it's not that. I don't think there is an answer, except to keep going through until you come out the other side. And cursing, of course."

"You don't seem to be doing any cursing. I've never heard you say anything worse than *shit*."

"Well, as you pointed out yesterday, I only lost an aged father, as expected. What happened to you is intrinsically more curse-worthy. Will you still move back to Cockayne, do you think?"

"There's no point in staying in Leeds, is there? I hadn't even got round to finding a job, or even thinking about one. Staying home to write a history of Cockayne took it for granted that Martin would be bringing in a salary. On the other hand, I'm hardly going to qualify for a place of my own, am I? The thought of moving back in with Mum and Dad on a permanent basis...I thought I was past that. I thought I'd moved on, spread my wings, become the owner of my own destiny. Silly me."

"The elders are breaking some of the bigger houses into flats when they fall vacant," Canny told her. "Cockayne may be stuck in the nineteenth century, but it has twenty-first century demographics. A place of your own wouldn't be out of the question, by any means—and a job shouldn't be too had to find either. The Mill always needs new blood."

"Not the blood of historians. I guess I could answer to *haddock and chips twice*, but Ellen wouldn't want her smart-mouthed little sister in the shop, showing her up. My Mum's idea of seeing me settled, of course, would be the same as your Mum's. If Lissa Lo hadn't broken your heart we could probably kill two birds with one ring, but I can't live with competition like that. Not without plastic surgery and a personality transplant."

"Don't go fishing for compliments, Alice," Canny said. "They're far nicer when they're spontaneous. Besides which, given my extreme ugliness and lack of athleticism, you're probably much more comfortable with my studied indifference."

"That's true," she countered, calmly. "We ought to be turning round, I suppose, or we'll be bumping into the A64—the ridge runs out in a couple of hundred yards. Do you know, I haven't been up here for years. Were there more sheep around when I was a kid, or have I just sugar-coated the memory?"

They both stopped as she spoke, and turned back in their tracks. "No," Canny said. "There really were more sheep. We ran down the flocks in the nineties—not commercially viable in the modern meat trade. We were lucky in the foot-and-mouth epidemic, though. It passed us by, and the stud-value of our rams rocketed afterwards. The farm-manager reckons that we ought to re-think the whole operation. Import some rare breeds, start a proper conservation program. Mind you, it's only five years ago that he wanted us to get into transgenics and cloning."

"It all seems quite serene now we're looking at it backwards," she said—meaning the Great Skull. "When we get back to the brow, it'll be just a few black rocks jutting through the turf, with no shape at all. Pity about the house, though—doesn't matter what angle you look at it from, it's gargoyles all around."

"It may be mock-Gothic," Canny said, "but it's mock-*Yorkshire* Gothic. In a thousand years time it'll be one of the seven wonders of the county, along with the Grand Hotel in Scarborough and our half of the Humber Bridge."

"Not to mention the wind farm on Wuthering Heights," Alice said. "You know, Canny, even for a lord of the manor and recently-reformed playboy, you're a seriously weird person."

"That's it," he said. "Pile on the insults. I'm the universe, remember. You have one hell of a grudge to pay back."

"It was a compliment," she told him. "A spontaneous one—the nicest kind."

"I knew that," he admitted. "But I was hoping that you wouldn't point it out, so that when I got around go telling you how impressed I am with the way you're handling all this, I could pretend to be exercising extraordinary generosity."

"I'm not doing it to impress you," she said, sharply. "I'm just doing the best I can."

"I know," he said. "I really do understand. Isn't that a police car heading for the village? Your family liaison officer, do you think?"

"Could be," she agreed. "Shit—if Mum rings your house and the creepy butler tells her we're out walking on the ridge, our Ellen will...no, actually, she won't. She'll make allowances. And she thinks you're a saint, even if she's the only person in the village who does."

"She's right," Canny said.

"I know. Better hurry anyway, though. There might be news—I'll just have to take the risk of being in time for church. I hope you find the book interesting, Canny—you're probably the only reader it's ever going to have. If you're as much of an expert as you pretend, you could finish it for him. Monument to his genius, etc. If you're not too busy being a big cog in a little wheel."

"I'll think about it," Canny promised, insincerely.

CHAPTER TWENTY-FOUR

Canny had to go to London the following day, but he drove into Leeds first to collect Bob Stanley's report on Lissa Lo and her ancestry.

"It was easier than I expected," Stanley reported, as he passed over a remarkably bulky file. "Her mother, grand-mother and great-grandmother all married relatively high-profile guys, and several journalists in search of background took the trouble to follow the paper trail back to the nineteenth century—including a number of highly efficient Japanese and Singaporean researchers. Let me know if you need more."

"I will," Canny said. "Thanks, Bob. Send me the bill and I'll settle up."

"Not the kind of work your father used to ask for," the detective observed.

"Not exactly," Canny agreed, "but it demands the same kind of discretion. Must rush—got to drive to London and the M1 will be hell, at least until junction 32."

This prophecy proved, alas, to be all-too-accurate—and the traffic built up again as he approached the M25, with the result that he was running late all day. He had no opportunity to study the file until the day's business was belatedly concluded, at which point he was finally able to retire to the flat. The last phase of his day's journey was the slowest of all, even though rush hour was long past. The flat was located in one of the residential terraces off Marylebone High Street, but the subterranean garage in which the Bentley's parking-spot was reserved was five minutes walk away—which always caused problems when he had paperwork to transport. It was ten-thirty before he got in, eleven before he started turning the pages of Stanley's report. There was no time left to plough through it all that night, and he was too tired to give it his full attention.

Canny tried to absorb as much of the story as he could by scanning each document in a matter of seconds. The method left him hazy on matters of details but allowed him to build up a composite sketch in which a clear pattern seemed to be discernible. He had already anticipated its broad outlines, but he was grateful for the solid support that hard data lent to his conjectures.

It wasn't just the procession of the centuries that altered the rewards of luck, he deduced. Cultural contexts varied just as much—and even more so when sex-differences were factored into the calculation. The direction in which the male Kilcannons had been steered by their lucky streak was entirely expectable in the context of the north of England; the direction in which Lissa Lo's female ancestors had been steered by theirs was just as expectable in their own context. The greatest luck conveniently available to Lissa's mother, maternal grandmother and half a dozen others before them had been luck in contracting marriages. The model was the natural product of a multigenerational Cinderella story, whose meteoric stars—in striking contrast to the wives of the Earls of Credesdale—were all makeshift Prince Charmings.

Lissa's back-story lacked the steadiness and coherency of Canny's, because her family's house percentage had never worked as smoothly. Canny couldn't be certain whether that was due more to the innate conservatism of his own forebears or to the fact that Lissa's ancestors had lived in such interesting times, but he figured that the combination probably leaned in favor of the latter. The luck carried forward by Lissa's female ancestors did seem to be transferable to their spouses, but only in the short term; the consorts drafted by Dame Fortune enjoyed remarkable prosperity immediately before and immediately after their marriages, but once their daughters were born their disability became obvious—more than one had died with extraordinary abruptness.

Canny could see the logic of that. Mummy had been an invaluable asset to Daddy in terms of the contribution she made to his own welfare, let alone the upbringing of his son; the continued utility of a patriarch in the Far East was, from the viewpoint of a female's luck, far less obvious. Lissa's own father had died while she was still in infancy—a pattern that could be extrapolated back to the sixth generation with only minor temporal variations. Only in remoter ages, before the advent of the nineteenth century, had the material protection afforded by warlords been a sufficiently significant factor to sustain the male adjuncts long enough to see their daughters married. Or so it seemed.

The fact that Lissa's foremothers tended to die a good deal younger than Canny's forefathers gave him slight pause for thought, but it wasn't difficult for him to come up with plausible explanations. Given the way the world worked, even in the supposedly-enlightened West, a man needed far less luck to establish him in long-sustainable comfort than a woman. If the females in Lissa's ancestry had used their lucky streaks more recklessly, it was probably because they had always had to. It couldn't have been as easy for her ancestors as it had been for his to maintain a balance between self-restraint and self-indulgence. No wonder her oral traditions were more sensitive to issues of yin and yang—and no wonder her defiant attitude to family tradition seemed reckless even to him.

The way that Lissa seemed to be using her ration of luck at present suggested to Canny that her mother might not have much left of her own portion—but if Lissa's lucky streak was allegedly fated to run dry in the same way that Canny's was, when her mother's luck ran out entirely, the experiment she had proposed to him began to seem even riskier. Lissa appeared to be hoping that a child whose heredity was lucky on both sides might renew her own luck more prodigiously than any child produced in accordance with tradition.

In essence, Canny guessed, Lissa was hoping for a miracle child: a superheroic Cinderella, with *more* than a double dose of shareable luck, by virtue of some kind of chemical or alchemical synergy. Such hope—and such recklessness—might be more in keeping with her traditions than his...but it seemed to Canny to be perfectly conceivable, if not rather probable, that the vital genes—or their metaphysical equivalent, if it turned out that his materialist assumptions were false—would not work in association at all. Even if they did, it might not follow that both the miracle child's parents would benefit equally. If chance should dictate that the child was a boy, and that Canny was the parent who benefited from his son's remarkable inheritance...what would Lissa do then?

He tried to haul himself back from the wilderness of conjecture to the contents of the documents Bob Stanley had gathered for him, but it wasn't easy. How, Canny wondered, did Lissa interpret the demographics of her own bloodline? Did she expect that he would follow the examples of her father and grandfather by dying almost as soon as his appointed task was complete? Did she really imagine herself as some kind of queen bee, relative to whom he was a mere disposable drone? Was she simply taking it for granted that her child would be a daughter rather than a son, or did she have some magic or technology in mind that would enhance her chances? If so, did she also have some magic or technology in mind that might assist in his removal from the scene? If not, what would the consequences be if she were to give birth to a boy who would be heir apparent to Can's wealth, if not to his titles?

Canny decided, on due reflection, that he dared not hope, let alone assume, that Lissa was planning to share the fruits of her experiment with him. She hadn't bothered to put up any sort of pretence that she was looking for a long-term relationship, so she presumably intended to take the child for herself, even if it turned out to be a boy. If she did intend to take sole custody of the child, there would be little that Canny could do, in spite of his title and all his connections, to prevent her doing so. But would that matter? Did legal custody of a luck-bearing child have anything to do with the distribution of its gift? There was nothing in the Kilcannon archives to help him with that; it was a possibility as yet untested.

How much would it matter, he wondered, if the child's luck—however exceptional it might prove to be—were to be used entirely to Lissa Lo's benefit? He could go on to have other children, with other women...but that might not suffice to renew the family streak.

The worst-case scenario, it seemed to him, was that he might lose his gift along his first-born child, having sacrificed his own opportunities on the altar of Lissa Lo's divine or diabolical beauty. But was that possibility any more than a phantom of superstition? If the streak really were a mere matter of a gene carried on his Y-chromosome, he ought not to be any worse off for having participated in Lissa Lo's experiment, even if she tried to cheat him...always provided that she didn't intend to do him any physical harm. He couldn't believe that she did...but he wasn't entirely sure that what he could or couldn't believe was the best guide to action in his particular case.

He could almost hear his father's ghostly voice saying: "Play safe. It isn't worth the risk. It's a bad bet."

He was too tired to give the matter sensible consideration. He had to go to bed, to sleep.

Tuesday was entirely taken up by meetings, and so was Wednesday. There seemed to be dozens of acquaintances to renew and cement, dozens more to make for the first time and set firmly in their intended pattern. It was surprisingly exhausting work, but it had to be done. In order to make sure that the house percentage of his business interests didn't begin to wane or go astray, he would have to be as careful and as vigilant as Henri Meurdon. The process of establishing himself as the new central cog in the many-spoked wheel did, however, have a certain innate fascination to compensate him for the fierceness of his concentration. It was easy enough to think of it all as some vast game, more like mah-jongg than poker, and every bit as demanding of expertise and practice.

Had he been more confident of his luck, the decisions he was called upon to make would have been simple enough, but as the hours went by he realized that he could not escape the toils of psychological probability. He had not had the slightest atom of real evidence that his luck was running low, but the conviction that it might be was irresistible, and it changed the pattern of his thinking very markedly. Now that he dared not take it for granted that bright streaks would deliver him from any threatened disaster, the problem of redeploying his money to insulate his share portfolio against the stock market's continued decline—not to mention the possibility of a flood of demands to fulfill his obligations as a Lloyd's underwriter—seemed quite intractable. The income from the estate would hold up reasonably well whatever happened, but it seemed now to be a tiny proportion of his fortune. The value of his property portfolio, which had soared with the boom, also seemed reasonably foolproof—except for the possibility of a crash, which he no longer dared to rule out.

He listened dutifully to a great deal of advice, and soon began to wish fervently that there was some discernible consistency in it—but he consoled himself with the thought that the supposed expertise of his inconsistent advisers was evidence that there was nothing accurately calculable in the shape of the future.

Talking to various bank-managers in Leeds, Canny had easily been able to sustain the illusion that his casual suggestion to Lissa that he was wealthy enough to live indefinitely on his resources without any supernatural injection of luck had been the simple truth. Two days of talking to brokers, underwriters and London estate agents, by contrast, gave him a very different impression. Yes, he was rich—but he was also living in a world where sudden reversals of fortune were not merely possible but had recently become routine. The financial world was full of foam, and no one really knew which bubbles were likely to burst, or when. Nothing was safe any more. He was as fireproof as anyone could be in twenty-first century Britain, and could probably live in relative comfort until he died no matter what might come to pass—but relative comfort was not an obviously worthy aim for the scion of a very long line of hardened gamblers, and could not seem so in the hubbub of the metropolis.

In the heart of the City of London, the devil's engine-room, Canny quickly came to understand very well why other recently-elevated earls, who must have been just as determined as he had been to get rid of all the mumbo-jumbo—to eat and drink like normal gluttons and to avoid sticking blades in agonizing places—had soon come to feel an irresistible pressure to comply with the demands of tradition.

He also began to understand much better what enormous relief those other fledgling earls must have felt when their bizarre endeavors began to pay off—and why his father had spent as much time as possible in the infinitely less fevered environments of Credesdale House and the village of Cockayne.

The trouble with being a lucky Kilcannon, Canny quickly realized as he made his way around the labyrinthine toils of London, was that it raised the expectations of everyone with whom one came into contact, as well as one's own—and the expectations of his metropolitan contacts were already wilder than common sense allowed. Perfectly ordinary ill-luck would become, for a Kilcannon, evidence of slackness and inferiority—and while that might be cause for gentle commiseration in Leeds, the only emotion it could generate in the City was contempt. If it would be difficult to suffer the effects of ordinary luck in the secret recesses of his own thoughts, it would even more difficult to suffer them in the arenas of high finance.

In Leeds, the thought of the self-mutilatory aspect of the rituals that were supposed to complete his compact with Dame Fortune—once he had fulfilled the basic requirement of siring a son—had seemed rather ridiculous. In London, however, it was easy enough to see self-mutilation as a matter of routine: a trivial cost that everyone involved in the life of the City expected to pay, if not by way of knives and flames, then by way of drug addiction, stress and the crushing burdens of the need to conform, the need to succeed and the need to show no weakness. Superstition was everywhere, and all-consuming.

Was this, Canny wondered as he went through the motions of his schedule, the stuff of which all magic had always been made? Was the real basis of all occult belief little more than a kind of cosmic fruit-machine, which paid off enough people enough of the time to keep them all coming back for more, even though the inevitable sum of all their endeavors was a massive house percentage in favor of the devil? Was his own consciousness of that fact, and his conviction that he was on the devil's side, really an advantage, or just a kind of cosmic irony? Might it be better, in fact, to be moderately unlucky all the time without ever suspecting—let alone believing—that there was any way to beat the odds, than it was to be as certain as one could be that there *was* a way to beat the odds without knowing how, exactly, the trick was worked?

He was tempted to wind down on the Wednesday evening by dropping into Victoria Club or one of its rivals, but he knew that the intention to stay for an hour was likely to slide inexorably into a fierce determination to make a night of it, even if he started losing—as he feared that he might.

In any case, he still had reading material to keep him busy, even when he'd exhausted the revelations of Bob Stanley's report. He had also brought the typescript of Martin Ellison's unfinished book, which was something of a jigsaw puzzle in itself. There he could read deft clinical analyses of the psychology of the belief that good luck came in threes, or that lucky streaks had to be ridden while they were hot. There he could read explanations for the common delusion that so many losers maintained, not merely as a public performance but also in the privacy of their own skulls, that they were actually breaking even. There he could read scrupulously-deciphered accounts of the mythological imagery that persuaded male gamblers to perceive luck as a fickle and capricious female, as deadly as a female black widow spider, as exacting as any vampiric muse, and yet quite irresistible to anyone with balls.

Lissa Lo would doubtless have loved that particular chapter—and laughed contemptuously at the allegation that even female gamblers saw Lady Luck in much the same terms.

CHAPTER TWENTY-FIVE

On Thursday Canny finished early in the afternoon, without any further appointments or an engagement for dinner. He expected to feel relief, glad that he finally had some time to himself, but as soon as he was alone he realized that the time would not be easy to fill. While he had been forced to squeeze his reading and his thinking into the interstices of a riot of obligations their produce had seemed precious, but now that there was plenty of time available he found himself easily distracted and convinced of the uselessness of his own speculations. When his doorbell rang, therefore, he was by no means as annoyed by the unexpected interruption as he might have anticipated.

The voice that came over the intercom seemed to be muttering away incomprehensibly in some unknown language, but it was punctuated with the name of "Miss Lo". Canny's heart leapt then. He had not by any means made up his mind what he wanted to do about Lissa Lo's interest in him, let alone her proposition, but the prospect of carrying the agenda further by action rather than reflection was suddenly irresistible.

"I'll come out," he said.

He fetched a jacket from the wardrobe rather than put on the one he'd worn to his meetings. He paused by the mirror in the hallway to check that his hair was properly combed. When he finally went out into the street he found a black limousine insouciantly parked on the double yellow line in front of the building, with a chauffeur who might have been Malaysian or Filipino silently holding the door open for him.

He got in without an instant's hesitation, incapable of any other feeling than joyful anticipation.

The limousine joined the long queue crawling westwards along Marylebone Road heading for the Westway, then turned south along Wood Lane, heading towards Hammersmith in order to take the flyover leading to the M4. The vehicle's lack of success in avoiding traffic could hardly be deemed unlucky, given the inevitable density of the traffic, and the rear seat was exceedingly comfortable. Once the car had actually moved on to the M4, it gathered speed rapidly.

When Canny asked the driver where they were going, his only reply was a shake of the head, presumably intended to indicate that the man's English was insufficient to permit him to understand the question, let alone give an intelligible answer. Canny accepted his fate meekly. It did not matter where they were going; all he really wanted to know was how long it would take to get there.

They turned off the motorway at Slough and headed for Windsor, but not quite as far as the castle. On the edge of Old Windsor they turned south, skirting the Great Park before moving onto the A30. Ignoring Ascot and the M3, they went through Chobham but turned right before reaching Woking.

Canny had been to Bisley more than once, but he did not know the area at all well. As dusk fell he lost his bearings completely, but relaxed when the car turned off into a private road through a wood. He had seen dozens of similar roads, each of which led with the utmost discretion to one of the thousands of country houses that were neatly tucked away in the secret coverts of the home counties, as if located in some parallel world unapprehended by the peasantry and the middle class. It wasn't one that he had ever visited, so far as he could remember, but he didn't care what its name was. He only cared about who might be awaiting him there.

He was inside the house, and had actually been introduced into the drawing-room, before the slightest suspicion hit him that he had assumed too much—but a split second before he moved around the high-backed armchair to look at the woman who was sitting there his vision was blurred by a streak.

It was a dark streak, but if it was a warning, it had come too late. It occurred to him that if it really were *his* streak, and not merely something of which he was a passive observer, it might not have been able to manifest itself until he came within range of another energy-source.

Either way, his stomach lurched more vertiginously than the force of such a tangentially-visible streak could normally have contrived. An unexpected chill of pure terror momentarily startled his brain. He couldn't understand why. There didn't seem to be anything unduly threatening in the situation, now that the initial surprise was over.

He was staring at an older version of Lissa Lo—a version so much older, in spite of what he knew about her actual age, that he was reminded of the climax of the movie version of *Lost Horizon*. Had the girl in the story also been called Lo Chen? No, he remembered; the character in the book had been Lo-*Tsen*.

At any rate, it was as if he were looking at a Lissa Lo who had abruptly faded into antiquity when years that she had long defied had caught up with her in a precipitate rush.

"Won't you sit down, Lord Credesdale," the old woman said. Bob Stanley's report had told him that she called herself Lo Chen nowadays, although she had worn other names in the past. Perhaps, he thought, the chauffeur had not intended to deceive him when he mumbled incoherently about "Miss Lo"—but if so, Canny had certainly taken the opportunity to deceive himself.

Canny let himself fall into the matching armchair on the far side of the hearth, trying to conceal the fact that his legs had become weak. The fireplace was open, but it looked as if no fire had been lit there for forty years and more. Unlike Credesdale House, this edifice was fitted with central heating and double glazing.

There was no conspicuous Oriental theme to the general decor, but Canny didn't know whether that made it more or less likely that the house actually belonged to Lissa or her mother.

"Are you not taking a risk, Madame Lo?" he asked, although he felt even as he said it that it was a horribly corny line.

"Madame is sufficient," she told him. "It will avoid incongruity—so far as incongruity can any longer be avoided. To answer your question, as honestly I hope you will answer mine: yes, I am taking a risk that I would rather not take. We are both weaker than we have been in the past, I think, although you still have the hope of becoming strong again. That might reduce the chance of catastrophe, although the omen we both experienced a few moments ago does not bode well. Were your meetings with my daughter attended by similar ill-effects?"

"No," Canny admitted, readily enough. "I had no sense of being in competition with Lissa, even when she told me that she knew what I was—and she, it seems, had no sense of being in competition with me, even when she revealed what she is. Consciously or unconsciously, you seem to feel differently—but it seems to me, now that I've recovered from the discomfort, that it was just a flash of anxiety, not a readjustment of the world's order. How did you find out that Lissa had approached me? Did she tell you?"

"I have not seen my daughter for some time," Lo Chen told him. "She is avoiding me, for reasons you will doubtless understand. It was foolish of you to hire detectives to discover what you might have found out easily enough by yourself. Had I done likewise, you would probably have been alerted to my counter-investigation, but I found most of what I needed to know in Burke's *Peerage* and the data assiduously collected by the Church of Latter Day Saints. A wonderful toy, the Internet, do you not think?"

"It's changing the face of modern gambling," Canny said, "but the Kilcannons are traditionalists. I've been very wary of it, although I'm thinking of setting up an on-line trading facility—my father could never have brought himself to disappoint the family stockbroker, but we live in an age when middlemen are fast becoming redundant. Did you really bring me here to discuss the Internet?"

"Your father lived a long time," the not-so-old woman observed, as if it were a matter of little consequence, suitable for polite chitchat. "I shall not live nearly so long. There appears to be a significant difference between the balance of power within our families, Lord Credesdale. Between father and son, the father seems always to have the upper hand. Between mother and daughter...is that because we are female, do you suppose, or because we are from what you call the East?"

"It's pure guesswork," Canny said, "but I'd go for the female line of descent being the more relevant variable. Kilcannon luck has never been overly concerned with handsome features, but Lissa's beauty is truly magical—as yours must once have been. The demands exacted of fortune by a daughter like Lissa must be powerful. I do understand, from my own experience, why she might feel disinclined to spend too much time in your company—and I think that her motives might be more intense than mine ever were, for good reasons."

"I agree," the old woman said. "Nor is the difference apparent only within the family."

The point was a trifle understated, but Canny saw the implication immediately. "You think she has the upper hand over me, too. You think she intends to plunder my luck as avidly as she's recently plundered yours—and you think she'll succeed."

"I believe that she will try."

"Without wishing to be rude," Canny said, "I'm not sure that I can understand why that prospect should disturb *you*. If she really could parasitize my luck, might that not release the pressure on yours?"

"I am a mother. Without wishing to be rude, I hope that you can understand that not all motives are purely or narrowly selfish."

Canny nodded his head, conceding the point.

"Perhaps you cannot listen to reason, and are therefore forgivable," Lo Chen continued. "She refuses to listen, which is quite a different thing. You know, I suppose, that she will take your child away, if you allow her to conceive it. You would probably never see it."

"It seems very likely," Canny admitted, "but I've dared to hope otherwise. Having had good luck all my life, it's difficult to suppress such hopes—as you must know. If you brought me here to try to talk me out of it, you couldn't have had more than a very frail hope of success—but if you planned something more forceful, you must have done so in the full awareness that however dangerous a peaceful meeting might be, attempted murder would be even more dangerous. Although not as effective as the birth of a son in the longer term, a direct threat to my life would probably reignite my power. So, at least, precedent suggests." He felt a little foolish talking about attempted murder in such seemingly-civilized circumstances, but the dark streak was still worrying him; if it had been a warning, there must be some danger.

"Power?" she echoed, ignoring his clumsy accusation. "Do you really think of it as power?"

He hesitated before answering. "Yes," he said, finally. "It's difficult to think of it as anything else. A few of my ancestors appear to have considered it as much a curse as a gift, but none ever denied that it's a kind of power."

"Did my daughter tell you about her fascination with the uncertainty principle—the arcane mysteries of quantum mechanics?"

Canny was surprised by that particular twist in the conversation's wayward flow, but it seemed to be safer ground than debating the politics of murder. "Yes," he said. "I'd had thoughts along the same lines myself, although I'm a biologist by training. Perhaps that *is* what we are: privileged observers, whose wishes, needs or appetites are slightly more powerful than those of our competitors. Perhaps we simply have more authority to shape the world than people who can't see as keenly."

"To *shape* the world?" The woman's features were expressionless, but her eyes were sparkling, as if the empty grate were filled with blazing logs whose ardent light was reflected there. "Have you not considered the alternative perspective, in which the effect we have is purely disruptive?"

"What do you mean?" Canny parried.

"Suppose, for a moment, that we are not imposing our own preferred observations at all, but merely subverting or interrupting the influence which other observers have. In that case, it would not be the directive force of your desire that guides a ball into a particular slot on a roulette wheel, but merely an ability to spoil the diffuse forces of desire that might otherwise have guided it to a neighboring slot."

"Isn't that a distinction without a difference?" Canny challenged her.

"Is it? Perhaps. But in the long run, the distribution of results always complies with that predicted by probability theory. You do not have the power to make the ball fall into a particular slot once in every ten spins of the wheel, or even once in every twenty."

"No, but when my luck is running smoothly I can make reasonably sure that my bet is down when it does turn up there, once in every thirty-seven spins or so. The cosmic balance always comes out more-or-less even in the end, but you and I can establish ourselves among those who win more often than they lose. Is there any point to this hair-splitting?"

"If there is," Lo Chen pointed out, "you have far more to gain or lose by its making than I have. A fuller understanding of our curse might work to your benefit for forty years—perhaps more, if modern medicine continues to make such strides."

"So you *do* think it's a curse?" Canny said, warming to the game. "Isn't it mere pessimism to speak of it in those terms rather than calling it a gift or a power?" In the meantime, he took what comfort he could from her admission that she had little to gain or lose by this encounter, in purely personal terms.

Would that make her less likely to do something silly, because she had so little to gain, he wondered—or would it make her more likely to act recklessly, because she had so little to lose?

The room seemed rather dark, although the sun hadn't quite set—but that was because the lamps were inefficient. So, at least, he tried to assure himself. He couldn't put that puzzling dark streak, or the unreasoning flash of terror that had followed it, out of his mind. Nor could he avoid the awareness that no one knew where he was, and that if anything were to happen to him while he were here, he would have vanished without trace.

CHAPTER TWENTY-SIX

"Would you say, Lord Credesdale," Lo Chen said, calmly, "that you and your ancestors have been happier than the human average?"

"I've no idea, and no way of guessing," he answered, although he remembered the answer he had given when Lissa had interrogated him about the portraits on the stair at Credesdale, as well as his labored ruminations in the library on that very subject. "I know that very few of them have died young, or lived in poverty—but wasn't it one of the founders of Western philosophy who said that the best thing of all was not to be born at all, and after that to die young? I'll admit that my forefathers don't always seem to have used their luck as wisely as I or they could have wished...but you know as well as I do what extremes of misfortune our fellow men sometimes suffer, and my ancestors always contrived to avoid those. If they weren't happy, I suspect that the fault was in them, not in their stars; it's a fate I've so far avoided, and hope to avoid in future, no matter what offence it may cause to the cosmic balance."

"And you think that sleeping with my daughter will help secure your future happiness?"

"In the short term, certainly. In the long term...well, if I have to lose her, I suppose I must cling to the hope that the poet was right who said that it's better to have loved and lost than never to have loved at all. What do you want from me, Madame? Do you really believe that you can talk me out of taking part in Lissa's scheme? Or that you can prevent me by force without the risk of disrupting your own reality far more direly than that twinge we both felt when I realized that I'd been duped?"

"I mean you no harm, Lord Credesdale," Lo Chen stated, reminding him that he had openly insulted her by suggesting that she might. "My forebears have never scrupled to hire assassins, but not for such a purpose as this. It is not for your benefit that I brought you here, but that does not mean that you cannot benefit from what I have to say to you. My fears are for Lissa, and for others associated with our family by habit and circumstance—not because I dread that she might fail in what she is trying to achieve, but because I wonder what might happen if she succeeds."

"I've been wondering about that myself," Canny confessed.

"So you should. It is, I suppose, inevitable that you should think of your ability to cheat the odds as a gift rather than a curse, as power rather than responsibility, but I had hoped for better from my daughter. You think that you are the one who has been seduced, but it is her—not by you, not even by your own curse, but by the world you represent. You believe, I suppose, that you have not the power to stand in her way—that you are helpless to resist her seduction, because you are incapable of wanting to resist. Perhaps that is so, but I will say this: you have the responsibility to act like a man, and not a slave of passion."

The old woman paused momentarily as if to assess the impact this statement had on Canny—but Canny had no difficulty remaining impassive in the face of such a silly cliché.

"I know that you will do nothing because I ask you to," Lo Chen went on, "and will not readily put your trust in anything I might tell you. That is as it should be. Even so, you know that you must think for yourself as wisely as you can, and weigh scrupulously in your mind possibilities of which you have so far been careless. Because my daughter thinks, as you do, in terms of power, she believes that she can add your power to hers, and thus acquire the one ability that you seem to have and she does not: the ability to renew herself so prodigiously that she need not suffer the same fate as her mother. You have, I suppose, deduced that for yourself?"

Canny nodded.

Lo Chen continued. "She believes, as you presumably do, that the dangers inherent in your meeting are those which might stem from conflict—from your simultaneous striving to make events come out the way you want them to, when your interests inevitably diverge. She also believes, as you presumably do, that no such conflict will arise between you until she attempts to exclude you from the life and luck of the child she intends to conceive. Perhaps you are both right—and perhaps one or other of you will be able to contrive a result of that eventual conflict other than your both sustaining injury—but you must consider the possibility that you are both wrong."

"I've tried," Canny assured her. "What are you getting at?"

"What I believe, and suggest to you in all honesty," the old woman said, "is that the greatest danger lies not in conflict but in collaboration. What I believe is that desire unchecked is hazardous in one mind, let alone in two, and that when two desires are joined in a simultaneous subversion of the consensus of observation, there can be no outcome but catastrophe."

"Black lightning," Canny said, to show that he could at least understand what she was saying. "Things fall apart. Lissa said something about the illusion of Maya...."

"She didn't mean it," Lo Chen said, sadly. "I do. The world is indeed more dream than its solidity implies, and...."

At that moment, the drawing-room door opened, and the chauffeur reappeared.

"Madame...," he began—but Madame had already guessed. Canny felt her alarm and frustration in his head and in his stomach, and once again he saw the world blur, darkly. He still had no idea why.

But it's still power, he thought, stubbornly. *The power of premonition, the gift of warning. It's still a kind of power, no matter what Cassandra thought. The terror part is purely subjective and unreasoning—something to be mastered, not indulged.*

"She's coming, isn't she?" he said. "She's found out what you've done, and she's not pleased. But it's *you* she's in conflict with, not me. It's the two of you who are tempting the black lightning with your mutual hostility." He was trying to reassure himself, but the rising nausea forbade him to do it. Even if it were the conflict between Lo Chen and Lissa that was threatening to upset the world, there could be no guarantee that he would not be the one hurt by the strike. In any case, if Lo Chen's judgment could be trusted, collaboration might be just as dangerous as conflict. The only thing that was certain was that he wasn't in control. He felt certain now that his own streak really was dormant, narcotized by the lack of an appropriate sharer.

Even as Canny felt the unreasoning disturbance growing in magnitude within him, though, he found a space in which to think: *Is this the same sickness I've felt before, or something different, something new? Do the old rules still apply, or have I crossed the line into a whole new dimension of chance? How urgent is this warning?*

He could already hear the sound of a car's engine, louder and more distinct than the only competing exterior sound: the purr of a 747 beginning its final descent towards Heathrow.

Although Canny had told himself, as sternly as he could, that the terror was purely subjective, it was still perversely tangible. There was nothing obvious to be afraid of, and yet there was fear in the air.

"Go now," said the old woman, who must have felt it at least as keenly. "There are matters to be settled here that don't concern you."

Canny didn't want to go. He wanted to make a sarcastic remark about the fact that she seemed fearful enough of conflict *now*—but the anxiety in the air was still pressing upon his receptive mind. He felt his own superstitious fears breaking through the bonds of discipline to which he had tried so hard to subject them. He actually had to fight to stay where he was, and force his legs to be still.

He fought as the car door slammed, and continued the

struggle as the door to the house opened—and then he realized that it didn't matter whether he won the fight or not, because the confrontation was now inevitable. He couldn't relax, although the agitation no longer seemed like terror; the whole room seemed slightly dark now, as if smoke were seeping into it from some invisible fire.

Then the door to the room flew open, and Lissa came in. She looked at Canny, and she looked at her mother—and her own anger must have begun to abate then, as she saw that no one was hurt or under any immediate threat of harm. She too had been uncertain how to read her premonition.

It's just confusion, Canny thought. *It's the effect of the three of us being so close together that our anxieties can overlap. It's feedback.*

The disturbance began to ebb away as he realized that it was just a freak of circumstance, a collision of uncertainties. Canny felt it shrink, and become controllable. He felt that he had won his fight, even though he knew that he had merely brought it to a stalemate.

"Mother," Lissa said, calmly, "I do understand that you have my best interests at heart, but I doubt that you are the best judge of what they are, at present."

"I meant no harm," Lo Chen said, stiffly. "I am merely attempting to assist Lord Credesdale to make a better judgment as to how his own interests might best be served."

"He can do that himself, Mother," Lissa stated, flatly. Then she turned to Canny. "I'm sorry about the warning signals," she said. "I think I may have been unreasonably anxious, and that the echoes of my anxiety were amplified—but I assure you that you were never in the slightest danger. Your own good fortune may be at a low ebb, but you have mine to protect you now. No harm will come to you while I have the power to prevent it—that I promise you. Even if Mother wanted to defy me, she could not."

"I'm glad to hear it," Canny said, trying to sound calm although the contents of her speech seemed to him a trifle bizarre.

"I think my mother and I need to talk in private now, Canny," Lissa said. "It's best that you don't stay any longer—and I think it would be best for all three of us if you didn't talk to my mother again. We have what the Americans call *issues*...but that's a private matter. I'm sorry you were dragged all the way out here for no good reason. Would you like Mother's chauffeur to drive you back to town, or would you prefer to take the train? We're only a short walk from Frimley station."

"The train will be fine," Canny assured her. Oddly enough, now that the moment of false panic had passed, his determination to remain had ebbed away. He didn't think that it would be dangerous, any longer, to be in the company of the two women—but now that Lissa had asked him to go, he couldn't see any reason to take sides with her mother. He hadn't wanted to come here in the first place, and he didn't think that Lo Chen could tell him anything that he couldn't work out for himself. He had given the matter at least as much thought as she had.

"I'll be in touch as soon as I can," Lissa promised. "At the very least, I'll call. If you're in London for long, I might be able to drop in."

"I'm due back in Yorkshire tomorrow," Canny said, regretfully. "I can come back again next week, if you want to fix a date."

"I can't. Don't change your plans—not yet. I still have to rearrange things, sort things out. All this has come up rather suddenly. It's complicated—but I'll do everything possible to move things on. Be patient, please."

"I will," Canny promised. "Let me know when you can." He got up, feeling only a little unsteady on his feet, and maintained his dignity with the utmost care as he made to leave the room.

"It's not the contest that you have to fear, Lord Credesdale," Lo Chen said. "It's the sum of your efforts—the combination of your destructive potential. You have no power to create, only to blur and obliterate. Think about that."

"Canny thinks about little else, Mother," Lissa Lo said. "He knows all about the politics of risk—but he's not a coward. If he and I were really to combine our forces, really to work *together*...what might we not accomplish? Did she tell you that I would steal your heart and steal your child, Canny? Did she tell you that I would use and discard you, and have you killed if you became troublesome?"

"Actually, no," Canny said, waiting by the door. "Nothing nearly so lurid."

"Lissa....," Lo Chen began—but Lissa cut her off.

"Good," the model said. "We're still within the bounds of sanity, then. I won't, Canny. I won't steal your child. I won't discard you. I want to work together—to see what we might really *do*, if we can only put all this stupid superstition aside. That's what you want, isn't it? That's what we both want. Am I lying, Mother? Am I?"

"Think about the consequences, Lord Credesdale," Lo Chen said, stubbornly. "Just think—that's all I ask."

"Me too," Lissa said. "That's all *I* ask—but I know that you can see the opportunities as well as the dangers, the possibilities as well as the threats. Go on, Canny—it's getting dark, and I haven't seen my mother for quite some time. There are things we need to settle."

Canny nodded to both of them before he went through the open doorway and closed the door behind him, He made his way to the main door of the house, keenly aware of the insistent beating of his heart. He cursed when the catch proved difficult, but there was no one to see the evidence of his tremulousness.

The car in which Lissa had arrived was skewed awkwardly across the drive. The headlights were still on, although the motor had been turned off, and the driver's door was wide open. Canny marched past it, not pausing until the reached the gate-post at the entrance to the driveway. Then he paused to draw breath and look back.

He still felt a slight constriction in his belly but he wasn't sure whether it was the echo of the streak or a common-or-garden stitch. His head was aching, but that too might have been entirely natural—and the gathering night was moonless, too dark to permit the perception of any inglorious blur.

The house stood up as steadily as it had for centuries, unassailably peaceful. The terror *had* been unreasoning—unless it had been a premonition of a disaster that three of them, having been forewarned, had contrived to avert.

Canny understood the psychology of that phenomenon too; no matter how hard his ancestors had tried to disbelieve that the terror associated with dark streaks was a symptom without a cause, they could never be sure of what *might* have happened if they hadn't handled themselves carefully. There was always a temptation to believe that the gift had allowed impending disaster to be avoided.

How lucky the Kilcannons were, to know of so many perils to which common men were oblivious!

There was no need for this, Canny admonished himself, sternly. *You could have stayed where you were. We could all have talked it over like civilized people.*

He didn't know whether he dared to believe that, either.

When he came to the roadway he realized that he didn't know which way to turn to get to Frimley station. In the other direction, he guessed, the road would probably lead to Brookwood.

Did it matter much which way he turned? Probably not, he decided—so he picked a direction at random, feeling no particular need to depend on his unusual luck to make the right choice for him.

CHAPTER TWENTY-SEVEN

By the time Canny got off the underground at Bond Street it was eleven o'clock. He dropped into a Pizza Hut and placed an order for a large ham and mushroom; there was a slight delay on deliveries but they promised to get it to him by half past.

He walked back to the flat in something of a daze, not noticing until he had actually set foot on the bottom step that someone was sitting beside the door. It was Alice Ellison.

"I buzzed the guy upstairs and asked him to let me wait inside but he wouldn't," Alice said, apologetically.

"How long have you been waiting?" he asked, as he opened the main door.

"Not long. A couple of hours."

"Why didn't you call?"

"I did. The second time, I could hear your mobile ringing inside the flat, where you'd left it."

Canny hadn't realized until she told him that he had been in so much of a hurry when Lo Chen's chauffeur had called that he hadn't picked up his phone from the side-table where he'd left it, beside the chair on whose back he'd draped the jacket he'd been wearing earlier in the day. Now, having opened the apartment door, he saw it lying there in full view, impossible to miss. "Damn," he said. "Sorry. I didn't even know you were in London."

"I wasn't. I drove down today."

"To see me?" Canny was genuinely surprised, although he remembered telling her that she could. "I'm due back tomorrow—Mummy or Bentley could have told you that if you'd asked."

"I did. They did. Not the point."

"You were in that much of a hurry? Then I'm doubly sorry to have kept you waiting. Can I get you a drink? I've no food in, but I've ordered a large pizza—they should be delivering it in ten or twenty minutes."

"Ham and mushroom?" she asked.

"How the hell did you know that?"

"You're a Yorkshireman. Yes, I will have a drink. Scotch, with soda if you have it. And ice, if you have that."

"No problem," he said, picking the scotch from the sideboard and hastening into the kitchen. "The fridge is fine, and well-stocked with essentials—it just doesn't have any food in it. I've been eating out. On business, mostly."

"So why the pizza?" The question floated back from the living-room.

"Except tonight," he said, as he pulled the ice tray out of the freezer and twisted it to release the blocks. "Tonight, I missed dinner entirely."

He distributed six cubes of ice in two glasses, poured two generous helpings of whisky over the ice and added a splash of soda to one glass. By the time he'd carried them back through she had taken off her light raincoat—an unnecessary precaution, given that the weather down south had not yet shown any sign of turning autumnal—to expose a black silk blouse and a knee-length skirt.

"Sorry," she said, as she took the proffered glass. "I'm in mourning."

"I know," he said. "You don't need to apologize."

"You might want to withhold judgment on that. So was it a five o'clock that dragged on and on, or was it Lissa Lo imposing her diet on you?"

"Neither," Canny told her, wryly. "It was Lissa Lo's mother trying to warn me off. She thinks that associating with me won't do Lissa's career prospects any good at all. I thought for a moment or two that she was going to have me bumped off, but she settled for giving me a good talking to. Did your parents give Martin a hard time when you first took him home?"

"Mum and Dad never gave anyone a hard time. They approved of Martin, just as they'd approved of Ellen's Jack and Lydia's Ken, albeit in a slightly more deferential fashion. They'd have approved of you, if Ellen had ever managed to get you into her knickers—even if there was no question of you ever condescending to make an honest woman of her."

Canny took a sip of whisky. "Was she trying?" he asked.

"Not all the time. At fifteen, sixteen and seventeen, maybe—albeit sporadically, given that you were away at school most of the time. At fourteen she hadn't started to care, and after she turned eighteen she'd had to give up, partly because you never seemed to come home again after you went to Cambridge but mainly because she was nursing Marie. Then she married Jack. Had you honestly forgotten? I know you weren't home much, being caught up in the social whirl of Ampleforth and all that, and probably had other offers even in the village, but Ellen was never as subtle as some and she always reckoned that she had a chance—of a night to remember, that is, not anything serious. She always reckoned that you wanted to, but were too afraid of what your Dad might do if he found out you'd been fucking the commoners."

"Dad would have been blazing mad if he'd ever caught me at it," Canny agreed. "It wouldn't have mattered who with—Ellen wouldn't have been any less in his eyes than a royal princess. A man of principle, my Daddy. So yes, I kept to my best behavior while I was home and sowed my precious few wild oats elsewhere. And no, I hadn't really forgotten—I'd just got into the habit of setting it aside, and remembering our encounters in happier and more innocent times. Not that it sounded so innocent when you blurted it out in front of your Mum."

"I told you—she wouldn't disapprove. Not that she's got fewer principles than your Dad, you understand—just that they're slightly different."

Canny observed, slightly to his surprise, that Alice's glass was empty. "Do you want another?" he asked.

"Please. So, did Mama Supermodel get through to you? Are you going to stop stalking her daughter?"

"That's a bit personal, isn't it?" he asked, before setting his own glass down and taking hers back into the kitchen.

"I thought we were allowed to ask one another questions like that," she said, raising her voice slightly to make herself audible. "Insults and all. I thought we had a deal. If I'd wanted bullshit, I could have stayed with Mum and Dad in Cockayne."

"Sorry," he said, as he broke out more ice. "I guess it's been a trying evening. I forgot I was doubling for the universe's whipping boy. You want to kick me in the balls, maybe? Spit in my face and put a curse on me?" He finished off with a squirt of soda.

The doorbell sounded as soon as he got back into the other room.

"I'll steal half your pizza," she said. "I haven't eaten either."

Canny collected the pizza and paid the delivery boy, adding a three pound tip even though the youth had only had to drive his bike a couple of hundred yards.

"That's okay," Canny said. "If I'd been here when you arrived there'd have been time to take you out for a proper meal. You need a plate, or can we eat straight out of the box?"

"Might as well save on the washing up," she said. "Mind you, now you're a lord you really ought to give up eating haddock and chips out of the paper and pizza out of the box."

"I suppose so," he agreed. "That was a no to spitting in my face, then? And the rest?"

"I wouldn't take a train all the way from Leeds to King's Cross and a tube to Baker Street just to spit in your face, Canny," Alice said. "I hope you don't think that I'm stalking you."

"Nobody's stalking anybody, Alice. I said I'd be here if you needed someone to talk to, and I'm sorry it took me two hours to turn up. Bond Street's a fraction closer, by the way, and it's a nicer walk."

"It's not as easy to get to from King's Cross," she pointed out. "And I didn't really come to talk."

"Oh? Why did you come?"

"Well, you probably haven't noticed this, but my mood's been all over the place recently—angry one minute, weepy the next. I'm a little bit out of control, and I just can't seem to get a grip."

"No," he said, amiably, "I hadn't noticed. So you came down on a whim, is that it?"

"Sort of. Actually, I came down expecting the whim to pass, just like all the rest. I thought it would have gone by the time the train got to King's Cross, so that I could just catch the next train back. Then I thought it would be gone by the time I got here. Then I thought it would be gone by the time *you* got here. But it wasn't. Isn't."

"Oh," he said. "Could you elaborate slightly—I'm not following you."

"Sure. You probably don't know this, since your own dear departed was your father, but when you lose a husband grief tends to move through several different phases, one of which is the lustful phase—which can be very embarrassing, if you happen to be staying with your Mum and Dad in a village where everybody knows everybody else and your sister runs the local fish shop, even if the pangs don't last for very long. So I asked myself whether there was anywhere else I could go where I stood a fair to middling chance of passing through the mood and out the other side without undue distress—or, if it happened to last the distance, getting someone to fuck my brains out. You just sprang to mind."

Canny choked on a slice of pizza, and found himself quite unable to reply.

While he was coughing, Alice went on. "It did occur to me on the way down that as you were being chased by Lissa Lo with a view to her bearing your love-child, you might be a trifle uninterested in a short-arsed widow with crooked teeth, but I said to myself, what the hell? if he says no he says no, and— who knows?—maybe he'll be so steamed up by Lissa Lo being difficult that he'll welcome the opportunity. Least I could do, if so. No strings, of course. We can go home tomorrow, by our separate ways, and forget that it ever happened. Your Mummy will never know—and, more to the point, neither will mine."

Canny took a swig of whisky to help clear his windpipe, but it only seemed to make things worse. Alice didn't get up, as any normal person would have done, to thump him on the back or pretend to know how to do the Heimlich maneuver. She just continued nibbling at a slice of pizza, swallowing very carefully.

"I think what you're trying to say, given that you're not one for cursing," she said, "is *Jesus, Alice!* I seem to be getting that a lot lately, even though my favorite WPC gave me an excuse not to go to church on Sunday. They've caught the murderers, by the way. Thirteen and fourteen years old. Scrawny, too. Didn't even have a drug habit. Stealing for fun rather than profit, followed by sheer blind panic and a lucky swipe with the crowbar. Utter stupidity, not to mention futility. I have to confess that I feel slightly ignominious, but my feelings do seem to have got slightly on top of me. How about you?"

"I'm okay," Canny finally contrived to splutter.

"No, I mean, how about you getting on top of me? Am I on, or not? A simple one word answer will suffice—I don't need an explanation, let alone counseling."

Canny coughed again, at great length, but it was more to cover up the absence of a one-word answer than to save his life.

"I'll take that as a no, then," she said. "Well, Ellen would be pleased, if she were ever to find out—which she won't. It dents a girl's confidence, you know, to practically offer herself to a randy teenager, with no strings attached, and get no response. It's the sort of thing that can end up with getting hitched to a fish and chip shop. Maybe I should have tried then, and saved myself the embarrassment of trying now, but you never know how things will turn out, do you? You just never know."

"Alice...," Canny began, weakly—but he didn't know how to carry on.

"Precious few," she echoed, thoughtfully. "You sowed your *precious few* wild oats elsewhere, setting Ellen aside, and Heaven knows how many others. But you *were* interested—it's not as if you were queer. So what was it, Canny? Were you really that afraid of your father?"

"Actually, yes," Canny said, glad to be back on safer ground. "He was a stickler for the family rules, and we had rather a lot of them."

"And you still do," she observed. "The hell you copped from Lissa's mother is nothing to what Daddy would have said if he'd known about your supermodel pash."

"He met her," Canny said, quietly. "I told him everything, before he died. But you're right—if he'd been younger, stronger, fitter...he'd have given me hell, and then some. As it was—with no axe to grind on his own behalf, he contented himself with giving me advice. All well-intentioned, of course...I wish I could say that he didn't understand, but the real problem is that he understood only too well. He even understood the generation gap." He risked another small mouthful of pizza, and made certain that he chewed it thoroughly before washing it down with whisky.

"You really are hung up on her, aren't you?" Alice said, with more disgust than amazement in her voice. "The Barbie-doll exterior is all it takes—just that and a beckoning finger, no matter how condescending. You really are hooked."

"Not the way you think," Canny retorted, sharply. "I'm sorry, Alice, but you *don't* understand."

"So explain it to me. We seem to have all night, and if you're not going to fuck me you might as well talk to me. I reckon I'm in credit now so far as insults are concerned, but it's okay—just think of me as the universe. Poke me with a sharp stick or spit on me if you've nothing else on offer."

"I can't," he said, baldly.

"Oh, come on Canny—impotence doesn't stretch all the way to your tongue. You mean it's against the rules. Well, fuck the rules if you won't fuck me. Tell me how it is, between you and the most beautiful woman in the world. Explain to me exactly how you came to be more interested in her mind than her body."

"I can't," he said, again, helplessly. He meant it. He wasn't trying to be difficult. He really didn't think that there was any way he could explain it to her. Not for the first time, he realized almost immediately that he had underestimated her.

"It's the Kilcannon luck, isn't it?" she said. "You have to pretend to be a monk to keep it flowing, is that the way it goes? Your Daddy would have hit the roof if he'd known you were spreading it around because he'd have thought you were imperiling the *real* family treasure."

Canny was too dumbfounded to hide his reaction. He knew, even though he didn't say a word, that he'd given himself away.

"Oh, shut your mouth, Canny," Alice said, bitterly. "How did I guess? I'm Martin Ellison's wife—widow. He talked to me. The psychology of gambling, the psychology of superstition, the legendry of luck. He didn't just write those notes down when I told him about all the things they say in the village about the lucky Kilcannons—he explained why it was interesting, and what the logic of it all must be. You confirmed it when you mentioned rules. So I know, you see, why you wouldn't fuck Ellen even when she wanted you to—and I'm going to tell myself that you won't fuck me for exactly the same stupid, superstitious, selfish reason, because it's a hell of a lot better than having to think that you just don't want to. If that's okay with you, of course."

Canny looked a her long and hard, and she met his stare. They each had a slice of pizza left, but he knew that the slices in question were fated to go to waste. Both their glasses were empty, but he didn't volunteer to refill them, even though there were certain kinds of conversations that were a lot easier to have while drunk.

"I never said no," he pointed out, eventually. "You jumped to that conclusion. Anxiety, you see—it's a corollary of the Oedipus Effect. You expect to fail in your enterprise, so you assume failure far in advance, and the assumption becomes a self-fulfilling prophecy. You're right about the rules—we have a thousand of them, and nine hundred and ninety of them are probably bullshit, only we've never been able to work out exactly which nine hundred and ninety, or whether there are any exceptions to the ten that work. One that seems sounder than the rest, for all sorts of reasons, is that the luck won't endure if other people know you've got it—but I just broke that one for you, and I'll break another if you need me to...or even if you just want me to. Not because I promised, but because you're worth breaking a few rules for."

"As many as you're breaking for Lissa Lo?" Her eyes were angry and accusing but her stare was slightly misted by excess moisture, which gave it a strangely poignant character.

"Jesus, Alice—you won. What more do you want?"

"You're right," she said, after a moment's hesitation. "Always been that way—littlest sister of three, always had to fight three times as hard and be three times as clever, and never knew when to stop. And you're right about other things too, which we won't go into. The others must never know, you realize—especially not Ellen."

"I realize," he said. "This is just between us."

"And completely self-contained," she added. "No strings, on either side."

"Neither of us can guarantee that," Canny said. "Some things, you can't anticipate or calculate—you just have to gamble. It is a gamble, Alice—you do know that? For both of us."

"Everything's a gamble, Canny," she said. "Those of us who don't have family rules just have to rely on the vagaries of chance. But you have to live, Canny—and sometimes, you have to give in to what you're feeling, no matter how it might look to your Mum or your sister or your family liaison officer. Martin would understand. He might not like it, but he'd understand. It's him I really need, really want...but you're the only one who could stand in for him, Canny—the *only* one."

"I know," he said, glad to have recovered his composure and the remnants of his conversational style. "I can't say that I've always been lucky *like that*, but I've always been lucky. I hope that you come out ahead, in the end. I really do."

Alice was busy unbuttoning her blouse.

"I'm sorry about the mourning-dress," she said. "I really am."

"I know," he said. "You really don't need to apologize."

CHAPTER TWENTY-EIGHT

The following morning, as Canny and Alice walked to the garage where the Bentley was locked up, Alice said: "You'd better drop me at King's Cross; that way I can arrive back in Leeds in a way that won't give anyone cause for alarm or suspicion."

"I'll take you to Leeds," Canny told her, phrasing it as a contradiction rather than a suggestion. "In the unlikely event that anyone from Cockayne sees you getting out of the car, I'm sure you can make up a plausible story about where I gave you a lift from that doesn't involve London or nights of blazing passion."

"Okay," she said, readily enough. "You can drop me at home. I need to pick up the mail, see to a few things. When I get back to Mum's, I'll tell her I spent the night there, with the answerphone on because I didn't want to talk to anyone. You know, I never needed to invent an alibi to cover up an infidelity— I never expected to be breaking that particular precedent in circumstances like this."

Canny didn't bother to point out that no infidelity had been involved. He used his keycard to let them in to the garage and opened the boot of the car to stow his suitcase while Alice got into the front passenger seat.

"A *lot* nicer than the mangy Citroen," she commented, when he joined her. "I feel like I've been promoted from skivvy to courtesan."

"You're fishing for compliments again," he pointed out. "And it's a very nice Citroen—Mummy wouldn't drive anything *mangy*."

"So I am," she admitted. "And I apologize to your Mum. Okay, so I'm an academic's widow, not a *femme fatale*. You want to talk about psychological probability? I can do that, if you want. It's going to be a long drive—starting from here at this time of day it'll probably take us an hour to get as far as Edgware."

"It's not that bad during the day since the congestion charge was introduced," he told her. "We'll have to stick to theoretical issues, mind. I've already tempted fate a little too far for one week."

"Fair enough," she said, readily enough. "One night of desperation isn't exactly a lifelong commitment—even I can see that it doesn't entitle me to be let in on the family secrets."

He turned right into Marylebone Road, and had no difficulty at all getting to the corner of Albany Street, where he turned north. There was a faint sheen of spilled oil dressing the surface of the road near the Royal College of Physicians, and the faint spectra sparked by the sunlight seemed uncommonly unobtrusive. It could almost have been a faint streak, but his stomach was only distressed because he hadn't had any breakfast.

"If it will ease your resentment any," he told Alice, "Mummy's been in the family for forty years, and she knows less than you've deduced. She doesn't ask and she doesn't guess—she just fits right in. The old sort, Bentley says—approvingly, of course. He doesn't ask either, and he keeps his guesswork strictly to himself, so far as I know."

"I thought all that went out with World War I," Alice said, with a hint of a sneer. "Well, your Dad might have managed to surround himself with the last of the dodos, but you won't. How many of the family secrets does Lissa Lo know?"

"Theoretical issues," Canny reminded her. "Safer ground." He turned into Camden Road, intending to turn left and join the M1 at junction 2, but the traffic was thickening now and his progress slowed

"Okay," Alice said. "I'm tamed, for the moment. I'm not about to bite the hand that fed me last night, let alone the other bits of your anatomy that helped me get by. Theoretical issues. The psychology of feeling lucky. The illusion that luck is on your side, that the omens are all favorable, that you only have to speculate to accumulate. Hard to dispel even if you lose— very difficult indeed if you win. You've read Martin's books, so you know the way it works. People who owe their success to a combination of hard work and good judgment often feel that they've just been lucky—it's a kind of modesty. By the same token, people who fail through laziness and bad judgment often attribute *that* to luck, so as to dodge the responsibility. It's very difficult, on either side of the average, to take a thoroughly realistic view. How am I doing, bearing in mind that I'm a mere historian?"

"Fine."

"Good. So an objective observer, looking at a family that had done well for centuries on end—not the Kilcannons, of course, since we're talking in purely theoretical terms—might be tempted to judge that however lucky the first in the line might have been to make his money and win his title, the advantage he passed on to his descendants was probably sufficient to keep them on the winning side as long as they didn't do anything too outrageously stupid. They might get a lot of benefit, of course, from maxims advising them to be abstemious in their lifestyles, and to weigh up risks with scrupulous care—but the actual operative effect of those kinds of rules might have nothing to do with any *magical* kind of luck. All they'd be doing is taking advantage of the corollary of the calculus of probability, which says that people who get a head start are far more likely to finish ahead than people who start from behind. Way back when, of course, its members wouldn't necessarily be able to figure that out—they'd probably be obsessed with notions of supernatural aid and judgment, completely unaware of the link between the protestant ethic and the spirit of capitalism. You can see how that might work, can't you?"

Canny agreed that he could see how it might work that way, in theory.

"Over time, of course," Alice went on, "the rules would acquire a mystique, and hence a power, of their own. The authority of ritual and symbolism. If the material rewards continued to roll in, that magical power and authority would be strengthened, even if the real causes of continued good fortune were perfectly ordinary."

"That's all in the book," Canny observed.

"So it is," Alice agreed. "But times change, Canny. A man who's read Martin Ellison has probably read more-or-less everything that's ever been written about the psychology, sociology and economics of risk-taking and wealth creation. As a theorist—and purely as a theorist, you understand—he'd be very skeptical indeed of that whole way of thinking, wouldn't he?"

"Yes, he would," Canny agreed—but said no more. He had more than one reason for letting her run with it. He was on the approach to the M1 now; the southbound morning rush was still in full flow, but the northbound carriageway was clear.

"Right," Alice said. "He wouldn't hold on to the theory without additional evidence, and he'd be very careful about the subjective element in the accumulation and interpretation of that evidence. Now, if Martin were here—sitting behind us, listening in—he'd probably be able to formulate some ideas as to what kind of evidence might be involved, even if he were skeptical of its value. He was very interested in the Oedipus Effect, as you know—particularly the phenomenon of self-deluding diviners. You remember all that, of course."

"Sure," Canny said. "Charlatans routinely fall for their own patter. Faith healers, astrologers, dowsers, tarot readers, spoon-benders...whether they start off with open and inquisitive minds or as dyed-in-the-wool con men, they all tend to end up believing in their own psychic powers. It's a variant of the fruit-machine principle. The surging sense of triumph with which the brain credits itself when a hit is scored outweighs the slow drip of disappointment generated by the failures. Even when the house percentage is as high as thirty or forty per cent, people keep playing the machines in the hope of hitting the jackpot. Prophets who are successful thirty or forty per cent of the time—even if that's less than you'd expect from random guessing—get such a buzz out of the sense of being right that they eventually become convinced of their innate power. So what?"

"So people who *feel lucky* may get that feeling even when they're not beating the odds at all, let alone when they are. They're just attributing too much weight to the sensations of triumph they get when they *are* right—but every hit they make becomes an item of evidence, a tangible proof of their power, a reason for continuing to believe in whatever they're doing, no matter how absurd. Then again, there's retrospective attachment of meaning—which is a corollary of the other aspect of the Oedipus Effect. Remember?"

"Of course. Also known as the oracle effect. People who believe that an oracle has the power to warn them if something is likely to go wrong are highly likely to consult one before any risky undertaking, and quite likely to visit on a regular basis just to make sure that disaster isn't lurking around the corner. Oracles, however, have a reputation for gnomic and ambiguous utterances, so if and when things do go wrong, it's often possible to look back at what they said and perceive—or construct—a meaning that was imperceptible at the time but seems obvious in hindsight. So people who believe in oracles, or omens, or whatever, are continually reconstructing the past in order to reveal warnings that they should have heeded, thus clocking up another potentially-infinite series of evidential samples to shore up their conviction that the oracles and omens never lie. They can also add in the instances when things worked out right, and disasters didn't occur, as firmer proofs that the oracles work. It's slightly paradoxical—effectively, they're claiming to know that the prediction was good because it didn't come true—but it all adds to a sense of conviction that the magic works."

"Exactly," she said. "More than enough to fool a credulous person, even today—but not a smart one. Not a sophisticated person who's read all the relevant books. *You* wouldn't fall for that kind of psychological trickery, would you?"

"No," said Canny, bluntly. "I wouldn't."

"A person as clever as you would need something extra. A person as clever as you would need a different and more powerful kind of evidence. A person like you would need the Road to Damascus Effect."

Canny was beginning to feel that he was sitting an examination—but that was okay, because he knew all the answers. This one, admittedly, made him feel a little less comfortable, but he did know it and he had taken due note of Martin Ellison's description of it.

"Named after the conversion experience that gave the world Saint Paul," he said, trying to sound laconic. "Maybe epilepsy, maybe some other altered state of consciousness—just so long as it involves nEurones firing spontaneously in the brain to produce a particular combination of effects. Firstly, exotic visual hallucinations, usually involving intense light, flashing or sustained. Secondly, an overwhelming impression of indubitability and significance. The nEurological basis of all religious experience, according to skeptics. In extreme cases, it turns a person's life around, infusing him—it's usually a him, but not always—with a strong sense of mission, at least until repetition of the experience fries his brains. In less extreme cases—and the spectrum probably extends all the way to the fringes of normality—people easily associate the flashes of light with moments of enlightenment, especially if they have lingering side-effects that summon up random memories or sensory impressions. In much the same way that people can easily imbue their dreams with oracular significance, people suffering that kind of hallucination can easily reconstrue them as premonitions, or even as active magical shocks, like the lightning bolts that come out of wizards' wands in cartoons. As before, whether they're retrospectively associated with fortunate outcomes or unfortunate ones, they acquire meanings that make them seem like items of evidence from which clear and reliable rules can be induced."

"Very good," she said. "Thanks—that's what I wanted to know."

"What's what you wanted to know?"

"That you see the flashes. Martin said you probably did, when I told him about the stories. NEurological disorders run in families, you see. Most seers don't have offspring, but those who do tend to pass on the so-called gift—the second sight."

"I never said...."

"Yes, you did, Canny," Alice told him. "You didn't quite realize that you were saying it, but you're not the only one who can import meaning retrospectively and convince yourself. I can do it too—and I know exactly what you meant. What about the supermodel? Does she see flashes too?"

Canny turned to stare at her in amazement—and realized, a moment too late, that he'd fallen into the trap.

"There you are," Alice said, quietly. "I'm psychic too. We haven't even got to Luton yet—by the time we're by-passing Coventry I'll even have convinced myself. Do you suppose it was being married to Martin that did it, or are you so very powerful that one night of reckless fucking was enough to sow the seed in me and bring it into flower in a matter of hours? Fertile ground, you see. Is that why she wants you to serve as a stud? She thinks that your flashes and her flashes will produce the next St Paul? And you're actually *thinking* about it? Jesus, Canny, have you no idea how much harm you could do to a kid by inflicting a double set of brain-buzzing genes on it? And suppose it worked! Suppose you did turn out a super seer—a St. Paul. Have you any idea what harm a kid like that might do to others, even if he turned out to have Lissa Lo's brain and your body instead of the other way round?"

"I thought this was a purely theoretical discussion," Canny muttered, although the rigid set of his mouth was caused by the fact that he suddenly saw what Lo Chen had been getting at—that the danger might not lie in the failure of Lissa's experiment, but in its success. The danger of competition spoiling their powers was one thing—the danger that their separate powers might really be combined in a single new individual was something else.

Except, he reminded himself, that Alice was talking about illusions—about things that might be taken as evidence for unusual luck and insight, but weren't. He had more than that to sustain his belief. He had the kind of evidence that Henri Meurdon's perfectly objective and utterly dispassionate computer had thrown up. He knew, too, that Lissa Lo and he could see the same flashes, and feel the same after-effects—which meant that they *had* to be objectively real, not just randomly-generated phantoms of some nEurological disorder from which they both happened to be suffering.

"I lied about the purely theoretical bit," Alice reported. "But at least you haven't broken any more of your stupid rules—although you might as well, now that most of the secret's out. If you were to tell me the whole story, you might do yourself some good—and you needn't worry about it going any further."

Canny didn't reply immediately. He needed a little time to recover his composure. "Why do you want to know?" he asked, eventually, keeping his voice perfectly level, and even contriving a slight tone of levity.

"You mean am I just a nosey bitch, or do I have an agenda?"

"If you want to put it like that," he agreed.

"Well," she said, "I'm not sure you'd trust my answer, either way. I'm not sure you'd even trust me to be able to give an honest answer if I wanted to."

"So I'm supposed to make my own guess—figuring, of course, that I'll be lucky."

"If you want to put it like that," she said.

"Now you're fishing for insults," he told her. "You're inviting me to be cynical about your motives, for last night as well as today. You shouldn't do that, Alice. Fortunately, I'm not a cynic. I think you're doing this because you have my best interests at heart. I think you felt sorry for me, that day you saw me at Daddy's funeral, and were afflicted by a sudden rush of nostalgia for the old days. I think your own tragedy intensified that feeling of empathy considerably. I think you really do feel that I'm in some sort of danger, not so much from Lissa Lo as from myself—from my suddenly-increased conviction that the family rules really do matter, and that terrible things might happen if I don't start paying obsessive attention to them. Not that you think Lissa isn't dangerous, mind—but it's not just jealousy. You really do think that she might mess up my head, if I let her. You want to protect me from all of that."

"Oh, fuck off, Canny," Alice said, exasperatedly. "I'm not your fucking Mummy. I'm only interested in your body, and it's just a phase I'm going through—a wayward mood. I told you that."

"You lied," Canny said. "All the omens say so, and they're never wrong. Besides which, you always curse at least twice as hard when you're bluffing. It's what gamblers call a tell."

She fell silent then, for a while.

"Funny thing, that," she said. "Martin was the world's foremost expert on psychological plausibility—or damn near—and yet he was a lousy card player. You could have taken him to the cleaners any day of the week, with or without your lucky streak."

"Understanding doesn't always give you control," Canny said, "any more than control always gives you understanding."

"Very neat," she said. "That's your way of putting us in boxes, is it? Me, because I had Martin, understanding without control. Lissa Lo, because she didn't have you, control without understanding. So she's your ideal mate, and I'm a fucked-up floozy in mourning-dress."

"It's not a competition, Alice," he said. "You don't have that kind of agenda, remember? If you want to get me out of her clutches, it's purely for my own good. You're still grieving—just passing through the phases until you come into clear psychological waters again."

"Absolutely," she said. "It's all just theoretical discussion. So tell me, if you can set aside the mind-bending effects of your mild nEurological disorder—what other evidence might a person have, to convince him that he and his family were blessed with unnatural good luck? Purely hypothetically, of course."

"It's all to do with patterns," Canny told her, after a brief pause for thought. "We're preprogrammed to look for them, even where they can't exist—and we see them, even when we know they're an illusion. Suppose, for instance, that I were a casino manager with a computer that logs every bet my clients make and accumulates the data over time. How many clients do I have, do you think? Hundreds of thousands overall, but maybe only a few hundred regulars—let's say five hundred. How many of those would you expect to come out ahead on a fairly regular basis, given that they're always betting against the house percentage? It's nowhere near half, if you do the calculation, even though the house percentage on most games is only a few per cent—but it's not that tiny either. You could probably identify a dozen, maybe more. And would you then just shrug your shoulders and say: *well, that's probability for you*? Chance would predict that only a dozen would come out ahead on that sort of long-term basis, and here's a dozen guys, so that's the end of the story. No, you wouldn't. You'd start asking yourself, because you couldn't help yourself, why *these* guys, and not a dozen others? You'd start looking more closely, at the patterns innate in their betting habits, the patterns inherent in their attitudes of mind...*anything* that might give you a clue to the magic, even though you know full well that the magic isn't there, because magic doesn't exist. It's all in the patterns, Alice—the patterns we can't help but find, even when they're not really there. Except, of course, for the ones that are."

"The curves," she said. "The Poisson distribution. Fractals. The Fibonacci sequence. All the little miracles of mathematics—the magic of numbers."

"Those too," He admitted.

"And after everything you've said," Alice challenged him, "you really do believe there's more?"

"I know there is," he said. "I suppose I would say that, if I really were suffering from a mild nEurological disorder, one of whose definitive symptoms was an unjustifiable sense of conviction—but I'd still know. The question isn't whether I'm a fool to believe in the Kilcannon luck, Alice—the question is, how do I find out what's actually necessary to its maintenance, and what isn't, without testing it to destruction? That's the question that Daddy faced, when he wanted to marry against the rules; it's the question that every earl in the line has faced, as soon as his father died. It's pointless trying to convert me to your kind of skepticism, Alice, because the faith is incarnate in my flesh and blood, hardwired into my brain if not engraved in my DNA by the letters of sacred tetragrammaton. The point is to figure out what's really necessary and what's not—and which risks are worth taking, and which aren't. So far, I've risked more for you than I have for Lissa Lo, by the way, and I'm adding to that margin with every sentence I say to you."

"Perhaps you should have dropped me at King's Cross, then," she told him, soberly. "That would have been the safe way to play. Your confidence might not be dented yet, but we're only just past Milton Keynes. I may already be half way to delivering you from your pact with the devil You're a captive audience, after all. If I play my cards right, Helen of Troy won't get a look in—it'll be dear, sweet Marguerite all the way."

"I think you're confusing the Goethe and Marlowe versions of *Faust*."

"You think *I'm* confusing? Try listening to yourself some time."

"I do," Canny assured her. "And you're right—sometimes, I don't make a lot of sense."

"I don't believe that there's anything supernatural about your good luck, Canny," Alice said, flatly. "I don't think you have any rational grounds for believing in it either, no matter how much supposed evidence you've collected. I think that when you find yourself saying that you *know* something, when you also know that it's false, it's time to reappraise what you think the word *know* actually means."

"I'd already gathered that you thought all that," Canny told her. "Ellen's not the only Proffitt sister who isn't very big on subtlety, even if you're a little smarter than her. I must introduce you to Lo Chen some time—I'm sure that you and she could have a fascinating discussion about nEurological disorders, the practical implications of Heisenberg's uncertainty principle and the symbolism of yin and yang. But that kind of skepticism is no good to me, Alice—believe me, I've tried and tried, and I just can't get the thin end of the wedge into my head. If I'm mad, the problem isn't to find a cure, because there isn't one—not even the love of a good woman. The problem is to find the best way of living with my madness. Except that, to me it's not madness at all—it's pure magic. It's *luck*—the honest-to-goodness real thing that everybody wants and hardly anyone can have."

After a long pause, she said: "I'm not a good woman, and it wasn't love...which is a stupid thing to say, given that this isn't about me at all, or even Lissa Lo. It's about you. I admit that. Do you suppose that Stevie Larkin sees flashes, too?"

"I doubt it," Canny said. "It wouldn't be very convenient in the middle of a football game. It was bad enough when I used to turn out for the village cricket team. I was a lucky player, of course—most of my edges went straight through the slips for four and you'd never believe the number of times I was dropped on the boundary—but the problem was that I always looked it. I never looked as if I'd actually *earned* my runs. I was a clown. Stevie isn't. He's the real thing. He got to where he is because he can play, end of story."

"And you envy him that?"

"Of course. It cuts both ways, though—when we used to bump into one another on the Riviera, and he had to ask me to translate for him, he always thought that he was the fraud and I was the real deal. He never suspected that I thought exactly the same. It all depends on your point of view. He thinks he's infinitely luckier than me, because chance not only gave him the ability to play football but a world in which playing football to that sort of standard is the nearest you can get to godhood without having to learn to play the guitar. To him, every match that passes without some bastard berserker of a central defender crashing into his ankle and taking it all away from him is another pat on the back from generous fate."

"But you don't think so. You let him take the credit for his skill, while refusing to take any credit for your own."

"Oh, I take the credit," Canny assured her. "You have no idea how good I feel every time I collect the house percentage—or, if you do, it's a *theoretical* idea. I give myself credit—it's just that it's a different kind of credit from the kind that Stevie Larkin deserves."

"I don't think so," Alice declared.

"I know—but I have to make my own judgments and decisions, don't I? I have to figure things out for myself."

After a pause, she said: "I really wish I could help, Canny. I really do think you need it."

"You have helped," he told her, sincerely. "You probably will again. Won't you?"

"Yes," she said, unresentfully. "I suppose I will. But I ought to warn you that I won't give up. I'll never believe in the Kilcannon luck—not in the way that you do—and I'll never believe that it will work any better as a *folie à deux*."

"That's okay," he assured her. "That's the deal. You can insult me, curse me, call me mad. You can play court jester to your heart's content."

"Bastard," she said. "I'm serious."

"I know," he told her. So, in my own peculiar way, am I. Shall we stop for breakfast at the next services? I'm starving."

"Me too," she said.

CHAPTER TWENTY-NINE

Canny dropped Alice at the house in Leeds. "How do you feel?" he said, as she got out of the car.

"Better," she assured him. "Much more relaxed than I did this time yesterday. Like a cow with bloat whose belly's just been punctured by the vet's giant hypodermic."

"That's a truly repulsive analogy."

"I know. I'm sorry. I'm sorry about going on at you so much—it was just more bloat, more hot air. I'm okay now. I'll see you back in Cockayne."

"Sure," he said. "Take care."

"I always do, she assured him.

It only required a further twenty minutes to drive back to Cockayne. Bentley had the usual stack of telephone messages for him, and the mail that had accumulated over the previous few days was unusually prolific—a further effect of his father's death.

"I'm afraid some of it's urgent," the butler said.

"I can see that," Canny told him. "I'll do what I can before lunch. Will Mummy be in?"

"No, sir. Lady Credesdale is out until dinner."

Canny took time out to shower and change his clothes before he started work on the mail, but that only took him twenty minutes. When he did sit down he set aside all the items that Bentley had opened and sorted for him, directing his immediate attention to one item that stood out from all the rest: a package marked with instructions CONFIDENTIAL—TO BE OPENED

BY ADDRESSEE ONLY and EXTREMELY URGENT.

This legend was handwritten with a marker pen. Bentley told him that it had been delivered earlier that morning by a courier service.

"You could have opened it," Canny said.

"I could not," the butler contradicted him, severely. "Even if the labeling is a mere publicity ploy, concealing some ludicrous commercial special offer, I am bound to take it seriously.

"Well," Canny said, "if it's a bomb, I'm never going to forgive you for not taking the blast." He tore open the package.

It wasn't a bomb. It was a mobile phone.

Canny's first thought was that Bentley had been right, and that it was some kind of promotional offer—an impression heightened rather than dispelled by the fact that there was nothing accompanying the handset but a single piece of paper containing a handwritten instruction to call a number that obviously belonged to another mobile phone.

Canny was inclined to drop the phone, the instruction and the packaging into the bin, but he hesitated. There was an electrical sensation in the air, and a certain fugitive darkness. He didn't know whether he was being warned to ring the number, or to avoid ringing it, and his conversation with Alice about nEurophysiological disorders was still all-too-fresh in his mind, but he still believed in the reality of the Kilcannon luck.

In the end, he thumbed the number into the keypad.

"Lord Credesdale," said a male voice that contrived to be flat, businesslike and menacing at the same time. "We had hoped to hear from you sooner." The voice was slightly accented, but Canny had no idea what kind of accent it was. He had to presume that it was Eastern European, but if he hadn't been pointed towards that conclusion in advance he wouldn't have been able to draw it with any confidence.

"I've just got back from London," Canny said. "What do you want?"

"We want a million Euros, Lord Credesdale, by five o'clock this evening—and your silence, of course."

Canny felt his body react to the words—or to the muted streak that came with them. The shock was dull, and only subtly nauseating, but he had no idea whether its half-hearted quality was a consequence of the diminution of his ability or the relatively low level of the danger with which he was faced.

"And what do I get in return?" Canny asked, trying to keep his voice level. His eyes, meanwhile, met Bentley's inquisitive gaze.

The voice that replied to that inquiry wasn't the same one. It was easily recognizable, in spite of its strained tone, as Stevie Larkin's.

"Canny? Is that you?"

"It's me," Canny confirmed. "What is this, Stevie?" The question was necessary, even though he knew perfectly well what it was. He needed confirmation.

"I've been kidnapped, Canny. I was in the country for secret talks. I took an opportunity that came up to go home to see the family. They boxed the car in, shot out the rear window to show me they meant business. God only knows why they contacted you—I *told* them to ring my agent. I can get the money, Canny—but they insist that you have to raise it for me. I'm truly sorry."

"It's okay, Stevie," Canny said. "I understand why. It's me they're after, not you. They won't hurt you, if I do what they say. I'll get you out, Stevie—depend on that."

"They say they'll do my knee, Canny," Stevie told him, plaintively. "That's all—but it'd mean that I'd never play again. They know what it's worth to me. The club's insured, but that's not the point. Do you understand, Canny? If I have to pay a million Euros to keep my knee, I'll do it, no matter how hard it is to get the money together. I'm good for it, Canny. Just do as they say, and I'll see you right. Can *you* get the money?"

"I don't know, Stevie," Canny said. "I hope so. I'll certainly try, as hard as I can."

The other voice came back. "You can get the money, Lord Credesdale. Five o'clock. Ring back, and we'll give you further instructions. Don't involve the police. If anything goes wrong,

Mr Larkin's career is over—and it won't end there. You do understand that, don't you, Lord Credesdale? This is business, not war—but you were the one who raised the stakes." The accent was still indecipherable, but Canny couldn't believe that any member of the Uzbekistani mafia would be quite that polished. He was dealing with authentic Europeans, not displaced tartars, more likely Magyars or Czechs than Bulgars or Chechens—not that it mattered.

Canny didn't bother to complain that he wasn't the player who had raised the stakes, let alone the one who had started the game in the first place. He wasn't the one who was setting the rules, either—and he had no idea how far his luck could now be trusted, if at all. He was fairly certain, though, that the threat was serious. If he were callous enough to refuse to help Stevie out, they'd not only cripple the footballer but go after someone else until they struck the right nerve. They'd be ripping open a hornets' nest if they went after Lissa Lo's face, but they probably didn't even know about her. If Stevie's knee didn't do the trick, they'd turn their attention to the village.

"I'll try to get the money," Canny said, as calmly as he could. "You don't have anything against Stevie—there's no need to hurt him. I'll try as hard as I can to get you what you want."

"That's good," the voice said, grimly. "If you deliver, and keep quiet, no one will get hurt. A million Euros in notes—Euros, sterling or US dollars are acceptable, but nothing else. Ring us as soon as you've got it together, not before. When we have it, Mr. Larkin will be released. It's a simple business transaction, nothing more."

Canny had to figure that the kidnapper was almost certainly lying—he didn't need any kind of gift to work that out—but the game still had to be played out.

When Canny had put the phone down he still had to answer Bentley's inquisitorial stare, but that was the easy part. "Trouble," He said. "Bad trouble. I need to raise a lot of money very quickly. Utmost discretion required. No police—and Mummy mustn't suspect a thing. You'll have to cover for me if anyone asks. I need you to do that, Bentley—but the less you actually know, the better. Okay?"

"Yes sir," Bentley said, dutifully.

"Good," Canny said. He picked up the mobile phone and put it into his left-hand jacket pocket—his own phone was in the right-hand pocket—before moving to the land-line and phoning Maurice Rawtenstall at the mill.

He didn't have time for diplomatic niceties. "It's Lord Credesdale, Maurice," he said. "I need the slush fund—all of it. Pounds, dollars and Euros. I'll try to get to back to you within the week. No questions—and if anyone else asks, no answers."

"Of course, Lord Credesdale," was the answer he got, after a few seconds hesitation. "How would you like the money delivered?"

Canny made sure that his sigh of relief was inaudible. For a moment or two, the politeness and sheer matter-of-factness of Rawtenstall's reply seemed utterly bizarre—but he *was* Lord Credesdale now, and it probably wasn't the first time that a Lord Credesdale had telephoned the mill to demand a large sum of cash, with no questions asked.

"I'll collect it in an hour or so," Canny said. "How much is there?"

"I don't know the exact sum," Rawtenstall said. "About a hundred and fifty thousand."

That would be pounds, Canny knew. He had a further fifty thousand in his own safe. Given that a million Euros was currently equivalent to seven hundred thousand pounds, that would leave him with a further half million sterling to raise.

He phoned the first of the three Leeds banks with which the family had accounts and asked to talk to the senior manager. "This is Lord Credesdale," he said, again. "We met last week. I need to raise a considerable sum in cash by five o'clock this afternoon. Sterling, dollars and Euros are all acceptable. How much can you let me have?"

The manager didn't bother to query his use of the term "considerable sum", or quibble about practicalities. "I can probably let you have a hundred thousand immediately," the manager said. "I ought to be able to raise a quarter of a million by five, although it might be a close-run thing."

"Would that involve obtaining cash from other banks in the city?" Canny wanted to know.

"Yes it would."

"I'll have to go to Lloyd's and HSBC myself. If you can obtain cash from other parts of your own organization, that would be more convenient. I know there's no time to transfer notes from London or Birmingham, but Manchester's not so far away."

"I might be able to raise two hundred thousand without troubling the other institutions you mention," the manager said. "I might, however, have to draw on other sources to which they would have recourse in their turn, reducing their own capacity to help you. How much do you need?"

"Too much. Start raising what you can. I'll get on to them directly, and I'll come back to you if it looks as if there might not be enough. This has to be handled with the utmost discretion, though."

"Of course, sir. Will you be collecting the money in person?"

"Yes. I'll be in touch."

By the time Canny had made two further phone calls, the entire half million had been promised. He was astonished, and slightly appalled, by how easy it had been.

"I always thought the title was so much meaningless gibberish," he said to Bentley. "This is the twenty-first century, for Heaven's sake."

"Yours is a name that commands a great deal of authority, sir," Bentley told him. "The country is doubtless replete with aristocrats whose credit rating is derisory, but the Earls of Credesdale have a reputation that stretches back further than anyone can remember—and their dealings, though always profitable in the long run, haven't always been orthodox."

It wasn't just Henri Meurdon who had a powerful computer and a healthy measure of curiosity, Canny realized. He was, indeed, living in the twenty-first century. Seven hundred thousand pounds wasn't that big a deal, and he wasn't short of collateral—but the real point at issue was that all four of the men he'd called had heard abundant rumors of the Kilcannon luck, and had the means to investigate its arithmetic. One thing they didn't know, of course, was that his luck was supposed to be at a low ebb just now—but he didn't know himself how crucial the rules, or how reliable the superstitious fears, might really be.

"They all think I'm putting it into some crooked deal, don't they?" Canny said. "They think it's all slush fund."

"I'm sure they don't know what to think," Bentley told him. "But they know better than to make difficulties. They have confidence in you, sir—as have I."

"Even though you know it's simple blackmail?"

"Simple, sir?" the butler replied, cocking an eyebrow. "I turned a conscientiously deaf ear to everything you said, of course—and the exact nature of your relationship with Mr. Larkin is none of my business—but I can't quite believe that it's *simple*. If I were permitted to speculate, I'd hazard a guess that this has something to do with the other sum of money you recently lost, and I'd feel obliged to ask whether you might be in danger of losing more than mere money."

"They already had to fall back on Plan B," Canny said. "Obviously, that was just a stopgap. The rap on the knuckles they got from the Union Corse didn't put them off—quite the reverse, in fact. But things will work out. Maybe matters have taken a slight turn for the worse, but they'll improve. They always do, don't they? I'm a Credesdale, after all. One of Fortune's favorites."

"Luck sometimes runs out, sir," Bentley said, baldly—not because he knew anything about the rules, but because he was no more immune to the seductions of proverbial wisdom than anyone else.

"Yes it does," Canny agreed. "Even the longest lucky streak in the world has to run out eventually, no matter how carefully you consult the oracles or how often you pass along the road to Damascus. But you can't live your life with that expectation, can you? You have to play the cards as they're dealt, the best way you can. And there's a certain comfort in knowing that the world has so many people in it who are willing to hand over every currency note they have because you, your father, and your grandfather before you, have never let them down."

"It might have been exactly that knowledge," the butler pointed out, "that attracted the wrong kind of people—people, that is, who are selective in paying attention to the many aspects of your family's reputation."

"I have to go to the library now, Bentley," Canny said. "Then I have to drive to the mill, and then into Leeds. Could you possibly unpack my suitcase for me—it's on the bed."

"Would you like me to come with you, sir?"

"No," Canny said. "They're not going to put up with that, are they? And no, I don't want a gun. I just want to hand over the money, and get Stevie Larkin out. He says he'll pay me back, and he means it. With luck, I'll come out of this without suffering any loss at all—and he'll still have five more years at the top of his game. It's just business. There's no need for any heroics."

Bentley nodded, not bothering to issue any further warnings or pleas. By the time Canny had emptied the safe in the inner sanctum, the suitcase on his bed was empty. Canny carefully compared the space he filled with the space that still remained, and figured that he ought to be able to fit the money into the suitcase easily enough, provided that the bills were of suffi-ciently large denomination.

It wasn't until he had cleaned out the safe at the mill and started to drive into Leeds that the silver Toyota settled in behind him. For a few minutes he worried that it might be the police, or someone else that Bentley had altered to his plight, but he put the thought aside. It had to be one of the kidnappers, making certain that he was on schedule.

Gathering the cash proved to be no trouble at all. Its suppliers looked at him inquisitively, but not one of them asked him whether anything was wrong, or when they might expect to get their money back. They were all men for whom discretion was not merely a habit but a necessity; not one of them gave the slightest indication that there was anything particularly unusual about handing over six-figure sums in cash at a couple of hours notice. Perhaps, he thought, it really was the kind of thing they were likely to do twice or three times a month. If so, the black economy must be a great deal larger than he had ever dared to imagine.

When he had accumulated the whole million, he wasted no time phoning the number again, while the Bentley was still sitting in the employees' car park underneath the bank.

"I've got it," He said.

"Of course. Take the A58. When you get to Collingham, ring again for further instructions. Are you being followed?"

Canny didn't hesitate. "Yes," he said. "A silver Toyota. Nothing to do with me. Do you want me to lose it?"

"No. It's ours." The line went dead.

The rush hour traffic was just beginning to build up, but Canny got on to the A58 without any difficulty. He didn't see the silver Toyota again until the Roundhay roundabout, but after that it stuck to his tail like glue as he went past Scarcroft and through Bardsey. Its windscreen was slightly shadowed but he had a clear enough view in his rear-view mirror to see that it only had one occupant: a tall person wearing a baseball cap.

He rang the number again as soon as he reached Collingham, before getting to the junction with the A659. There would, he knew, be three main routes to choose from at that point—one leading west to Harewood, one east to Boston Spa and the third north to Wetherby.

He was ordered to take the western route, but only as far as the golf course, where there was a second turn-off to Wetherby. Once on that road he was directed to turn left towards Sicklinghall. Between Sicklinghall and Harrogate, he knew, there was a great deal of open country, all relatively low-lying.

At least, he thought, the kidnappers had been polite enough to stash Stevie in Yorkshire, instead of making him drive all the way to Nelson or Clitheroe.

CHAPTER THIRTY

There were far lonelier spots up on the windswept moors than any available between Kirkby Overblow and Spofforth, but Canny figured that the Bentley wouldn't be nearly as conspicuous in this relatively prosperous territory. The foot-and-mouth epidemic hadn't hit as badly here as it had further East, but there were farms here, as there were almost everywhere else, that had never been restocked because their broken-hearted proprietors had found better things to do with the ministry's compensation.

It was to one such abandoned farm that Canny was guided by the blandly sinister voice. The windows of the house had been boarded up, but the barn, emptied of its contents after disinfection, had probably never been locked. The door stood ajar, and as Canny guided the Bentley up the long curving drive someone came out to watch him approach.

The silver Toyota followed him no further than the gate, in which it paused so as to block the entrance—or, from Canny's point of view, the exit.

The waiting man pulled the barn door open and waved the Bentley through.

There was plenty of room inside for Canny to park the car without getting too close to the pale blue Datsun that was discreetly tucked away under the rim of the hayloft, beside a row of empty stalls. The place seemed uncannily tidy; all the straw that must have been strewn around it when it was a hive of activity had been swept away and burnt. There was a certain amount of clutter up in the loft—he could see planks of old wood; a few large drums, some of which were still wound around with fragments of fencing-wire; an ancient water-butt; and a couple of oil drums—but everything that had been worth taking away must have been removed.

Canny switched off the engine. He could see Stevie Larkin sitting in the back seat of the Datsun, alone. The footballer was gagged, and he was shifting awkwardly, clearly unable to raise a hand to reply to his reassuring salute. Canny deduced that his hands were secured behind his back.

There was a second person standing by the blue car, dressed in a loose-fitting sweater and jeans, wearing a ski-mask—but the man who was now closing the door that he had opened to let the Bentley through was not masked in any way. He would be easily recognizable if Canny—or Stevie—ever bumped into him again.

Canny didn't know how bad a sign that was, but he was sure that it couldn't be good. The kidnappers probably intended to leave the country as soon as they could, once they had the cash, but they still had reason enough not to advertise their identities.

The androgynous figure by the Datsun was toting a gun so heavy that it required the support of a shoulder-strap—some kind of sub-machine gun, Canny guessed. The man at the door only had an automatic pistol, which he carried as if it weighed hardly anything at all. He was a tall man, with light brown hair cut very short—but more like an old-fashioned crew-cut than a modern razor cut—and pale blue eyes. His grey suit looked far from new, but it seemed to have been made to measure. His polo-necked shirt wouldn't have got him into a high-class restaurant in a conservative county like Yorkshire, even though it was white, but it was neat enough.

Canny opened the door and slowly climbed out of the Bentley. The heavy gun swung to point at him; the slight figure's finger was hovering close to the trigger.

"The money?" said the man by the door, who didn't bother to make any exaggeratedly threatening gesture with his own weapon. Canny recognized the voice that had guided him.

"In the boot," Canny said. "Let Stevie out of the car, will you—I want to make sure he's all right."

"He's all right where he is," the man with the pistol assured him. "Open the boot."

"It's open," Canny said. "Help yourself."

The kidnapper opened the boot and looked down at the suitcase. "You open it," he said.

Canny shrugged, and went to release the locks on the case, before unzipping it and flipping back the lid to expose the bundles of cash inside. "Three hundred and eighty sterling," he said. "That just over five hundred and thirty-two thousand Euros. There's a further two hundred and sixty thousand in actual Euros. There's also two hundred and twenty-eight thousand US dollars. Grand total, at today's exchange rates, one million Euros."

"It's always best to do business with businessmen," the man with the pistol observed, as he stepped up beside Canny to take a look. "They have the means to lay their hands on the money, and they know how easily it comes and goes. Better by far than dealing with loose cannons like sports agents or football clubs. Phone." As he spoke the last word he put out his hand.

Canny handed over the mobile phone that had arrived by courier. "Far better," he agreed. "You can let Stevie go now. Put the cash in the Datsun and drive away. Simple as that."

The tall man took the phone and put it in his pocket. Then he ran his left hand over Canny's pockets, removing Canny's own mobile. He put that one in his breast pocket, for want of any other convenient place of storage. Then he continued patting Canny down, presumably to make sure that he wasn't carrying any kind of weapon. When he was satisfied he motioned to Canny to back away from the car, then began probing in the suitcase, riffling through wads of bills at random.

"It's all there," Canny told him. "No bombs, or purple dyes. Just cash. You've got what you wanted. It's over."

The tall man didn't answer; he went on patiently checking the contents of the case for two more minutes before he flipped the lid down again and zipped it up. "For myself," he said, in the end, "I agree. This is what we wanted. I'm satisfied." He wasn't looking at Canny, though—he was looking at his companion.

Canny felt a prickling sensation in his skin, but he knew that it wasn't anything supernatural. It was a perfectly natural symptom of fear. The atmosphere in the barn was dark, but that was mostly because its unglazed windows were so small and high-set. There was plenty of light to see by, but it was dull light, almost leaden. It didn't seem to be laden with any kind of potential—but Canny couldn't know whether that was any indication of his safety or a symptom of the diminution of his luck.

He swallowed a lump in his throat, but he felt relatively tranquil. He had acquired the habit long ago of remaining calm in the face of apparent danger. Even if the present danger turned out to be real, the habit was still in force. He was glad of it. He didn't want to be terrified. He didn't want to be shot, but he didn't want to be terrified of being shot whether he ended up dead or not.

"We've met before," Canny said, to the person in the ski-mask. "In my hotel in Monte Carlo. You made the sensible decision then. You hesitated, but you took the money and left."

"That was a mistake." The voice wasn't deep, but Canny had abandoned his last suspicion that its owner might be a woman even before the muffled figure reached up with his left hand to pull the ski-mask from his head. The man was young—probably no more than twenty-one or twenty-two—but he had enough five o'clock shadow to leave no doubt as to his sex. His eyes were dark, although his hair was the same mousy shade as his companion's. The removal of the mask seemed to Canny to be an unmistakably bad sign.

"No it wasn't," Canny said. "It was the right thing to do, once you'd heard that my father was seriously ill. As your friend says, you need to deal with businessmen in a businesslike way. Complications are awkward for everyone."

"It got my brother killed," the young man said, flatly.

"That was my mistake," Canny said, readily enough. "When

you took the money, I assumed that was what you were after, so I told the casino that someone might be hanging around targeting their customers. I didn't realize that he was only there to tell you when I left. By the time the casino's guardians figured that out...I suppose they felt that they ought to set an example anyway. The money did belong to one of their customers, after all. I didn't know. It's not as if I hired a hitman. As I said, you have what you wanted. It's over now."

"He was my brother," the young man said.

"You don't want this to get out of hand," Canny said, addressing the tall man although he was still looking at the other. "This can't be part of your plan. Just let us go, and go your own way."

"In the old socialist days," the tall man said, "we had discipline, order, hierarchy. Then everything collapsed. Now, the young people don't know how to take orders any more. They don't understand that personal sacrifices have to be made for the common good. They're Westernized—individualists, committed to their own agendas. A tragedy—but what can you do? They're still our children."

"I'm not your son!" the young man retorted, although the words hadn't been addressed to him. He was still speaking English, though, so that Canny could understand him. "What do you care, whether he lives or dies? You've got your money. Anyway, your socialist conscience shouldn't give you any trouble. He's a filthy aristocrat as well as a bloated capitalist."

"It's bad for business," the tall man said—but it was obvious that he didn't care enough to make any very strenuous effort to prevent his companion from exacting the vengeance due to him. He was staying well clear of the potential line of fire.

Canny searched in vain for any kind of light; the air was dead and still. For the first time since his father had died, he felt the void that the rules had promised: the absence of any premonition, any inspiration, any crack in the fabric of mechanical causality.

"This is foolish," Canny said. "People in your line of work

need to avoid publicity. The last thing you need is an Interpol manhunt spurred on by the tabloid press. Even if you restrict yourself to shooting me and let Stevie live, this is the kind of story that'll rattle round the world. Take the money, and let us go."

He could see that the would-be killer was hesitating, just as he had in the hotel room. He really hadn't made up his mind—not completely. The decision could go either way. All it required was a slight nudge by Lady Luck, a fortunate flip of the decisive coin—but Canny still couldn't see the kindly light, the small benign spark of momentary deconstruction.

Shit! he thought. *Is this what it's like to go naked in the world, with no help but human hands? Is this sort of sensation what terrified my ancestors into marriage and paternity, with all that the rules had loaded into them, in the desperate hope of getting back to a more comfortable way of being?*

Until that moment, the young man's hand hadn't actually settled on the trigger of the obscenely intimidating gun. Now it did.

Canny couldn't bear to look at his would-be assassin any longer. He half-turned to look at the tall man, whose stance was quite relaxed. The automatic pistol was pointing idly at the ground—but the pale blue eyes were utterly bleak and devoid of fellow-feeling. The older and wiser gangster didn't feel in the least sorry for Canny, or afraid for himself.

There was a sound like a popping cork.

The thought sprang into Canny's mind that it was an absurd noise for such an ugly and powerful weapon to make—but then, as he swiveled his eyes to look for one last time into the eyes of his murderer, he realized that the young man's finger hadn't tightened on the trigger.

Caught up in the residue of his hesitation, the finger didn't even convulse as the young man's head was jerked to one side by an oblique impact.

There was hardly any blood. There was no exit wound, and no fountain effect where the bullet had gone in, somewhere above the right temple.

Then, it seemed, there were enough corks popping to signal a twenty-first birthday: a veritable cacophony of fizzing champagne.

The young man was hit for a second time before his falling body hit the ground. The other must have been hit four or five times, in the chest as well as in the face.

Now they were both bleeding, but with an odd decorum. The red tide simply flowed out of them on to the floor, forming ever-widening circles on the scrubbed and scoured floor.

Canny looked up at the hayloft, where a man in a dark blue boiler suit was standing on the platform rim, holding a pistol with an absurdly long barrel. It seemed impossible that one man could have fired so many times, with such amazing accuracy— but there had been only the one shooter. The man in the brown raincoat who was now emerging from the clutter had no weapon in his gloved hands.

While the boiler-suited assassin was reloading his weapon the second man said something in French, which Canny didn't quite catch—except for the word "Toyota". The shooter nodded before setting himself on the ladder.

Stevie Larkin was barging about in the back of the Datsun, trying to maneuver his bound hands into a position from which they could grip the inner handle—but it was all to no avail. The door didn't respond. It probably had a child-lock.

Canny was in no hurry to let Stevie out; he stood where he was until both of his unexpected allies had descended to floor-level. He was still marveling at the absence of any sign of their impending intervention. His old habits persisted in their effect, though—he was possessed nevertheless by a sense of the inevitable, an acute consciousness of his entitlement to his amazing good fortune. He was also slightly ashamed of the fact that he had triumphed only by remaining completely passive, letting fate take care of him. He would have liked to be able to feel proud as well as relieved, by virtue of having done something slightly heroic.

"You cut that rather fine," Canny said—in English, because he didn't know the French for "cut it fine".

"Yes, that is so," the man in the raincoat agreed, in the same language, but speaking with a very noticeable accent. "We had intended to wait until you and Monsieur Larkin had departed, so that you would not be placed in danger."

"Very thoughtful," Canny said, drily. "And you'd have had the million Euros too."

The man in the raincoat had even darker eyes than the young man with the heavy gun. He looked Canny up and down before saying: "From which we would have taken our standard commission, before returning the remainder to you. I hope you will have no objection if I do that in any case."

"How much?" Canny asked.

"Ten per cent," the other replied. "It would have been higher, had you not already made a down payment."

Canny had to raise a hand to request that Stevie Larkin be patient, because the footballer was writhing around with increasing urgency. He ventured a small laugh. "You mean the cash you recovered from my win at the casino? You're treating that as payment for protection—membership in the club?"

"In expectation of further commerce, Monsieur le Comte. Not criminal commerce, I hasten to add. We have many potential interests in common, all *above board*, as you say."

"We have earls in England, not *comtes*," Canny said. "But I take your point. Ten per cent is perfectly satisfactory. Take Euros, if you wish, or the dollars, if you prefer." He didn't doubt that what the other said about their future commerce not necessarily being criminal was true. Unlike the kidnappers, who were fledglings in the world of organized crime, the Union Corse had been around long enough to have moved a substantial fraction of its wealth into legitimate businesses.

"You've been following them all along, haven't you?" Canny said. "You could have taken them any time. You didn't have to let them kidnap Stevie, or put the bite on me. You could have taken them out before they made a move."

"We did not know what they planned to do, Monsieur. Had they not involved you...the footballer is not our responsibility. Had it not been your money, I would not feel honor bound to settle for ten per cent and the hope of a fruitful association in the future—but we have a reputation to uphold." He went to the door as he spoke, and opened it by a crack in order to look out, then opened it much wider. Over his shoulder, Canny could see the Toyota approaching, with a different driver at the wheel.

"I shall take my money, with your permission," the dark-eyed man said, soberly. "Then, I think you and Monsieur Larkin should go. We shall tidy up here—you need have no fear that the bodies will be discovered, unless by some freak of outrageous chance." As he spoke he knelt down beside the body of the tall man, which was already beginning to stink horribly, and fished something out of his breast pocket: Canny's mobile phone, smashed by a bullet. Had it not been for the other four that had struck the dead man down, the stolen phone might have saved his life. "Sorry, Monsieur," the Frenchman said. "Shall I dispose of this too?"

"If you like," Canny said. "The raincoat and the boiler-suit are mistakes, though—they won't pass for casual wear nowadays, even in Yorkshire."

"I doubt if we can keep them clean enough to take them away with us," the other said, as he began removing bundles of banknotes from the suitcase in the Bentley's boot.

Canny finally went to the Datsun and opened the rear nearside door from the outside. He removed Stevie's gag.

"Fucking hell, Canny, what's the fuck's going on?" Stevie demanded. "You took your time. You bring the SAS with you, or what?" He offered his wrists, which were secured by duct tape. Canny began stripping it away, unwinding it as it came loose. As soon as Stevie's hands were free the footballer began rubbing his right thigh with his left hand. There was obviously nothing wrong with his knees.

"Or what," Canny said. "Don't take this the wrong way, Stevie, but it would probably be best for everyone concerned if you forgot what you'd seen here—or anything that happened to you since your car got boxed. It's not the Toyota or the Datsun, I assume?"

"No—it was a hired beamer. They left it where it was. They moved it off the road and locked it up, although the hole in the back windscreen would have let anyone in who wanted to steal it. It *might* be still there."

"I'll give you a lift back," Canny said. "If it's gone, I'll take you wherever you want to go."

"How much is he taking?" Stevie asked, as the man in the raincoat zipped up the suitcase again.

"A hundred thousand," Canny said. "Euros, not pounds. Don't worry—I'll stand the loss. It was me they were after, not you. It was just bad luck that you got caught up in it." He opened the front passenger door of the Bentley to let Stevie in, then went back to the boot and locked the suitcase. Both his saviors were busy lifting the third body out of the front seat of the Toyota. He had been shot in the head—by a single bullet, so far as Canny could tell. He must have been keeping a look-out in the wrong direction as his killer approached.

"I thought you were dead, for sure," Stevie said, as Canny climbed back into the Bentley's diving-seat. "Me too—I nearly pissed myself. Who the fuck *were* those people? And who are the guys who bailed us out?"

"I forgot to ask," Canny told him, dryly. "Believe me, Stevie, there are things you're better off not knowing. I'm truly sorry you got mixed up in this—but it'll be something to tell your grandchildren, if you can keep your mouth shut that long." He put the car into gear and eased it out of the barn. The man in the boiler-suit closed the door behind him, without bothering to make any gesture of farewell.

"Does this have anything to do with Lissa Lo?" Stevie asked, as they passed through the gate and turned on to the road.

"Nothing at all," Canny assured him, although he couldn't help wondering whether the protection that Lissa had offered him on the previous evening might have had *something* to do with the Union Corse hit-man's fortunate presence. "Why would you think it might?"

"I don't know," Stevie said. "Ever since that night when we all bet on that zero, things have been a little crazy. The newspapers are still banging on about her and me being an item, although it was pure coincidence that we both turned up at your Dad's funeral. You know that, right?"

"Pure coincidence," Canny echoed.

"We didn't even leave together," Stevie said. "You know that, right?"

"She had nothing to do with your being kidnapped, Stevie." Canny said. "The publicity might have helped to call their attention to you, but there'd have been publicity enough if you'd turned up on your own, with all the transfer rumors going round. You were just unlucky that our friendship became a notch tighter at the wrong moment—but it all worked out okay. Nobody got shot. Nobody even pissed himself."

"You must have nerves of steel, then—that's all I can say. If I'd been looking down the barrel of that chopper...friends, you say? We're friends?"

Canny realized that Stevie actually thought that being counted a friend by an earl was a big deal—even though the loyal readers of every tabloid in the land would reckon Canny the luckier man for having made a friend of a star like Stevie.

"We're more than friends, Stevie." he said, coolly. "We were friends even before you put that bet on zero. Now, we've been saved by the Union Corse from being slaughtered by the Albanian mafia—from now on, we're practically blood-brothers."

Stevie thought about that fir a moment or two, before daring to say: "Were they *really* the Albanian mafia?"

Canny felt free to laugh at that. "If they weren't," he said, "they were the next worst thing. Globalization, eh? What's the world coming to? You don't mind if we stop off at Cockayne on the way to pick up your car, do you? I'll feel a lot better when that money's in a safe—I'll have to get it back to the banks first thing in the morning, though, or the interest payments will suck me dry."

Stevie was silent for a few minutes, while the Bentley whizzed through Sicklinghall and Canny steered towards Wetherby. "Thanks, Canny," he said, finally. "I really couldn't see any reason why you should stick your neck out, you know—and *a million Euros*. You might have lost the lot."

"True," Canny said—although now that it hadn't happened, he was flooded by the conviction that it couldn't possibly have happened, and that he must have been an utter fool ever to have had a moment's anxiety. "Well, next time you get kidnapped, you know where to come—but leave it for a while, will you? And keep quiet about this one. In my experience, it always pays not to advertise one's implication in multiple murders."

"Is that what it was?" Stevie asked, hesitantly. "I was thinking of it as a daring rescue."

"One man's daring rescue is another's multiple murder," Canny said. "And to answer the unspoken question, no—I haven't been a witness to very many multiple murders. None, in fact, before today. And you're right—if I'd had an atom of sense I'd have pissed myself when that kid decided to blow me away. You will keep quiet, though—as a friend?"

"We're more than friends, mate," Stevie said. "Anything you need that I can provide, you only have to ask."

CHAPTER THIRTY-ONE

By the time Canny finally got home after delivering Stevie Larkin safely to his original destination, Bentley was in a complete stew. The butler was acting far more like an anxious mother than Canny's actual mother, who was swanning around the house in blissful ignorance, and he was doubtless doubly stressed by the necessity of keeping her out of the loop.

"You could have telephoned, sir," Bentley complained, when Canny had assured him that everything was fine.

"Actually, I couldn't," Canny told him. "Somebody took my mobile, as well as the one they sent me, and it stopped a bullet. Lucky he was holding at the time instead of me, eh?"

The butler didn't think that was at all amusing, and got himself caught up in an absurd internal struggle to determine the most polite way to make further enquiries. In the end, he settled for the astonishingly anodyne: "There are such things as public telephones, sir."

"Never use them," Canny told him, as he sank gratefully into the armchair in the drawing-room that his mother would have been using if she'd been there. "Never have any change, let alone one of those silly cards. But you're right—I should have asked Maurice to tip you off when I dropped the money at the mill before driving Stevie to Bolton. I sort of took it for granted that he would, even though he didn't know that you were worried, not having known that I'd been in any danger himself...sorry, I'm babbling."

"I expect you've had a stressful day, sir," the butler observed, sarcastically.

"Not one of my better ones," Canny confessed, wondering why his heart had begun to hammer again, and why the atmosphere in the room seemed to have grown a little darker, as if fate were mocking him by saying *oh, here's a warning I forgot to give you earlier.*

"But it all worked out in the end. Mr. Larkin's knees are in perfect working order."

"He's fine. I ended up a hundred thou down—Euros, mercifully, not pounds—and I think I might have been drafted as a money-launderer for the Riviera mob...although that might not be such a bad thing, given that I'll probably get the hundred thou back in no time, with abundant interest. On the other hand, it could have been a lot worse. The psychopath who wanted to kill me is safely underground, and if I'm reading between the lines with sufficient accuracy, I made a lucky guess when I told Alice Ellison to spread it around that Stevie's on the brink of signing for Leeds United. All things considered, I guess I came out ahead of reasonable expectation. I'm truly sorry about not phoning, though. Could you possibly arrange for Securicor to pick up some bundles of cash at the mill, first thing tomorrow? They have to go back to three Leeds banks as soon as humanly possible."

Bentley accepted the apology and promised to make the necessary arrangements—but he couldn't resist having one last dig. "Is life going to be *exciting* from now on, sir?" he asked, making the prospect of excitement seem like the innermost circle of hell, in a manner that no one but a true Yorkshireman could ever have contrived.

"I don't know," Canny said. "History suggests that things will soon calm down, especially if I follow Daddy's dying advice and get married—with or without your help in locating a suitably old-fashioned bride. But we're living in the twenty-first century now, and I'm not sure that history is any longer a reliable guide to the future. For the time being, at least, I'm inclined to suspect that the excitement will get worse before it gets better—or vice versa, depending on your point of view. Do you think you'll be able to stand it, or should I start looking for a younger man?"

"Your father communicated a few dying wishes to me, to, sir," Bentley said, with a sigh. "He asked me to look after you, in case your devil-may-care attitude should lead you into trouble. I promised that I would do my best, circumstances permitting. I fear, therefore, that I shall have to resist any attempt to replace me with every passive-aggressive weapon known to modern psychiatry."

"According to legend, Bentley," Canny told him, "the devil *may* care. On the other hand, he might not. Either way, we all have to decide which chances to take and which to pass over. I'm not about to start passing on all but the safe ones—not yet, anyway. I'm sorry if you disapprove. Sometimes though, you take the Jeeves act just a little too far, if you don't mind me saying so. I need to go to bed now—it's been a long and eventful day, and even your ear-bending skills pale into insignificance by comparison with some of the abuse I've endured since my alarm failed to go off this morning."

"Perhaps you forgot to set it, sir." Bentley suggested, in a manner that almost suggested that he'd had his own copies of the library keys for many years.

"Perhaps I did," Canny agreed.

Canny was certainly tired, but he found himself returned to that awkward condition in which mere exhaustion wasn't nearly sufficient to carry him over the threshold of oblivion. His mind was still far too active to let go of consciousness, even if it fell into delirium. Oddly enough, though, it wasn't the memory of looking death in the face that came back to haunt him; it was Alice Ellison's sarcastic account of the illusions that might be born of flashes of apparent light.

At the time, he'd rejected the account, not merely because the family luck had the statistical evidence of Henri Meurdon's computer to support it, but also because Lissa Lo had confirmed the objective reality of the streaks that lesser mortals couldn't perceive. Now that he was in reduced mental circumstances, though, doubt began to nibble away at both convictions.

How often had he played roulette or *chemin de fer*, rather than poker, in Meurdon's casino? And how often had he played more than one game in the course of a single twelve- or sixteen-hour session? Given that the only thing Meurdon could conveniently tabulate was the record of the chips that he bought and cashed in, how could Meurdon know that his winnings were as consistent in games of chance as they were in games of skill? Wasn't it possible—probable, even—that Meurdon had been reading more into the figures than could be legitimately deduced, perhaps because he wanted to be convinced himself that luck really did exist, and could be tamed?

Then again, how much did Lissa Lo's claims really amount to, even if they were honest? She saw streaks when he saw flashes, but how could either of them know that they were the same streaks? More importantly, how could either of them know, given that the streaks coincided with similar events, that the flashes of light and clouds of darkness were not reflexive physiological responses to similar circumstances and similar anticipations? They had both seen streaks when zero came up on Meurdon's wheel, while Stevie Larkin and the other players had apparently remained oblivious to any deconstruction of the moment, but might that only mean that they had similar nEurological disorders, likely to react to surges of excitement—or surges of anxiety—in the same pathological fashion?

Might Alice, in fact, be right? Might the Kilcannon gift, and other gifts like it, be nothing more than a concatenation of exotic symptoms produced by nEuronal weak spots in brains under stress: moments of literal enlightenment, in which the uninvolved but ever-watchful rational mind could not help but look for patterns and meanings...and which might indeed have a genetic basis transmissible from father to son, even for thirty generations and more.

But the numbers can't lie, he told himself, over and over again, as his mind struggled to let go of the continuity of waking thought. *Everything else can, and probably does, but the numbers can't. No matter how much psychological arith- metic might differ from the real thing, money in the bank is real. We do win. The percentage is there. Either the devil cares, or our lucky star keeps right on shining. One way or the other, we've always been ahead of the herd.*

He knew, though, that he was trying harder to convince himself than he had ever had to do before—and harder by far than he had ever tried to convince himself of the opposite conclusion.

There had been times aplenty when he had lain awake telling himself that it as all mumbo-jumbo, all tomfoolery, all superstition—but never on a day when he had been within seconds of getting wasted by a sub-machine gun.

On a day like that, anyone would cling with all his might to the faith that he really did have an edge over the laws of chance, and that fate really was looking out for him, forever moving in mysterious ways to protect him from harm.

In the morning he rang Maurice Rawtenstall with exact instructions as to how the cash he'd brought back from his excursion was to be redistributed. Then he rang Henri Meurdon.

"I just wanted to say thanks, Henri," He said. "Your friends came through for me. It was tight, but they've tidied everything up."

It was an hour later in Monte Carlo than in England, but the casino manager kept strange hours, and the call had obviously woken him up. "Don't thank me, Monsieur Kilcannon...Lord Credesdale," he said. "I did nothing. I am glad to know that it worked out well."

"As well as could be expected," Canny corrected him. "I can see now why you approved of my pattern of play. My attitude and style seem to fit in very well with the general ambiance of your operation."

"I am merely an employee, Mons...Lord Credesdale."

"There's nothing mere about you, Henri. May I ask you something?"

"Of course."

"How many others did you find, when your computer churned out its results?"

There was a pause at the other end while Meurdon collected himself. "I am sorry, Lord Credesdale," he said, eventually. "I cannot tell you that. I am neither a doctor nor a lawyer, but even so...I am bound by duty to keep certain information confidential. I am sure that you understand."

Canny understood the careful implication that if anyone else were to ask, Meurdon would not be giving away any information about *him*—except, of course, that "anyone" didn't mean *anyone* in an absolute sense. Canny was protected now, by people who thought that he was worth protecting—a category that obviously extended far beyond a faithful butler and a curious supermodel.

"I think I understand a little better than I did before," Canny agreed. "I think I understand, for instance, why you egged me on to take that seat at your roulette table, although it wasn't a dare. I understand curiosity, and its corollaries—and I really *do* understand. I certainly don't hold it against you. The casino business is built on the vagaries of psychological probability. It's essentially predatory, feeding on false beliefs and true ones alike. It's the business we Kilcannons have been in since time immemorial. I like your style too, Henri, and your attitude to the news your computers deliver. If you find that there are loaded dice out there, and you don't have a set yourself, the logical move to make is to find the guys who do and bet on them. I wish you the best of luck, Henri—I really do."

"The sentiment is mutual, Lord Credesdale. Shall we be seeing you at the casino again in the future? You are, as you know, always welcome."

"Thanks. Maybe next year. For the time being, I have other business to attend to. I need to get a much firmer grip on the reins of Daddy's affairs, not just to steer them through the inevitable disruption caused by his death but to make sure that everyone knows that I'm in charge, and that the whole enterprise is in safe hands. It's not the work of a few days, or even a year. When a man in Daddy's position dies, there are always complications—and when a man like me steps into his shoes, there's a certain amount of wearing in to be done."

"I understand, Lord Credesdale," Meurdon said. "We shall be delighted to see you again, when you have time to spare for leisure. I shall always be glad to be of service."

When he'd rung off, Canny thought that it might be well worth traveling down to the Riviera again, when he could spare to time, to have a quiet chat with Henri Meurdon about the mysteries of probability—but he decided, on due reflection, that it would probably be pointless. Meurdon was a practical man, not a theorist. Asked about matters of causation and meta-physical significance he would simply shrug his shoulders in his stylish Gallic fashion, and suggest that it might be better not to trouble one's mind with such issues.

From a casino manager's point of view, it was enough to know that a pattern existed, and to follow it as long as it held—and, doubtless, to be ready to abandon it the moment it disintegrated and dissolved into the chaos of chance—but Canny's needs were greater than that.

Lissa's right, he thought, as he began compiling his time-table for the day. *There's only one way to find out where the limitations are, and that's to test them. And that's why Alice is wrong—it really isn't Lissa's body that had me hypnotized; it's her courage and determination. When all appearances are set aside, we're two of a kind.*

CHAPTER THIRTY-TWO

What Canny had told Henri Meurdon was true. Stepping into his father's shoes really had committed him to a long wearing-in process that would not permit him to walk comfortably for some considerable time. He had a great deal of work still to do, not merely to familiarize himself with a complex set of new routines but to instill confidence in a host of collaborators. Taking the money out of the mill and the three banks had not assisted this enterprise, and putting it back the following morning, although it saved him a small fortune in interest payments, did not add credence to the supposition that he knew what he was about. The fact that his own safe was now empty, and the mill's slush fund more than twenty thousand down, was a further inconvenience requiring urgent attention. He set about making the necessary repairs with a will, and succeeded in making up the lost financial ground in less than a fortnight, but restoring the cracks in his image was a slower and more arduous task.

He had few interruptions. Lissa Lo didn't call, and Alice left the district to visit her in-laws and make arrangements for Martin Ellison's funeral in the Gloucestershire village of Cherington, where the psychologist had been born and raised.

Canny went to the funeral, where he was able to exchange a few words with Alice, much as she had been able to do with him at his father's funeral, but the first claim on her attention was that of her in-laws, and the promise he made to visit her in Leeds when she returned to await the trial of her husband's murderers was unattached to any firm date. He also went to the big party that Leeds United threw to celebrate Stevie Larkin's signing, and exchanged a few words with Stevie—but Stevie's attention was likewise claimed by his new idolaters, and the promises the two of them made to get together for a quiet evening were unlikely to materialize in the near future, given that the season was in full swing.

Lissa Lo didn't attend either function—disappointing Canny slightly, although there was not the slightest reason to expect her presence. He was able to keep approximate track of her movements by surreptitiously reading his mother's weekly magazines, but the model had retreated to the Olympian world from which she had briefly descended; he couldn't help wondering, and fearing, that he might have been relegated to the status of a cryptic note in her overflowing diary.

Three more weeks passed, during which Leeds United won twice in the premiership and drew once. Canny spent ten days out of the twenty-one in London, but he found it far more difficult to feel at home there than he had before his father's death. During his troubled teens he had been quite unable to imagine that he would ever feel more comfortable at Credesdale House than he did in Cambridge or the capital, but now that the title had alighted upon him like a confidential raven on his shoulder he found all kinds of unexpected corollaries arising in his mind and body alike.

He saw no flashes of dubious inspiration, nor did the world ever seem to grow more ominously dark than was explicable in terms of ordinary weather—in that respect, at least, his brain had become quiet and meek—but the absence of deconstructed moments was compensated by the slow reconstruction of his everyday life, which seemed to be urging him into an inexorable process of personal metamorphosis, whose ultimate result he could not yet foresee.

It was all illusion, of course; he told himself that a thousand times—but he was no longer sure of the exact extent to which illusion and reality overlapped, or in what strange ways they might exchange their roles in the souls of the unwary.

When he was at home, Canny spent a good deal of time in the library—not because he was studying but because it was the only place where he was fully insulated from his mother's questions and solicitations. Whenever the heavily-laden walls began to shrink in upon him like a prison he went for walks across the estate, sometimes into Cockayne but more often in the opposite direction. Sometimes he drove around the north of Leeds to Ilkley, so that he could walk from March Ghyll to Fewston Rest; occasionally he went further still, to Brown Bank Head and Pock Stones Moor. On Barden Fell he was able to rejoice in the bite of the wind that blew from the west, all the way from the Atlantic. It was, he knew, the kind of wind that carried people off who went unwisely on to Ilkley Moor without a hat, and turned them into food for worms before recycling their atoms into human flesh once more—but that prospect could not intimidate any true Yorkshireman, whether or not he had the devil's luck to shield him.

He dropped into the fish-and-chip shop in the village once a week, to say hello to Ellen and refuse Jack's last few offers to give him one more game for the village team before the season ended. Once it had ended, though, there was a residuum of subtle resentment in the way Jack would wrap his haddock—as if the new earl had let the side down by not lending it his unequivocal blessing. Promises to turn out in 2004 were blatantly inadequate compensation, even had they been sincere. He was careful not to be too obvious in asking after Alice.

"I think she's okay now," Ellen told him, when a month had passed after Martin's funeral, during which Alice had not returned to Cockayne. "She was rocky for a bit, but she seemed to find her feet again all of a sudden. I only hope the trial doesn't set her off again. We're still waiting for a place to fall vacant in the village, but I'm not so sure she still wants it badly enough to force her way in ahead of the waiting list. Do you know who else was making enquiries? That Stevie Larkin. Dad thinks he's got no chance—says the elders won't make exceptions for a football player, no matter how much they think of him in Leeds—but

Jack reckons they might make an exception, seeing as he's a friend of yours. Don't you, Jack?"

Jack, who was busy lowering a fresh bath of chips into the batter with clinical concentration, contented himself with a nod.

"He *is* a friend," Canny confirmed, although he knew that Ellen was fishing for gossip. "I wouldn't ask the elders to make any exceptions on that account, though. It was probably only a whim. He'll likely want to buy a place of his own—somewhere big. Come to think of it, the House might be just the thing, if I were thinking of selling it."

"You wouldn't!" The expression on Ellen's face was a thing to behold.

"I couldn't," Canny reassured her. "It's what they call *entailed*—not really mine at all, although I've got a life interest in it. It belongs to the family; I can't sell it, and when I die, it has to go to my son no matter what. I'm obliged to have a son, you see, to make sure that there's someone it can go to. *Noblesse oblige* and all that."

"Better be getting on with it then, hadn't you?" Ellen said, boldly—mainly to scandalize her husband, who was still standing guard over his chips like a mother goose keeping watch on her chicks. "You're not getting any younger. You missed out on all three of us by dragging your feet, but there must be someone out there who'll take you on."

"It's okay," Canny assured her. "Mummy and Bentley are both on the lookout. They spend hours poring over the social calendar, searching for coming-out parties in Beverley, Harrogate and Richmond. It's only a matter of time before they fix me up. It's such a comfort not to have to bother with all that oneself. Yorkshiremen don't do flirting, do they Jack?"

Jack maintained a proper silence in the face of that provocation.

"Our Marie's not spoken for yet," Ellen said—but that was a step too far for her husband, who practically barged her out of the way as he raced to the side of the mushy peas simmering on the hotplate, apparently fearful that disaster might be about to overtake them. When Canny's order was ready it was Jack who packaged up the haddock and chips and handed them over, saying: "Don't know how long I'm going to be able to get proper fish, milord. All but extinct, they say. Quotas aren't working—but if you ask me, the Hull boys are the only ones observing the quotas. The Icelanders and Norwegians don't care, and there's boats coming all the way up from Spain to poach. Who'd have thought it? When you and I were lads, we thought the fish would last forever, didn't we?"

"Yes Jack," Canny said, with a straight face. "I remember thinking exactly that, more than once. The Soviet Union will come apart, I used to think, and the Space Age will be over, but the haddock and the cod will endure forever. You can't rely on anything, these days—except cricket and taxes."

When the next day's business in Leeds was done he drove through Shipley all the way to Keighley Moor, just for a change, but the wind was hardly blowing at all. The sky was grey, its leaden clouds reaching down to touch the summits of all the surrounding hills, so that he seemed to be surrounded by stubborn obscurity. When he drove back, he found a Lexus that he had never seen before blocking the entrance to the stable which normally held the Bentley. His mother took the unprecedented step of coming out to meet him.

"You've got visitors, Can," she told him, in a voice that could have vitrified a wart.

"So I see," Canny said, gently. "Even if I couldn't see, you didn't have to come out to warn me. That's Bentley's job."

"No it isn't," she said. "Not in this case. There's some warnings only I can give you, and that fact that I know you won't listen doesn't let me off the hook."

"Don't be silly, Mummy," he said, still trying to keep the least trace of harshness out of his voice. "Did you mean the plural? Exactly how many visitors are there?"

"She brought her bodyguard with her this time—and a maid too. Can you imagine?"

"It's tradition, Mummy," Canny said. "You ought to approve.

In the good old days, when the entire aristocracy left London at the weekend to go to spiffing country-house parties, every young man took his manservant and every young lady her maid, Bodyguards were optional, mind. We've got plenty of room—it's no trouble." Secretly, he was pleased. If Lissa had brought servants and luggage, that implied an intention to stay for more than a fleeting visit.

"She'll break your heart, Can," Lady Credesdale was trying to keep a straight face, as befitted a dour Yorkshirewoman. but she couldn't help the dread showing through. "She's not our sort."

"Perhaps she will," Canny admitted. "But you're wrong about her not being our sort. She's more our sort than anyone I've ever met, or am ever likely to met. Anyway, I have to find out. There's no other way."

When he got indoors, Bentley was hovering inside the door, waiting to intercept him in his turn. "The lady's in the library, sir," he said. "I tried to explain...."

"That's all right," Canny said. "I'm the one who left the door unlocked."

Lissa Lo was not only in the library but in the inner sanctum, although Canny was certain that he hadn't left *that* door unlocked. This time, she was sitting *behind* the desk, in a chair that no one but a male Kilcannon had sat on since some lesser contemporary of Thomas Chippendale had carved and uphol-stered it. She had obviously told the truth about her lock-picking abilities.

"I expected a slightly warmer welcome," she observed, when Canny paused in his stride, with the desk still between them. "Last time I was here there was a funeral on—I didn't realize that it was like this all the time. Perhaps I should have called. Turning up unexpectedly with the full set of paraphernalia is a trifle impolite."

"How's your mother, Lissa?" he asked.

"Alive, if not exactly kicking," Lissa assured him. "She's not so very old, chronologically speaking, but her attitudes are ancient. The trouble with growing old—even if it's all in the mind—is that people lose interest in the future and become bogged down in the past. All change comes to seem threatening, and even retaining things exactly as they are seems a poor second best to the impossible quest of returning to a nostalgia-tinted past. I'm sorry she tried to throw the fear of God into you—she tries it with me all the time, so I'm used to it, but she must have taken you by surprise. Did she get to you?"

"No, she didn't," Canny said. "But I did get to myself, a little. I'm sorry about the cold welcome you got from Mummy and Bentley. They think you're some kind of *femme fatale*. They're right, of course, in a way—and they can't help resenting your influence over me. They've grown old too, and can't help seeing the future as a mass of ominous threats backed by the inevitability of death. It's understandable, if not entirely forgivable."

"They're only parents and servants, after all," Lissa said, dismissively. "Deconstructed any good moments lately?"

"I'm afraid not. I've glimpsed a few shadows, but my gift does seem to have become quiet, just as Daddy always said it would. I can't really complain about the way my luck's running, though. I'm not ahead of the game, but I'm not far behind it either. Perhaps the last few weeks have been one of these intervals when one needs fortune's prejudice just to stave off disaster."

"I've heard tell about those—but only from mother, of course. Well, things are looking up for you now. I'm sorry to have deprived you of my radiant presence for so long, but I really have had to move heaven and earth to cut the time as short as I have. You have no idea how hard I've had to work to create a year-long gap in my schedule, or even to make sure that no one will come looking for me for the next two weeks...not that they'd find me if they did, unless your crabby mother and her loyal servants start blabbing."

"They won't," Canny assured her. "Discretion is a way of life here. Do you think that two weeks will be a long enough gap, to begin with?"

"Long enough to destroy the world, I suppose, if we bring down your black lightning—or blast my illusion of Maya into the stuff of shattered dreams. Long enough, by the same token, to bring something special into the world for which the future will be eternally grateful. I love standing at the crossroads, knowing that whichever road I take will lead to a better place, don't you?"

"I've never been quite that confident," Canny admitted. "Afterwards, when the nausea's relented, I get the rush, but beforehand...perhaps I've never really *known*, even in a purely psychological sense. Perhaps I've always been conscious, at the back of my mind, of the fact that it could all go wrong—that at any moment, Lady Luck might cast me aside like a worn-out sock in favor of some new toy boy."

"It's not a fact," she said. "It's a fiction. You've let the burden of past superstitions weigh you down, Canny. You've let talk of deals with the devil seep into your conscience. You've started to grow old before your time by letting your father take too greedy a command of the family well. That's the way it's supposed to be in my homeland too, but globalization has all-but-obliterated traditional deference in the space of a single generation. God bless America, the land of youth and *Vanity Fair*! Not to mention *Cosmopolitan*, *Vogue*, *Time*, and *Life* and all the rest. Even *Hello!* and *OK!*. They made me what I am, and there was nothing my darling mother could do about it. You should be grateful for that. You *are* grateful, aren't you?"

"Daddy was always horrified by the idea that the family secret would ever come out," Canny observed, "and I can understand why. He was afraid that the hatred and envy people already felt for the Kilcannon luck would be further intensified. But that's not the kind of world we're living in now, is it? Today's world is just a vast spectrum of opportunities to be exploited. People don't hate success the way they used to—they idolize it, and try to copy it. I suppose they always hoped it would rub off—even in the Middle Ages, they thought that the mere touch of a king's hand might cure scrofula, and regarded some kinds of marriages as matters of magical alchemy, from which divinely-favored offspring might be born. I'm not so sure that this hasn't happened before, Lissa—but I don't know what the results were if it has. On that point, at least, history is vague."

"History's always vague," she told him. "Everything is vague, until people like us make an effort to see it clearly. If you won't confront the shadows, they'll consume you. If you do— the brightness is there, if only you look hard enough."

"Not according to Martin Ellison," Canny said. "According to him, it's all a matter of nEurological disorders—nEurones firing in the brain, sometimes at random but more often in response to stress, producing flashes of illusory light and surges of emotion that consciousness strives to rationalize as best it can."

"Martin Ellison is dead," Lissa said, baldly. "He was born unlucky, unlike us. He was so envious of what we have that he tried to argue it out of existence—but we're still here, with the world at our feet. You know that, and I know that you know it. We both know that no matter what anyone might say—including your father and my mother—you're with me on this. I'm willing to take risks that might improve our situation even further, and so are you. Your mother might think of it as a matter of her poor boy being unable to resist a wicked woman's temptation, but we know that's not the way it is. We know that it's better to live in hope than fear, and that people like us are far better equipped by nature to do it than fortune's fools. We have to do this, because we'll never forgive ourselves if we don't."

Canny remembered what his father had said about his never being able to forgive himself if things went awry, because he would always know that he could and should have done better. According to his father, there was a special Hell reserved for people of the Kilcannon kind, into which every one of them must fall who went in search of a special Heaven...but it hadn't stopped him, in his own young days, and perhaps he would have succeeded had he only had the right kind of help.

"It's never easy to forgive," he said. "But we do to have

think it through, even so. We have to consider the future—what happens *after* we contrive the ultimate orgasm."

She smiled, wryly but gloriously. "You have my word that I won't try to cut you out if there is a child," she said. "Mother lied about that. I won't marry you, but I have no intention of bearing a child who doesn't know his father. I always intended to share whatever rewards the adventure brings—not just because it would be stupid to turn co-operation into competition, but because it's the more courageous thing to do."

It wasn't as simple as that, and Canny knew it—but he wasn't sure how much even Lissa thought she knew about what might happen if she did bear the child of another of her kind.

Lissa rose to her feet with astonishing grace, and came around the desk to stand before him. It was, he supposed, all a matter of knowing how to walk.

She tilted her face, and invited him to take her in his arms and kiss her. It was as if he were in the front row of a widescreen cinema, looking at her in a close-up more intimate than any of which ordinary vision was capable.

He accepted the unspoken invitation.

When a couple of minutes had passed she detached herself, presumably having dispelled the last lingering doubts about his readiness to co-operate.

"I'm glad the old witch didn't make any lasting impression," she said. "She's clever—but she's the older generation. Closer to your age than mine, of course, but not part of our world, not a party to our modernity."

"She did make a lasting impression," Canny told her, blandly. "She told me that I have a responsibility to act like a man and not a slave of passion. She was right. I won't go into this telling myself that I'm helpless to resist. It has to be what I want to do, and what I need to do."

That was easy enough to say while the world remained in focus, he knew. He still feared that the black lightning and terror might come, if and when they overstepped the limits of uncertainty's tolerance, and knew that lust would not help him then—

but Lissa was right. To go forward together was the courageous thing to do, and to face whatever came of it as a couple rather than as individuals in competition was the right thing to do.

And even if it is lust, Canny thought, *there's nothing mere about it. Whether it's true love or not, it may still be more than equal to whatever the darkness can deliver.*

"And *is* it what you want and need to do?" Lissa asked, smiling because she already knew the answer.

"It is," he said.

CHAPTER THIRTY-THREE

Dinner was very civilized, all things considered, although the food was little better than mediocre. Canny brought up the last bottle of the '73 Pomerol in honor of their newly-founded tradition, and Lissa drank two glasses with evident relish, although she refused dessert and left the greater part of the main course on her plate.

"Miss Lo and her companions will be staying for a few days," Canny told Bentley, while the table was being cleared. "She doesn't want to be disturbed while she's here, and she doesn't want her presence here to be discussed outside these walls. If anyone asks for her on the phone, or in the village, you're to deny that she's in the house. I know that I can rely on the discretion of everyone on the staff, but if anyone making deliveries should catch sight of her, or either of her companions, you might need to have a quiet word. Can you do that?"

"I believe so, milord," Bentley said, with just a hint of sarcasm. "Provision has already been made for her maid and... manservant. Which room shall I make up for the lady?"

"Have her cases placed in the master bedroom—and put her car inside one of the stables, out of sight."

"Yes sir."

Lissa made no comment on this exchange; she obviously trusted her own servants' discretion, and fully expected Canny to have sufficient power over his.

When his mother had gone resignedly to her bedroom, leaving them alone in the drawing-room, Lissa seemed to become slightly uncomfortable for the first time. Now that her timetable had run its course and her objective was immediately before her, her puritanical habits began to reassert themselves. She was afflicted by a procrastination that he had not seen in her before.

"I suppose my mother spun you the usual line," she said. "We can't actually *do* anything—all we can contrive is to *undo* the work of the consensus, and that only momentarily. For which reason, collaboration is infinitely more dangerous than conflict, because we might undo so much that the consensus loses its grip for more than a moment."

"That's what she said," he confirmed.

"But you don't believe it?"

"I believe that she believes it."

Lissa nodded. "Me too. But the world's still here. The apocalypse isn't so cheaply bought."

"Step on a crack, break your mother's back," Canny quoted. "That's what the local kids used to say—but no one could remember anyone's mother ever having broken her back. Our fears do tend to be exaggerated—*our* fears more than most, I suspect. Unlike the average superstition, the mother's back thing didn't even need a single instance of coincidence to set it off—all it had to do was rhyme. According to the bullshit in the library, no one who saw black lightning ever lived to tell the tale...but that calls into question everything anyone's ever said about it. People who benefit from the white lightning are bound to fear the black, even if they never catch a glimpse of it...even if it doesn't really exist. On the other hand...."

"If there were such a thing," she finished for him, "and nobody who saw it ever lived to tell the tale, we'd have exactly the same absence of evidence."

"But as you say," he added, returning the compliment, "the world's still here. If it's ever been seriously disrupted, the consensus has always got a grip again, one way or another. The way I figure it, Lissa, you and I are the only ones taking a big risk, and we're entitled. We're adults, after all. My mother says you'll break my heart, and she might be right...but it's my heart. The other earls might have been paranoid about the succession, but that was the pressure of conventional expectation as much as the desperate desire to do anything that might be necessary to renew their good fortune. I'm going into this with open eyes, just like you. You have no need to feel guilty about your seductive powers."

"I don't," she assured him.

"This is just between the two of us," he went on. "We're responsible for our own risks, just as your mother said. I had to make an adult decision. Well, that's what I've made. If one or both of us loses the gift, or life itself, as a consequence of tempting fate a little too far...well, it's a risk we take. It's a risk everybody takes, at every one of life's turning-points. We're not so different from the average man and woman—just a little bit luckier. Sometimes, we can see the light, and that obliges us to fear the darkness—but for at least twenty-three hours, fifty-nine minutes and fifty-nine seconds of every day, we take what fate throws our way, just like everybody else. The rewards of being the most beautiful woman in the world may flow a little more strongly and constantly than the interest on the Kilcannon investments, but you don't need to bathe in the blood of innocent virgins to maintain it any more than I need to sacrifice them to the Great Skull. We're only human. We can allow ourselves to be human."

"Is that what we're doing?"

"Yes," he said, refusing to raise the issue of whether they were both being human in exactly the same way.

Lissa hesitated for a moment before saying: "I'm sorry for what I said about it being just an experiment, not a love-match."

Canny knew better than to raise the issue of whether she was sorry because it wasn't true, or because it was.

"I've always been alone," Lissa continued, after a pregnant silence. "Mother wouldn't like to hear me say it, but it's true. I've always been alone. Now, for the first time, there really are two of us—not bound together like conjoined twins fighting one another for access to a single blood supply, but independent individuals with our own hearts and minds, willing and able to make a coherent team. If we can only overcome our fear that simply being together might precipitate disaster...it might be good for us, in more ways than one."

In a way, he was glad that she had admitted that she *did* feel the fear, even though she gave the impression of someone who was stalling, making conversation because she wasn't quite ready to get down to action. The light in the room was steady and electric; there were no awkward shadows gathered in the corners, no smoky hazes forming up in the coverts—none, at least, that Canny could see. His mind was still quiet, untroubled by the phantasmagoric spin-off of any hereditary glitches that might be lurking in his cerebral cortex.

"I know what you mean," he said, mildly. "Daddy and I were never close. How could we be? I never fought him with the kind of ferocity you seem to have brought to competition with your mother, but not a day went by when I wasn't aware of the tension between us. You're right—it's because he and I were so tightly bound together that we were always alone. And you're right about the other thing, too. If we can make a coherent team, a real couple, it might be good for us in more ways than one. Even if playing double or quits were to end up quits, with our lucky streaks shattered forever, we'd still be able to understand one another better than most."

"We're not going to lose, Canny." she said. "We can't. That's the whole point."

"True," he conceded, readily enough. "We're not. We've never been destined for loneliness, no matter what our ancestors thought and feared—our kind may be rare, but there are others around—and if competition between beings of our kind is invariably disastrous, how come I'm the thirty-second earl? We're all in competition all the time, simply by being here, and the world isn't getting any less crowded. We're entitled to try— to run our own risks, and damn the consequences." *And you are one of the ten most beautiful women in the world*, he didn't add, *and my blood's as red as any in Yorkshire.*

"In that case," she said, softly, "we might as well go to bed."

The first time was awkward, as Canny had fully expected—not because their somewhat-limited experience had left them unprepared but because first times always were awkward. Because they both knew that, they hastened into the second with all due determination.

That was when Canny finally became able to feel that he had been carried away, and that it was good to have been carried away...because, after all, nothing terrible was going to happen.

Canny had never found it difficult to focus his attention during sex, because he always tried to make the most of it, for obvious reasons, but there had always been an excessive attentiveness in his focusing: an element of calculation that he had never been able to set aside. He had tried to set it aside more than once, most recently with Alice Ellison, but he had never quite succeeded. He had always hoped—*known*, Lissa Lo would probably have said—that it would be different with anyone with whom he embarked upon a longer-term relationship, but he had always feared, too, that setting aside the calculative hyperconsciousness might also set aside the intensity of the focus.

It didn't.

He had not the slightest difficulty in absorbing himself entirely in the sensations of Lissa's intimate presence: the touch sensations most of all, but the sight of her too, and the scent. He was too close to her now to take full account of the fact that she was very probably the best-looking woman in the whole world, but there was no doubt in his mind that she was the most exquisitely tangible. He lost himself in her presence, and forgot that there was anything else in the universe but her and the sensory pathways that carried her into his mind, where his consciousness of her seemed to float upon an infinite ocean of subliminal response.

There was no fear, because there was no longer any scope in Canny's supersaturated awareness in which fear could take form. For the first time in his life he felt that he was in a place where he had no need of luck, nor any premonition of anything to come.

He seemed to be in a moment that could not be deconstructed, no matter how temporary it might prove to be. He seemed to be in a state of mind that was secure against all anxiety, all thought, and all sensation—except for the sensation of being with Lissa Lo, and the sensation that she was with him, answering to his own touch, his own movement, his own emotional agitation.

There was no desperation in the way he clung to the moment, nor any effort needed to prolong it now that the first release of purely physical pressure had liberated him from that vulgar kind of need.

It was all he could have wished for.

While it lasted, it was all he could possibly need.

It didn't seem to last forever, or even for very long, but when it was over he felt sufficiently content to reflect that nothing ever did last forever, or—in the context of forever—even for very long.

When his train of thought began to move again, slowly, it moved in a new way: serene; uplifted; majestic. True love or not, it was as imperious as it was exhilarating.

Then, and only then—at least for Canny—the special effects began.

If it was a streak it was like none he had ever experienced before, but it was certainly bright. It was a kind of light he had never seen, or thought possible, of a color he had never before been able to perceive. If the world blurred at all, it did so very discreetly, as if it wanted to slip into soft focus but didn't quite dare, and therefore trembled on the brink, protractedly.

Canny didn't doubt that the tremor was pregnant with all manner of possibilities—all of them good and some of them miraculous—but he wasn't in the least inclined to exert any mental effort to precipitate them from the mist. He was, for the moment, languidly satisfied with the unapprehended, the unanticipated, the unrealized.

Perhaps, he thought, *this isn't an experience unique to people of my kind. Perhaps anyone and everyone can get to this state of satisfaction with a world hesitating on the brink of conclusive settlement. Perhaps it's a grail worth seeking, a prize worth keeping, a memory never to be surrendered.*

What it certainly was not, it seemed to him, was a deconstruction of the moment. It appeared to him to be the inverse of that: an enhancement of the moment; an elevation of the moment to a new expressiveness and a new expansiveness.

Perhaps, Canny continued, gladly following his train of thought, *the bright streaks have never been more than detritus, products of the decay of this very ordinary kind of light, this very ordinary kind of luck.*

It seemed, in his present state of mind, an amazing thought— but it didn't seem absurd.

Perhaps, he concluded, as the train ran on towards its terminus, *this is the first time that I've ever really seen what my gift was intended to let me see, the first time I've ever contrived to draw upon its full potential and isolate the crystallized reward from the echoes of its chaotic collapse.*

In the ancient world, Canny recalled, as the swell of thought calmed again, romantic love had been regarded as a kind of madness—the very antithesis of a secure base for an actual relationship. Romantic love could only lead to tragedy, because it cut across all the careful boundaries that constituted society's order; it could have no consequence but disgrace and ruin, and disgrace and ruin could have no further consequence but lifelong penance, or death. His ancestors—all the ancestors of all humankind, in fact—would have regarded the modern mythology of romance, which supposed love to be a maker rather than a breaker of marriages, was a lunatic folly, a universal flirtation with disaster.

But the world had changed.

The old order had passed, because its rigidity no longer served any purpose. The old boundaries had melted, because social unity no longer had to be secured by designating outsiders and enemies. The old terrors could be set aside, because there was nothing any longer to be feared more than fear itself.

Romantic love had seemed to the ancients to be a super-natural force, which carried people away in spite of all the resistance that reason could muster—to the extent that some Romantic fantasists had been prepared to assert, and perhaps to believe, that the only love that could ever satisfy a human heart was the love of a supernatural being, untainted by any of the frailties of flesh or constraints of everyday life.

Perhaps, Canny thought—knowing that he was being self-indulgent—*they were right*.

"Did you see it?" Lissa Lo asked him, in a whisper, when she had found a voice capable of carrying the question.

"Yes," he said, glad that she had seen it too. They were still entwined within one another's arms, and Canny was still glorying in the miracle of her presence, the marvel of her substance.

"No nausea," she said. "No vertigo. Just...the sum of what we have—what we are."

"Synergy," he said.

"We were right," she said. "We've made a child. I know it. I feel it. We've made a child."

That, Canny knew, was an imaginative step too far. He had educated himself in biology, and he knew that conception was far from instantaneous. If one of his sperm were fortunate enough to reach Lissa Lo's womb, and to find an egg waiting there, avid for fertilization, it would not do so for several hours yet.

If *that* union were eventually to be secured, it would happen tomorrow, perhaps around noon, when the sun was as high in the sky as the autumnal season allowed. They would not be in bed then, but they would surely be together—walking hand-in-hand, perhaps, on Cockayne Ridge, with the mythical terrain of the Land of Ease spread out before them, shallow moor succeeding shallow moor to the ascendant horizon.

And if that were to happen, how could it be other than a miracle child? If it were a boy, bearing his Y-chromosome, could it not also carry her gift on the X, or in the autosomes?

It would, he felt certain, be a boy. Did Lissa know that? Did she understand that it was the most fortunate outcome?

As a geneticist, Canny had to hope, and desire, that the child would be a boy—because a girl could not be carrying his lucky Y chromosome.

On the other hand, he realized, he was also bound, as a geneticist, to hypothesize that if Lissa's talent had always been passed down to her from mother to daughter, never displaying itself in any son, then it had to be a sex-limited gene, not a sex-linked one: a gene whose expression his Y-chromosome would suppress and prevent. Even if the child were a boy, his gift might find itself in competition with hers. Even if he and she were not in conscious competition—even if they really were united by heart and mind alike—their genes might be in conflict, locked in an age-old struggle to determine the sexual characteristics of the embryo they were sculpting.

So, at least, Canny was bound to think *as a geneticist.*

Was there, he wondered, a third possibility? A freak with a second X-chromosome as well as a Y, somatically female but genetically male, or a true hermaphrodite. Didn't occult tradition suggest that true miracle children combined the key features of both sexes?

No, he concluded, after a moment's reflection. It wasn't possible...*if it were a matter of genetics.* Either the genetic complement of the double X would suppress the expression of the genes favoring maleness, or the genes on the Y-chromosome would suppress those favoring femaleness; any confusion of the two could only be disruptive, obliterating potential rather than creating it.

If, on the other hand, it were a matter of magic, or miracle, or even madness....

That was unthinkable, or so he had to suppose. If genetics didn't hold the key, then it had to be something to do with the arcane mysteries of quantum mechanics: the bizarre and seemingly-paradoxical relationship between observers and events, and the manner in which the vagueness of potentiality was rendered down into the concrete certainty of reality. It had to be science—not magic; not mumbo-jumbo; not superstition; not blind terror, but something else. Something explicable, if only one could get one's head around it...but not the Road to Damascus Effect, not a mere matter of some nEuro-physiological disorder rumbling way in the brain like tremors in the earth's crust. It had to be explicable, but it also had to be real. The numbers couldn't lie. They could flatter and deceive, induce all kinds of illusions, appeal to all kinds of psychological predispositions, but they couldn't lie to a computer or a balance sheet. At the end of the day, something actually had to happen; at the end of the day, there had to be an authentic interaction, a meeting and melding of skewed probabilities, a collision of discreet destinies.

There really is no need to be afraid, Canny said to himself, silently, trying as hard as he could to mean it.

"There really is no need to be afraid," Lissa Lo said, aloud, her words overlaying his thought with uncanny neatness. "We can be together. We really can. It'll be our child, no matter whether it's a girl or boy. It's our good fortune, our triumph."

The culmination of our love, Canny added, still not daring to say the words aloud in case they fell victim to some cosmic stutter that would shatter their meaning. *The tie that will bind us together forever.*

After that, as if to prove the point, he slept—and never doubted, as he slipped away, that Lissa would sleep too, cradled in his arms: his world, his future, his fate.

CHAPTER THIRTY-FOUR

Canny and Lissa got up late, thus avoiding his mother's presence at the breakfast table. Indeed, Lady Credesdale had already gone out by the time they came down, obviously as keen as Canny to avoid an embarrassing confrontation.

Canny expected Bentley to be in his stiffest and most formal mode, and was not disappointed—but the butler was careful to overplay the role, moving it towards caricature; although he never actually cracked a smile, his eyes were by no means unamused. Even so, Canny thought it best to take a walk in order to remove themselves from the retainer's mildly discomfiting presence.

Fortunately, the weather was fine—what might have been described as an "Indian summer" in the days before global warming had caused the advent of autumn to be delayed on a routine basis.

They didn't linger long in the garden, but made haste to climb the hill, ignoring the disapproving specter of the Great Skull. Canny felt in need of a literal elevation to suit their emotional state, and Lissa seemed to be in complete agreement.

They walked along Cockayne Ridge hand-in-hand, with the gentle undulations of the dale spread out before them and the moors standing out with unusual clarity in the distance. The green horizon was clear cut against the blue sky, unconfused by any trace of atmospheric haze.

The beauty of the day didn't seem to Canny to be a coincidence, but he didn't think that the judgment was any mere illusion or acceptance of superstition. He preferred to think of it as indulging the dream, prolonging the moment.

It seemed to him that he had been sure, even before he awoke, that the day would be bright, with no clouds descending to shroud the tops of the hills and draw a veil around the Land of Cockayne. He counted the fact that he had been right as a testament to their shared luck, their communal good fortune.

"You can't see it at all from up here, can you?" Lissa observed, as they looked down at the slate roof of Credesdale House.

"See what?" he asked, momentarily puzzled.

"That skull-shaped rock-formation."

"The resemblance is partly a matter of perspective," he told her. "If you look out of the attic window over there, it doesn't look nearly as sinister as it does when you look up at it from ground-level. From up here, you can see that the slope isn't as sheer as it seems from below, and the apparent foreshortening works the other way around. You can see the rocks easily enough, but there's only one vantage-point from which they combine to form anything like an inverted skull. It's right over there, but you have to be careful—the slope is at its steepest just at that point. You could hurt yourself if you slipped. I slid all the way down once and nearly broke my leg."

"But you were lucky, and escaped with no more than a few superficial bruises," she said.

"Very lucky—but even if I *had* broken my leg, everyone would have told me how lucky I was not to break my neck."

"I'll be careful," she promised. "I'm good at keeping my balance."

Canny refused to let go of her hand, although there wasn't the least hint of a dark streak in the blue sky and his stomach was settled.

Lissa went right to the edge, pulling him along in her wake, and looked down.

"I see what you mean," she said. "From this angle, the eyes aren't round and the mouth's too thin. If I hadn't seen it from below, I wouldn't ever have been able to think of it as an inverted skull. Why didn't your remotest ancestor—or one of the nearer ones—build his house up here, free of that ominous stare?"

"Too exposed. The hillside provides shelter from the wind. It's mild now, but when it's blowing a gale...."

Lissa shook her head. "It wasn't that," she said. "The person who built the original house wanted the skull there. He wanted it as a *memento mori*...or perhaps a symbol, of his imagined guilt. Your rules forbid any interference with it, right?"

"Right," he confessed.

"If one of my ancestors had been in his place, it would definitely have been the guilt, but yours seem to have seen things rather differently. It's a *memento mori*, isn't it?

"Probably," Canny agreed. "But they suffered from the guilt too—perhaps they weren't as different from your foremothers as you think. It would probably need more fingers than I've got to count the Earls of Credesdale who convinced themselves that they really had made tacit pacts with the devil—and made human sacrifices of their own sons in so doing. *The luck of the devil* has always been more than a way of speaking in my family, even in the Age of Enlightenment. Daddy always denied that he took it seriously, of course, and I dare say that his father did the same—but I sometimes wonder whether I might be the first to be entirely free of that kind of anxiety."

"But you *are* entirely free of it?"

"Oh yes," he said. "Whether genes are involved or not, the Kilcannon luck is just an accident of happenstance. There's nothing to feel guilty about. You and I haven't done anything wrong. Whatever comes of this, we haven't done anything *wrong*."

Lissa came back from the edge, drawing him with her to safer ground. She turned her face up to his then, inviting a kiss. He felt the same impulse—the same causeless whim—and smiled at the coincidence.

This, he thought, must be the moment of conception.

And suddenly, he knew that it was.

Black lightning was a myth after all, he thought. The streak was bright—brighter than any he had ever seen. It dazzled him, blinded him, and catapulted him into a new way of seeing, a whole world of exotic sensation.

There was no tremor in his guts, no sword-thrust of pure objectless terror. The world, as it fell apart, did not darken in any way, even metaphorically; although it lost all trace of color, it did not even become grey, let alone black.

The world lost the *possibility* of color, just as it lost the possibility of mass, of space, of time—but a world there was...or a Heaven.

If the moment was, indeed, deconstructed it gained in timelessness what it lost in coherency. The flash, if flash it was, seemed to go on indefinitely.

Canny had the opportunity to remember reading, somewhere, that what seemed to human senses to be a single lightning flash was actually thousands of nanosecond-long flashes, united by the persistence of vision.

He also had the opportunity to reflect on the impossibility of his actually *perceiving* all that he saw and heard and felt, given that if the world had really been deconstructed his sensory apparatus and his brain must have fallen apart along with everything else. In any case, he knew, such an event was quite incapable of sensory expression. He knew, therefore, that anything that he believed he saw or felt could be no more than a reconstruction *after* the event: a kind of dream or confabulation; a belated attempt to grasp the ungraspable.

Canny could not doubt, though, that he was in a privileged position of some kind, in spite of the fact that he must have fallen apart along with everything else—and that what he constructed or reconstructed in his mind *en route* to Damascus was a kind of truth as well as a kind of warning, a kind of luck as well as a kind of terror.

No man can ever know what death is like, he thought, *no matter what effort he puts into the business of dying. No man can ever know what it is to be devoid of any appreciable existence, as what was once his self dissolves into a mere mist of potentialities.*

The thought was only part of his realization, which cut much deeper than thought itself—or that poor shadow of thought that was all he had been able to experience, until now.

It seemed that the kind of luck that allowed some favored individuals to avoid overmuch infliction of the pain of loss also allowed them to imagine, and even to believe, that they knew what *loss* was really like. Perhaps it was an incentive, provided by their genes and by their physical make-up, for those occasions when fear lost its force. So, at least, Canny tried to explain it to himself, when he was far enough removed from the pure horror of it to be able to think about it at all.

Illusion or not, he believed that he had felt the world dissolve around him, falling apart under a kind of stress that—for whatever reason—it couldn't endure. He believed, too, that he had felt the world reconstitute itself again, gracefully finding a new accommodation. There was no thunderous explosion, no violent tremor of any kind; from the viewpoint of the cosmos, it was no more than a reflexive twitch, too brief even to be described as a shudder, a frisson or a flicker. From the viewpoint of the cosmos, the concrete reality beyond the fabrications of human sensation, it was almost nothing.

It might, indeed, have been nothing at all—but between the moment in which Lissa Lo stumbled, having been suddenly transfixed by the conception of a miracle inside her womb, and the moment in which he snatched her back from the edge of the Great Skull, so that she could not tumble down the slope at risk to life and limb, he saw the future far more clearly than he had ever sensed it before, not as a shadow of unrealized possibilities but as a soaring arc of light, full of promise and actuality.

He saw Lissa give birth to a son, for which result she had hoped as fervently as he—because she too had realized that only a boy could possibly combine her gift with his. He saw the three of them together, coming gradually to the triumphant realization that her heritage had neither been suppressed nor diluted, having been transmitted not by genes at all but by the benign influence of the maternal environment. He shared in their discovery, by careful reasoning and investigation, of the fact that her maternal ancestors had been—*until that miraculous moment*—a chain of natural clones, who had required the intervention of a paternal sperm only as a trigger to the development of anomalous egg-cells which carried a full complement of maternal genes rather than a selective half. He shared in the revelation that she, alone of all her ancestors, had contrived to undo the perverse curse that usually rendered the conventionally-endowed egg-cells of her kind infertile. This had not been accomplished by means of any intervention of twenty-first century technology, but by sheer good fortune, thus allowing the extraordinary generosity of her womb—whose compensatory effect had prevented the damaged cell-line from becoming extinct—to work upon a hybrid embryo for the first time in many, many generations.

He saw that their son was greatly loved, and that Lissa had never intended to steal him away, or to use him as a conduit by means of which to drain Canny's luck as she had drained her mother's. He saw that Lissa was *not* a vampire, intent on giving birth to a unique child in order to have the means of remaining young herself for far longer than her resources would otherwise have permitted. He saw that Lissa was a loving human being, whose desire had always been to maximize the resources on which all three of them might draw, as a team whose like had never been seen before in human history. He saw that they became so extraordinarily fortunate, as their son grew to manhood, in qualitative as well as quantitative ways, that they helped the world to change even faster than it had begun to change of its own accord, so that the twenty-first century hastened towards an inevitable singularity at which everything became...incalculable, if not quite unimaginable.

And then...the present reasserted itself again. *A* present, at any rate. Not, he suspected, the one that they had left behind for an interval of time far briefer than the duration of a *real* lighting flash, but another, imposed by some censorious, fearful and *old* consensus.

Canny stumbled then, and they both fell—but they fell safely, on soft and level ground.

Lissa's eyes, which had been momentarily closed, opened again. They looked into his.

But they did not see him.

The moment she opened her eyes—her dazed, haunted, uninformed eyes—he knew the truth. She didn't have to say a word. She only had to look at him to tell him that she could not see him, and never had been able to see him, because she was not the person she had been before.

She had been a new Eve: Eternity's Eve, the mother of the future. Now, she was Lilith, cast out of Eden screeching in mortal anguish for the fate of her child, and all her children.

She did not hate him; she simply did not know him. He was a stranger, unimportant in her eyes. There was no longer anything special about him, anything attractive. In her heart and mind, he had ceased to exist.

From his own point of view—and, more significantly, the point of view that had been Lissa Lo's—the reflexive *tic* by means of which the universe had readjusted itself was almost everything. It had destroyed her, and in so doing, it had destroyed him. It had destroyed him more utterly by leaving him more-or-less untouched than it would have done by altering him as it altered her. Whether that ought to be regarded an accident of minimalism, or an ironic punishment, he did not care to judge. He did ask himself why—how could he help it?—but he knew that it was an unanswerable question. There was no *why*. None of this was deliberate. The universe was not actively intervening to save itself from the disruptive power of a potential miracle-child. It was just a matter of *confusion*: an amplification of echoes, whose feedback could not be sustained.

It was all a matter of luck.

What had taken place was such a trivial reconstruction of the world that the only thing destroyed in her was quite intangible: a mere phantom of electrical states in the brain and the chemical transactions that produced them. Her image could not disappear from millions of photographs in thousands of magazines; her physical presence was far too complex a knot to be unraveled—but what remained of her in the world was not what she had been.

The object of universal destruction had been the moment of their child's conception, and all that went with it: not merely the moment at which the head of the sperm penetrated the egg-cell, but all the intangible components of its causality: the illusion, the ambition, the desire, the hubris, the curiosity. She had been the prime mover in all of that, and she was the one who bore its loss.

Canny had to wonder, when he realized that, how much real cause he had for regret in the judgment handed down to him by the reconstruction—the callous, contemptuous judgment that his role had been so passive, so slightly relevant, that his memory did not warrant erasure or perversion.

In a way, that was the worst thing of all.

The woman in his arms looked into his eyes, dizzy with confusion, and he knew that Lissa—the Lissa he had known, and loved—had gone. The new one knew who he was, in the sense that she knew his name, and knew that they had met once or twice—but she did not *know* him. They had not made a child, nor had she ever had any intention of so doing. She did not know what she was doing here, and had no memory of what had happened—to him, at least—the previous night.

It was all in her eyes, all in the animating intelligence of her startled gaze.

I'll win her back, he thought. *Whatever it takes, I'll win her back. We can still be together. We can try again.* Even the thought was enough to set off an aftershock of darkness and nausea, though. He knew that the die had been cast, and that the wager was lost, and that there was no way to turn back time.

There was more, and worse, to come.

While he looked down at her, and saw what he saw, Lissa Lo began to age. Her face changed—perhaps not as much as the face of the Lo-Tsen who unwisely ran away from Shangri-La, but quite visibly. Perhaps, when her face had ceased to change, she looked no older than her true age—but if so, then Lissa had not merely seemed far younger than she really was, but had actually been much younger than she actually was, in body and attitude alike.

It was, he supposed, all a matter of knowing how to walk.

He looked up then, at last, and saw Lo Chen standing there, flanked by Lissa's bodyguard and maid.

Lo Chen looked younger by far than she had when she confronted him in the house at Frimley. She still looked older than her daughter—her clone—but no older than she really was.

"I've come to take her home," Lo Chen said. "She will need to rest—to recover herself. Fortunately, she has no commitments for a while, and will not be missed.

"You knew, didn't you?" Canny said. "You knew all along that this would happen. You wanted it to happen. You weren't trying to put me off—you knew that I'd be more likely, not less, to want to go ahead."

"Don't be ridiculous, Lord Credesdale," Lo Chen said. "I was warned, of course, else I would not be here. You saw and felt the warning yourself, when I summoned you. You saw what I saw, felt what I felt—but you did not understand, any more than I did. How could I possibly have *known*? How could you imagine that I *wanted* this? Am I not her mother, closer to her than any mother ever could be to a cuckoo-child? You know nothing; you understand nothing. We do not need you. We never have. No good could ever come of our knowing you, and there was always more danger in collaboration than competition. I played fair with you, Lord Credesdale. I urged you to see sense."

"I have seen sense," Canny murmured. "It's gone, now."

"May I take her?" Lo Chen asked—although it wasn't really a question, and it was in fact the bodyguard who stepped forward and lifted Lissa up in his arms, ready to carry her down the slope to the Lexus that was no longer hidden in the stable but parked in the yard, ready to depart. Canny didn't doubt that

Lissa's suitcases would be in the boot, fully and neatly packed.

"Shall I call Dr Hale in Cockayne and ask him to take a look at her?" Canny asked. Lissa had not broken any bones when she fell, and hadn't even sustained any obvious bruises, but her eyes were wild and confused and she didn't seem able to speak. She knew that something had happened to her but she didn't know what. It would probably take her a while to catch up with the world as it now was—but she would do it.

"That's not necessary," Lo Chen said. "It's not western medicine that she needs. She's had too much of that these last few years. You do know, don't you, that you won't be able to see her again—not because I forbid it, but because she doesn't wish to? You do understand that the folly is ended?"

"Yes," Canny said. "I know."

He did know. Just as he had known that the day would be fine, Canny knew what had happened to Lissa even in the absence of any blatant evidential confirmation in word or gesture. He knew, as soon as he had perceived and understood the deconstruction of the moment, what it was that had been leeched out of reality and substituted by a subtle poison, calculated to thin the blood of passion and life and prevent the coagulation of desire and purpose. He *knew*, far more precisely than he had ever been able to judge the oracular quality of any of his premonitory streaks. For once, his mind had been stripped absolutely bare by the presence and force of the reality that made him what he was, and he could not put up the slightest resistance to the exactitude of its revelation.

He knew *everything*.

He even knew that Alice Ellison, summoning the shade of her dead husband, would curl her lip as she referred him to the second aspect of the "Road to Damascus Effect": the irresistible sensation of conviction that sometimes accompanied the sensory hallucinations generated by the spontaneous firing of unruly nEurons. This, she would argue, was the basis of the most powerful prophetic illusions of them all—the illusion of communication with God, the source of a faith that could never be dismantled or corroded by rational argument or subsequent experience.

But Canny had neither seen nor heard from God. He had conceived no faith. What he knew—and it was true—was something far more intimate, and perhaps far more trivial...although it did not seem so.

He knew that he had lost Lissa Lo. She was gone, and in her place was someone else: someone who would never have dared to suggest the experiment that had brought them together, the project that really had enabled them to move the world. She had been replaced by someone who could never have wanted *him*, for any reason whatsoever. All of that had been sucked from the marrow of her being, not by her mother-vampire but by jealous fate; she was not merely different now from what she had been before but less.

But she hadn't fallen down the slope. She hadn't broken her bones on the unforgiving rocks of the Great Skull. She hadn't fractured her own skull, or even broken her heart.

In an way, she had been lucky.

So had he.

Canny knew that all the people in Cockayne would continue to think that he was a lucky Kilcannon, and would always say that he had the luck of the devil. Everyone would think that, and say that—with one possible exception. And they would be right. By every conceivable standard, except his own private conviction, they would be right.

He was lucky not to have broken his arm when he fell—and even if he *had* broken his arm, he would have been lucky not to kill himself. He was lucky to find himself unchanged, given that he might have been changed—and even if he *had* been changed, he would have been lucky not to have been erased. He was lucky to have loved and lost, given that he might never have loved at all, and there was even a sense—albeit a cruelly ironic one—in which he was lucky to have been the loser, when he might have been the lost. He was lucky that he had not been struck by the black lightning, even though he was lucky enough, perhaps, to have found out what the phrase really meant, to those who could read the ancient wisdom in the way that the ancient wisdom was intended to be read.

Lissa was lucky too, in a way. In another way, of course, she was not—but that other way was no longer possible, let alone material.

That was the trouble with luck, Canny thought, as he watched Lo Chen follow the bodyguard and is burden down he hill, followed in her turn by the patient maid; it was rarely unambiguous. Even when you sat at a roulette table and placed a bet, when there seemed to be no alternatives available but winning or losing and nothing at stake but mere money, luck was by no means unambiguous. Sometimes, winning led to trouble. Sometimes, losing led in the opposite direction. The house percentage was all that was perceptible and calculable, but that was only a fraction of the whole phenomenon of luck, by no means its greater part merely because it was calculable.

The greater part was what he and Lissa had found, or at least glimpsed, within the last twenty-four hours...the part that their bargain with fate had refused, in the end, to sanction.

Lucky at cards, unlucky in love, declared one of the clichés that poor Martin Ellison had been so assiduous in collecting, so interested in understanding. But who was really qualified to judge, at the end of the day, exactly how lucky or unlucky Lissa Lo had been when the moment of conception of her miracle child had killed her? It had, after all, placed a clone in her place, who would doubtless carry her career forward when she had rested a while, perhaps to even greater heights of success, and make a spectacular marriage with an entirely suitable husband.

Perhaps, Canny thought, that was calculated in the accounts of the idiot cosmic mind, not as a loss but as a gain, not as a punishment but as a reward, not as misfortune but as salvation. But that was to fall, yet again, into the trap of thinking that there as some kind of justice in what had happened, or some kind of reasoning. There wasn't. It was just a matter of exotic cause-and effect, of freakish accident, or utter confusion.

There was not a mark on Lissa's lovely body, let alone any evidence of a cause of "death"—but Canny knew that the violation of cause and effect had always been her domain as well as his; and he had always known, although he had refused to voice the knowledge of late, how much luck everyone needed merely to maintain the miracle of life within the frail envelope of flesh. That was especially true, he now understood, in a world where every moment that passed might be deconstructed and reconstructed, blotted out and rewritten, dissolved into uncertainty and crystallized out again as something not merely certain but inevitable...something that could never have been otherwise than it was.

CHAPTER THIRTY-FIVE

Canny went down the hill after Lo Chen, and caught up with her in the yard, as the bodyguard was laying Lissa down in the back seat. It was the maid, not Lo Chen, who got in with her, to make sure that she would be as comfortable as possible. Lo Chen made ready to get into the front passenger seat, from which she could direct the driver, but she turned to Canny again before she did so. "I could not know what would happen, any more than I can know exactly what did happen," she told him, before adding her own question: "Do *you* know what happened?"

It was an honest question. She didn't know. She wondered if he did. He wondered, in his turn, whether she would pity him if he told her everything. He decided, after only a moment's reflection, that she wouldn't.

"Yes," he said. "I know what happened. I remember the world as it was, and am a stranger in this one."

She didn't tell him that he was talking nonsense, although she might well have been entitled to do so. "We are all strangers in the world," she told him. "Your kind and mine more than many others. We all live in the world we construct by common consent, and we all long for worlds that might have been and might yet be, had we only the wit to realize their potential. We all believe that we know the world for what it is, for that is the price of its existence, but the only real power we have is the power of hindrance and interruption; to mistake that for the power of creation is vanity. We are neither artists nor architects, you and I, but merely skilful fugitives who sometimes contrive to hide—for a little while—from the oppressions of implacable causality."

"You knew that something like this would happen," he said, not to be put off, "even if you didn't know exactly what it would be—and you wanted it to happen. You knew that whatever happened would hurt her, slow the pace of your own deterioration. You wanted her to over-reach herself, to stumble, to fall. Your ancestors kept no written records, but you have your legacy of accumulated experience."

"How could I know more than the darkness could tell me?" Lo Chen retorted, reinforcing her insistence. "If there had been any more to know, she would have known it too. You were there when the dark streak terrified us all. You know that I had no more ability to read it than you did."

Canny didn't believe her. He could not doubt that Lissa Lo had been diminished by the failure of her bold experiment, and that her diminution was matched by an increase in her mother's portion of their family fortune. In due course, Lo Chen would die as his own father had died, but in the meantime, Lissa would be a more obedient and patient child, a more docile partner in the game of chance. But he, too, had known no more than he could read in the darkness, and had not even taken proper heed of the darkness while Lissa's radiance had blotted it out...and he had always been an obedient and patient son, unable to challenge his father's authority in any but the pettiest rebellions.

His mother arrived home in the Citroen just as the Lexus drove away; the two vehicles passed one another in the driveway.

"What happened, Can?" Lady Credesdale asked, as she got out of her car. "I thought your friend was going to stay for a few days."

"Lissa had a slight accident, Mummy," Canny told her, soothingly. "She's not hurt—just a little confused. She didn't want me to go with her. It really wasn't my fault, but I don't think she'll want to see me again."

"That's no great loss," his mother said, blissfully unaware of her own brutality. "I could tell during dinner that she didn't really like you—that she was just amusing herself. You didn't really think that there was anything between you, did you?"

"I'm not a mind-reader, Mummy, except for the occasional flash of insight," he said. "Most of the time, I can't even imagine what people might be thinking. But whatever there was between us is gone know. Strange, isn't it, how these things can evaporate in a moment, without the ghost of a reason?"

"It was all in your mind, Can," his loving mother told him, seemingly making every effort to be kind in spite of the harshness of the judgment. "I'm surprised she accepted your invitation. If you want my opinion, I think she was hoping to get together with that footballer without the press finding out. Did you know that he's playing for Leeds now? Of course you did—you went to the party, didn't you? I think she was hoping to set up an assignation here, out of the reach of prying eyes. They probably planned it when they came to Daddy's funeral."

"That's not how it was, Mummy."

"You take after your father when it comes to women, Can," the dowager Lady Credesdale went on, relentlessly. "He was always a fool for a pretty face. Do you think I never saw the look in his eye when he turned away from me to follow some silly bit of skirt with that moony expression? Do you think I didn't understand that he always felt *trapped*?"

"He didn't feel trapped by you, Mummy," Canny told her, truthfully. "He felt trapped by the weight of tradition, the legacy of a thousand years of expectation and custom."

"You don't have to spare my feelings, Can," she said. "For once, I'm not trying to spare yours. She didn't want you, no matter how much you wanted her—and it wasn't really her you wanted anyway. It was her image, what she stood for. But that's no way to manage your life, Can. You can probably use the title as a hook to snare pretty girls, if that's what you want, but what kind of pretty girls will you catch? It's not the right way to do it, and there'd so much more to life than that. You have to see sense, Can—even if you can't resist the temptation to look sideways for the rest of your life every time a bit of fluff drifts by, you have to be sensible. Not because it's what Daddy would have wanted, but just because it *is* the sensible way to do things. She's not our sort, Can—not because she's Oriental, but because she's not part of *our world*. You do see what I mean, don't you?"

"I understand what you mean, Mummy," Canny assured her. "I'm sure Daddy would be proud of you, if he could hear you— but you're free of him now. You're free of his expectations, his restrictions, his superstitions. I'm not—but you are. Think on that. You can be anything you want to be, now."

"Don't be silly, Canny," she said, after a pause. "People can't be anything they want to be. They can only be what nature made them. We're what we are, you and I, and you need to accept that."

"How about you, Bentley?" Canny asked, when the butler came out of the house to meet them as they moved towards the door. "Are you what nature made you?"

"Certainly, sir," was the inevitable answer. There was nothing caricaturish in Bentley's manner now; the spark of satire seemed to have vanished, for the moment, with the world that had inspired it—although it would doubtless reassert itself in time.

"Mummy reckons that Lissa Lo was only scouting the place out to see if it would make a convenient hideaway for meeting Stevie Larkin on the sly," Canny told him. "Is that what the gossips are saying in the kitchen?"

"It's not for me to speculate, sir," Bentley observed, shrewdly.

"Well," Canny said, "at least we had our one night stand. No one an take that away from us." He didn't know, in fact, whether that *had* been taken away from the realm of objective reality by fate's hasty reshuffle, but he did know that Bentley was too discreet to confirm or deny any judgment he might have made— and that his mother would have made scrupulously certain that she had no information on the subject one way or another.

"Actually, sir," Bentley said. "Mr. Larkin did phone. He didn't mention Miss Lo, but he did mention the possibility of you and he meeting up. He seemed strangely anxious that you might not return the call, although I can't imagine why. Perhaps he thinks that you still haven't replaced your mobile phone—or perhaps you forgot to give him your new number."

"I haven't got around to circulating the new number," Canny admitted. "I'll ring him later to fix something up."

"I hope he won't be too disappointed to hear about Miss Lo's accident," Lady Credesdale put in.

"He'll cope," Canny assured her. "If any reporters should call, Bentley, you'd better deny that Lissa Lo was ever in the house. It doesn't matter whether they believe you or not. We don't know where she is, and we know nothing about any accident."

"Yes sir."

In the event the paparazzi never did come calling; Lissa and Lo Chen had covered their tracks so well that no discoverable evidence now remained that Lissa Lo had visited Credesdale House since the funeral of the thirty-first earl. Her image could still be found in back issues of *Cosmopolitan* and *Hello!* tucked away in the magazine-rack, but of her physical presence and eager vitality there was no trace whatsoever.

Lo Chen never phoned to report on her condition, nor did Lissa contact Canny herself. It was as if he had never met her.

By the time three days had passed, Canny actually began to wonder whether he had imagined the details of their brief affair—but he knew that the fantasy was too self-indulgent. He knew what had happened, and he knew *everything* that had happened, in the world that now was as well as the world that had been.

He had seen it in her eyes.

He wondered, too, whether he ought to reckon himself lucky that the universe in which he had lived the greater part of his life had chosen to conserve him and destroy her, preserving itself for his memory while obliterating itself from hers.

What a privilege that was, if only he could ignore the pain!

The despotic Imperium of actuality had refused to produce any kind of child by means of their ill-starred union, but its blind, unreasoning, utterly confused reflex had let him live while she died. If there had been an element of competition in their collaboration, he had won, in spite of all the odds stacked against him. Even Lo Chen had been convinced, when she handed down her deceptive warning, that Lissa might hold the upper hand—but she had not reckoned with the Kilcannon luck, which had held in spite of its alleged dormancy, just as it had when Stevie had been kidnapped.

Unless, of course, it was Lissa's luck that had protected him, as she had sworn that it would, while his was impotent to intervene. Or perhaps—a much more extravagant unlikelihood—it had been the luck of his own nascent miracle-son, in spite of the fact that his existence had been so infinitesimally brief.

If, as Canny had quoted only recently—from Sophocles, he now remembered—the best thing was not to be born at all, and after that to die young, perhaps the child had been the luckiest of all the Kilcannons. Perhaps he had reached out from the ephemeral moment of his almost-existence to let his father know that. At the same time, the child might have protected his mother from the knowledge that she had not, after all, been favored by the luck of the chromosomal draw. Perhaps the child had been more powerful than either he or Lissa had been able to imagine—and perhaps his awesome prescience had informed him that, although existence was a thing to be avoided, blissful ignorance ought sometimes to be reserved for those who needed it.

But that, of course, was asking *why* again, and there was no *why*. It was all just a matter of chance, of quantitative probability, with no qualitative dimension at all. It was all horribly unfair, but the cosmic balance knew nothing of fairness; it was not that sort of balance.

On the fourth day he met up with Stevie Larkin for a meal in a restaurant in Leeds. They were together for five hours, during which time Lissa Lo's name wasn't mentioned once. They talked about exchange-rates, Italy, guns, football, organized crime, friendship and fish and chips. It was a welcome, if temporary, relief.

By the time Canny secluded himself in the library at Credesdale on the following day, however, he had relegated Stevie to the status of a mere revenant—an illusion of reconstitution, who had not the means to know that he was just a copy, and not a real thing at all. It was possible to convince himself, for a moment or two, that his own Lissa Lo had never actually existed at all—except as a hallucinatory element of his curse—but each such momentary success only served to increase the darkness of the returned conviction that blasted the truth into his reluctant brain time and time again.

The inescapable truth was that Lissa had not only existed in the flesh, but that she had been the finest thing the old world—the true world—had contained...until he had broken the rules, precipitating her destruction, and the destruction of all the children he and she might have had.

What a power he had to spoil, to diminish, to subvert, to impoverish!

What an expert he was at interference, at prevention, at annihilation!

Lucky Canny Kilcannon!

Lucky Killer Kilcannon, possessed of the power to blast universes apart, inflicting scars upon them that could never be fully healed.

Did he dare to hope, he wondered as he turned the pages of the ancient diaries, that there was another universe somewhere in the infinite manifold of potential universes, existing in parallel to this one, in which Lissa had not changed but that *he* had forgotten that he had ever loved *her*?

No, he didn't. He couldn't.

Once, he might have dared, but not now. He knew better. He had been cured of that kind of daring. He would have to find another if he were to live as a man and not a slave of chance.

CHAPTER THIRTY-SIX

As soon as Canny heard from the ever-reliable Bentley that Alice Ellison was back in Cockayne again to visit her parents he walked down to the village and knocked on the door of the Proffitt house. This time, Mrs Proffitt didn't seem in the least surprised to see him.

"She's gone to see our Ellen at the fish shop," she said.

"Of course," Canny said, nodding his head. "I should have looked in on my way past, shouldn't I?"

Jack Ormondroyd was alone behind the counter, the shop having only just opened for the evening shift. He shouted for Ellen and Alice to come out as soon as he saw Canny walk in.

"Hello, Canny," said Ellen. "Haddock and chips, is it? Bit early for you."

"Actually," Canny aid, "I was looking for Alice. There's something up at the house that I need her to take a look at."

Ellen raised a quizzical eyebrow but Jack's face remained deliberately set. Alice also seemed surprised by the baldness of the declaration, and her expression was tinged by suspicion—as if she feared that he might be about to let something slip about her excursion to London.

"You want to hear the latest about the trial?" She said, although it must have sounded just as unlikely to her as it did to everybody else. The trial of her husband's murderers was still more than a month away, and there would be no news until it actually started.

"That too, of course," he said, "and to find out how you are. I thought you might ring. I left a message on your answer-phone three or four days ago."

"Sorry," she said, as she ducked under the counter. "Been a bit distracted. I won't be long, El."

Once they were out on the street, she said "Is this wise? Everyone will see us."

"So what," Canny said. "I won't say we've nothing to hide, but I don't see that hiding it commits us to avoid speaking to one another for the rest of our lives. We made promises, remember? I'd be there if you needed me, and you'd be there if I needed you."

She seemed surprised by the implication. "Why?" she said. "What's happened to you? Nothing that our Ellen's heard about."

"Nothing that your Ellen could have heard about," Canny said. "But there's more to the world than passes for gossip in the local chippy."

Alice looked swiftly from side to side, but they were already outside the village boundary, and there was no one within earshot. Now that the county was back on Greenwich Mean Time, evening came early; the dusk was already closing in on them

"Does this have owt to do with Lissa Lo?" Alice guessed, reverting just for a moment to a way of speaking she'd polished away during the last decade.

"Yes," he said.

"She let you down?"

"In a manner of speaking."

"Not gently?"

"No, not gently."

"Right." She thought about that for a few moments, and then said: "Some people might think you've got a fucking nerve, Canny Kilcannon, coming crying to me because some super-model you've been mooning over has kicked you into touch. What am I supposed to be—the fucking consolation prize?"

"No," he said. "It's not like that. As I said in the shop, there's something at the house that I need to show you." He wasn't absolutely sure whether or not he was lying about the matter of her being the consolation prize, but they were both living in a world where he had never had a chance of establishing a fruitful relationship with Lissa Lo.

"What is it?"

"You'll see. But I did want to talk to you, and I was surprised when you didn't call back. *Doesn't run away, our Alice*—that's what Ellen said. You're the one person I can talk to with some slight show of honesty, and I needed that. You have come home, though—I'm grateful for that."

Alice didn't bother to assert, angrily or otherwise, that her only reason for returning to Cockayne was to see her mother, father, sister and niece. "Well then," she said, as they made their way along the Crede beneath a sky patched with cloud, "tell me about Lissa Lo—with some slight show of honesty."

"She was here last week—but I don't think Ellen found out about it."

"She didn't mention it—and she would have, if she'd known. What happened?"

"She had a slight fall on the Ridge. She wasn't hurt, but she was shaken up a bit. Martin would probably have judged that she had a flash—a slight nEurophysiological shock, due to a hereditary condition."

"Whereas you think she had a premonition?"

"No. Nothing so simple. But it did change things. It changed all sorts of things. Her mother had to come and take her way. She'll be back at work in no time, I dare say. But it changed things."

"So you keep saying. What is it you want, Canny? If it's a replay of that night of passion, I guess I owe you that...although it might have been more convenient if you'd come over to Leeds."

"For something that you claimed was no big deal," he observed, "I believe you're letting that prey on your mind a little."

"No I'm not," she lied.

"I wanted to tell you that you were right," he said, as they arrived at the gate of Credesdale House.

"About what?"

"About everything. Everything you said about the Kilcannon lucky streak—about what I might take as evidence to convince me that it was real, including the flashes of apparent light in my brain. It was all true."

"I know that. You gave it all away—a lousy performance, for a man with your reputation as a poker player."

"But it wasn't the whole truth."

"Well, I gathered you probably thought that too. And at the end of the day, why not? You're an earl, and you probably have assets worth several million pounds, including a mill that's moved with the times more cleverly than most, and a whole fucking village to play lord of the manor in. I can see why you might think that the Kilcannon luck is real. I'm not going to try to talk you out of it."

"I nearly got shot the day I brought you back to Leeds from London," he said. "I went to pay a million Euros ransom to the people who robbed me in Monte, but it was a trap—they wanted to kill me as well as taking the money. I walked out without a scratch, and most of the million was back in the bank first thing."

"Ellen should *really* have heard about that," was Alice's immediate response to this news. "She must be getting sloppy in her old age—either that or you're becoming a world-class secret-keeper. What ransom? Who were you supposed to be ransoming?"

"Stevie Larkin. Nobody knows about it, and we'd both appreciate it if you kept quiet about it. If they dig up the three bodies, they'll probably find little bits of my mobile phone embedded in one of them, along with several bullets. I didn't kill them, and Stevie could testify to that, but the people who did kill them don't appreciate publicity."

"So what the fuck are you telling *me* for?" she demanded, as he let them into the house.

"I thought we'd settled that. I can talk to you. You can talk to me. We don't worry about being insensitive. We just help one another along."

"Where to?" was her counter to that. Her timing was accidental, but no less neat in consequence; they had just reached the library door. Canny opened it, and ushered her in. Then he opened the second door, and the third. He could tell that she was impressed by all three rooms.

"Cool," she observed. "Very cozy—especially if you're a world-class secret-keeper." Then she took note of the fact that there were two chairs in the inner sanctum, one on either side of the table. "Is that where Lissa Lo sat?" she demanded.

"Twice," the confirmed, scrupulously. "The last time, she sat in my chair." Having said that, he sat down in the chair at which he'd just pointed. She took the other, meekly enough.

Canny pointed to the open cupboard. "Those," he said, "are the Kilcannon family diaries. They go all the way back to the mid-eighteenth century. They contain as complete a record as was then recoverable of the Kilcannon family legends, stretching all the way back to the Middle Ages. I asked Bentley to order me some dynamite today, by the way."

The abrupt change of subject took her by surprise, as it had been intended to do. "Dynamite?" she echoed. "Why?"

"One of the things you'll find out when you read the diaries," he said, "is that there are very explicit instructions about the necessity of preserving the Great Skull."

She must have remembered, then, what she'd said about a couple of judiciously-placed sticks of dynamite—but that wasn't the theme she took up. "Am I going to read them?" she asked.

"You'll have to, won't you. if you're going to write a history of the Kilcannon streak?"

She stared at him, not knowing quite what to say. "What I suggested," she reminded him, "was that I might write a history of Cockayne. The mill and the village—not the family."

"True," he said. "That would be an interesting book too. But it might not sell as well as a history of the Kilcannon luck, complete with a record of all its rituals and regulations. That wouldn't just appeal to historians, you see—it would find a public avid to try out all the formulas and spells, no matter how carefully you analyzed it in terms of the theory of psychological probability. You wouldn't just be writing a history of reckless superstition—you'd be laying the groundwork for a burgeoning industry."

She paused for a moment before saying: "Isn't one of those regulations an instruction that the secrets should never be revealed to a living soul?"

"Of course—but the reading public won't mind that, and few of its members will be such connoisseurs of paradox as to realize that the fact that they're reading all about the magic is a cast-iron guarantee that it will never work again, if it ever did."

"Why would you want me to write a book like that?" Alice asked. "I'd be grateful for the opportunity, I suppose—but I don't believe in the Kilcannon luck. You do, don't you?"

"Yes," he said. "I do. Even now. I'll still believe in it when I've blasted the Great Skull to smithereens and broken most of the other rules in the books. It's the superstition I don't believe in. I want to banish that—to eliminate it from consideration, so that the luck can be free from all the paranoid crap that presently surrounds it. It's a bold move, I admit, but I'm in a reckless mood just now, and I don't think it's the kind of mood that might evaporate if I take a few more walks on the moors or a train to King's Cross. It would be a lot of work, mind. You'd have to spend a lot of time here. You might be able to get a flat in the village, of course, but if not you'd probably have to stay here at the house. It wouldn't be entirely your book, either—it would be a collaboration, a joint venture. Would you mind that?"

"I'd have to think about it," Alice said, warily.

"Of course you would," Canny said. "After all, people would be bound to talk, wouldn't they? You're a widow and I'm a single man. You know what the villagers are like, even without Ellen to egg them on. It would probably ruin your reputation, even if you did manage to get a flat. People would be keeping track of your comings and goings every day of the week, always speculating. We'd probably have to get married, eventually, just to save Jem and Madge's blushes."

He would rather have been able to shocked her as profoundly as she'd one shocked him, but she was too wary for that—and the effect would, in any case, have been considerably ameliorated by the fact that she didn't have a mouthful of ham-and-mushroom pizza.

"If that's a proposal, you bastard," she said, eventually, "it's the most dreadful one I ever heard. Even Martin had the grace to *ask*."

"So will I, when the time comes," Canny assured her. "I'm not making conditions, Alice. I'm just pointing out the logic of the situation. I want you to write this book. If the collaboration brings us closer together, that will be an added bonus. If you want to make conditions that will allow you to do it without getting too close, that's fine—but the diaries have to stay in the house. They're entailed. They have to be preserved here for my son, whether or not he's your son too. He'll have to make his own decisions about how to carry matters forward. You don't have to give me an answer until you're ready, of course—you can have all the time you need to reach a reasoned decision, not just about the book but everything."

"You bastard," she said, again. "Do you really think I want to be somebody's *second choice*?"

"I'd be yours," he pointed out. "But no, I don't. And I don't think it's a relevant issue. It's not the right way to look at things, because it isn't true. London's preyed on my mind too—and not just because you made me choke on a pizza and then hit me right between the eyes with all that stuff about the Road to Damascus effect. I need you, Alice. I need you more than anything I've ever needed in my life."

"You needed Lissa Lo."

"No I didn't. I never thought I *needed* her, not for an instant. She and I had a lot in common, including some of the same privileges and delusions, but that didn't mean that we needed one another. Quite the reverse, in fact. It meant that we ought to have avoided one another. I see that now, and so does Lissa. What we both needed, and still need, is someone to balance out our outlandish convictions, someone to provide an anchor in the real world."

"An anchor? You're sure you don't mean a millstone round your neck?"

"Jesus, Alice," he complained. "You could let up a *little* bit. I just offered to let you write a book that you're probably better qualified to write than anyone else in your line of work, and suggested that if collaborating on it didn't prove too terrible an experience, we might want to take the relationship further. *Killing two birds with one ring* certainly isn't one of my expressions. And nothing I've said is anything like as indecent a proposal as the one you made me."

"That's true," she conceded, eventually. "In fact, you're right. I really ought to stop letting it all out on you, just because I can't say anything to Mum and Dad, or Ellen...or anyone else, really. You're the one who's providing the anchor, not me. This need thing seems to be mutual. And you're right about taking it slowly, leaving the age-old decent interval. We need to know that we wouldn't drive one another completely crazy, and working together on the book would certainly put that to the test. Okay, I'll come clean. I really wanted you to ask me do this, or something like it, and I feel a little stupid now for pretending so hard that I didn't. Fuck Lissa Lo—or not, I really don't want to know about that right now. Shit, who am I to complain—the luckiest man in Yorkshire thinks that getting off with me might count as an extension of his lucky streak, How lucky is that? Now I'm babbling. A gentleman would probably have interrupted by now to save me from further embarrassment."

"We don't have to do that any more," he told her. "From now on, we can let our vulnerabilities show. We don't have to do anything reckless, like telling one another the whole truth, but we can stop hiding quite as determinedly as we were before. Okay?"

"Fine. You do realize that our Ellen is going to kill me, don't you? She's bound to twig, probably long before anyone else."

"She'll be happy for you," he told her. "She was telling me just the other day how unlucky and unwise I'd been to let all three of you slip through my fingers. She offered me Marie, but I don't think she was serious. If you tell her all about it she'll be so grateful for the gossip that she won't even think of being annoyed. Not that there's any rush, mind. For now, all that you need tell her about is the possibility of writing the book, and getting access to all the Kilcannon family secrets. That's all I intend to tell Bentley."

Alice squinted slightly as she looked into his eyes, and Canny made a mental note to get a more powerful bulb for the desk lamp before they attempted any serious work in the inmost part of the library. She seemed to be able to see him clearly enough, though. "You've changed," she said. "I can't quite put my finger on it, but you're different."

"No I'm not," he told. "The world's different, but I'm not. I've been through a few things—a close brush with death, a close brush with its opposite—but I'm the same. Not just the same luck, but the same style...except that it's not really a style at all. It's just a habit—a matter of taking things to much for granted. Maybe I should have learned better, but that kind of habit is hard to shake, and when you get right down to it, it's not something a sane man would want to shake. It's part of my luck—my real, measurable, authentic luck. Sometimes, you see, psychology really does reflect probability. Some of us really do have a house percentage to draw on, whether or not we follow the rules. You won't cure me of that, Alice, and you shouldn't want to."

"You're wrong, you know," Alice said. "Ellen's going to be really, *really* pissed when she finds out that we're screwing around. She was always the glamorous one, you know. I was just loud. She might not have been serious about Marie—although it might help set poor Jack's mind at rest—but if Marie thought she had a chance...."

"What do you mean, *set poor Jack's mind at rest*?"

"Ellen always swore she was his, and I always knew that she was telling the truth, but Jack was never that certain. Why do you think it took him so long to make an honest woman of her? Let's not get into that, though. Are you sure it's me you want?"

"I can talk to you," Canny said, truthfully.

"Fucking Yorkshireman," she retorted. "Romantic as a stone skull."

"Snap," he came back, wishing that he didn't feel quite so much like a cheat, when he was really nothing of the kind. He was being as honest as he could be, and as honest as the world would ever let him be. Everything else was just a pattern of phantoms in his skull, with no real referent in the world they shared—just a symptom of some wayward nEurological disorder.

He could still see the future, although it wasn't as clear as it once had been. He *would* marry Alice, in St Peter's—not for a while yet, but when all the inconveniences were out of the way and the traditional decent interval had elapsed. Stevie Larkin would be his best man, Ellen Ormondroyd would be her maid-of-honor and Marie would be a bridesmaid—who would probably try harder than most to make use of the bridesmaid's traditional *droit-de-demoiselle* in respect of the best man. Alice would bear a child the following year: a son, who would renew and eventually inherit his father's gift and title, as well as the royalties from his mother's books, many more of which would follow successfully in the wake of her fascinating account of the secrets of the Kilcannon fortune. Canny would love his son as much as any father could, and share their common funds with him as liberally as he could bear to do. He would love his wife very dearly too, and share far more with her than his father had ever shared with his mother. They would make the most of their life together, and that was all there was to it. There as no need for anxiety, no need for pain, no need to regret anything that had not happened and never could have.

They would be happy together.

If Canny ever had his portrait painted, he would smile. He

would know himself far too well to frown, or to look like the kind of guilty fool who might have made a pact with the devil. He would live to an over-ripe old age, and keep what looks he had a little longer than nature intended. He would labor long and hard in the vineyards of chance and reap therefrom an abundant crop. He would keep his journal as best he could—save that he would refrain from recording any blatant impossibilities or obvious symptoms of madness—and he would maintain his library for those who came after him, even though he felt even now that it was more like a prison than a fount of wisdom, and more like a tomb than a key to life.

In the end, he knew, he would feel a great deal better than he had felt for the last few days. He would never forget, or forgive, but he would become distanced, and calm, and appropriately grateful for the luck he had had in the past, and the luck he would have in the future.

On his deathbed, he would tell his son not worry about the black lightning.

"The black lightning is nothing but the dark between the stars," he would say. The whole cosmos is black lightning, with just a few scattered specks of starry light and cold grey dust. The void isn't empty, you see: it's a seething mass of potential particles, potential universes. It's nothing because it hasn't become anything yet, but the potential is always there. It isn't anything to be afraid of. Look for the light, son—always look for the light—and don't be afraid to be dazzled. It won't let you down. You're a Kilcannon, and it will never let you fall too far, or hurt yourself too badly, no matter how many times you stumble."

While this reverie possessed him, he looked into Alice's eyes. In the dim light her pupils had grown large, and they were full of mystery and potential.

"Life itself defies the darkness," he said, aloud. "Life is light, even if it's just a random freak of chance or a reaction to stress."

"Just what I was thinking myself," Alice said, dryly. "Sometimes, Canny, you can be a bit of an idiot."

"Sorry," he said. "I was just thinking. You'll get used to it—I hope."

"I hope so too," she said.

So he carried on. And on. And on. He didn't make any resolutions he couldn't keep, but he did make one that he could. One thing he would certainly never do again, he resolved—under any circumstances whatsoever—was bet on zero on any spinning wheel, or its equivalent in any glossy mirror of whirling fate...not because he feared that it might not come up for a second time, but because he could be absolutely certain that it would. From now on, he intended to stick to positive numbers: the ones that counted.

ABOUT THE AUTHOR

Brian Stableford was born in Yorkshire in 1948. He taught at the University of Reading for several years, but is now a full-time writer. He has written many science-fiction and fantasy novels, including *The Empire of Fear*, *The Werewolves of London*, *Year Zero*, *The Curse of the Coral Bride*, *The Stones of Camelot*, and *Prelude to Eternity*. Collections of his short stories include a long series of *Tales of the Biotech Revolution*, and such idiosyncratic items as *Sheena and Other Gothic Tales* and *The Innsmouth Heritage and Other Sequels*. He has written numerous nonfiction books, including *Scientific Romance in Britain, 1890-1950*; *Glorious Perversity: The Decline and Fall of Literary Decadence*; *Science Fact and Science Fiction: An Encyclopedia*; and *The Devil's Party: A Brief History of Satanic Abuse*. He has contributed hundreds of biographical and critical articles to reference books, and has also translated numerous novels from the French language, including books by Paul Féval, Albert Robida, Maurice Renard, and J. H. Rosny the Elder.

www.ingramcontent.com/pod-product-compliance
Lightning Source LLC
Chambersburg PA
CBHW030932260626
47169CB00002B/443